ABOUT THE EDITORS

JAMES ELLROY was born in Los Angeles in 1948. His L.A. Quartet—
The Black Dahlia, *The Big Nowhere*, *L.A. Confidential*, and *White Jazz*—
were international bestsellers. *American Tabloid* was a *Time* Novel of
the Year in 1995; his memoir *My Dark Places* was a *Time* Best Book
and a *New York Times* Notable Book for 1996. His novel *The Cold Six-
Thousand* was a *New York Times* Notable Book and a *Los Angeles Times*
Best Book for 2001. He lives on the California coast.

OTTO PENZLER is the proprietor of the Mysterious Bookshop in New
York City, the founder of the Mysterious Press, and creator of the
publishing firm Otto Penzler books. He is the editor of many books
and anthologies and has been the recipient of the Edgar Award. He
lives in New York City.

THOMAS H. COOK is the author of eighteen books, including two
works of true crime. His novels have been nominated for the Edgar
Award, the Macavity Award, and the Dashiell Hammett Prize. He lives
in New York City.

The Best American
CRIME WRITING
2005

Edited by
THOMAS H. COOK AND
OTTO PENZLER

*With an Introduction
and an Original Essay by*
JAMES ELLROY

AN ECCO BOOK

HARPER PERENNIAL

HARPER PERENNIAL

THE BEST AMERICAN CRIME WRITING 2005. Copyright © 2005 by Thomas H. Cook and Otto Penzler. Introduction and "Choirboys" copyright © 2005 by James Ellroy. All rights reserved. Printed in the United States of America. No part of this book may be used or reproduced in any manner whatsoever without written permission except in the case of brief quotations embodied in critical articles and reviews. For information address HarperCollins Publishers, 10 East 53rd Street, New York, NY 10022.

HarperCollins books may be purchased for educational, business, or sales promotional use. For information please write: Special Markets Department, HarperCollins Publishers, 10 East 53rd Street, New York, NY 10022.

FIRST EDITION

Designed by Love Dog Studio/Brian Mulligan

Library of Congress Cataloging-in-Publication Data is available upon request.

ISBN-10: 0-06-081551-5
ISBN-13: 978-0-06-081551-6

05 06 07 08 09 WBC/RRD 10 9 8 7 6 5 4 3 2 1

Contents

PREFACE

THE YEAR 2004 WAS profoundly political. Thus it was not surprising that a great deal of newspaper and magazine space was given over to the Democratic primaries and, later, to the presidential campaign. Nonetheless, the best of our nation's crime writers were not silenced by the crashing symbols of our quadrennial bash. Amid all the hoopla, they made their voices heard, and the finest of those voices have been gathered into this, the fourth volume of *Best American Crime Writing*.

As in previous editions, the tone of those voices vary tremendously.

There is sadness in the voice of Peter Landesman as he relates the tragic plight of "The Girls Next Door." In "Stalking Her Killer," Philip Weiss's voice seems eternally haunted by a murder that was solved . . . but never punished. Comic irony pervades Jonathan Miles's tale of bar-brawling, while the irony of Neil Swidey's "The Self-Destruction of an M.D." is very dark indeed. Bruce Porter, Justin Kane, and Jason Felch record a similarly dark descent in "A Long Way Down" and "To Catch an Oligarch." A similar descent leads to murder in Debra Miller Landau's riveting "Social Disgraces."

There is, as always, variety in subject matter as well, from the gentlemanly art of stealing silver in Stephen J. Dubner's "The Silver Thief," to simple larceny in Skip Hollandsworth's "The Family Man," to the maddening antics of Internet hackers described in Clive Thompson's "The Virus Underground," and finally to the terrible slaughter both threatened and envisioned by Lawrence Wright's "The Terror Web."

Apprehension, or the lack of it, is the subject of three of our distinguished contributors. Robert Draper chronicles the inexcusable escape of a group of deadly terrorists in "The Ones that Got Away," while Craig Horowitz's "Anatomy of a Foiled Plot" details the fortunate capture of a group of criminals before they had a chance to commit their awesome crime.

Finally, there are certain pieces that simply defy categorization. Jeff Teitz's "Fine Disturbances" portrays in finely nuanced detail the intuitive brilliance of a great tracker. In "Mysterious Circumstances," David Grann investigates the death (by murder or misadventure) of the world's foremost collector of Sherlock Holmes memorabilia.

Here then, and with great pride, we present this year's collection of the *Best American Crime Writing*, tales that will delight and sadden you, inspire both awe and disbelief, but always stories that display, in full color, the variety of human malfeasance, and thus the poles not only of criminal experience, but the whole checkered history of our kind.

In terms of the nature and scope of this collection, we defined American crime writing as any factual story involving crime or the threat of a crime by an American or Canadian and published in the United States or Canada during the calendar year 2004. We examined a huge array of publications, though inevitably the preeminent ones attracted many of the best pieces. All national and large regional magzines were scanned, as well as nearly two hundred so-called little magazines, reviews and journals.

We welcome submissions by any writer, publisher, editor, agent or other interested party for *Best American Crime Writing 2006*. Please send a tear sheet with the name of the publication in which the article appeared, the date of publication and, if possible, the address of the author or representative. If first publication was in electronic format, a hard copy must be submitted. Only articles actually published with a 2005 publication date are eligible. All submissions must be made by December 31, 2005; anything received after that date will not be read. This is not capricious. The nature of this book forces very tight deadlines which cannot be met if we are still reading in the middle of January.

Please send submissions to Otto Penzler, The Mysterious Bookshop, 129 West 56th Street, New York, NY 10019. Submitted material cannot be returned. If you wish verification that material was received, please send a self-addressed stamped postcard. Thank you.

INTRODUCTION

THE CHALK OUTLINE. Blood patterns. The sleep-fucked men standing by. The punk flanked by two squadroom bruisers. He's blinking back flashbulb glare. He's got one finger twirling. He's flipping the square world off.

Don DeLillo called it "the neon epic of Saturday night." It's *Crime*. It's the bottomless tale of the big wrong turn and the shortcut to Hell via cheap lust and cheaper kicks. It's meretricious appetite. It's moral forfeiture. It's society indicated for its complicity and dubious social theory. It's heroism. It's depravity. It's justice enacted both vindictively and indifferently. It's our voyeurism refracted.

We want to know. We need to know. We *have* to know. We don't want to live crime. We want our kicks once removed—on the screen or the page. It's our observer's license and innoculation against the crime virus itself. We want celebrity lowlifes and downscale lives in duress. We want crime scenes explicated through scientific design. We want the riddle of a body dumped on a roadway hitched to payback in the electric chair.

We want it. We *get* it. Filmmakers, novelists, and journalists keep us supplied. They know how much we want our bloodthirsty thrills and how we want them circumscribed. Movies, TV, novels, and stories. Dramatic arcs. Beginnings, middles, and ends. Most crime is fed to us fictionally. The purveyors exploit genre strictures and serve up the kicks with hyperbole. We get car chases, multiple shootouts, and limitless sex. We get the psychopathic lifestyle. We get breathless excitement—because breathless excitement has always eclipsed psychological depth and social critique as the main engine of crime fiction in all its forms.

Herein lies the bullshit factor. Here we indict the most brilliant suppliers of the crime-fiction art. I'll proffer indictment Count number one—and cringe in the throes of self-indictment.

In the worldwide history of police work there has never been a single investigation that involved numerous gun battles, countless sexual escapades, pandemic political shake-ups, and revelations that define corrupt institutions and overall societies.

Count number one informs all subsidiary counts. That sweeping statement tells us that we are dealing with a garish narrative art. It's underpinnings are realistic. Its story potential is manifest—and as such, usurped by artists good, great, fair, poor, proficient, and incompetent. Crime fiction in all forms is crime fiction of the imagination. That fact enhances good and great crime fiction and dismisses the remainder. Crime fiction fails the reader/viewer/voyeur in only one way: It is not wholly true. And that severely fucks with our need to know.

True-crime TV shows, feature documentaries, full-length books and reportage. Revised narrative strictures.

You must report the truth. You can interpret it and in that sense shape it—but your factual duty is nonnegotiable.

As crime reader/viewer/voyeurs, we now cleave to this: our need to know has metamorphosed. We want less breathless excitement and more gravity. We still hold that observer's license and innoculation card—but we're willing to get altogether closer now.

And, with that, a reward awaits. True-crime writing offers a less kineticized and more sobering set of thrills—chiefly couched in human revelation. A simple bottom line holds us: *This Really Happened.* The violated child, the crackhead dad, the cinderblock torture den. We're rewarded for getting close. We're buttressed in our safety. This isn't me, It's not my kid, I'm not going there.

We get to say those things. But we say them with less smugness. The missing boyfriend or girlfriend. The cast of predators nearby. The cops with instincts and no hard leads. Real-life stand-ins for us.

It hurts a little now. It's a DNA transfusion. We're bone-deep with pathos and horror. Their world is now our world. We mate with victims and monsters. We see justice ambiguously affirmed and subverted. Heroes greet us. Evil is subsumed by goodness as more evil thrives. We came for kicks and got something more. Welcome to the true-crime riches of this book.

—James Ellroy,
January 11, 2005

The Best American Crime Writing

2005

Peter Landesman

THE GIRLS
NEXT DOOR

FROM THE *New York Times Magazine*

THE HOUSE AT 1212 ½ West Front Street in Plainfield, New Jersey, is a conventional midcentury home with slate-gray siding, white trim and Victorian lines. When I stood in front of it on a breezy day in October, I could hear the cries of children from the playground of an elementary school around the corner. American flags fluttered from porches and windows. The neighborhood is a leafy, middle-class Anytown. The house is set back off the street, near two convenience stores and a gift shop. On the door of Superior Supermarket was pasted a sign issued by the Plainfield police: "Safe neighborhoods save lives." The store's manager, who refused to tell me his name, said he never noticed anything unusual about the house, and never heard anything. But David Miranda, the young man behind the counter of Westside Convenience, told me he saw girls from the house roughly once a week. "They came in to buy candy and soda, then went back to the house," he said. The same girls rarely came twice, and they were all very young, Miranda said. They never asked for anything beyond what they were purchasing; they certainly never asked for help. Cars drove up to the house all day; nice cars, all kinds of cars. Dozens of men came and went. "But no one here knew what was really going on," Miranda said. And no one ever asked.

On a tip, the Plainfield police raided the house in February 2002, expecting to find illegal aliens working an underground brothel. What the police found were four girls between the ages of fourteen and seventeen. They were all Mexican nationals without documentation. But they weren't prostitutes; they were sex slaves. The distinction is important: these girls weren't working for profit or a paycheck. They were captives to the traffickers and keepers who controlled their every move. "I consider myself hardened," Mark J. Kelly, now a special agent with Immigration and Customs Enforcement (the largest investigative arm of the Department of Homeland Security), told me recently. "I spent time in the Marine Corps. But seeing some of the stuff I saw, then heard about, from those girls was a difficult, eye-opening experience."

The police found a squalid, land-based equivalent of a nineteenth-century slave ship, with rancid, doorless bathrooms; bare, putrid mattresses; and a stash of penicillin, "morning after" pills and miso-prostol, an antiulcer medication that can induce abortion. The girls were pale, exhausted, and malnourished.

It turned out that 1212 ½ West Front Street was one of what law-enforcement officials say are dozens of active stash houses and apartments in the New York metropolitan area—mirroring hundreds more in other major cities like Los Angeles, Atlanta, and Chicago—where under-age girls and young women from dozens of countries are trafficked and held captive. Most of them—whether they started out in Eastern Europe or Latin America—are taken to the United States through Mexico. Some of them have been baited by promises of legitimate jobs and a better life in America; many have been abducted; others have been bought from or abandoned by their impoverished families.

Because of the porousness of the United States-Mexico border and the criminal networks that traverse it, the towns and cities along

that border have become the main staging area in an illicit and barbaric industry, whose "products" are women and girls. On both
sides of the border, they are rented out for sex for as little as fifteen
minutes at a time, dozens of times a day. Sometimes they are sold
outright to other traffickers and sex rings, victims and experts say.
These sex slaves earn no money, there is nothing voluntary about
what they do, and if they try to escape they are often beaten and
sometimes killed.

Last September, in a speech before the United Nations General
Assembly, President Bush named sex trafficking as "a special evil,"
a multibillion-dollar "underground of brutality and lonely fear," a
global scourge alongside the AIDS epidemic. Influenced by a coalition of religious organizations, the Bush administration has
pushed international action on the global sex trade. The president
declared at the United Nations that "those who create these victims and profit from their suffering must be severely punished" and
that "those who patronize this industry debase themselves and
deepen the misery of others. And governments that tolerate this
trade are tolerating a form of slavery."

Under the Trafficking Victims Protection Act of 2000—the first
U.S. law to recognize that people trafficked against their will are
victims of a crime, not illegal aliens—the U.S. government rates
other countries' records on human trafficking and can apply economic sanctions on those that aren't making efforts to improve
them. Another piece of legislation, the Protect Act, which Bush
signed into law last year, makes it a crime for any person to enter
the United States, or for any citizen to travel abroad, for the purpose
of sex tourism involving children. The sentences are severe: up to
thirty years' imprisonment for each offense.

The thrust of the president's U.N. speech and the scope of the
laws passed here to address the sex-trafficking epidemic might suggest that this is a global problem but not particularly an American
one. In reality, little has been done to document sex trafficking in
this country. In dozens of interviews I conducted with former sex

slaves, madams, government and law-enforcement officials, and anti-sex-trade activists for more than four months in Eastern Europe, Mexico, and the United States, the details and breadth of this sordid trade in the United States came to light.

In fact, the United States has become a major importer of sex slaves. Last year, the CIA estimated that between eighteen thousand and twenty thousand people are trafficked annually into the United States. The government has not studied how many of these are victims of sex traffickers, but Kevin Bales, president of Free the Slaves, America's largest antislavery organization, says that the number is at least ten thousand a year. John Miller, the State Department's director of the Office to Monitor and Combat Trafficking in Persons, conceded: "That figure could be low. What we know is that the number is huge." Bales estimates that there are thirty thousand to fifty thousand sex slaves in captivity in the United States at any given time. Laura Lederer, a senior State Department adviser on trafficking, told me, "We're not finding victims in the United States because we're not looking for them."

ABDUCTION

In Eastern European capitals like Kiev and Moscow, dozens of sex-trafficking rings advertise nanny positions in the United States in local newspapers; others claim to be scouting for models and actresses.

In Chisinau, the capital of the former Soviet republic of Moldova—the poorest country in Europe and the one experts say is most heavily culled by traffickers for young women—I saw a billboard with a fresh-faced, smiling young woman beckoning girls to waitress positions in Paris. But of course there are no waitress positions and no "Paris." Some of these young women are actually tricked into paying their own travel expenses—typically around $3,000—as a down payment on what they expect to be bright, prosperous futures, only to find themselves kept prisoner in Mexico before being moved to the United States and sold into sexual bondage there.

The Eastern European trafficking operations, from entrapment to transport, tend to be well-oiled monoethnic machines. One notorious Ukrainian ring, which has since been broken up, was run by Tetyana Komisaruk and Serge Mezheritsky. One of their last transactions, according to Daniel Saunders, an assistant U.S. attorney in Los Angeles, took place in late June 2000 at the Hard Rock Cafe in Tijuana. Around dinnertime, a buyer named Gordey Vinitsky walked in. He was followed shortly after by Komisaruk's husband, Valery, who led Vinitsky out to the parking lot and to a waiting van. Inside the van were six Ukrainian women in their late teens and early twenties. They had been promised jobs as models and babysitters in the glamorous United States, and they probably had no idea why they were sitting in a van in a backwater like Tijuana in the early evening. Vinitsky pointed into the van at two of the women and said he'd take them for $10,000 each. Valery drove the young women to a gated villa twenty minutes away in Rosarito, a Mexican honky-tonk tourist trap in Baja California. They were kept there until July 4, when they were delivered to San Diego by boat and distributed to their buyers, including Vinitsky, who claimed his two "purchases." The Komisaruks, Mezheritsky, and Vinitsky were caught in May 2001 and are serving long sentences in U.S. federal prison.

In October, I met Nicole, a young Russian woman who had been trafficked into Mexico by a different network. "I wanted to get out of Moscow, and they told me the Mexican border was like a freeway," said Nicole, who is now twenty-five. We were sitting at a cafe on the Sunset Strip in Los Angeles, and she was telling me the story of her narrow escape from sex slavery—she was taken by immigration officers when her traffickers were trying to smuggle her over the border from Tijuana. She still seemed fearful of being discovered by the trafficking ring and didn't want even her initials to appear in print. (Nicole is a name she adopted after coming to the United States.)

Two years ago, afraid for her life after her boyfriend was gunned down in Moscow in an organized-crime-related shootout, she found herself across a cafe table in Moscow from a man named Alex, who explained how he could save her by smuggling her into the United States. Once she agreed, Nicole said, Alex told her that if she didn't show up at the airport, "'I'll find you and cut your head off.' Russians do not play around. In Moscow you can get a bullet in your head just for fun."

Donna M. Hughes, a professor of women's studies at the University of Rhode Island and an expert on sex trafficking, says that prostitution barely existed twelve years ago in the Soviet Union. "It was suppressed by political structures. All the women had jobs." But in the first years after the collapse of Soviet Communism, poverty in the former Soviet states soared. Young women—many of them college-educated and married—became easy believers in Hollywood-generated images of swaying palm trees in Los Angeles. "A few of them have an idea that prostitution might be involved," Hughes says. "But their idea of prostitution is *Pretty Woman*, which is one of the most popular films in Ukraine and Russia. They're thinking, This may not be so bad."

The girls' first contacts are usually with what appear to be legitimate travel agencies. According to prosecutors, the Komisaruk/Mezheritsky ring in Ukraine worked with two such agencies in Kiev, Art Life International and Svit Tours. The helpful agents at Svit and Art Life explained to the girls that the best way to get into the United States was through Mexico, which they portrayed as a short walk or boat ride from the American dream. Oblivious and full of hope, the girls get on planes to Europe and then on to Mexico.

Every day, flights from Paris, London, and Amsterdam arrive at Mexico City's international airport carrying groups of these girls, sometimes as many as seven at a time, according to two Mexico City immigration officers I spoke with (and who asked to remain anonymous). One of them told me that officials at the airport—

who cooperate with Mexico's federal preventive police (PFP)—work with the traffickers and "direct airlines to park at certain gates. Officials go to the aircraft. They know the seat numbers. While passengers come off, they take the girls to an office, where officials will 'process' them."

Magdalena Carral, Mexico's commissioner of the National Institute of Migration, the government agency that controls migration issues at all airports, seaports, and land entries into Mexico, told me: "Everything happens at the airport. We are giving a big fight to have better control of the airport. Corruption does not leave tracks, and sometimes we cannot track it. Six months ago we changed the three main officials at the airport. But it's a daily fight. These networks are very powerful and dangerous."

But Mexico is not merely a way station en route to the United States for third-country traffickers, like the Eastern European rings. It is also a vast source of even younger and more cheaply acquired girls for sexual servitude in the United States. While European traffickers tend to dupe their victims into boarding one-way flights to Mexico to their own captivity, Mexican traffickers rely on the charm and brute force of "Los Lenones," tightly organized associations of pimps, according to Roberto Caballero, an officer with the PFP. Although hundreds of "popcorn traffickers"—individuals who take control of one or two girls—work the margins, Caballero said, at least fifteen major trafficking organizations and one hundred and twenty associated factions tracked by the PFP operate as wholesalers: collecting human merchandise and taking orders from safe houses and brothels in the major sex-trafficking hubs in New York, Los Angeles, Atlanta, and Chicago.

Like the Sicilian Mafia, Los Lenones are based on family hierarchies, Caballero explained. The father controls the organization and the money, while the sons and their male cousins hunt, kidnap, and entrap victims. The boys leave school at twelve and are given one or two girls their age to rape and pimp out to begin their training, which emphasizes the arts of kidnapping and seduction.

Throughout the rural and suburban towns from southern Mexico to the United States border, along what traffickers call the Via Lactea, or Milky Way, the agents of Los Lenones troll the bus stations and factories and school dances where under-age girls gather, work, and socialize. They first ply the girls like prospective lovers, buying them meals and desserts, promising affection and then marriage. Then the men describe rumors they've heard about America, about the promise of jobs and schools. Sometimes the girls are easy prey. Most of them already dream of El Norte. But the theater often ends as soon as the agent has the girl alone, when he beats her, drugs her, or simply forces her into a waiting car.

The majority of Los Lenones—80 percent of them, Caballero says—are based in Tenancingo, a charmless suburb an hour's drive south of Mexico City. Before I left Mexico City for Tenancingo in October, I was warned by Mexican and United States officials that the traffickers there are protected by the local police, and that the town is designed to discourage outsiders, with mazelike streets and only two closely watched entrances. The last time the federal police went there to investigate the disappearance of a local girl, their vehicle was surrounded, and the officers were intimidated into leaving. I traveled in a bulletproof Suburban with well-armed federales and an Immigration and Customs Enforcement agent.

On the way, we stopped at a gas station, where I met the parents of a girl from Tenancingo who was reportedly abducted in August 2000. The girl, Suri, is now twenty. Her mother told me that there were witnesses who saw her being forced into a car on the way home from work at a local factory. No one called the police. Suri's mother recited the names of daughters of a number of her friends who have also been taken: "Minerva, Sylvia, Carmen," she said in a monotone, as if the list went on and on.

Just two days earlier, her parents heard from Suri (they call her by her nickname) for the first time since she disappeared. "She's in Queens, New York," the mother told me breathlessly. "She said she was being kept in a house watched by Colombians. She said they take her by car every day to work in a brothel. I was crying on the phone, 'When are you coming back, when are you coming back?'" The mother looked at me helplessly; the father stared blankly into the distance. Then the mother sobered. "My daughter said: 'I'm too far away. I don't know when I'm coming back.'" Before she hung up, Suri told her mother: "Don't cry. I'll escape soon. And don't talk to anyone."

Sex-trafficking victims widely believe that if they talk, they or someone they love will be killed. And their fear is not unfounded, since the tentacles of the trafficking rings reach back into the girls' hometowns, and local law enforcement is often complicit in the sex trade.

One officer in the PFPs antitrafficking division told me that ten high-level officials in the state of Sonora share a $200,000 weekly payoff from traffickers, a gargantuan sum of money for Mexico. The officer told me with a frozen smile that he was powerless to do anything about it.

"Some officials are not only on the organization's payroll, they are key players in the organization," an official at the U.S. Embassy in Mexico City told me. "Corruption is the most important reason these networks are so successful."

Nicolas Suarez, the PFP's coordinator of intelligence, sounded fatalistic about corruption when I spoke to him in Mexico City in September. "We have that cancer, corruption," he told me with a shrug. "But it exists in every country. In every house there is a devil."

The U.S. Embassy official told me: "Mexican officials see sex trafficking as a United States problem. If there wasn't such a large demand, then people—trafficking victims and migrants alike—wouldn't be going up there."

When I asked Magdalena Carral, the Mexican commissioner of migration, about these accusations, she said that she didn't know anything about Los Lenones or sex trafficking in Tenancingo. But she conceded: "There is an investigation against some officials accused of cooperating with these trafficking networks nationwide.

Sonora is one of those places." She added, "We are determined not to allow any kind of corruption in this administration, not the smallest kind."

Gary Haugen, president of the International Justice Mission, an organization based in Arlington, Virginia, that fights sexual exploitation in South Asia and Southeast Asia, says: "Sex trafficking isn't a poverty issue but a law-enforcement issue. You can only carry out this trade at significant levels with the cooperation of local law enforcement. In the developing world the police are not seen as a solution for anything. You don't run to the police; you run from the police."

BREAKING THE GIRLS IN

Once the Mexican traffickers abduct or seduce the women and young girls, it's not other men who first indoctrinate them into sexual slavery but other women. The victims and officials I spoke to all emphasized this fact as crucial to the trafficking rings' success. "Women are the principals," Caballero, the Mexican federal preventive police officer, told me. "The victims are put under the influence of the mothers, who handle them and beat them. Then they give the girls to the men to beat and rape into submission." Traffickers understand that because women can more easily gain the trust of young girls, they can more easily crush them. "Men are the customers and controllers, but within most trafficking organizations themselves, women are the operators," Haugen says. "Women are the ones who exert violent force and psychological torture."

This mirrors the tactics of the Eastern European rings. "Mexican pimps have learned a lot from European traffickers," said Claudia, a former prostitute and madam in her late forties, whom I met in Tepito, Mexico City's vast and lethal ghetto. "The Europeans not only gather girls but put older women in the same houses," she told me. "They get younger and older women emotionally attached. They're transported together, survive together."

The traffickers' harvest is innocence. Before young women and girls are taken to the United States, their captors want to obliterate their sexual inexperience while preserving its appearance. For the Eastern European girls, this "preparation" generally happens in Ensenada, a seaside tourist town in Baja California, a region in Mexico settled by Russian immigrants, or Tijuana, where Nicole, the Russian woman I met in Los Angeles, was taken along with four other girls when she arrived in Mexico. The young women are typically kept in locked-down, gated villas in groups of sixteen to twenty. The girls are provided with all-American clothing—Levi's and baseball caps. They learn to say, "United States citizen." They are also sexually brutalized. Nicole told me that the day she arrived in Tijuana, three of her traveling companions were "tried out" locally. The education lasts for days and sometimes weeks.

For the Mexican girls abducted by Los Lenones, the process of breaking them in often begins on Calle Santo Tomas, a filthy narrow street in La Merced, a dangerous and raucous ghetto in Mexico City. Santo Tomas has been a place for low-end prostitution since before Spain's conquest of Mexico in the sixteenth century. But beginning in the early nineties, it became an important training ground for under-age girls and young women on their way into sexual bondage in the United States. When I first visited Santo Tomas, in late September, I found one hundred and fifty young women walking a slow-motion parabola among three hundred or four hundred men. It was a balmy night, and the air was heavy with the smell of barbecue and gasoline. Two dead dogs were splayed over the curb just beyond where the girls struck casual poses in stilettos and spray-on-tight neon vinyl and satin or skimpy leopard-patterned outfits. Some of the girls looked as young as twelve. Their faces betrayed no emotion. Many wore pendants of the grim reaper around their necks and made hissing sounds; this, I was told, was part of a ritual to ward off bad energy. The men, who were there to rent or just gaze, didn't speak. From the tables of a shabby cafe midblock, other men—also Mexicans, but more neatly dressed—sat scrutinizing the girls as at an auction. These were buyers and renters with an interest in the youngest and best-looking. They nodded to the girls they wanted and then followed them past a guard in a Yankees baseball cap through a tin doorway.

Inside, the girls braced the men before a statue of St. Jude, the patron saint of lost causes, and patted them down for weapons. Then the girls genuflected to the stone-faced saint and led the men to the back, grabbing a condom and roll of toilet paper on the way. They pointed to a block of ice in a tub in lieu of a urinal. Beyond a blue hallway the air went sour, like old onions; there were thirty stalls curtained off by blue fabric, every one in use. Fifteen minutes of straightforward intercourse with the girl's clothes left on cost 50 pesos, or about $4.50. For $4.50 more, the dress was lifted. For another $4.50, the bra would be taken off. Oral sex was $4.50; "acrobatic positions" were $1.80 each. Despite the dozens of people and the various exertions in this room, there were only the sounds of zippers and shoes. There was no human noise at all.

Most of the girls on Santo Tomas would have sex with twenty to thirty men a day; they would do this seven days a week usually for weeks but sometimes for months before they were "ready" for the United States. If they refused, they would be beaten and sometimes killed. They would be told that if they tried to escape, one of their family members, who usually had no idea where they were, would be beaten or killed. Working at the brutalizing pace of twenty men per day, a girl could earn her captors as much as $2,000 a week. In the United States that same girl could bring in perhaps $30,000 per week.

In Europe, girls and women trafficked for the sex trade gain in value the closer they get to their destinations. According to Iana Matei, who operates Reaching Out, a Romanian rescue organization, a Romanian or Moldovan girl can be sold to her first

transporter—who she may or may not know has taken her captive—
for as little as $60, then for $500 to the next. Eventually she can be
sold for $2,500 to the organization that will ultimately control and
rent her for sex for tens of thousands of dollars a week. (Though the
Moldovan and Romanian organizations typically smuggle girls to
Western Europe and not the United States, they are, Matei says,
closely allied with Russian and Ukrainian networks that do.)

Jonathan M. Winer, deputy assistant secretary of state for international law enforcement in the Clinton administration, says, "The
girls are worth a penny or a ruble in their home village, and suddenly they're worth hundreds and thousands somewhere else."

CROSSING THE BORDER

In November, I followed by helicopter the twelve-foot-high sheet-
metal fence that represents the United States Mexico boundary from
Imperial Beach, California, south of San Diego, fourteen miles
across the gritty warrens and havoc of Tijuana into the barren hills
of Tecate. The fence drops off abruptly at Colonia Nido de las
Aguilas, a dry riverbed that straddles the border. Four hundred
square miles of bone-dry, barren hills stretch out on the United
States side. I hovered over the end of the fence with Lester Mc-
Daniel, a special agent with Immigration and Customs Enforcement. On the United States side, "J-e-s-u-s" was spelled out in rocks
ten feet high across a steep hillside. A fifteen-foot white wooden
cross rose from the peak. It is here that thousands of girls and young
women—most of them Mexican and many of them straight from
Calle Santo Tomas—are taken every year, mostly between January
and August, the dry season. Coyotes—or smugglers—subcontracted
exclusively by sex traffickers sometimes trudge the girls up to the
cross and let them pray, then herd them into the hills northward.

A few miles east, we picked up a deeply grooved trail at the fence
and followed it for miles into the hills until it plunged into a deep

isolated ravine called Cottonwood Canyon. A Ukrainian sex-trafficking ring force-marches young women through here, McDaniel told me. In high heels and seductive clothing, the young women trek twelve miles to Highway 94, where panel trucks sit waiting. McDaniel listed the perils: rattlesnakes, dehydration, and hypothermia. He failed to mention the traffickers' bullets should the women try to escape.

"If a girl tries to run, she's killed and becomes just one more woman in the desert," says Marisa B. Ugarte, director of the Bilateral Safety Corridor Coalition, a San Diego organization that coordinates rescue efforts for trafficking victims on both sides of the border. "But if she keeps going north, she reaches the Gates of Hell."

One girl who was trafficked back and forth across that border repeatedly was Andrea. "Andrea" is just one name she was given by her traffickers and clients; she doesn't know her real name. She was born in the United States and sold or abandoned here—at about four years old, she says—by a woman who may have been her mother. (She is now in her early to mid-twenties; she doesn't know for sure.) She says that she spent approximately the next twelve years as the captive of a sex-trafficking ring that operated on both sides of the Mexican border. Because of the threat of retribution from her former captors, who are believed to be still at large, an organization that rescues and counsels trafficking victims and former prostitutes arranged for me to meet Andrea in October at a secret location in the United States.

In a series of excruciating conversations, Andrea explained to me how the trafficking ring that kept her worked, moving young girls (and boys too) back and forth over the border, selling nights and weekends with them mostly to American men. She said that the ring imported—both through abduction and outright purchase—toddlers, children, and teenagers into the United States from many countries.

"The border is very busy, lots of stuff moving back and forth," she said. "Say you needed to get some kids. This guy would offer a woman a lot of money, and she'd take birth certificates from the United States—from Puerto Rican children or darker-skinned children—and then she would go into Mexico through Tijuana. Then she'd drive to Juarez"—across the Mexican border from El Paso, Texas—"and then they'd go shopping. I was taken with them once. We went to this house that had a goat in the front yard and came out with a four-year-old boy." She remembers the boy costing around five hundred dollars (she said that many poor parents were told that their children would go to adoption agencies and on to better lives in America). "When we crossed the border at Juarez, all the border guards wanted to see was a birth certificate for the dark-skinned kids."

Andrea continued: "There would be a truck waiting for us at the Mexico border, and those trucks you don't want to ride in. Those trucks are closed. They had spots where there would be transfers, the rest stops and truck stops on the freeways in the United States. One person would walk you into the bathroom, and then another person would take you out of the bathroom and take you to a different vehicle."

Andrea told me she was transported to Juarez dozens of times. During one visit, when she was about seven years old, the trafficker took her to the Radisson Casa Grande Hotel, where there was a john waiting in a room. The john was an older American man, and he read Bible passages to her before and after having sex with her. Andrea described other rooms she remembered in other hotels in Mexico: the Howard Johnson in Leon, the Crowne Plaza in Guadalajara. She remembers most of all the ceiling patterns. "When I was taken to Mexico, I knew things were going to be different," she said. The "customers" were American businessmen. "The men who went there had higher positions, had more to lose if they were caught doing these things on the other side of the border. I was told my purpose was to keep these men from abusing their own kids." Later she told me: "The white kids you could beat but you couldn't mark. But with Mexican kids you could do whatever you wanted. They're untraceable. You lose nothing by killing them."

Then she and the other children and teenagers in this cell were walked back across the border to El Paso by the traffickers. "The border guards talked to you like, 'Did you have fun in Mexico?' And you answered exactly what you were told, 'Yeah, I had fun.' 'Runners' moved the harder-to-place kids, the darker or not-quite-as-well-behaved kids, kids that hadn't been broken yet."

Another trafficking victim I met, a young woman named Montserrat, was taken to the United States from Veracruz, Mexico, six years ago, at age thirteen. (Montserrat is her nickname.) "I was going to work in America," she told me. "I wanted to go to school there, have an apartment and a red Mercedes Benz." Montserrat's trafficker, who called himself Alejandro, took her to Sonora, across the Mexican border from Douglas, Arizona, where she joined a group of a dozen other teenage girls, all with the same dream of a better life. They were from Chiapas, Guatemala, Oaxaca—everywhere, she said.

The group was marched twelve hours through the desert, just a few of the thousands of Mexicans who bolted for America that night along the two thousand miles of border. Cars were waiting at a fixed spot on the other side. Alejandro directed her to a Nissan and drove her and a few others to a house she said she thought was in Phoenix, the home of a white American family. "It looked like America," she told me. "I ate chicken. The family ignored me, watched TV. I thought the worst part was behind me."

IN THE UNITED STATES: HIDING IN PLAIN SIGHT

A week after Montserrat was taken across the border, she said, she and half a dozen other girls were loaded into a windowless van. "Alejandro dropped off girls at gas stations as we drove, wherever there were minimarkets," Montserrat told me. At each drop-off there was somebody waiting. Sometimes a girl would be escorted to the bathroom, never to return to the van. They drove twenty-four hours a day. "As the girls were leaving, being let out the back, all of them fourteen or fifteen years old, I felt confident," Montserrat said. We were talking in Mexico City, where she has been since she escaped from her trafficker four years ago. She's now nineteen, and shy with her body but direct with her gaze, which is flat and unemotional. "I didn't know the real reason they were disappearing," she said. "They were going to a better life."

Eventually, only Montserrat and one other girl remained. Outside, the air had turned frigid, and there was snow on the ground. It was night when the van stopped at a gas station. A man was waiting. Montserrat's friend hopped out the back, gleeful. "She said goodbye, I'll see you tomorrow," Montserrat recalled. "I never saw her again."

After leaving the gas station, Alejandro drove Montserrat to an apartment. A couple of weeks later he took her to a Dollarstore. "He bought me makeup," Montserrat told me. "He chose a short dress and a halter top, both black. I asked him why the clothes. He said it was for a party the owner of the apartment was having. He bought me underwear. Then I started to worry." When they arrived at the apartment, Alejandro left, saying he was coming back. But another man appeared at the door. "The man said he'd already paid and I had to do whatever he said," Montserrat said. "When he said he already paid, I knew why I was there. I was crushed."

Montserrat said that she didn't leave that apartment for the next three months; then for nine months after that, Alejandro regularly took her in and out of the apartment for appointments with various johns.

Sex trafficking is one of the few human rights violations that rely on exposure: victims have to be available, displayed, delivered, and returned. Girls were shuttled in open cars between the Plainfield, New Jersey, stash house and other locations in northern New

Jersey like Elizabeth and Union City. Suri told her mother that she was being driven in a black town car—just one of hundreds of black town cars traversing New York City at any time—from her stash house in Queens to places where she was forced to have sex. A Russian ring drove women between various Brooklyn apartments and strip clubs in New Jersey. Andrea named trading hubs at highway rest stops in Deming, New Mexico; Kingman, Arizona; Boulder City, Nevada; and Glendale, California. Glendale, Andrea said, was a fork in the road; from there, vehicles went either north to San Jose or south toward San Diego. The traffickers drugged them for travel, she said. "When they fed you, you started falling asleep."

In the past several months, I have visited a number of addresses where trafficked girls and young women have reportedly ended up: besides the house in Plainfield, New Jersey, there is a row house on Fifty-first Avenue in the Corona section of Queens, which has been identified to Mexican federal preventive police by escaped trafficking victims. There is the apartment at Barrington Plaza in the tony Westwood section of Los Angeles, one place that some of the Komisaruk/Mezheritsky ring's trafficking victims ended up, according to Daniel Saunders, the assistant U.S. attorney who prosecuted the ring. And there's a house on Massachusetts Avenue in Vista, California, a San Diego suburb, which was pointed out to me by a San Diego sheriff. These places all have at least one thing in common: they are camouflaged by their normal, middle-class surroundings.

"This is not narco-traffic secrecy," says Sharon B. Cohn, director of anti-trafficking operations for the International Justice Mission. "These are not people kidnapped and held for ransom, but women and children sold every single day. If they're hidden, their keepers don't make money."

IJM's president, Gary Haugen, says: "It's the easiest kind of crime in the world to spot. Men look for it all day, every day."

But border agents and local policemen usually don't know trafficking when they see it. The operating assumption among American police departments is that women who sell their bodies do so by choice, and undocumented foreign women who sell their bodies are not only prostitutes (that is, voluntary sex workers) but also trespassers on U.S. soil. No Department of Justice attorney or police vice squad officer I spoke with in Los Angeles—one of the country's busiest thoroughfares for forced sex traffic—considers sex trafficking in the U.S. a serious problem, or a priority. A teenage girl arrested on Sunset Strip for solicitation, or a group of Russian sex workers arrested in a brothel raid in the San Fernando Valley, are automatically heaped onto a pile of workaday vice arrests.

The United States now offers five thousand visas a year to trafficking victims to allow them to apply for residency. And there's faint hope among sex-trafficking experts that the Bush administration's recent proposal on Mexican immigration, if enacted, could have some positive effect on sex traffic into the United States, by sheltering potential witnesses. "If illegal immigrants who have information about victims have a chance at legal status in this country, they might feel secure enough to come forward," says John Miller of the State Department. But ambiguities still dominate on the front lines—the borders and the streets of urban America—where sex trafficking will always look a lot like prostitution.

"It's not a particularly complicated thing," says Sharon Cohn of International Justice Mission. "Sex trafficking gets thrown into issues of intimacy and vice, but it's a major crime. It's purely profit and pleasure, and greed and lust, and it's right under homicide."

IMPRISONMENT AND SUBMISSION

The basement, Andrea said, held as many as sixteen children and teenagers of different ethnicities. She remembers that it was underneath a house in an upper-middle-class neighborhood on the West Coast. Throughout much of her captivity, this basement was where she was kept when she wasn't working. "There was lots of scrawling on the walls," she said. "The other kids drew stick figures, daisies, teddy bears. This Mexican boy would draw a house with sunshine. We each had a mat."

Andrea paused. "But nothing happens to you in the basement," she continued. "You just had to worry about when the door opened."

She explained: "They would call you out of the basement, and you'd get a bath and you'd get a dress, and if your dress was yellow you were probably going to Disneyland." She said they used color coding to make transactions safer for the traffickers and the clients. "At Disneyland there would be people doing drop-offs and pickups for kids. It's a big open area full of kids, and nobody pays attention to nobody. They would kind of quietly say, 'Go over to that person,' and you would just slip your hand into theirs and say, 'I was looking for you, Daddy.' Then that person would move off with one or two or three of us."

Her account reminded me—painfully—of the legend of the Pied Piper of Hamelin. In the story, a piper shows up and asks for one thousand guilders for ridding the town of a plague of rats. Playing his pipe, he lures all the rats into the River Weser, where they drown. But Hamelin's mayor refuses to pay him. The piper goes back into the streets and again starts to play his music. This time "all the little boys and girls, with rosy cheeks and flaxen curls, and sparkling eyes and teeth like pearls" follow him out of town and into the hills. The piper leads the children to a mountainside, where a portal opens. The children follow him in, the cave closes and Hamelin's children—all but one, too lame to keep up—are never seen again.

Montserrat said that she was moved around a lot and often didn't know where she was. She recalled that she was in Detroit for two months before she realized that she was in "the city where cars are made," because the door to the apartment Alejandro kept her in was locked from the outside. She says she was forced to service at least two men a night, and sometimes more. She watched through the windows as neighborhood children played outside. Emotionally, she slowly dissolved. Later, Alejandro moved her to Portland, Oregon, where once a week he worked her out of a strip club. In all that time she had exactly one night off; Alejandro took her to see *Scary Movie 2.*

All the girls I spoke to said that their captors were both psychologically and physically abusive. Andrea told me that she and the other children she was held with were frequently beaten to keep them off-balance and obedient. Sometimes they were videotaped while being forced to have sex with adults or one another. Often, she said, she was asked to play roles: the therapist's patient or the obedient daughter. Her cell of sex traffickers offered three age ranges of sex partners—toddler to age four, five to twelve, and teens—as well as what she called a "damage group." "In the damage group they can hit you or do anything they wanted," she explained. "Though sex always hurts when you are little, so it's always violent, everything was much more painful once you were placed in the damage group.

"They'd get you hungry then to train you" to have oral sex, she said. "They'd put honey on a man. For the littlest kids, you had to learn not to gag. And they would push things in you so you would open up better. We learned responses. Like if they wanted us to be sultry or sexy or scared. Most of them wanted you scared. When I got older I'd teach the younger kids how to float away so things didn't hurt."

Kevin Bales of Free the Slaves says: "The physical path of a person being trafficked includes stages of degradation of a person's mental state. A victim gets deprived of food, gets hungry, a little dizzy and sleep-deprived. She begins to break down; she can't think for herself. Then take away her travel documents, and you've made her stateless. Then layer on physical violence, and she begins to follow orders. Then add a foreign culture and language, and she's trapped."

Then add one more layer: a sex-trafficking victim's belief that her family is being tracked as collateral for her body. All sex-trafficking operations, whether Mexican, Ukrainian, or Thai, are vast criminal underworlds with roots and branches that reach back to the countries, towns, and neighborhoods of their victims.

"There's a vast misunderstanding of what coercion is, of how little it takes to make someone a slave," Gary Haugen of International Justice Mission said. "The destruction of dignity and sense of self, these girls' sense of resignation. . . ." He didn't finish the sentence.

In Tijuana in November, I met with Mamacita, a Mexican trafficking-victim-turned-madam, who used to oversee a stash house for sex slaves in San Diego. Mamacita (who goes by a nickname) was full of regret and worry. She left San Diego three years ago, but she says that the trafficking ring, run by three violent Mexican brothers, is still in operation. "The girls can't leave," Mamacita said. "They're always being watched. They lock them into apartments. The fear is unbelievable. They can't talk to anyone. They are always hungry, pale, always shaking and cold. But they never complain. If they do, they'll be beaten or killed."

In Vista, California, I followed a pickup truck driven by a San Diego sheriff's deputy named Rick Castro. We wound past a tidy suburban downtown, a supermall and the usual hometown franchises. We stopped alongside the San Luis Rey River, across the street from a Baptist church, a strawberry farm, and a municipal ballfield.

A neat subdivision and cycling path ran along the opposite bank. The San Luis Rey was mostly dry, filled now with an impenetrable jungle of fifteen-foot-high bamboolike reeds. As Castro and I started down a well-worn path into the thicket, he told me about the time he first heard about this place, in October 2001. A local health care worker had heard rumors about Mexican immigrants using the reeds for sex and came down to offer condoms and advice. She found more than four hundred men and fifty young women between twelve and fifteen dressed in tight clothing and high heels. There was a separate group of a dozen girls no more than eleven or twelve wearing white communion dresses. "The girls huddled in a circle for protection," Castro told me, "and had big eyes like terrified deer."

I followed Castro into the riverbed, and only fifty yards from the road we found a confounding warren of more than thirty roomlike caves carved into the reeds. It was a sunny morning, but the light in there was refracted, dreary, and basementlike. The ground in each was a squalid nest of mud, tamped leaves, condom wrappers, clumps of toilet paper and magazines. Soiled underwear was strewn here and there, plastic garbage bags jury-rigged through the reeds in lieu of walls. One of the caves' inhabitants had hung old CDs on the tips of branches, like Christmas ornaments. It looked vaguely like a recent massacre site. It was eight in the morning, but the girls could begin arriving any minute. Castro told me how it works: the girls are dropped off at the ballfield, then herded through a drainage sluice under the road into the riverbed. Vans shuttle the men from a 7-Eleven a mile away. The girls are forced to turn fifteen tricks in five hours in the mud. The johns pay fifteen dollars and get ten minutes. It is in nearly every respect a perfect extension of Calle Santo Tomas in Mexico City. Except that this is what some of those girls are training for.

If anything, the women I talked to said that the sex in the United States is even rougher than what the girls face on Calle Santo Tomas. Rosario, a woman I met in Mexico City, who had been trafficked to New York and held captive for a number of years, said: "In America we had 'special jobs.' Oral sex, anal sex, often with many men. Sex is now more adventurous, harder." She said that she believed younger foreign girls were in demand in the United States because of an increased appetite for more aggressive, dangerous sex. Traffickers need younger and younger girls, she suggested, simply because they are more pliable. In Eastern Europe, too, the typical age of sex-trafficking victims is plummeting; according to Matei of Reaching Out, while most girls used to be in their late teens and twenties, thirteen-year-olds are now far from unusual.

Immigration and Customs Enforcement agents at the Cyber Crimes Center in Fairfax, Virginia, are finding that when it comes to sex, what was once considered abnormal is now the norm. They are tracking a clear spike in the demand for harder-core pornography on the Internet. "We've become desensitized by the soft stuff; now we need a harder and harder hit," says ICE Special Agent Perry Woo. Cybernetworks like KaZaA and Morpheus / through which you can download and trade images and videos—have become the Mexican border of virtual sexual exploitation. I had heard of one Web site that supposedly offered sex slaves for purchase to individuals. The ICE agents hadn't heard of it. Special Agent Don Daufenbach, ICE's manager for undercover operations, brought it up on a screen. A hush came over the room as the agents leaned forward, clearly disturbed. "That sure looks like the real thing," Daufenbach said. There were streams of Web pages of thumbnail images of young women of every ethnicity in obvious distress, bound, gagged, contorted. The agents in the room pointed out probable injuries from torture. Cyberauctions for some of the women were in progress; one had exceeded $300,000. "With new Internet technology," Woo said, "pornography is becoming more pervasive. With Web cams we're seeing more live molestation of children." One of ICE's recent successes, Operation Hamlet, broke up a ring of adults who traded images and videos of themselves forcing sex on their own young children.

But the supply of cheap girls and young women to feed the global appetite appears to be limitless. And it's possible that the crimes committed against them in the United States cut deeper than elsewhere, precisely because so many of them are snared by the glittery promise of an America that turns out to be not their salvation but their place of destruction.

ENDGAME

Typically, a young trafficking victim in the United States lasts in the system for two to four years. After that, Bales says: "She may be killed in the brothel. She may be dumped and deported. Probably least likely is that she will take part in the prosecution of the people that enslaved her."

Who can expect a young woman trafficked into the United States, trapped in a foreign culture, perhaps unable to speak English, physically and emotionally abused and perhaps drug-addicted, to ask for help from a police officer, who more likely than not will look at her as a criminal and an illegal alien? Even Andrea, who was born in the United States and spoke English, says she never thought of escaping, "because what's out there? What's out there was scarier. We had customers who were police, so you were not going to go talk to a cop. We had this customer from Nevada who was a child psychologist, so you're not going to go talk to a social worker. So who are you going to talk to?"

And if the girls are lucky enough to escape, there's often nowhere for them to go. "The families don't want them back," Sister Veronica, a nun who helps run a rescue mission for trafficked prostitutes in an old church in Mexico City, told me. "They're shunned."

When I first met her, Andrea told me: "We're way too damaged to give back. A lot of these children never wanted to see their parents again after a while, because what do you tell your parents? What are you going to say? You're no good."

Correction

An article on January 25 about sexual slavery referred erroneously to the film *Scary Movie 2*. A Mexican woman who was being held as a sex slave in the United States could not have been taken to see it by her captor; by the time the movie came out in 2001, she had already escaped and returned to Mexico.

"The Girl Next Door," an article about the importing of women and girls to the United States for sexual slavery, has generated much discussion since it appeared in the *Times Magazine* on January 25. In response to questions from readers and other publications about sources and accuracy, the magazine has carried out a thorough review of the article.

On the issue of sources, the writer, Peter Landesman, conducted more than forty-five interviews, including many with high-ranking federal officials, law enforcement officers, and representatives of human rights organizations. Four sources insisted on anonymity to protect their professional positions. A magazine fact-checker also interviewed all relevant sources, many of them both before and after publication. Some readers have questioned the figure of ten thousand enforced prostitutes brought into this country each year. The source of that number is Kevin Bales, recommended to the magazine by Human Rights Watch as the best authority on the extent of enforced prostitution in the United States, who based his estimates on State Department documents, arrest and prosecution records, and information from nearly fifty social service agencies.

In the course of this review, several errors were discovered in specific details. One, an erroneous reference to the release date of *Scary Movie 2*, was corrected in the magazine last Sunday.

On the question whether women imported through Cottonwood Canyon, California, could have been wearing high heels, the original source, when pressed, acknowledged that his information was hearsay. The article should not have specified what the women were wearing, and the anecdote should have been related in the past tense, since the trafficking ring was broken up in 2001.

The woman in her twenties known to her traffickers as Andrea recalled an incorrect name for the hotel to which she was taken in Juarez, Mexico. The Radisson Casa Grande had not yet opened when she escaped from her captors.

After the article was published, the writer made an impromptu comment in a radio interview, noting that Andrea has multiple-personality disorder. The magazine editors did not learn of her illness before publication. Andrea's account of her years in slavery remained consistent over two and a half years of psychotherapy. Her therapist says that her illness has no effect on the accuracy of her memory. Her hours-long interview with the author, recorded on tape, is lucid and consistent.

An independent expert consulted by the magazine, Dr. Leonard Shengold, who has written books and papers about child abuse and the reliability and unreliability of memory, affirms that a diagnosis of multiple-personality disorder is not inconsistent with accurate memories of childhood abuse. Because multiple-personality disorder has been associated with false memory, however, the diagnosis should have been cited in the article.

The magazine's cover showed a nineteen-year-old nicknamed Montserrat, who escaped from a trafficker four years ago. An insignia on her school uniform had been retouched out of the picture by the magazine's editors to shield her whereabouts. The change violated the *Times*'s policy against altering photographs.

PETER LANDESMAN *is a journalist, award-winning novelist, and screenwriter. A contributing writer to the* New York Times Magazine, *his journalism has also appeared in* The New Yorker *and the* Atlantic Monthly. *His journalism typically takes him inside underground networks that traffick in weapons, refugees, sex slaves, and stolen and forged art and antiquities. He lives in Los Angeles.*

Coda

I spent five months in Mexico, the United States, Moldova, Russia, and Ukraine for this piece, among victims, police, and federal agents and trafficking networks, carrying out what was at times an emotionally and physically harrowing investigation. "The Girls Next Door"—cited by the Overseas Press Club for Best International Reporting on Human Rights Issues and the most requested and widely read *New York Times* story of 2004, and the most thoroughly fact-checked in the history of the *New York Times Magazine*— sparked a national conversation, and a wave of controversy. The story made people feel terrible, and the attacks against it were organized. And yet the truths the story laid out were incontrovertible. While the controversy was bolstered by little more than blog-esque ad hominem rhetoric and unsubstantiated and at times hysterical disbelief, in the real world—the corridors of power in Washington, D.C.; Mexico City; Rome; and London (among other capitals), and in the streets where girls and young women are "disappeared" inside these networks—the story has had a profound and tangible effect:

Government officials continually report to me the many ways the story changed policy inside the Department of Justice and the Bush administration, which had believed sex trafficking to be a problem in Asia and Eastern Europe but not in the United States. Multiple federal and state task forces and initiatives were established in the story's wake. Two weeks after publication, Mexican and United States authorities performed simultaneous raids on one of the trafficking networks the story identifies. Its victims held captive in New York City and Mexico were rescued and entered into a witness protection program. The infant of one of them—held by the traffickers as collateral in Mexico—was also saved. The principles in the network were arrested and are now being tried in the United States. That same week, a sex trafficking ring operating near Disneyland—another place the story identified—was broken up, its principles arrested. Federal authorities have since surveilled and raided the San Diego trafficking network exposed by the story, rescuing dozens of its captives. Cities such as Los Angeles have begun to train its police officers to recognize sex trafficking when they see it. Embarrassed by the story's revelations, the Mexican government— through its intelligence agency, CISEN—founded a task force to fight sex trafficking in Mexico.

But perhaps most importantly, "The Girls Next Door" sparked a national conversation about sex slavery, the use and captivity of thousands of foreign girls and young women in America. I am frequently buttonholed by NGO experts and government officials—including a number of Justice officials and federal prosecutors, and one high official from the Department of Health and Human and Services—that this article was not only groundbreaking in its accuracy, but represented a watershed moment in the understanding of this barbaric economy.

Robert Draper

THE ONES
THAT GOT AWAY

FROM GQ

THE LITTLE WHITE BOAT meant nothing to them. Out here in the Gulf of Aden on this soupy October morning, what first came to mind was, *How the hell do they live in this heat?* That, and *How much farther to freaking Bahrain?* Somewhere along the way—during the great ship's two-month voyage from Norfolk, Virginia, across the Atlantic, into the Mediterranean, and at last through the Suez Canal toward the northern Arabian Gulf—the whiff of danger had settled into the crew's nostrils. It would not be fair to say that they were unready. But you would have to say that they were, in the end, unprepared.

There were 293 of them, male and female, twenty-two-year-old doe-eyed peacetime recruits from flyspeck towns in Wisconsin and North Dakota and Texas. They were trained for a kind of warfare that, after today, would become virtually obsolete. For at their disposal aboard the 505-foot-long ship were all the tools for superpower combat. Tomahawk and Harpoon cruise missiles. SM-2 surface-to-air missiles, Spy-1 multifunction radar. A Phalanx close-in weapons system. Torpedoes and rapid-fire multibarrel cannons.

They were girded, it would seem, for Armageddon. Shielded by all this high-tech weaponry, the ship's crew lined up outside the galleys for an early lunch of fajitas; and when they observed the puttering approach of the little white boat, they responded, as any giant would, with serene obliviousness. Trusting its puniness, they dropped their guard.

The two men aboard the little white boat looked happy. They were waving and saluting—or was that a salute? And calling out in greeting—or was that a Muslim prayer? It was hard to tell from the destroyer's great height, looming 148 feet above the water. The crew believed the two men to be harbor garbage collectors, though they could just as easily have been selling trinkets and snacks like so many other vendors bobbing across the water. Or they could have been fish merchants, which was what the two men had told neighbors they were, though no one had ever seen them at the Aden fish market, just as no one had ever seen them at the mosques, the qat-vending stands, the bakeries, the beaches. . . . Only a few furtive appearances from behind the wall they had erected around their cinder-block house overlooking the harbor. Elsewhere—Bangkok, Nairobi, Afghanistan—the two men had been seen plenty. But those in the intelligence community who were paid to track their whereabouts had failed to follow them here, to the shabby district of Madinat ash Sha'b on the southern coast of Yemen. And now, on the morning of October 12, 2000, the two men had taken leave of the neighborhood that never knew them, slid their little white boat down a ramp and into the water, revved the outboard motor, and commenced an unhurried path eastward across the bay, toward the USS *Cole*.

And the little white boat? There was nothing unusual about it, nothing at all. In fact, it had plied these waters just a month earlier—from the inlet to the harbor and back—without incident, seemingly without purpose, trolling right past the Yemeni naval base. There had been another time before that, too: January 3, 2000, when another man launched the little white boat toward another

American destroyer, only to see it sink within minutes because the bomb it was carrying was too heavy. No one aboard that particular American ship, *The Sullivans*, ever saw the skiff submerge, or saw it being retrieved the next day, or saw it being subsequently reinforced with fiberglass while the C-4 plastic explosives were compacted into a neat five hundred-pound bundle. No, the little white boat gave away nothing. Not then, not now, nine months later, with its two bearded passengers coming ever closer to the *Cole*, rounding the hull toward the rear of the ship, calling out and waving.

Was that a wave? Was that a prayer? Was it garbage they were looking for? All unasked. But the answer came anyway as the little white boat and the two happy men detonated into a million pieces, and the massive American destroyer roared in pain.

In that instant, the world went asymmetric. Seventeen sailors lay dead, another thirty-nine wounded, and America suddenly needed Yemen to explain what had gone wrong. *Yemen?* What did we know of Yemen? Where did it stand, this dog-poor Muslim country that had been driven from our herd when it sided with Saddam Hussein in the 1991 Gulf War and only after a decade's worth of economic sanctions had been brought to heel? We would, alas, soon find out—beginning with Yemen's president, Ali Abdullah Saleh, who immediately blamed the explosion on a technical mishap inside the *Cole*, and later on the Egyptians, and later still on the Israelis. Still, to show the Americans that his government would leave no stone unturned, President Saleh dispatched his Political Security Organization—the thuggish plainclothes domestic intelligence unit that reports directly to Saleh—to rampage through Aden and collar "every man with a beard," as one Yemeni government official would say.

When FBI agents arrived in Aden two days later and requested that those behind bars be extradited to the United States for prosecution, President Saleh informed them that the Yemeni constitution forbade this. When the FBI demanded to join the interrogations, the PSO refused on the grounds of national sovereignty. When the

FBI agents asked for interview transcripts, they were handed pages that read like Dadaist poetry. And when the FBI suggested that certain Islamic extremists in the Yemeni government be investigated in connection with the crime, the PSO agents smiled and did nothing.

In late November 2000, the Yemeni government suddenly announced that the case of the USS *Cole* bombing had been solved, that all ten perpetrators were in custody. The investigation was shut down, and a trial was set for the following January. The Americans protested that this was lunacy: the plot's two alleged overseers, after all, men with direct ties to Osama bin Laden, were still at large. So the Yemeni government agreed to delay the trial for a year. Then it delayed the trial for another year. By that time, it was November 2002; one of the two alleged *Cole* masterminds was in American hands, and the United States was strongly urging Yemen to proceed with trial. As of April 10, 2003, the ten *Cole* suspects were still in prison, awaiting formal charges.

As of the next morning, they were not.

HERE, NOW, grinning for the cameras, stands America with Yemen—a marriage not quite from hell, but ever so far from heaven. It would be unfair to cast all blame on the war bride. After all, no sitting American president has ever deigned to set foot on Yemeni sand—though in 1986, then vice president George H. W. Bush briefly touched down to commemorate the opening of an oil refinery there by a Texas petroleum firm.

As it has turned out, the deserts of Yemen are largely petro-barren, and its government has been known to meddle in corporate profits; and so since there is no point in Americans trying to make any money there, there has seemed little point in paying it much mind at all. Except, of course, when we have no choice. In the two years since President George W. Bush proclaimed "either you are with us or you are with the terrorists" and President Saleh dashed off to Washington to pledge his country's allegiance to the war on terror, the United States has supplied Yemen with Special Forces training, Coast Guard patrol boats, an FBI office and a fraction of the economic aid it gives to the far tinier nation of Jordan. About its new ally, the U.S. State Department offers only this: "Any counter-terrorism cooperation will be judged on its continuing results." Though far more American travelers have been killed in, say, Mexico than in Yemen in recent years, the State Department warns Americans not to go there.

Then again, Yemen *is* bin Laden country. Osama's father hailed from the southeastern tribal stronghold of Hadhramawt, and Osama himself plucked his fifth and favorite wife from the town of Ibb. "Even when bin Laden was in Afghanistan," says Edmund Hull, the U.S. ambassador to Yemen, "he always imagined Yemen as a fallback." And after the routing of the Taliban last year, the worry was so great that Al Qaeda would regroup in bin Laden's ancestral homeland that, in the words of one U.S. official, "we began looking around Yemen for a tall guy with a cane."

Bin Laden would be at home in Yemen in more ways than one. Though President Saleh has denounced Al Qaeda almost as strongly as he has Israel—"I am for jihad, for resistance, for arms and money to be sent to fight the Jews," he once declared by way of supporting a Palestinian homeland—his "instinctive tendency," as one U.S. official puts it, "is to seek accommodation" with Islamic extremists and with the tribal leaders who have long harbored terrorists in the lawless Empty Quarter that covers a vast swath of the country. Once upon a time, travel writers spoke of Yemen as a cradle of civilization, the nexus of the frankincense trade, the land of Noah's son and the dominion of the Queen of Sheba. No longer. To talk about Yemen today is to talk about terrorism.

But that is America doing the talking. "You've been here for a while," a Yemeni acquaintance said to me while I was there. "Do we seem like a nation of terrorists to you?" And the only honest reply was no, Yemen did not seem that way. On the night of my arrival, I could hear the chattering of automatic gunfire somewhere below the window of my heavily guarded hotel in Sanaa. But this was only the revelry of a wedding party, which I caught up to the next morning, in the Wadi Dhahr valley, where grapes and pomegranates and qat flourish. On a peak overlooking a former sultan's winter palace, the bridegroom and his tribal brethren staged an elaborate jambiya sword fight to the furious rhythm of a *tasa* drumbeat. Several men standing around the dancers still toted their Kalashnikovs from the night before. When I told one of them I was an American, he hesitated for only a moment before replying with the word I heard more often than any other during my two weeks in Yemen: "Welcome."

I was welcome here, but so was the Palestinian organization Hamas, which maintains an office in Sanaa. To the U.S. government, Hamas is a terrorist organization; to most Yemenis, it is a resistance movement. For that matter, to the Arab world, the honey produced in the Hadhramawt region is a peerless aphrodisiac. To the U.S. government, Yemeni honey merchants are terrorist money launderers. Which truth prevails? Teetering between the exotic and the horrific became my psychic tightrope walk. While shuffling through the spice-scented thousand-year-old alleyways of the Sanaa souk, tangled up in the foot traffic of beggars and silversmiths and qat procurers—a claustrophobic bustle not that different from the one that suddenly coalesced around the U.S. embassy last year, screaming, "Death to America!"—I clung to the admonition *Sometimes, usually, nearly always, a little white boat is just a little white boat.*

And they, no doubt, thought of me: *Sometimes, after all, an American man in Yemen is not an FBI agent.* In this uneasy way, we trusted each other—though relieved, if we were to be honest with ourselves, that our governments did not.

THE PRISON was not a prison. It might have been helpful, from the American point of view, to know this—that the ten conspirators believed responsible for the deaths of seventeen American sailors were being held in a mere interrogation center, situated on the first floor of the Aden headquarters of the PSO, a sullen two-story building the British had constructed sometime before 1967, when the South Yemen socialists escorted the colonialists out of the country at gunpoint. Whatever the building had once been, it had since taken on the PSO's own shadowy personality. Individuals were brought there without charges and were detained for unspecified periods. Many were not treated kindly. Amnesty International had asked to inspect the building to determine whether torture took place there. Lawyers demanded to meet with jailed clients. Family members showed up in tears; all were turned away. No one could get into this prison unless the PSO had dragged him there.

Getting out, by comparison, was a snap.

The ten men were not equal partners in crime. One of them, Jamal al-Badawi, the accused USS *Cole*–plot field coordinator, was a highly regarded sheik and, along with Fahd al-Quso, an Al Qaeda camp habitué. The eight others, however, were mere crooked cops and civil servants who had supplied al-Badawi and al-Quso with phony identification and credit references. One prisoner's sole offense was that of preparing the *Cole* suicide bombers a farewell lunch the day before the attack. Though the FBI agents saw little sport in crucifying marginal offenders ("We're interested in quality, not quantity," said a top U.S. official), they saw no profit in quibbling. Justice of a kind would be served. All ten would be tried together. All were up for the death penalty. In the meantime, all ten occupied the same cell. And it was a lucky thing for the rest that one of them was good friends with a certain uniformed man named Hussein al-Ansi. Around Aden, al-Ansi was described as a mustachioed lout who enjoyed crashing diplomatic parties. Among the FBI, he was believed to be the foremost obstructionist in the USS *Cole* investigation. Here in the PSO building, he was chief.

And he was all they needed. For this prison had no surveillance cameras. No motion detectors. No electric fences. No watchtowers. What it did have was a hole, dug by hand through a concrete bathroom wall. And so through this hole, out into the coastal air, across a vacant lot and over the low perimeter fence, down the street, beyond the forbidding gates of the PSO headquarters and into a waiting taxicab galloped ten men with a plan, with one good friend and with only the moon smiling down on them—unless it, too, turned away.

Later that afternoon of Friday, April 11, 2003, while the Yemeni government was denying that any prisoners had escaped, roadblocks barricaded every major road in Aden while the PSO reprised its every-man-with-a-beard burlesque. But the USS *Cole* Ten—the only suspects Yemeni authorities had ever apprehended in connection with the bombing—had already disappeared into the creases of the southern Arabian desert, much as the two happy suicide bombers had scattered themselves over the Gulf of Aden three years before. Disappeared, to this day, they all remain.

THE QAT leaves I had been chewing for the past half hour began to achieve the expected effect. My extremities trembled, my stom-. ach performed somersaults, and I jawed like a jackass about matters of which I was extravagantly ignorant. "You have to understand," I was saying. "Very few Americans can even find Yemen on a map. They only hear about Yemen when there's an incident like the USS *Cole* bombing."

The five young Yemeni journalists I was talking to passed more leaves my way. "Why is it," one of them asked, "that America is so preoccupied with hunting down people who it thinks are terrorists while it allows Israel to pursue blatant acts of terrorism against the Palestinian people?"

"America's never going to view Israel the way you do," I said. "It's the only reliable democracy in the Middle East, and it's one of the most loyal allies we have."

"What do you think about the fact that no Jews were killed when the World Trade Center was attacked?"

It was Friday, the holy day. The five of them—and almost every-one else in Yemen—had been chewing qat leaves for hours. Golf ball-size convexities formed in their right cheeks. The qat was of very high quality, I was told. No DDT or other pesticides. We sat cross-legged and barefoot on a carpeted floor in a room whose only adornments were photographs of assassinated former leaders of Yemen. I had fallen into the journalists' company while pursuing the mystery of the USS *Cole* escapees. The young reporters were eager to help, but in truth they knew less than I did. None of them had been to the prison, and no Yemeni official would speak to them about the investigation. As the sunlight ebbed, the sounds of traffic in the disordered streets of Sanaa gave way to the muezzin's final call to prayer. "Let's take a fifteen-minute break," said the lean-faced *Yemen Observer* writer as he stood up and brushed the qat rem-nants off his traditional Yemeni blazer, skirt, and ornamental belt.

As soon as they returned from their prayer session in the hallway, I took the offensive. I wanted to know why Yemen—which the United Nations had recently ranked as 148th out of 174 nations in terms of economic development—did not throw out President Saleh after twenty-five years in power. I wanted to know what it suggested about Yemen's supposed free press that journalists who impugned the president or Islam were summarily hauled off to un-derground prisons by the PSO. As the qat buzz shivered through me like an electric eel, I concluded my discourse with a rousing, "The government's not going to hand you more rights—*you've* got to fight for them!"

The journalists nodded listlessly. Then one of them asked, "Do you think it's right that the CIA launches Predator drone missiles into Yemen and murders suspected terrorists extrajudicially, the way the Israeli army does?"

So it went for hours, a congenial impasse, until the best we could do was rhapsodize about qat, the opiate of the Yemeni masses—how it spurred a man to perform like a gladiator in the bedroom, weep for the absence of his mother, or produce seamless poetry on deadline. What qat could not do was make a Yemeni and an American see the world in remotely the same way.

No, no, no, I was constantly assured by both United States and Yemeni officials, there has been much progress. Things are changing. Al Qaeda is on the run here and cannot regroup. Jailed extremists are renouncing jihad in exchange for probation. The Imams are toning down their oratory. American aid is trickling in. And so why focus on the prison? Bring it up and everyone gets nasty again. Like interior minister Rashad al-Alimi, Yemen's top law-enforcement official. "It's our negligence," he said, "but the Americans have their fingerprints on this, too. We wanted to put [the ten suspects] through the legal system. Try them in the courts and then move them from the interrogation center to a maximum-security prison. But who was delaying this? The Americans. They said no, leave them there, leave them there."

To which an official at the U.S. embassy replied, "Frankly, we weren't aware they'd been transferred there to begin with."

And so we arrive where we began, blown back into the Gulf of Aden, staring out at the little white boat. To trust or not to trust? So the PSO chief in Aden and all the prison's guards were sacked immediately following the jailbreak. So the taxi driver who drove the ten men away was interrogated. So a government commission was assembled to straighten the whole mess out. Where were the indictments? Why had the entire matter become classified? And why had none of the fugitives been apprehended?

"We have sources saying they're at a certain location," the interior minister assured me. "My people are on the ground, and they're trailing them."

That was in July. Sound familiar? To Clint Guenther, the FBI's logistical coordinator for the USS *Cole* investigation, the jailbreak episode "didn't surprise me one bit, considering that the cooperation we'd always gotten from the Yemen government was shoddy at best. I truly believe that they didn't want us to know everything."

And that was the way it was going to be. Just as America would see bin Laden's ghost behind every beard, just as it would browbeat with its Predator bombings and extort with its foreign-aid budget, so too would Yemen insist that its extremists are a dying breed, and chafe at the slightest accusation to the contrary. Better, then, to stand together for the cameras, grin our grins—enemies kept closer, terrorized into friendship—and say nothing, absolutely nothing, about the prison.

EXCEPT THAT I wanted to visit it. And so one evening I flew from Sanaa with my translator, Khaled al-Hammadi, to the port town of Aden.

The flight attendant's mascara began to drip the moment she stepped onto the runway. At eight in the evening, the temperature exceeded ninety, and the air leeched itself to our pores. Khaled haggled with a cabdriver before we stepped into his vehicle—which, like most Yemeni taxis, resembled an oil spill. I hung my head out the window, pretending there was a cool breeze and that I was in my swimsuit, prostrate before the waves.

When we checked into our beachside hotel, the clerk politely explained that, as a foreigner, I would be assessed a higher room rate than would Khaled. (This informal "visitor's tax" in Yemen applies not only to hotels but also to plane tickets and restaurant meals. It's the country's small contribution to global-wealth redistribution.) Having endured an alcohol-free week in conservative Sanaa, I made for the hotel bar, where I drank Heineken from a can and watched an episode of Arabic-subtitled *Friends* in the company of several Jordanian businessmen.

When I knocked on Khaled's hotel door later that evening, I found another man in the room. He introduced himself as Haydar and showed me his PSO identification card. Haydar was short, with a trim mustache and intense eyes—a sort of Arabian Errol Flynn, except that he was pronouncedly duck-footed and had sweated completely through his olive silk shirt. He explained that foreign journalists were not to be wandering around Aden without a "minder" from the Ministry of Information. I suggested that this was ridiculous, that I had been interviewing cabinet officials un-fettered all week long in Sanaa and that President Saleh's aides had given me their blessings to travel to Aden. Did I have documenta-tion of this, Haydar wanted to know. No, I confessed, I did not, but he was free to call them. Haydar told us not to leave the hotel grounds that evening, shook our hands, and said good night.

The next morning, Haydar was already making himself com-fortable in the lobby when I showed up for breakfast. "Hello, Robert!" he called out in English and sprang to his feet to shake my hand. I had people to see that morning, and Haydar informed me that he would escort me in his pickup truck. The interview subject, a powerful newspaper publisher, was not daunted by Haydar. He closed the door on the PSO agent's nose. When I finished my interview, Haydar was dutifully standing outside, having sweated through his natty blue long-sleeve shirt. He was waiting to hear from the new Aden PSO chief about my visiting the prison. In the meantime, he offered with a shrug, would I like a tour of Aden?

We killed time by driving through the old market in Crater, bumping along the old British-built boulevards past sagging and blistered storefronts and then finally around an immense cistern that had been dug perhaps two thousand years ago and now was dry. At one point, Haydar's pickup truck broke down, and he fret-ted over the carburetor in the 110-degree heat while Khaled and I tried to control our laughter. He was actually a decent sort, not one of the PSO's musclemen, and though he said he was from the mountains in the north and ill-suited to Aden's stifling humidity, he maintained a kind of futile dignity in his neatly trimmed mustache and his fine sweat-stained clothes.

There wasn't much to see in the raggedy old coastal city, so Hay-dar ferried us back to the hotel. We sat in deck chairs at the water's edge, watching a procession of young Yemeni women stride slowly through the waves in their head-to-toe *sharshafs* like ebony apparitions. At last Haydar's cell phone rang. He strode off for some privacy, kicking up sand and mopping his brow.

When he returned, I could tell by his face that the news was not good. Khaled translated: The new Aden chief was irate at Haydar. *What was this American journalist doing in Aden anyway? And you took him on a tour? No, he cannot see the prison. Do not let him leave the hotel grounds. Escort him to the airport tomorrow morning.*

"I am sorry, Robert," Haydar said. Then he bent down, reached for my neck, and kissed me on both cheeks with his sweaty lips.

The next morning, a few minutes after the mascara-stained Yemen Airways flight attendant welcomed me aboard, I lay my forehead against the aircraft window—a portrait of stupefaction, gaping at the dunes, which swirled like caramel question marks in the almighty nothingness below. Thinking: *The prison is not a prison. The little white boat is not just a little white boat. The alliance is not an alliance.* Then the plane thrust heavenward, and the question marks melted under the Arabian sun.

Now in his eighth year as GQ *writer-at-large,* ROBERT DRAPER *is also the author of the novel* Hadrian's Walls *(Knopf, 1999) and the biography* Rolling Stone Magazine: The Uncensored History *(Doubleday, 1990). He is at work on a book about the Bush presidency for the* Free Press. *Draper resides in Asheville, North Carolina.*

Coda

And then, fully eleven months after their escape, in a single week in March of 2004, all ten suspects were magically recaptured in the mountains of Abyan province dominated by tribal factions. A "security trial" was staged for five of them in a Sanaa courtroom in early July. At some point during the course of the trial, the defendants were awarded attorneys but were not permitted to speak with them outside of court. The sentences came down in September: five to ten years for four of the defendants, and the death penalty for the plot's on-the-ground coordinator, al-Badawi, who hollered out, "This is an unjust verdict! This is an American verdict!"

For me, the proceedings were quintessentially Yemeni. But al-Badawi had a point: American diplomats attended the trial and were quick to praise its outcome, and once again it seemed that Yemen's eagerness to please both sides had produced slapstick consequences. I left the country as most Western journalists have, awed and confounded—and oddly reluctant to return to my world of shallow, banal mysteries.

Skip Hollandsworth

THE FAMILY MAN

FROM *Texas Monthly*

WHEN MOTHERS SAW TODD BECKER in the carpool line at the elementary school in Stonebridge Ranch, an upscale bedroom community in McKinney, north of Dallas, they'd occasionally stop chatting on their cell phones and do a double take. Becker was a good-looking young guy in his early thirties, with neatly cut hair and brown eyes. He wore khaki pants and crisp T-shirts. He had a pleasant smile, his teeth very white and straight.

But it wasn't his looks, the mothers later said, that were the most attractive part about him. Around Stonebridge Ranch, Todd Becker was known as the family man, a devoted husband who always took the time to eat lunch with his sweet blond wife, Cathy, and a doting father who coached his children's soccer teams and took them to their ballet lessons. Some of the mothers were impressed that he liked to go to the school and read stories to his children's classes. Others noted that he was happy to let the neighborhood kids swim in his backyard pool or jump on the trampoline. He was pleasant and soft-spoken, never one to talk too much about himself. He rarely had more than a beer or two at parties. He took his family to

Sunday services at the Lutheran church not far from his home, and at the Stonebridge Country Club, where he was one of the top tennis players, he never threw his racket when he was losing. "Let's face it," one mother would later say. "A lot of women around Stonebridge Ranch wished their own husbands were more like Todd."

At his $280,000 two-story custom-built home on Fallen Leaf Lane, in Stonebridge's Autumn Ridge neighborhood, where he had turned the living room into an extra playroom for the kids, Becker always led the family in a prayer at dinner. At bedtime, he would kiss his children good-night and tell them to sleep well. Then, he would kiss his wife good-night and tell her to sleep well too. Then, he would get into his minivan or his Ford Expedition, back out of the driveway, and head off to commit some of the most daring, professionally executed burglaries that law enforcement authorities have ever seen.

Todd Becker made his living by stealing the cash out of safes from stores, restaurants, and businesses throughout Texas and Florida, where he had lived before moving to Texas. He and his small band of employees would pry the safes open with crowbars, slam them apart with sledgehammers, hack into them with concrete saws, or cut them open with torches. Many times they'd yank the entire safe out of the floor and carry it away to be opened at a more discreet location, occasionally inside Becker's own garage. Becker would split up the loot with his team and then take his cut to his bedroom, hiding the money under some clothes in his closet. He'd shower, comb his hair, and be downstairs by the time his kids awakened, ready to fix them pancakes and drive them to school. When a torrent of gun-wielding police officers arrived at his house one morning in late 2002, bursting through his front door and stepping over children's toys to arrest him, his neighbors stood in their front yards, cups of coffee in their hands, their mouths open. A few of them later told the cops that they had made a terrible mistake.

"We said there is no way he could be a thief," one neighbor re-called. "He's just like the rest of us."

A few months ago, while the thirty-three-year-old Becker was still out on bond, he allowed me to come see him. When I walked up to his house, he greeted me at the door, gave me a friendly hand-shake, and said with a half-smile, "Well, here's my crime den." He led me to his dining room table, made of burnished cherry, while his youngest daughter, aged two, watched Barney in the family room and Cathy, who's thirty-five, made coffee. It was a couple of weeks before Halloween, and Cathy had decorated the front of their house, as she did every year, with pumpkins and plastic skele-tons hanging from a tree and a sign on the front door that read: AU-TUMN GREETINGS FROM THE BECKERS. Next to the sewing machine in the kitchen were Halloween costumes that she was making for their four children. "Usually, I'm in charge of the neighborhood Hal-loween parade," she told me with a slight shrug of her shoulders. "But this year I thought someone else should do it." As she talked, Becker flipped through a scrapbook to a page that showed pictures of his wife and children in costumes from a previous Halloween parade, cheerfully marching down the street with their neighbors. Then he turned the page and showed me photos of birthday parties that he and Cathy had thrown for their kids. "Not what you were expecting, huh?" Becker asked me.

Nor the authorities. According to police detectives, burglars are typically impoverished young males looking for money to buy drugs. Wearing sweatshirts with hoods, they amateurishly smash through store windows and grab what they can while the alarms are blaring. "You don't find these guys meticulously planning out their crimes so that they can live an all-American lifestyle in a nice neighborhood with a nice family," said Bill Hardman, a detective from Fort Pierce, Florida, one of the many cities plagued by Becker. "They want crack or guns. But Todd Becker was one of a kind—a clean-cut yuppie daddy who bought dolls for his children."

What especially intrigued the cops about Becker was the way he chose his accomplices. Like the Old West outlaw Jesse James, who also had a love of snatching money out of safes and strongboxes, Becker relied mostly on kinfolk to help him: his two half brothers, his brother-in-law, a step-nephew, and a childhood friend. Unlike Jesse James, however, he didn't choose them because they were experienced criminals or good with guns. (Becker didn't allow weapons of any kind to be used during his burglaries. He didn't even allow guns in his home, fearing that his children might find them and accidentally shoot themselves.) He picked relatives and friends who happened to be down on their luck, involved in unhappy relationships, or stuck in dead-end jobs, if they had jobs at all. One brother who worked for Becker had a job on the side performing as an "entertainer" on a subscription Internet sex site, and another worked part-time as a Santa's helper at a mall. His childhood friend was battling a weight problem. Becker even used his own sister Kim, who was dancing at a strip club in Florida, to work as a lookout on one of his burglaries, telling her that he hoped the money she made on the venture would encourage her to quit stripping and lead a more stable life. "Maybe to someone else, none of this makes any sense, but you've got to understand Todd," said Kim, a perky single mother of five. "He had created this really happy life for himself in the suburbs, with church and soccer and good schools and all that. And I think he wanted all the rest of us in his family to experience what he had."

Indeed, Becker was a new kind of American criminal, so intent on improving his life and the lives of his fellow family members that he would often tune the radio in his vehicle to the nationally syndicated show of self-help counselor Dr. Laura Schlessinger as he drove through various shopping centers with his team, scouting out potential businesses to rob. He talked to his accomplices about the dangers of drinking and drug abuse. He encouraged them to save their money for the future. "I really thought I was helping out everyone who went to work for me, helping them put some money together and get a new start with their lives," Becker told me, staring out his dining room window. "It's still hard to believe just how it all turned out."

HE WAS literally an altar boy at a Lutheran church in Port St. Lucie, the small city on Florida's east coast where he was raised. When he signed up for junior tennis tournaments, he would inform the tournament directors that he could not play matches on Sunday mornings because he had to attend church. "Todd never smoked cigarettes, and he would have only one beer at high school parties," recalled one of his Florida friends; Jeff Drock. "And he wouldn't even drink that." What amazed almost everyone who got to know Todd Becker during his teenage years was that he never tried to have sex with girls. He said that he wanted to save himself for marriage.

If he had gone into the ministry, none of his childhood friends would have been surprised. But during Becker's adolescence, his father, William Becker, began having run-ins with the law. A former police officer from Detroit, the elder Becker had quit the force in the sixties to sell encyclopedias door-to-door, then moved to Florida to sell video games during the era when Pac-Man and Donkey Kong were the biggest sellers. Although he had been decorated as a cop for fighting crime, he apparently went the other way when it came to making money as a salesman. He spent some time in jail for business fraud during Becker's youth, and when he got out, he had trouble finding steady employment.

While Becker's father went through his legal problems, Becker's mother worked at Domino's delivering pizzas, but her income was hardly adequate to support herself and her three children, of whom Becker was the eldest. "I think the family was evicted out of a couple of houses," said Todd's half brother Dwayne Becker, one of four sons from William Becker's first marriage who were raised by their mother in another home. "And I remember Todd said he was never going to live this way again, and maybe that explains him a little."

Becker told me he began to steal simply to help out his family. He swiped tennis balls from a tennis club because he didn't want his mother to use her money on him. To pay for gasoline for his car, he stole money from a country club. By his junior year in high school, he was stealing radar detectors out of cars and selling them for fifty to sixty dollars each and taking his siblings to the mall to buy clothes. Two years later, Becker enrolled at the University of Central Florida, in Orlando, on a tennis scholarship. But after hurting his neck, he quit the team and dropped out of school in 1989, just after his freshman year. He returned to Port St. Lucie to attend junior college, where he ran across a guy who told him that he knew about some Apple computers that could be stolen from a warehouse. "That was when Apple computers cost four thousand dollars, which sure beat radar detectors," Becker said.

Becker did get arrested a couple of times in his late teens and early twenties, but either the charges were dropped or he was given a minor probated sentence. When he met Cathy, in 1992, at a night-club on the beach frequented by college students, he told her on their first date about his past burglaries. But he also talked about his love for family and his intentions to go straight. Cathy had been raised in West Texas by her mother after her father, a crop duster, had died in a plane crash. She too wanted a stable family life after having been moved from home to home, and she found herself drawn to Becker's old-fashioned sincerity, especially when he told her his goal was to own a family-friendly business, like a Chuck E. Cheese's. "Todd really wanted to be Ward Cleaver, and he wanted Cathy to be June," said another of Becker's half brothers, Bill Becker. "And they lived in the perfect community, where they could walk around at night and not have to worry about the wrong elements."

Still, Becker could not get away from the fact that he possessed a special gift for burglary. To pay for his and Cathy's 1993 wedding, for instance, he slipped out one night and quickly burglarized a couple of computer stores. Six months after the marriage, when he learned Cathy was pregnant, he committed a few more burglaries so they could rent a nice house in a quiet neighborhood on the Florida coast.

Cathy believed Becker when he kept promising that his next burglary would be his last, but as criminals like to say when describing their pasts, one thing led to another, and soon Becker was a full-time burglar, focusing on computer companies located in out-of-the-way business parks throughout Florida. He asked Dwayne, a part-time construction worker who was then hanging out at bars in the afternoons, drinking and playing darts, to help him break into businesses, and he persuaded Bill, a Grizzly Adams look-alike who had been unsuccessfully trying to build a career as a manager of Holiday Inn restaurants, to allow the stolen computers to be stored in his garage. Although he could have found other professional burglars to work as his accomplices, Becker told me that he decided to work with family members and friends because he felt they would not squeal on anyone else if they ever got arrested. He said he also thought it might be nice to boost the fortunes of his family, especially those Beckers who were facing personal or financial challenges. As a favor to his sister Kim, Becker asked her husband, Danny Birtwell, an electrician who had shown little competence in the workforce—"He was a complete idiot," Kim told me—to work with him. And he also recruited a friend from his old high school tennis team, Paulo Rodrigues, who had become somewhat disheartened because he was seriously overweight (Becker estimated he weighed three hundred pounds) and because he had a rather mundane job as a salesman at Mattress Giant.

It seemed to be the unlikeliest of operations, this partnership between a fastidious young suburban dad and his unambitious relatives. Initially, they looked more like the Marx Brothers than Butch Cassidy's Wild Bunch. The beer-drinking Dwayne occasionally broke into the wrong businesses. Danny once fell off a roof while trying to get into an office building. After one burglary, while the team was unloading the computers from Becker's car, Danny accidentally locked the keys inside the vehicle. Unwilling to damage his own car, Becker called a locksmith in the middle of the night. When Danny took a break from the burglary business, complaining that he had been working too hard, Becker brought in Kim to work one job with him. She wore a cute sweat suit, brushed her hair back into a ponytail, and hid behind some bushes to look for cops. When Becker was ready to leave with a stack of computers, she sprinted to the minivan, her enhanced breasts bouncing like beach balls.

Against all odds, Becker kept himself and his employees one step ahead of the cops. He taught his guys how to pry open the front door of a business with a crowbar without shattering the glass or tearing the door frame, thus allowing the door to shut behind them and preventing a cop or security guard driving by from realizing that a burglary was in process. He showed them how to cut certain phone lines, which would disconnect most alarm systems. To make sure they hadn't tripped a silent alarm, Becker would have everyone pile back into the car after cutting the phone lines, drive fifteen minutes in one direction, and then return. If no police officers had shown up by that time, they would break in.

Becker told me that he and his team made $2 million in a ten-year span selling their stolen computers to fences (other criminals who purchase stolen goods). He was doing so much work that police departments all over Florida had begun to share information in an attempt to find the computer thief. Becker figured that the cops had to be thinking about him: Because of his earlier arrests, his name was in their databases. What's more, Cathy wanted to find a place for the family to live where they wouldn't always have to look over their shoulder, a place where they could be anonymous.

So Becker did exactly what so many nineteenth-century lawbreakers once did to hide out from the long arm of the law. He moved to Texas. And just like the outlaws of old, Becker decided to hide out on a ranch.

WELL, IT was called a ranch. At the edge of almost every large American city there is a development like Stonebridge Ranch: a master-planned community, filled with just the right amenities for the upper middle class, including eighteen-hole golf courses, a large community swimming pool, hike-and-bike trails surrounding man-made ponds, and strategically placed shopping centers. All the neighborhoods are given lofty names (Eldorado, Stone Canyon), and the custom-built houses that line the uncracked streets look nearly identical, with nearly identical trees planted in the front yards and nearly identical SUVs sitting in the driveways. In such communities can be found the newest generation of Americans bonded together by their striving for entitlement. The setting couldn't have been more perfect for Todd Becker.

In 1996, Becker put down $56,000 for his new home, which Cathy loved because it had a second-floor catwalk. ("Perfect for decorating for Christmas," she told me.) They added a chandelier to the living room, and on a dining room wall they hung vases from which poured fake ivy. On another wall they placed photos of themselves holding each of their children. "He was a very caring, loving neighbor, friendly to everyone," said Kathy Scherer, who lived on the same street and who believed Becker's story that he worked in "computer consulting," one of those nineties catch-all phrases that could mean absolutely anything. He helped clean up one neighbor's house when it was toilet-papered by some kids. He used his extra-long ladder to help another neighbor put up Christmas lights. He tracked down another neighbor at work to let him know that his burglar alarm was going off and that he'd be happy to check the house out for him. Parents appreciated the way he never yelled at the kids on the soccer teams he helped coach, and the elders at the Lutheran church near the Becker home appreciated the $500 checks he deposited in the collection plate.

Cathy, meanwhile, babysat anytime someone needed her. She

generously gave money to a friend on the block who was running in a charity race to raise funds for breast cancer research. She taught vacation Bible school at the church, and she made sure to invite the neighborhood kids over for her children's birthday parties, for which she brought in petting zoos and pony rides. "What can I say? We loved them," said neighbor Jodi Anderson. "My husband works for a defense contractor, and he used to be in the navy, so he's trained to be a little skeptical of people. He can always spot the bad seed. But he never thought twice about Todd. He told me that he wished he could find a job like Todd's so he could be around the house more."

Becker still held on to his dream of opening a Chuck E. Cheese's. He also talked with Cathy about someday owning a Stride Rite children's shoe store and perhaps a tanning salon. With his new Stonebridge Ranch lifestyle, however, he knew he wouldn't be going straight anytime soon. On his way to Texas, as a matter of fact, he had committed a couple of computer burglaries in Louisiana and Mississippi to get a jump-start on his upcoming mortgage payments. To help out the other members of his family, he used some of his burglary earnings to buy a restaurant near Port St. Lucie called Big Al's Catfish House, changed the name to Becker Boys Big Al's, and hired Bill to manage it. But the restaurant failed. He then opened a check-cashing and quick-loan business called Treasure Coast Cash Company, which he had his father run. That company shut down after the State of Florida charged the elder Becker with loan sharking.

To cover his debts and to pay his father's legal fees, Becker found himself forced to carry out even more burglaries, and it wasn't long before he was flying in his old burglary buddies to help him plunder from Texas's computer companies. During one job, his brother-in-law Danny stumbled across a small safe in the corner of a store, pulled it from the floor, and carried it out to the minivan. When they got the safe open, they found more than $10,000 inside. Becker, always one to look for new entrepreneurial opportunities, took a breath. His career in crime was about to take a major step forward.

IN THE annals of American crime, few criminals have been romanticized like those who can get into a safe. Almost since moviemaking began, Hollywood has loved producing films about a gentleman burglar leaning his ear against a safe and trying to decipher its combination. The reality, however, is that safecrackers cannot compete with today's manufacturers, who can build safes with electronically controlled locks. Bank safes, surrounded by reinforced vaults and state-of-the-art security systems, are virtually impossible to penetrate. But smaller safes and ATMs found inside many businesses can be broken apart or dislodged from their moorings. They can be *stolen*—which is exactly what Becker decided to do.

He did not have to be told that compared with the pilfering of computers, safe-stealing would be a high-risk, noisy business. The sound of a sledgehammer pounding into the bolts holding a safe to the floor or the ear-splitting whine of a gasoline-powered saw slamming into a steel safe could be heard dozens of yards away. What's more, most businesses with safes—at least safes with substantial money—are located in busy commercial sections of cities rather than remote business parks, increasing the likelihood of eyewitnesses and cops.

But as far as Becker could tell, about the only criminals willing to steal safes were stupid kids who would drive stolen pickups through the plate-glass windows of convenience stores and frantically try to dislodge the safe behind the counter before the cops arrived. He became convinced that he could beat the cops by carefully planning his burglaries, spending days scouting locations, looking for stores that his team could get into and then get away from without causing too much disturbance. He studied stores on the Internet to see what kind of cash transactions they did. He particularly looked for stores that cashed payroll checks, as well as stores owned by foreign-born shopkeepers, because they tended not to trust American banks and thus were likely to keep more money in their own safes.

Becker's team was also ready to make some more money. Although Dwayne's life had improved somewhat through the computer thefts—he had used his earnings to buy a Mercedes—he remained in dicey financial shape. To make extra money, Dwayne's new girlfriend had persuaded him to perform sex acts with her in front of a camera attached to their computer, which were then shown on an Internet sex site. (Viewers who paid to watch the not-particularly-good-looking couple could e-mail them and request that they try new positions.) Meanwhile, Bill was still having trouble keeping a steady job in the restaurant business, and Danny was still relying on the money Kim made as a topless dancer. Paulo Rodrigues was still fat.

Becker brought in one more family member: his step-nephew Julian Gavin, whose mother had married Bill. Julian was a raw-boned, chain-smoking country boy who liked to take his mother "mudding" (driving her in his pickup through big mud pits). He was also, by his own admission, a crack-cocaine user who had been drifting through life ever since his fiancée had died in a car crash. A concerned Becker told Julian that he could get a new start in life with the money he would make robbing safes. ("Since I had nothing else to lose at the time," Julian would later tell a police detective, "I took him up on the offer.")

According to police reports, Becker also recruited a Stonebridge Ranch neighbor, forty-three-year-old Joey Thompson, an unhappy salesman of heavy equipment with no past criminal record. Becker told me that Joey, depressed after losing $60,000 in the stock market, had come to him to talk about new career opportunities. Like Becker, Joey loved Stonebridge Ranch and didn't want to lose his home. "Whatever you're doing, I want in," Becker recalled Joey saying. Taking pity on his sad-sack neighbor, Becker replied, "Well, I've got something, but it might not be exactly what you're expecting."

Becker told his team that he would keep 65 percent of whatever was found in a safe; whoever was working with him on that particular job would receive the rest. (Typically, Becker would commit a burglary with either one or two members of his team.) Becker said he would pay all expenses and that he would purchase all the burglary tools, including two-way radios with headsets so that everyone could remain in contact during the heists. He promised they would hit the businesses only late at night, when no one would be there, thus avoiding the need to use guns and hold anyone up. And if anyone was arrested, he said, he would pay for his bail and his lawyer.

Whether he liked it or not, Becker was coming into his prime as a criminal mastermind. After spending the day substitute-teaching for his daughter's kindergarten class or playing shortstop for a Stonebridge Ranch league softball team, shouting out encouragement to his teammates, he would find himself sitting at his dining room table, sketching diagrams about how he could get into his next target. On Sunday nights, when he and Cathy watched *The Sopranos*, the HBO series about the fictional mob family that lives in a nice suburban neighborhood in New Jersey, he would instantly spot the mistakes that Tony Soprano and his mobsters were making when they committed their crimes.

For his own burglaries, he had his guys wear light-colored T-shirts or polo shirts, along with shorts or regular jeans, because he thought that anyone wearing too much black at night would look suspicious. He rented green or blue minivans for the burglaries because they blended in with traffic and were hard for potential eyewitnesses to remember. He also did all the driving, because he had learned how to stay calm, no matter what, when dealing with the cops. While casing a location in Dallas, for instance, Becker and his team were pulled over by a police officer. Becker lowered the window of the minivan and pleasantly told the officer that he was giving his out-of-town brothers a sightseeing tour. The officer, unable to detect anything suspicious, smiled back and told them to be careful because several burglaries had recently taken place in the area.

Regardless of Becker's ingenuity, it was hard to imagine that the Becker Crew, the name the cops would later give to Becker and his cohorts, would last long enough to make a name for itself. Julian, an eccentric sort, refused to wear baseball caps during the heists—he believed hats made a man go bald—which made him an easier target for identification. Dwayne would get so nervous that he constantly had to stop what he was doing to use the restroom. During one burglary, he unzipped his pants in the middle of the store and urinated on the floor. During another burglary, Paulo tried to lift a safe, lost his balance, fell on his back, and could not get up without assistance. On another job, the lumbering Paulo ran so slowly during a getaway that Becker was forced to drive toward him in the minivan to pick him up before he collapsed from exhaustion.

Becker told me that Danny was not quite focused during burglaries because he was worried about what Kim was doing in his absence. Occasionally, he would call her during a burglary just to make sure that she wasn't cheating on him with someone from the topless bar. As for Joey Thompson, he happened to own a high-powered torch that could cut through steel safes. Unfortunately, he wasn't as skilled with it as Becker had hoped. According to Becker, he and Joey broke into a company in Rockwall, a Dallas suburb. While using his torch, Joey burned the entire business to the ground.

The Becker Crew split time between Florida and Texas, going after safes in bingo halls, liquor stores, small supermarkets, self-storage businesses, camera shops, clothing outlets, gasoline stations, convenience stores, and restaurants, from Burger Kings to Red Lobsters. (A typical suburbanite, Becker didn't like to venture into the inner city because he was afraid of gangs.) If a safe could be moved, the Becker Crew would carry it into the back of the minivan, where it would be taken either to Becker's garage if they were in the Dallas area or to Bill's garage if they were working along Florida's east coast. Or sometimes they would dismantle the safe right in the minivan, remove the money, and then dump the safe out the back doors. One time Becker watched his team dump a safe in the parking lot of a Lutheran church in Florida. A Lutheran church! Becker's very own denomination! "Guys, please, show some respect!" Becker yelled.

Becker told me that during 2001 and 2002, he and his crew pulled $650,000 from as many as one hundred safes in Florida and Texas. Sometimes, he said, they would strike three or four times in one night, the money in each safe ranging from a few hundred dollars to $50,000 or more. Other times, weeks would pass before Becker would round up his guys and do a job. During that period, police departments in Texas and Florida were beginning to sense, by the similar way the phone lines were being cut and the front doors carefully opened and the in-store surveillance videotapes taken, that one group was probably responsible for the sharp increase in safe thefts. At one point, at least thirty local agencies were on the case.

But amazingly, despite numerous hair-raising escapes, the Becker Crew was never caught. In one foiled burglary attempt in Texas, in which an alarm was accidentally tripped, Julian escaped from the cops by jumping over a fence, only to find himself in a small pasture where he was chased by an angry horse that kept nipping at his rear end. In Florida, Becker and Julian broke into Norris's Famous Place for Ribs in Port St. Lucie and came across an unmovable, five-hundred-pound safe. They started cutting it apart with a gasoline-powered saw that Bill had rented for them. But before they could get through the steel walls, they ran out of gasoline. They had Bill bring them a can of gasoline, and then they started again. By daybreak, however, they had worn out their saw blade trying to get into the safe. They drove to Lowe's hardware store, waited for the store to open so they could purchase a new blade, returned to the scene of the crime, began again, and then saw a restaurant employee arriving. As they were fleeing, Becker suddenly realized that Julian had left the rented saw, which could be traced back to them, in the restaurant. Julian ran back inside, dashed past the startled employee, grabbed the saw, and raced out. As Becker pulled away in the mini-van, a few police cars were gathering on the street in front of the restaurant, setting up a morning rush-hour speed trap. The police didn't realize until Becker was long gone that a burglary had been attempted.

WHEN I ASKED Becker if he ever felt remorse about his chosen profession on Sunday mornings, as he sat in a church pew with his family, he told me that he constantly prayed for forgiveness. He said he also asked God to let him have one big score, so he could finally quit and fulfill his dream of living the noncriminal life. Although he did buy a few nice things for his family—a Rolex for Cathy and five-hundred-dollar porcelain dolls for his daughters on their birthdays—he was not that big of a spender. He was always trying to save money, he said, for that Chuck E. Cheese's franchise. When Becker took the family to Orlando for an expensive vacation at Disney World, he told me (and later told investigators) that he paid for the trip by having his Stonebridge Ranch buddy Joey fly there and meet him so that they could burglarize businesses at night after Becker had spent the day taking the children through the Magic Kingdom.

As for Cathy, there would be times during her Friday night bunco games with other mothers when the conversation would in-evitably turn to the challenges the women were facing in their marriages. Cathy would look searchingly for a moment across the table, not sure what to say. The women believed she simply had no complaints about her life. What she told me, however, was that she lived in constant fear that her husband would someday go to jail. "It preyed on my mind, every day," she said. "When Todd would leave for the night, I'd lie in bed, unable to sleep, about to throw up every single second."

At one point, Cathy got her residential real estate license and went to work for Coldwell Banker, vainly hoping that she could bring in enough income so that her husband would no longer feel a need to steal. She went to a counselor at the Lutheran church, telling him she wasn't sure how to deal with a problem in her marriage. But when the counselor asked exactly what that problem was, she didn't dare tell him. To use the self-help vernacular that she would hear on such television shows as *Oprah,* Cathy was the classic enabler. She had to admit that she loved the kind of life that Todd had provided for her. She could never convince herself that Todd, a man who truly loved his family and did everything he could to make their lives better, was any worse than those corporate executives, plenty of whom lived right there in Stonebridge Ranch, who ignored their kids and kept mistresses on the side and did their own bit of white-collar thievery, bending accounting rules or hiding income from the IRS. She knew that Todd would never harm anyone: after all, he tried to hit only businesses that had insurance, so the owners could recover their losses.

And, she liked to point out, if Todd were really that bad of a man, would he go to such trouble to try to improve the lives of those who worked for him? When he flew his accomplices to Texas to do burglaries, for instance, he always invited them to come to his house to play with the children and eat one of Cathy's home-cooked meals. It was as if he wanted to show them that they too could climb the ladder to . . . yes, suburban life! (After one dinner at Becker's home, Julian went outside to smoke a cigarette. A neighbor saw the wiry young man wearing a very unsuburbanish muscle shirt and called the police, thinking the Becker house was being burglarized.) Despite their attempts to get him to change the radio to a rock station during their scouting expeditions, Becker kept playing Dr. Laura, because he believed they could use her no-nonsense advice on improving relationships and raising children. When Dwayne asked Becker to invest $25,000 of his burglary earnings into the Internet sex venture, Becker refused, telling him that he didn't like those sex sites and that he believed Dwayne needed to do something more productive with himself.

The truth was that his lessons didn't seem to be catching on. Behind his back, the crew called Becker "Ken" and Cathy "Barbie." Despite Dr. Laura's admonitions about living an immoral life, the crew still liked to get drunk at topless clubs to celebrate successful burglaries. One night, Julian and the others persuaded Becker to come with them to the Lodge, one of Dallas's more famous topless nightclubs. For a while, Becker sat uncomfortably in a booth, then he went back outside to sit in his minivan. Julian eventually showed up with a woman he had met and promptly had sex with her nearby on the hood of the woman's car. Periodically, Julian would shout at the disgusted Becker, "I'm giving her the mustard, baby! I'm giving her the mustard!"

What Becker never could have imagined was that his desire to help his brothers would eventually lead to his own arrest. It wasn't a crack police investigation that exposed Becker. What brought him down was his own perplexing moral code. In July 2002 Dwayne's girlfriend frantically called the St. Lucie county sheriff's department and claimed that Dwayne had hit her and kicked her in the face and taken a six-pack of beer from her refrigerator. After Dwayne was jailed on a charge of aggravated battery, he tried to get Becker to bail him out.

Although Becker had promised his coworkers he would always take care of them if anything happened to them during one of his burglaries, he made it clear he was not going to help them if they got into their own trouble, like a drug arrest. And he was certainly not going to help out Dwayne for battering his girlfriend. "I had had conversations with Dwayne about hitting women," Becker told me. "I had said to him, 'What kind of man could do that?' I was disgusted with Dwayne. So I said no, I'm not bailing him out."

It was a tough decision. Becker knew that Dwayne was already somewhat disenchanted with him because of his lack of interest in his Internet venture. Dwayne had also been arguing with Becker about his share of the burglary proceeds, which he thought needed to be bigger. The fact that Becker would not bail him out was the last straw. An angry Dwayne impulsively contacted a police detective and said that he might know a thing or two about the mysterious safe burglaries that had been occurring around Florida. Indeed, Dwayne was so willing to talk that he forgot to arrange any kind of immunity deal for himself before making his confession.

When the cops located Julian and confronted him with the statements Dwayne had made, he did quickly cut a deal, perhaps because a few months earlier he'd been arrested for doing some burglaries on his own. Apparently, Julian had begun to believe he was as good as Becker and no longer needed him. In Orlando, in a single evening, he had attempted to steal the safes of a Dairy Queen, a check-cashing business, and a Steak and Ale—all of them located within a block of one another. An Orlando police officer saw Julian running from the last burglary, drove up beside him, and shot him with a stun gun, causing him to soil his pants. Julian realized that the only way he could avoid prison for his triple-burglary stunt was to betray the very person who had taught him how to do it.

And just like that, the Becker Crew was no more. Police officers descended on Todd and Cathy's dream home, yelling at them, "Where are the safes? Where is the money?" They found only a couple thousand dollars in the bedroom closet and around a hundred dollars in Cathy's purse, which she told them was money from her daughters' Girl Scout cookie sales. When Becker's five-year-old son watched the officers lead Becker away, he told his mother that the men were soldiers and that they wanted Becker to go away with them to fight terrorists. Cathy said, "I bet that's right," and then she burst into tears.

When police officers in Florida went looking for Bill, they found him working part-time as a Santa's helper at a mall because he was still having trouble finding a good job in the restaurant business. (He was also a very bad criminal: The cops found one of the stolen safes, which he had been too lazy to discard, in his garage.) As the police approached, he was wearing a Santa's hat and a bright green vest festooned with decorations of candy canes, telling children to smile for their photo with Santa. According to Bill, the police shouted, "Step away from the Santa booth!" During the arrest of Paulo in another part of Florida, the police found a sculpture of a purple dolphin, titled "Taking Flight," that had been taken from one of the Florida stores where a safe had been stolen. The sculpture was so beautiful, Paulo later said, that he just had to have it for his living room.

Becker was taken to Florida to be booked on state burglary charges. In the jail, he came across Dwayne. "We were sitting there by ourselves," Becker recalled, "and I said, 'What did I do to you that was so terrible that you had to do this to me?' I said, 'My kids love you—they jump on you. They call you Uncle Dwayne. They jump all over you.'" Becker paused, still stunned by the betrayal. "And there was nothing Dwayne could say. Nothing he could say."

FOR DAYS at Stonebridge ranch, people drove past the Becker house to gawk. Neighbors on the street talked about how Becker used to give each of them a nice bottle of wine for Christmas. Parents from the soccer teams that Becker helped coach wondered if the soccer league would let him coach again after he got out of prison. He was, after all, so good with the kids. "We definitely knew what he did was criminal," said Jodi Anderson, "but we did admire the way he pulled it off. It did take a lot of courage. And it's pretty hard to get away with something like that for so long in this neighborhood, where everyone knows your business."

Some neighbors withdrew from the Beckers, and one woman on the street told her children they could no longer play with the Becker children because their daddy was a burglar. Cathy told me she was so furious at what the neighbor had said that she marched up the street to where the woman and others were gathered one evening and shouted, "You hypocrites! I've seen you get drunk in front of your own kids. I know you smoke pot. I know you went swimming naked in someone else's pool!"

When investigators asked Becker to explain how he could maintain his Stonebridge Ranch lifestyle despite filing income tax returns that showed him earning less than six figures, Becker said that he had made money gambling in Las Vegas. (Becker had indeed done some gambling over the years in hopes that he could earn enough money to quit burglarizing.) But Becker quickly succumbed after hearing the evidence accumulated against him. Besides the state burglary charges he was facing, an IRS task force was charging Becker with money laundering and was planning to take away all his assets. M. Andrew Stover, an assistant U.S. attorney for the eastern district of Texas, met with Becker and told him that Cathy could well be prosecuted for conspiracy. "His reaction was amazing," said Stover. "He started crying and shaking—something you rarely see a major criminal do—and he said that all he wanted was to take care of his wife and family."

To keep his wife out of prison, Becker agreed to confess to everything he had done. His attorney, Mark Watson, of Dallas, also arranged that in return for a five-year federal prison sentence, Becker would reveal the names of the various fences around the country who had bought his stolen computers years before.

Dwayne, Bill, and Paulo received two-year sentences in Florida. The cases against Joey and Danny are still pending. Kim was never charged because the statute of limitations had expired for her particular criminal adventure. (Due to Becker's encouragement, she did quit dancing and now works as a waitress at an Italian restaurant.) Meanwhile, with his full immunity, Julian has disappeared from Florida. The rumor is that he has used his burglary money to help out members of his family, just as Becker used to do. Julian has allegedly purchased his father a Camaro and given money to his mother, who now has no income, with her husband, Bill, in jail. (When I talked to Becker about Julian's new life, he paused for a moment, then said, "I hope I had an effect on him, getting him to help out his family, because that's what it's all about.") Perhaps the greatest irony of all is that Dwayne, Becker's Judas, told me when I went to see him in Florida that as soon as he gets out of prison, he is going to get his dog back from his girlfriend and move to Tennessee. "I'm going to get started again," he said. "Find a nice house in a nice neighborhood and not drink or anything."

"It sounds just like the life Todd wanted you to live," I said.

There was a pause. "Well, no," said Dwayne. He paused again. "I don't know. Maybe."

I went to see Becker and his wife for the last time this past November, just before he left for federal prison. The IRS had decided not to confiscate his Stonebridge Ranch home, which still had a sizable mortgage, because real estate values had decreased in the area and the home would be difficult for the federal government to sell at a profit. As a result, Cathy and the children were going to be able to stay in the house. (Although Cathy, who has gone back to work as a real estate agent, said she was going to make the mortgage payments with her income, some detectives speculate that the Beckers still have a secret stash of stolen money.) When I walked through the front door, Cathy was busy decorating the house for Thanksgiving and Becker had just returned from his next-door neighbor's home, where the woman there had locked herself out of the house. "I used a flat-head screwdriver to pop open her back door," he said with a shrug.

Becker had been busy that week—cleaning out the attic so that Cathy wouldn't have to do it for the next five years, going to the school cafeteria to eat lunch with his children, and attending church. I asked Becker if he could imagine ever returning to the craft that he does so well. There are plenty of police detectives who believe he will go right back to burglary when he gets out of prison, because it's the only profession he knows. But Becker firmly insisted that this time, he was going to go straight. When I asked what he might do for a living after prison, he mentioned a seminar he had given a few months earlier to a group of detectives on the burglaries he had committed. The audience was so attentive that he had begun to ponder the idea of becoming some sort of paid consultant to police departments and businesses that wanted to know how to stop good burglars.

"I think that's a good idea, honey," said Cathy, coming in from the kitchen.

"There could be some money in it," Becker agreed. "We might finally get the money to open that Chuck E. Cheese's."

He grabbed Cathy's hand, and the two of them smiled at each other. For a moment, they looked just like Ward and June.

SKIP HOLLANDSWORTH has been a writer for Texas Monthly magazine for fifteen years. He is completing a history of the city of Austin in the year 1885, when a Jack the Ripper–like killer ripped apart seven women over the course of twelve months, sending the city into chaos, exposing one major political scandal after another, and setting off a rip-roaring and, at times, completely comic hunt for the killer.

Coda

When this story was published, many of the people who lived in Stonebridge Ranch called me to ask how much of what I had written was true. They had no idea about the extent of Todd Becker's criminal life. They simply assumed I was exaggerating. Many of them also refused to believe that Todd's neighbor Joey Thompson had been involved in the safe-stealing ring. They still didn't believe Joey was involved until Todd was brought back from Florida to Texas in 2004 to testify at Thompson's trial. Meanwhile, Kathy and the children still live their pristine suburban life in the home Todd had bought for them, and rumors are flying about how she is able to afford the mortgage payments. CBS has bought the rights to her life story, and a television movie about the Beckers might be made soon.

David Grann
———————————

MYSTERIOUS CIRCUMSTANCES

The Strange Death of a Sherlock Holmes Fanatic

FROM *The New Yorker*

RICHARD LANCELYN GREEN, the world's foremost expert on Sherlock Holmes, believed that he had finally solved the case of the missing papers. Over the past two decades, he had been looking for a trove of letters, diary entries, and manuscripts written by Sir Arthur Conan Doyle, the creator of Holmes. The archive was estimated to be worth nearly four million dollars, and was said by some to carry a deadly curse, like the one in the most famous Holmes story, *The Hound of the Baskervilles*.

The papers had disappeared after Conan Doyle died, in 1930, and without them no one had been able to write a definitive biography—a task that Green was determined to complete. Many scholars feared that the archive had been discarded or destroyed; as the London *Times* noted earlier this year, its whereabouts had become "a mystery as tantalizing as any to unfold at 221B Baker Street," the fictional den of Holmes and his fellow-sleuth, Dr. Watson.

Not long after Green launched his investigation, he discovered that one of Conan Doyle's five children, Adrian, had, with the other heirs' agreement, stashed the papers in a locked room of a château that he owned in Switzerland. Green then learned that Adrian had spirited some of the papers out of the château without his siblings' knowledge, hoping to sell them to collectors. In the midst of this scheme, he died of a heart attack—giving rise to the legend of the curse. After Adrian's death, the papers apparently vanished. And whenever Green tried to probe further he found himself caught in an impenetrable web of heirs—including a self-styled Russian princess—who seemed to have deceived and double-crossed one another in their efforts to control the archive.

For years, Green continued to sort through evidence and interview relatives, until one day the muddled trail led to London—and the doorstep of Jean Conan Doyle, the youngest of the author's children. Tall and elegant, with silver hair, she was an imposing woman in her late sixties. ("Something very strong and forceful seems to be at the back of that wee body," her father had written of Jean when she was five. "Her will is tremendous.") Whereas her brother Adrian had been kicked out of the British Navy for insubordination, and her elder brother Denis was a playboy who had sat out the Second World War in America, she had become an officer in the Royal Air Force, and was honored, in 1963, as a Dame Commander of the Order of the British Empire.

She invited Green into her flat, where a portrait of her father, with his walrus mustache, hung near the fireplace. Green had almost as great an interest in her father as she did, and she began sharing her memories, as well as family photographs. She asked him to return, and one day, Green later told friends, she showed him some boxes that had been stored in a London solicitor's office. Peering inside them, he said, he had glimpsed part of the archive. Dame Jean informed him that, because of an ongoing family dispute, she couldn't yet allow him to read the papers, but she said that she intended to bequeath nearly all of them to the British Library, so that scholars could finally examine them. After she died, in 1997, Green eagerly awaited their transfer—but nothing happened.

Then, last March, Green opened the London Sunday *Times* and was shocked to read that the lost archive had "turned up" at Christie's auction house and was to be sold, in May, for millions of dollars by three of Conan Doyle's distant relatives; instead of going to the British Library, the contents would be scattered among private collectors around the world, who might keep them inaccessible to scholars. Green was sure that a mistake had been made, and hurried to Christie's to inspect the materials. Upon his return, he told friends that he was certain that many of the papers were the same as those he had uncovered. What's more, he alleged, they had been stolen—and he had proof.

Over the next few days, he approached members of the Sherlock Holmes Society of London, one of hundreds of fan clubs devoted to the detective. (Green had once been chairman.) He alerted other so-called Sherlockians, including various American members of the Baker Street Irregulars, an invitation-only group that was founded in 1934 and named after the street urchins Holmes regularly employed to ferret out information. Green also contacted the more orthodox scholars of Conan Doyle, or Doyleans, about the sale. (Unlike Green, who moved between the two camps, many Doyleans distanced themselves from the Sherlockians, who often treated Holmes as if he were a real detective and refused to mention Conan Doyle by name.)

Green shared with these scholars what he knew about the archive's provenance, revealing what he considered the most damning piece of evidence: a copy of Dame Jean's will, which stated, "I give to The British Library all . . . my late father's original papers, personal manuscripts, diaries, engagement books, and writings." Determined to block the auction, the makeshift group of amateur sleuths presented its case to members of Parliament. Toward the end of the month, as the group's campaign intensified and its objections appeared in the press, Green hinted to his sister, Priscilla West, that someone was threatening him. Later, he sent her a cryptic note containing three phone numbers and the message: PLEASE KEEP THESE NUMBERS SAFE. He also called a reporter from the London *Times*, warning that "something" might happen to him.

On the night of Friday, March 26, he had dinner with a long-time friend, Lawrence Keen, who later said that Green had confided in him that "an American was trying to bring him down." After the two men left the restaurant, Green told Keen that they were being followed, and pointed to a car behind them.

The same evening, Priscilla West phoned her brother, and got his answering machine. She called repeatedly the next morning, but he still didn't pick up. Alarmed, she went to his house and knocked on the door; there was no response. After several more attempts, she called the police, who came and broke open the entrance. Downstairs, the police found the body of Green lying on his bed, surrounded by Sherlock Holmes books and posters, with a cord wrapped around his neck. He had been garroted.

"I WILL LAY out the whole case for you," John Gibson, one of Green's closest friends, told me when I phoned him shortly after learning of Green's death. Gibson had written several books with Green, including *My Evening with Sherlock Holmes*, a 1981 collection of parodies and pastiches of the detective stories. With a slight stammer, Gibson said of his friend's death, "It's a complete and utter mystery."

Not long after, I traveled to Great Bookham, a village thirty miles south of London, where Gibson lives. He was waiting for me when I stepped off the train. He was tall and rail-thin, and everything about him—narrow shoulders, long face, unruly gray hair—seemed to slouch forward, as if he were supported by an invisible cane. "I have a file for you," he said, as we drove off in his car. "As you'll see, there are plenty of clues and not a lot of answers."

He sped through town, past a twelfth-century stone church and a row of cottages, until he stopped at a red brick house surrounded by hedges. "You don't mind dogs, I hope," he said. "I've two cocker spaniels. I only wanted one but the person I got them from said that they were inseparable, and so I took them both and they've been fighting ever since."

When he opened the front door, both spaniels leaped on us, then at each other. They trailed us into the living room, which was filled with piles of antique books, some reaching to the ceiling. Among the stacks was a near-complete set of *The Strand Magazine*, in which the Holmes stories were serialized at the turn of the twentieth century; a single issue, which used to sell for half a shilling, is now worth as much as five hundred dollars. "Altogether, there must be about sixty thousand books," Gibson said.

We sat on a couch and he opened his case file, carefully spreading the pages around him. "All right, dogs. Don't disturb us," he said. He looked up at me. "Now I'll tell you the whole story."

Gibson said that he had attended the coroner's inquest and taken careful notes, and as he spoke he picked up a magnifying glass beside him and peered though it at several crumpled pieces of paper. "I write everything on scraps," he said. The police, he said, had found only a few unusual things at the scene. There was the cord around Green's neck—a black shoelace. There was a wooden spoon near his hand, and several stuffed animals on the bed. And there was a partially empty bottle of gin.

The police found no sign of forced entry and assumed that Green had committed suicide. Yet there was no note, and Sir Colin Berry, the president of the British Academy of Forensic Sciences, testified to the coroner that, in his thirty-year career, he had seen only one suicide by garroting. "One," Gibson repeated. Self-garroting is extremely difficult to do, he explained; people who attempt it typically pass out before they are asphyxiated. Moreover, in this instance, the cord was not a thick rope but a shoelace, making the feat even more unlikely.

Gibson reached in his file and handed me a sheet of paper with numbers on it. "Take a look," he said. "My phone records." The records showed that he and Green had spoken repeatedly during the week before his death; if the police had bothered to obtain Green's records, Gibson went on, they would no doubt show that Green had called him only hours before he died. "I was probably the last person to speak to him," he said. The police, however, had never questioned him.

During one of their last conversations about the auction, Gibson recalled, Green had said he was afraid of something.

"You've got nothing to worry about," Gibson told him.

"No, I'm *worried*," Green said.

"What? You fear for your life?"

"I do."

Gibson said that, at the time, he didn't take the threat seriously but advised Green not to answer his door unless he was sure who it was.

Gibson glanced at his notes. There was something else, he said, something critical. On the eve of his death, he reminded me, Green had spoken to his friend Keen about an "American" who was trying to ruin him. The following day, Gibson said, he had called Green's house and heard a strange greeting on the answering machine. "Instead of getting Richard's voice in this sort of Oxford accent, which had been on the machine for a decade," Gibson recalled, "I got an American voice that said, 'Sorry, not available.' I said, 'What the hell is going on?' I thought I must've dialled the wrong number. So I dialled really slowly again. I got the American voice. I said, 'Christ almighty.' "

Gibson said that Green's sister had heard the same recorded greeting, which is one reason that she had rushed to his house. Reaching into his file, Gibson handed me several more documents. "Make sure you keep them in chronological order," he said. There was a copy of Jean Conan Doyle's will, several newspaper clippings on the auction, an obituary, and a Christie's catalogue.

That was pretty much all he had. The police, Gibson said, had not conducted any forensic tests or looked for fingerprints. And the coroner—who had once attended a meeting of the Sherlock Holmes Society to conduct a mock inquest of the murder from a

Conan Doyle story in which a corpse is discovered in a locked room—found himself stymied. Gibson said that the coroner had noted that there was not enough evidence to ascertain what had happened, and, as a result, the official verdict regarding whether Green had killed himself or been murdered was left open.

Within hours of Green's death, Sherlockians seized upon the mystery, as if it were another case in the canon. In a Web chat room, one person, who called himself "inspector," wrote, "As for self-garroting, it is like trying to choke oneself to death by your own hands." Others invoked the "curse," as if only the supernatural could explain it. Gibson handed me an article from a British tabloid that was headlined: "CURSE OF CONAN DOYLE" STRIKES HOLMES EXPERT.

"So what do you think?" Gibson asked.

"I'm not sure," I said.

Later, we went through the evidence again. I asked Gibson if he knew whose phone numbers were on the note that Green had sent to his sister.

Gibson shook his head. "It hadn't come up at the inquest," he said.

"What about the American voice on the answering machine?" I asked. "Do we know who that is?"

"Unfortunately, not a clue. To me that's the strangest and most telling piece of evidence. Did Richard put that on his machine? What was he trying to tell us? Did the murderer put it on there? And, if so, why would he do that?"

I asked if Green had ever displayed any irrational behavior. "No, never," he said. "He was the most levelheaded man I ever met."

He noted that Priscilla West had testified at the inquest that her brother had no history of depression. Indeed, Green's physician wrote to the court to say that he had not treated Green for any illnesses for a decade.

"One last question," I said. "Was anything taken out of the apartment?"

"Not that we know of. Richard had a valuable collection of

Sherlock Holmes and Conan Doyle books, and nothing appears to be missing."

As Gibson drove me back to the train station, he said, "Please, you must stay on the case. The police seem to have let poor Richard down." Then he advised, "As Sherlock Holmes says, 'When you have eliminated the impossible, whatever remains, however improbable, must be the truth.'"

SOME FACTS about Richard Green are easy to discern—those which illuminate the circumstances of his life, rather than the circumstances of his death. He was born on July 10, 1953; he was the youngest of three children; his father was Roger Lancelyn Green, a best-selling children's author who popularized the Homeric myths and the legend of King Arthur, and who was a close friend of C. S. Lewis and J. R. R. Tolkien; and Richard was raised near Liverpool, on land that had been given to his ancestors in 1093, and where his family had resided ever since.

Nathaniel Hawthorne, who was the American consul in Liverpool in the eighteen-fifties, visited the house one summer, and he later described it in his "English Notebooks":

> We passed through a considerable extent of private road, and finally drove through a lawn, shaded with trees, and closely shaven, and reached the door of Poulton Hall. Part of the mansion is three or four hundred years old. . . . There is [a] curious, old, stately staircase, with a twisted balustrade, much like that of the old Province House in Boston. The drawing-room looks like a very handsome modern room, being beautifully painted, gilded, and paper-hung, with a white-marble fire-place, and rich furniture; so that the impression is that of newness, not of age.

By the time Richard was born, however, the Green family was, as one relative told me, "very English—a big house and no money." The curtains were thin, the carpets were threadbare, and a cold draft often swirled through the corridors.

Green, who had a pale, pudgy face, was blind in one eye from a childhood accident, and wore spectacles with tinted lenses. (One friend told me that, even as an adult, Green resembled "the god of Pan," with "cherubic-like features, a mouth which curved in a smile which was sympathetic, ironic, and always seeming to suggest that there was just one little thing that he was not telling you.") Intensely shy, with a ferociously logical mind and a precise memory, he would spend hours roaming through his father's enormous library, reading dusty first editions of children's books. And by the time he was eleven he had fallen under the spell of Sherlock Holmes.

Holmes was not the first great literary detective—that honor belongs to Edgar Allan Poe's Inspector Auguste Dupin—but Conan Doyle's hero was the most vivid exemplar of the fledgling genre, which Poe dubbed "tales of ratiocination." Holmes is a cold, calculating machine, a man who is, as one critic put it, "a tracker, a hunter-down, a combination of bloodhound, pointer, and bulldog." The gaunt Holmes has no wife or children; as he explains, "I am a brain, Watson. The rest of me is a mere appendix." Rigidly scientific, he offers no spiritual bromides to his bereaved clients. Conan Doyle reveals virtually nothing about his character's interior life; he is defined solely by his method. In short, he is the perfect detective, the superhero of the Victorian era, out of which he blasted with his deerstalker hat and Inverness cape.

Richard read the stories straight through, then read them again. His rigorous mind had found its match in Holmes and his "science of deduction," which could wrest an astonishing solution from a single, seemingly unremarkable clue. "All life is a great chain, the nature of which is known whenever we are shown a single link of it," Holmes explains in the first story, "A Study in Scarlet," which establishes a narrative formula that subsequent tales nearly always follow. A new client arrives at Holmes's Baker Street consulting room. The detective stuns the visitor by deducing some element of his life by the mere observation of his demeanor or dress. (In "A Case of Identity," he divines that his client is a shortsighted typist by no more than the worn "plush upon her sleeves" and "the dint of a pince-nez at either side of her nose.") After the client presents the inexplicable facts of the case, "the game is afoot," as Holmes likes to say. Amassing clues that invariably boggle Watson, the stories' more earthbound narrator, Holmes ultimately arrives at a dazzling conclusion—one that, to him and him only, seems "elementary." In "The Red-headed League," Holmes reveals to Watson how he surmised that an assistant pawnbroker was trying to rob a bank by tunnelling underneath it. "I thought of the assistant's fondness for photography, and his trick of vanishing into the cellar," Holmes says, explaining that he then went to see the assistant. "I hardly looked at his face. His knees were what I wished to see. You must yourself have remarked how worn, wrinkled and stained they were. They spoke of those hours of burrowing. The only remaining point was what they were burrowing for. I walked round the corner, saw the City and Suburban Bank abutted on our friend's premises, and felt that I had solved my problem."

Following the advice that Holmes often gave to Watson, Green practiced how to "see" what others merely "observed." He memorized Holmes's rules, as if they were catechism: "It is a capital mistake to theorize before one has data"; "never trust to general impressions, my boy, but concentrate yourself upon details"; "there is nothing more deceptive than an obvious fact."

Not long after Green turned thirteen, he carried an assortment of artifacts from local junk sales into the dimly lit attic of Poulton Hall. Part of the attic was known as the Martyr's Chamber and was believed to be haunted, having once "been tenanted by a lady, who was imprisoned there and persecuted to death for her religion," according to Hawthorne. Nevertheless, up in the attic, Green assembled his objects to create a strange tableau. There was a rack of pipes and a Persian slipper stuffed with tobacco. There was a stack of unpaid bills, which he stabbed into a mantle with a knife, so that they were pinned in place. There was a box of pills labelled: POI-SON; empty ammunition cartridges and trompe-l'œil bullet marks painted on the walls ("I didn't think the attic would stand up to real bullets," he later remarked); a preserved snake; a brass microscope; and an invitation to the Gasfitters' Ball. Finally, outside the door of the room, Green hung a sign: BAKER STREET.

Relying on the stray details sprinkled throughout Conan Doyle's stories, Green had pieced together a replica of Holmes and Watson's apartment—one so precise that it occasionally drew Holmes afi-cionados from other parts of England. One local reporter described the uncanny sensation of climbing the seventeen stairs—the same number specified in the stories—as a tape recording played in the background with the sounds of Victorian London: the rumble of cab wheels, the clopping of horses' hooves on cobblestones. By then, Green had become the youngest person ever inducted into the Sherlock Holmes Society of London, where members sometimes dressed in period costumes—in high-waisted trousers and top hats.

Though Holmes had first appeared in print nearly a century ear-lier, he had spawned a literary cult unlike that of any other fictional character. Almost from his inception, readers latched on to him with a zeal that bordered on "the mystical," as one Conan Doyle biogra-pher has noted. When Holmes made his début, in the 1887 *Beeton's Christmas Annual*, a magazine of somewhat lurid fiction, he was considered not just a character but a paragon of the Victorian faith in all things scientific. He entered public consciousness around the same time as the development of the modern police force, at a mo-ment when medicine was finally threatening to eradicate common diseases and industrialization offered to curtail mass poverty. He was the proof that, indeed, the forces of reason could triumph over the forces of madness.

By the time Green was born, however, the worship of scientific thinking had been shattered by other faiths, by Nazism and Com-munism and Fascism, which had often harnessed the power of technology to demonic ends. Yet, paradoxically, the more illogical the world seemed, the more intense the cult surrounding Holmes became. This symbol of a new creed had become a figure of nostalgia—a person in "a fairy tale," as Green once put it. The character's popularity even surpassed the level of fame he had attained in Conan Doyle's day, as the stories were reenacted in some two hundred and sixty movies, twenty-five television shows, a musical, a ballet, a burlesque, and six hundred radio plays. Holmes inspired the creation of journals, memorabilia shops, walking tours, postage stamps, hotels, themed ocean cruises.

Edgar W. Smith, a former vice-president of General Motors and the first editor of the *Baker Street Journal*, which publishes scholarship on Conan Doyle's stories, wrote in a 1946 essay, "What Is It That We Love in Sherlock Holmes?":

> We see him as the fine expression of our urge to trample evil and to set aright the wrongs with which the world is plagued. He is Galahad and Socrates, bringing high adventure to our dull existences and calm, judicial logic to our biased minds. He is the success of all our failures; the bold escape from our imprisonment.

What has made this literary escape unlike any other, though, is that so many people conceive of Holmes as a real person. T. S. Eliot once observed, "Perhaps the greatest of the Sherlock Holmes mysteries is this: that when we talk of him we invariably fall into the fancy of his existence." Green himself wrote, "Sherlock Holmes is a real character . . . who lives beyond life's span and who is constantly rejuvenated."

At the Sherlock Holmes Society of London, Green was introduced to "the great game," which Sherlockians had played for decades. It was built around the conceit that the stories' true author was not Conan Doyle but Watson, who had faithfully recounted Holmes's exploits. Once, at a gathering of the elite Baker Street Irregulars (which Green also joined), a guest referred to Conan Doyle as the creator of Holmes, prompting one outraged member to exclaim, "Holmes is a man! Holmes is a great man!" If Green had to invoke Conan Doyle's name, he was told, he should refer to him as merely Watson's "literary agent." The challenge of the game was that Conan Doyle had often written the four Holmes novels and fifty-six short stories—"the Sacred Writings," as Sherlockians called them—in haste, and they were plagued with inconsistencies that made them difficult to pass off as nonfiction. How, for instance, is it possible that in one story Watson is described as having been wounded in Afghanistan in the shoulder by a Jezail bullet, though in another story he complains that the wound was in his leg? The goal was thus to resolve these paradoxes, using the same airtight logic that Holmes exhibits. Similar textual inquiries had already given birth to a related field, known as Sherlockiana—mock scholarship in which fans tried to deduce everything from how many wives Watson has (one to five) to which university Holmes attended (surely Cambridge or Oxford). As Green once conceded, quoting the founder of the Baker Street Irregulars, "Never had so much been written by so many for so few."

After Green graduated from Oxford, in 1975, he turned his attention to more serious scholarship. Of all the puzzles surrounding the Sacred Writings, the greatest one, Green realized, centered on the man whom the stories had long since eclipsed—Conan Doyle himself. Green set out to compile the first comprehensive bibliography, hunting down every piece of material that Conan Doyle wrote: pamphlets, plays, poems, obituaries, songs, unpublished manuscripts, letters to the editor. Carrying a plastic bag in place of a briefcase, Green unearthed documents that had long been hidden behind the veil of history.

In the midst of this research, Green discovered that John Gibson was working on a similar project, and they agreed to collaborate. The resulting tome, published in 1983 by Oxford University Press, with a foreword by Graham Greene, is seven hundred and twelve pages long and contains notations on nearly every scrap of writing that Conan Doyle ever produced, down to the kind of paper in which a manuscript was bound ("cloth," "light blue diaper-grain"). When the bibliography was done, Gibson continued in his job as a government property assessor. Green, however, had inherited a sizable sum of money from his family, who had sold part of their estate, and he used the bibliography as a launching pad for a biography of Conan Doyle.

Writing a biography is akin to the process of detection, and Green started to retrace every step of Conan Doyle's life, as if it were an elaborate crime scene. During the nineteen-eighties, Green followed Conan Doyle's movements from the moment he was born, on May 22, 1859, in a squalid part of Edinburgh. Green visited the neighborhood where Conan Doyle was raised by a devout Christian mother and a dreamy father. (He drew one of the first illustrations of Sherlock Holmes—a sketch of the detective discovering a corpse, which accompanied a paperback edition of *A Study in Scarlet*.) Green also amassed an intricate paper record that showed his subject's intellectual evolution. He discovered, for instance, that after Conan Doyle studied medicine, at the University of Edinburgh, and fell under the influence of rationalist thinkers like Oliver Wendell Holmes—who undoubtedly inspired the surname of Conan Doyle's detective—he renounced Catholicism, vowing, "Never will I accept anything which cannot be proved to me."

In the early eighties, Green published the first of a series of introductions to Penguin Classics editions of Conan Doyle's previously uncollected works—many of which he had helped to uncover. The essays, written in a clinical style, began garnering him attention outside the insular subculture of Sherlockians. One essay, running more than a hundred pages, was a small biography of Conan Doyle unto itself; in another, Green cast further light on the short story "The Case of the Man Who Was Wanted," which had been found in a chest more than a decade after Conan Doyle's death and was claimed by his widow and sons to be the last unpublished Holmes story. Some experts had wondered if the story was a fake and even if Conan Doyle's two sons, in search of money to sustain their lavish life styles, had forged it. Yet Green conclusively showed that the story was neither by Conan Doyle nor a forgery; instead, it was written by an architect named Arthur Whitaker, who had sent it to Conan Doyle in hopes of collaborating. Scholars described Green's essays variously as "dazzling," "unparalleled," and—the ultimate compliment—"Holmesian."

Still, Green was determined to dig deeper for his now highly anticipated biography. As the mystery writer Iain Pears has observed, Conan Doyle's hero acts in nearly the same fashion as a Freudian analyst, piecing together his clients' hidden narratives, which he alone can perceive. In a 1987 review of Conan Doyle's autobiography, *Memories and Adventures*, which was published in 1924, Green noted, "It is as if Conan Doyle—whose character suggested kindliness and trust—had a fear of intimacy. When he describes his life, he omits the inner man."

To reveal this "inner man," Green examined facts that Conan Doyle rarely, if ever, spoke of himself—most notably, that his father, an epileptic and an incorrigible alcoholic, was eventually confined to an insane asylum. Yet the more Green tried to plumb his subject, the more he became aware of the holes in his knowledge of Conan Doyle. He didn't want just to sketch Conan Doyle's story with a series of anecdotes; he wanted to know everything about him. In the draft of an early mystery story, "The Surgeon of Gaster Fall," Conan Doyle writes of a son who has locked his raving father inside a cage—but this incident was excised from the published version. Had Conan Doyle been the one to commit his father to the asylum? Was Holmes's mania for logic a reaction to his father's genuine mania? And what did Conan Doyle mean when he wrote, in his deeply personal poem "The Inner Room," that he "has thoughts he dare not say"?

Green wanted to create an immaculate biography, one in which each fact led inexorably to the next. He wanted to be both Watson and Holmes to Conan Doyle, to be his narrator and his detective.

Yet he knew the words of Holmes: "Data! Data! Data! I can't make bricks without clay." And the only way to succeed, he realized, was to track down the lost archive.

"MURDER," OWEN Dudley Edwards, a highly regarded Conan Doyle scholar, said. "I fear that is what the preponderance of the evidence points to."

I had called him in Scotland, after Gibson informed me that Edwards was pursuing an informal investigation into Green's death. Edwards had worked with Green to stop the auction, which took place, in spite of the uproar, almost two months after Green's body was found. Edwards said of his friend, "I think he knew too much about the archive."

A few days later, I flew to Edinburgh, where Edwards promised to share with me his findings. We had arranged to meet at a hotel on the edge of the old city. It was on a hill studded with medieval castles and covered in a thin mist, not far from where Conan Doyle had studied medicine under Dr. Joseph Bell, one of the models for Sherlock Holmes. (Once, during a class, Bell held up a glass vial. "This, gentlemen, contains a most potent drug," he said. "It is *extremely* bitter to the taste." To the class's astonishment, he touched the amber liquid, lifted a finger to his mouth, and licked it. He then declared, "Not one of you has developed his power of perception . . . while I placed my *index* finger in the awful brew, it was my *middle* finger—aye—which somehow found its way into my mouth.")

Edwards greeted me in the hotel lobby. He is a short, pear-shaped man with wild gray sideburns and an even wilder gray beard. A history professor at the University of Edinburgh, he wore a rumpled tweed coat over a V-neck sweater, and carried a knapsack on his shoulder.

We sat down at the restaurant, and I waited as he rummaged through the books in his bag. Edwards, who has written numerous books, including *The Quest for Sherlock Holmes*, an acclaimed account of Conan Doyle's early life, began pulling out copies of Green's edited collections. Green, he said, was "the world's greatest Conan Doyle expert. I have the authority to say it. Richard ultimately became the greatest of us all. That is a firm and definite statement of someone who knows."

As he spoke, he tended to pull his chin in toward his chest, so that his beard fanned out. He told me that he had met Green in 1981, while researching his book on Conan Doyle. At the time, Green was still working on his bibliography with Gibson; even so, he had shared all his data with Edwards. "That was the kind of scholar he was," he said.

To Edwards, Green's death was even more baffling than the crimes in a Holmes story. He picked up one of the Conan Doyle collections and read aloud from "A Case of Identity," in the cool, ironical voice of Holmes:

> Life is infinitely stranger than anything which the mind of man could invent. We would not dare to conceive the things which are really mere commonplaces of existence. If we could fly out of that window hand in hand, hover over this great city, gently remove the roofs, and peep in at the queer things which are going on, the strange coincidences, the plannings, the cross-purposes, the wonderful chains of events, working through generations, and leading to the most *outré* results, it would make all fiction with its conventionalities and foreseen conclusion most stale and unprofitable.

After Edwards closed the book, he explained that he had spoken frequently with Green about the Christie's sale. "Our lives have been dominated by the fact that Conan Doyle had five children, three of whom became his literary heirs," Edwards said. "The two boys were playboys. One of them, Denis, was, I gather, utterly selfish. The other one, Adrian, was a repulsive crook. And then there was an absolutely wonderful daughter."

Green, he said, had become so close to the daughter, Dame Jean, that he came to be known as the son she never had, even though in the past Conan Doyle's children had typically had fractious relationships with their father's biographers. In the early nineteen-forties, for example, Adrian and Denis had cooperated with Hesketh Pearson on *Conan Doyle: His Life and Art*, but when the book came out and portrayed Conan Doyle as "the man in the street," a phrase Conan Doyle himself had used, Adrian rushed into print his own biography, *The True Conan Doyle*, and Denis allegedly challenged Pearson to a duel. Dame Jean had subsequently taken it upon herself to guard her father's legacy against scholars who might present him in too stark a light. Yet she confided in Green, who had tried to balance his veneration of his subject with a commitment to the truth.

Edwards said that Dame Jean not only gave Green a glimpse of the treasured archive; she also asked for his help in transferring various papers to her solicitor's office. "Richard told me that he had physically moved them," Edwards said. "So his knowledge was really quite dangerous."

He claimed that Green was "the biggest figure standing in the way" of the Christie's auction, since he had seen some of the papers and could testify that Dame Jean had intended to donate them to the British Library. Soon after the sale was announced, Edwards said, he and Green had learned that Charles Foley, Sir Arthur's great-nephew, and two of Foley's cousins were behind the sale. But neither he nor Green could understand how these distant heirs had legally obtained control of the archive. "All we were clear about was that there was a scam and that, clearly, someone was robbing stuff that should go to the British Library," Edwards said. He added, "This was *not* a hypothesis—it was quite certain in our own minds."

Edwards also had little doubt that somebody had murdered his friend. He noted the circumstantial details—Green's mention of threats to his life, his reference to the American who was "trying to bring him down." Some observers, he said, had speculated that Green's death might have been the result of autoerotic asphyxiation, but he told me that there were no signs that Green was engaged in sexual activity at the time. He added that garroting is typically a brutal method of execution—"a method of murder which a skilled professional would use." What's more, Green had no known history of depression. Edwards pointed out that Green, on the day before he died, had made plans with another friend for a holiday in Italy the following week. Moreover, he said, if Green had killed himself, there surely would have been a suicide note; it was inconceivable that a man who kept notes on everything would not have left one.

"There are other things," Edwards continued. "He was garroted with a bootlace, yet he always wore slip-on shoes." And Edwards found meaning in seemingly insignificant details, the kind that Holmes might note— particularly, the partially empty bottle of gin by his bed. To Edwards, this was a clear sign of the presence of a stranger, since Green, an oenophile, had drunk wine at supper that evening, and would never have followed wine with gin.

"Whoever did this is still at large," Edwards said. He put a hand on my shoulder. "Please be careful. I don't want to see you garroted, like poor Richard." Before we parted, he told me one more thing—he knew who the American was.

THE AMERICAN, who asked that I not use his name, lives in Washington, D.C. After I tracked him down, he agreed to meet me at Timberlake's pub near Dupont Circle. I found him sitting at the bar, sipping red wine. Though he was slumped over, he looked strikingly tall, with a hawkish nose and a thinning ring of gray hair. He appeared to be in his fifties and wore bluejeans and a button-down white shirt, with a fountain pen sticking out of the front pocket, like a professor.

After pausing a moment to deduce who I was, he stood and led me to a table in the back of the room, which was filled with smoke and sounds from a jukebox. We ordered dinner, and he proceeded to tell me what Edwards had loosely sketched out: that he was a longtime member of the Baker Street Irregulars and had, for many years, helped to represent Conan Doyle's literary estate in America. It is his main job, though, that has given him a slightly menacing air—at least in the minds of Green's friends. He works for the Pentagon in a high-ranking post that deals with clandestine operations. ("One of Donald Rumsfeld's pals," as Edwards described him.)

The American said that after he received a Ph.D. in international relations, in 1970, and became an expert in the cold war and nuclear doctrine, he was drawn into the Sherlockian games and their pursuit of immaculate logic. "I've always kept the two worlds separate," he told me at one point. "I don't think a lot of people at the Pentagon would understand my fascination with a literary character." He met Green through the Sherlockian community, he said. As members of the Baker Street Irregulars, both had been given official titles from the Holmes stories. The American was "Rodger Prescott of evil memory," after the American counterfeiter in "The Adventure of the Three Garridebs." Green was known as "The Three Gables," after the villa in "The Adventure of the Three Gables," which is ransacked by burglars in search of a scandalous biographical manuscript.

In the mid-nineteen-eighties, the American said, he and Green had collaborated on several projects. As the editor of a collection of essays on Conan Doyle, he had asked Green, whom he considered then "the single most knowledgeable living person on Conan Doyle," to write the crucial chapter on the author's 1924 memoir. "My relationship with Richard was always productive," he recalled. Then, in the early nineteen-nineties, he said, they had had a falling out—a result, he added, of a startling rupture in Green's relationship with Dame Jean.

"Richard had gotten very close to Dame Jean, and was getting all sorts of family photographs, having represented himself as a great admirer of Conan Doyle," he said. "And then she saw something in print by him and suddenly realized that he had been representing his views very differently, and that was kind of the end of it."

The American insisted that he couldn't remember what Green had written that upset her. But Edwards, and others in Holmesian circles, said that the reason nobody could recall a specific offense was that Green's essays had never been particularly inflammatory. According to R. Dixon Smith, a friend of Green's and a longtime Conan Doyle book dealer, the American played on Dame Jean's sensitivities about her father's reputation and seized upon some of Green's candid words, which had never upset her before, then "twisted" them like "a screw." Edwards said of the American, "I think he did everything he possibly could to injure Richard. He drove a wedge between Richard and Dame Jean Conan Doyle." After Dame Jean cast Green out, Edwards and others noted, the American grew closer to her. Edwards told me that Green never got over the quarrel with Dame Jean. "He used to look at me like his heart was breaking," he said.

When I pressed the American further about the incident, he said simply, "Because I was Jean's representative, I got caught in the middle of it." Soon after, he said, "the good feeling and cooperation by Green toward me ended." At Sherlockian events, he said, they continued to see each other, but Green, always reserved, would often avoid him.

Smith had told me that in Green's final months he often seemed "preoccupied" with the American. "He kept wondering, What's he gonna do next?" During the last week of his life, Green told several friends that the American was working to defeat his crusade against the auction, and he expressed fear that his rival might try to damage his scholarly reputation. On March 24, two days before he died, Green learned that the American was in London and was planning to attend a meeting that evening of the Sherlock Holmes Society. A friend said that Green called him and exclaimed, "I don't want to see him! I don't want to go." Green backed out of the meeting at the last minute. The friend said of the American, "I think he scared Richard."

As I mentioned some of the allegations of Green's friends, the American unfolded his napkin and touched the corners of his mouth. He explained that during his visit to London he had offered counsel to Charles Foley—whom he now served as a literary representative, as he had for Dame Jean—and discussed the sale of the archive at Christie's. But the American emphasized that he had not seen or spoken to Green for more than a year. On the night that Green died, he revealed with some embarrassment, he was walking through London with his wife on a group tour of Jack the Ripper's crime scenes. He said that he had learned only recently that Green had become fixated on him before his death, and he noted that some Sherlockians blurred the line between fandom and fanaticism. "It was because of the way people felt about the character," he said. Holmes was a sort of "vampire-like creature," he said; he consumed some people.

The waiter had served our meals, and the American paused to take a bite of steak and onion rings. He then explained that Conan Doyle had felt oppressed by his creation. Though the stories had made him the highest-paid author of his day, Conan Doyle wearied of constantly "inventing problems and building up chains of inductive reason," as he once said bitterly. In the stories, Holmes himself seems overwhelmed by his task, going days without sleep, and, after solving a case, often shooting up cocaine ("a seven-percent solution") in order to spell the subsequent drain and boredom. But, for Conan Doyle, there seemed to be no similar release, and he confided to one friend that "Holmes is becoming such a burden to me that it makes my life unendurable."

The very qualities that had made Holmes invincible—"his character admits of no light or shade," as Conan Doyle put it—eventually made him intolerable. Moreover, Conan Doyle feared that the detective stories eclipsed what he called his "more serious literary work." He had spent years researching several historical novels, which, he was convinced, would earn him a place in the pantheon of writers. In 1891, after he finished *The White Company*, which was set in the Middle Ages and based on tales of "gallant, pious knights," he proclaimed, "Well, I'll never beat that." The book was popular in its day, but it was soon obscured by the shadow of Holmes, as were his other novels, with their comparatively stilted, lifeless prose. After Conan Doyle completed the domestic novel *A Duet with an Occasional Chorus*, in 1899, Andrew Lang, a well-known editor who had helped publish one of his previous books, summed up the sentiment of most readers: "It may be a vulgar taste, but we decidedly prefer the adventures of Dr. Watson with Sherlock Holmes."

Conan Doyle was increasingly dismayed by the great paradox of his success: the more real Holmes became in the minds of readers, the less the author seemed to exist. Finally, Conan Doyle felt that he had no choice. As the American put it, "He had to kill Sherlock Holmes." Conan Doyle knew that the death had to be spectacular. "A man like that mustn't die of a pin-prick or influenza," he told a close friend. "His end must be violent and intensely dramatic." For months, he tried to imagine the perfect murder. Then, in December 1893, six years after he gave birth to Holmes, Conan Doyle published *The Final Problem*. The story breaks from the established formula: there is no puzzle to be solved, no dazzling display of deductive genius. And this time Holmes is the one pursued. He is being chased by Professor Moriarty, "the Napoleon of crime," who is "the organizer of half that is evil and of nearly all that is undetected in this great city" of London. Moriarty is the first true counterpart to Holmes, a mathematician who is, as Holmes informs Watson, "a genius, a philosopher, an abstract thinker." Tall and ascetic-looking, he even physically resembles Holmes.

What is most striking about the story, though, is that the two great logicians have descended into illogic—they are paranoid, and consumed only with each other. At one point, Moriarty tells Holmes, "This is not danger. . . . It is inevitable destruction."

Finally, the two converge on a cliff overlooking Reichenbach Falls, in Switzerland. As Watson later deduces from evidence at the scene, Holmes and Moriarty struggled by the edge of the precipice before plunging to their deaths. After finishing the story, Conan Doyle wrote in his diary, with apparent delight, "Killed Holmes."

As the American spoke of these details, he seemed stunned that Conan Doyle had gone through with such an extraordinary act. Still, he pointed out, Conan Doyle could not escape from his creation. In England, men reportedly wore black armbands in mourning. In America, clubs devoted to the cause "Let's Keep Holmes Alive" were formed. Though Conan Doyle insisted that Holmes's death was "justifiable homicide," readers denounced him as a brute and demanded that he resuscitate their hero; after all, no one had actually seen him go off the cliff. As Green wrote in a 1983 essay, "If ever a murderer was to be haunted by the man he had killed and to be forced to atone for his act, it was the creator, turned destroyer, of Sherlock Holmes." In 1901, under increasing pressure, Conan Doyle released *The Hound of the Baskervilles*, about an ancient family curse, but the events in the story antedated Holmes's death. Then, two years later, Conan Doyle succumbed completely, and began writing new Holmes stories, explaining, less than convincingly, in "The Adventure of the Empty House," that Holmes had never plunged to his death but merely arranged it to look that way so he could escape from Moriarty's gang.

The American told me that even after Conan Doyle died Holmes continued to loom over his descendants. "Dame Jean thought that Sherlock Holmes was the family curse," he said. Like her father, he said, she had tried to draw attention to his other works but was constantly forced to tend to the detective's thousands of fans—many of whom sent letters addressed to Holmes, requesting his help in solving real crimes. In a 1935 essay entitled "Sherlock Holmes the God," G. K. Chesterton observed of Sherlockians, "It is getting beyond a joke. The hobby is hardening into a delusion."

Several actors who played Holmes were also haunted by him, the American said. In a 1956 autobiography, *In and Out of Character*, Basil Rathbone, who played the detective in more than a dozen films, complained that because of his portrayal of Holmes his renown for other parts, including Oscar-nominated ones, was "sinking into oblivion." The public conflated him with his most famous character, which the studio and audience demanded he play again and again, until by the end he, too, lamented that he "could not kill Mr. Holmes." Another actor, Jeremy Brett, had a breakdown while playing the detective and was eventually admitted to a psychiatric ward, where he was said to have cried out, "Damn you, Holmes!"

At one point, the American showed me a thick book, which he had brought to the pub. It was part of a multivolume history that he was writing on the Baker Street Irregulars and Sherlockian scholarship. He had started the project in 1988. "I thought if I searched pretty assiduously I'd find enough material to do a single hundred-and-fifty-page volume," he said. "I've now done five volumes for more than fifteen hundred pages, and I've only gotten up to 1950." He added, "It's been a slippery slope into madness and obsession."

As he spoke of his fascination with Holmes, he recalled one of the last times he had seen Green, three years earlier, at a symposium at the University of Minnesota. Green had given a lecture on "The Hound of the Baskervilles." "It was a multimedia presentation about the origins of the novel, and it was just dazzling," the American said. He repeated the word "dazzling" several times ("It's the only word to describe it"), and as he sat up in his chair and his eyes brightened I realized that I was talking not to Green's Moriarty but to his soul mate. Then, catching himself, he reminded me that he had a full-time job and a family. "The danger is if you have nothing else in your life but Sherlock Holmes," he said.

———

IN 1988, Richard Green made a pilgrimage to Reichenbach Falls to see where his childhood hero had nearly met his demise. Conan Doyle himself had visited the site in 1893, and Green wanted to repeat the author's journey. Standing at the edge of the falls, Green stared at the chasm below, where, as Watson noted after he called out, "My only answer was my own voice reverberating in a rolling echo from the cliffs around me."

By the mid-nineteen-nineties, Green knew that he would not have access to the Conan Doyle archive until Dame Jean died— presuming that she bequeathed the papers to the British Library. In the meantime, he continued researching his biography, which, he concluded, would require no less than three volumes: the first would cover Conan Doyle's childhood; the second, the arc of his literary career; the third, his descent into a kind of madness.

Relying on public documents, Green outlined this last stage, which began after Conan Doyle started using his powers of observation to solve real-world mysteries. In 1906, Conan Doyle took up the case of George Edalji, a half-Parsi Indian living near Birmingham, who faced seven years of hard labor for allegedly mutilating his neighbors' cattle during the night. Conan Doyle suspected that Edalji had been tagged as a criminal merely because of his ethnicity, and he assumed the role of detective. Upon meeting his client, he noticed that the young man was holding a newspaper inches from his face.

"Aren't you astigmatic?" Conan Doyle asked.

"Yes," Edalji admitted.

Conan Doyle called in an ophthalmologist, who confirmed that Edalji's malady was so severe that he was unable to see properly even with glasses. Conan Doyle then trekked to the scene of the crime, traversing a maze of railroad tracks and hedges. "I, a strong and active man, in broad daylight, found it a hard matter to pass," he later wrote. Indeed, he contended, it would have been impossible for a nearly blind person to make the journey and then slaughter an animal in the pitch black of night. A tribunal soon concurred, and the *New York Times* declared: CONAN DOYLE SOLVES A NEW DREYFUS CASE.

Conan Doyle even helped in solving a case of a serial killer, after he spotted newspaper accounts in which two women had died in the same bizarre manner: the victims were recent brides, who had "accidentally" drowned in their bathtubs. Conan Doyle informed Scotland Yard of his theory, telling the inspector, in an echo of Holmes, "No time is to be lost"; the killer, dubbed "the Bluebeard of the Bath," was subsequently caught and convicted in a sensational trial.

Around 1914, Conan Doyle tried to apply his rational powers to the most important matter of his day—the logic of launching the First World War. He was convinced that the war was not simply about entangling alliances and a dead archduke; it was a sensible way to restore the codes of honor and moral purpose that he had celebrated in his historical novels. That year, he unleashed a spate of propaganda, declaring, "Fear not, for our sword will not be broken, nor shall it ever drop from our hands." In the Holmes story "His Last Bow," which is set in 1914, the detective tells Watson that after the "storm has cleared" a "cleaner, better, stronger land will lie in the sunshine."

Though Conan Doyle was too old to fight, many of his relatives heeded his call "to arms," including his son Kingsley. The glorious battle Conan Doyle envisioned, however, became a cataclysm. The products of scientific reason—machines and engineering and electronics—were transformed into agents of destruction. Conan Doyle visited the battlefield by the Somme, where tens of thousands of British soldiers died, and where he later reported seeing a soldier "drenched crimson from head to foot, with two great glazed eyes looking upwards through a mask of blood." In 1918, a chastened Conan Doyle realized that the conflict was "evidently preventable." By that time, ten million people had perished, including Kingsley, who died from battle wounds and influenza.

After the war, Conan Doyle wrote a handful of Holmes stories, yet the field of detective fiction was changing. The all-knowing detective gradually gave way to the hardboiled dick, who acted more on instinct and gin than on reason. In "The Simple Art of Murder," Raymond Chandler, while admiring Conan Doyle, dismissed the tradition of the "grim logician" and his "exhausting concatenation of insignificant clues," which now seemed like an absurdity.

Meanwhile, in his own life, Conan Doyle seemed to abandon reason altogether. As one of Green's colleagues in the Baker Street Irregulars, Daniel Stashower, relates in a 1999 book, *Teller of Tales: The Life of Arthur Conan Doyle*, the creator of Holmes began to believe in ghosts. He attended séances and received messages from the dead through "the power of automatic writing," a method akin to that of the Ouija board. During one session, Conan Doyle, who had once considered the belief in life after death as "a delusion," claimed that his dead younger brother said, "It is so grand to be in touch like this."

One day, Conan Doyle heard a voice in the séance room. As he later described the scene in a letter to a friend:

> I said, "Is that you, boy?"
> He said in a very intense whisper and a tone all his own, "Father!" and then after a pause, "Forgive me!"
> I said, "There was never anything to forgive. You were the best son a man ever had." A strong hand descended on my head which was slowly pressed forward, and I felt a kiss just above my brow.
> "Are you happy?" I cried.
> There was a pause and then very gently, "I am so happy."

The creator of Sherlock Holmes had become the St. Paul of psychics. Conan Doyle claimed to see not only dead family members but fairies as well. He championed photographs taken in 1917 by two girls that purported to show such phantasmal creatures, even though, as one of the girls later admitted, "I could see the hatpins holding up the figures. I've always marvelled that anybody ever took it seriously." Conan Doyle, however, was convinced, and even published a book called *The Coming of Fairies*. He opened the Psychic Bookshop, in London, and told friends that he had received messages that the world was coming to an end. "I suppose I am Sherlock Holmes, if anybody is, and I say that the case for spiritualism is absolutely proved," he declared. In 1918, a headline in the *Sunday Express* asked: IS CONAN DOYLE MAD?

For the first time, Green struggled to rationalize his subject's life. In one essay, Green wrote, "It is hard to understand how a man who had stood for sound common sense and healthy attitudes could sit in darkened rooms watching for ectoplasm." Green reacted at times as if his hero had betrayed him. In one passage, he wrote angrily, "Conan Doyle was deluding himself."

"One thing Richard couldn't stand was Conan Doyle's being involved with spiritualism," Edwards said. "He thought it crazy." His friend Dixon Smith told me, "It was all Conan Doyle. He pursued him with all his mind and body." Green's house became filled with more and more objects from Conan Doyle's life: long-forgotten propaganda leaflets and speeches on spiritualism; an arcane study of the Boer War; previously unknown essays on photography. "I remember once, I discovered a copy of *A Duet with an Occasional Chorus*," Gibson said. "It had a great red cover on it. I showed it to Richard and he got really excited. He said, 'God, this must have been the salesman's copy.'" When Green found one of the few surviving copies of the 1887 *Beeton's Christmas Annual*, with "A Study in Scarlet," which was worth as much as a hundred and thirty thousand dollars, he sent a card to a friend with two words on it: "At last!"

Green also wanted to hold things that Conan Doyle himself had held: letter openers and pens and spectacles. "He would collect all day and all night, and I mean night," his brother, Scirard, told me. Green covered many of his walls with Conan Doyle's family photographs. He even had a piece of wallpaper from one of Conan

Doyle's homes. "'Obsession' is by no means too strong a word to describe what Richard had," his friend Nicholas Utechin, the editor of *The Sherlock Holmes Journal*, said.

"It's self-perpetuating and I don't know how to stop," Green confessed to an antiques magazine in 1999.

By 2000, his house resembled the attic at Poulton Hall, only now he seemed to be living in a museum dedicated to Conan Doyle rather than to Holmes. "I have around forty thousand books," Green told the magazine. "Then, of course, there are the photographs, the pictures, the papers, and all the other ephemera. I know it sounds a lot, but, you see, the more you have, the more you feel you need."

And what he longed for most remained out of reach: the archive. After Dame Jean died, in 1997, and no papers materialized at the British Library, he became increasingly frustrated. Where he had once judiciously built his conjectures about Conan Doyle's life, he now seemed reckless. In 2002, to the shock of Doyleans around the world, Green wrote a paper claiming that he had proof that Conan Doyle had had a tryst with Jean Leckie, his delicately beautiful second wife, before his first wife, Louisa, died of tuberculosis, in 1906. Though it was well known that Conan Doyle had formed a bond with Leckie during his wife's long illness, he had always insisted, "I fight the devil and I win." And, to maintain an air of Victorian rectitude, he often brought along chaperones when he and Leckie were together. Green based his allegation on the 1901 census, which reported that on the day the survey was taken Conan Doyle was staying at the Ashdown Forest Hotel, in East Sussex. So, too, was Leckie. "Conan Doyle could not have chosen a worse weekend on which to have a private tryst," Green wrote. Yet Green failed to note one crucial fact also contained in the census report—Conan Doyle's mother was staying in the hotel with him, apparently as a chaperone. Later, Green was forced to recant, in a letter to *The Sherlock Holmes Journal*, saying, "I was guilty of the capital mistake of theorising without data."

Still, he continued to lash out at Conan Doyle, as Conan Doyle once had at Sherlock Holmes. Edwards recalled that, in one conversation, Green decried Conan Doyle as "unoriginal" and "a plagiarist." He confessed to another friend, "I've wasted my whole life on a second-rate writer."

"I think he was frustrated because the family wasn't coming to any agreement," Smith said. "The archive wasn't made available, and he got angry not at the heirs but at Conan Doyle."

Last March, when Green hurried to Christie's after the auction of the papers was announced, he discovered that the archive was as rich and as abundant as he'd imagined. Among the thousands of items were fragments of the first tale that Conan Doyle wrote, at the age of six; illustrated logs from when Conan Doyle was a surgeon on a Scottish whaling ship, in the eighteen-eighties; letters from Conan Doyle's father (whose drawings in the asylum resembled the fairies that his son later seized upon as real); a brown envelope with a cross and the name of his dead son inscribed upon it; the manuscript of Conan Doyle's first novel, which was never published; a missive from Conan Doyle to his brother, which seemed to confirm that Green's hunch had been right, and that Conan Doyle had in fact begun an affair with Leckie. Jane Flower, who helped to organize the papers for Christie's, told reporters, "The whereabouts of this material was previously unknown, and it is for this reason that no modern-day biography of the author exists."

Meanwhile, back at his home, Green tried to piece together why the archive was about to slip into private hands once more. According to Green's family, he typed notes in his computer, reexamining the trail of evidence, which he thought proved that the papers belonged to the British Library. He worked late into the night, frequently going without sleep. None of it, however, seemed to add up. At one point, he typed in bold letters: STICK TO THE FACTS. After another sleepless night, he told his sister that the world seemed "Kafkaesque."

Several hours before Green died, he called his friend Utechin at home. Green had asked him to find a tape of an old BBC radio interview, which, Green recalled, quoted one of Conan Doyle's heirs saying that the archive should be given to the British Library. Utechin said that he had found the tape, but there was no such statement on the recording. Green became apoplectic, and accused his friend of conspiring against him, as if he were another Moriarty. Finally, Utechin said, "Richard, you've lost it!"

ONE AFTERNOON while I was at my hotel in London, the phone rang. "I need to see you again," John Gibson said. "I'll take the next train in." Before he hung up, he added, "I have a theory."

I met him in my hotel room. He was carrying several scraps of paper, on which he had taken notes. He sat down by the window, his slender figure silhouetted in the fading light, and announced, "I think it was suicide."

He had sifted through the data, including details that I had shared with him from my own investigation. There was mounting evidence, he said, that his rationalist friend was betraying signs of irrationality in the last week of his life. There was the fact that there was no evidence of forced entry at Green's home. And there was the fact, perhaps most critically, of the wooden spoon by Green's hand.

"He had to have used it to tighten the cord" like a tourniquet, Gibson said. "If someone else had garroted him, why would he need the spoon? The killer could simply use his hands." He continued, "I think things in his life had not turned out the way he wanted. This Christie's sale simply brought everything to a head."

He glanced nervously at his notes, which he strained to see without his magnifying glass. "That's not all," he said. "I think he wanted it to look like murder."

He waited to assess my reaction, then went on, "That's why he didn't leave a note. That's why he took his voice off the answering machine. That's why he sent that message to his sister with the three phone numbers on it. That's why he spoke of the American who was after him. He must have been planning it for days, laying the foundation, giving us false clues."

I knew that, in detective fiction, the reverse scenario generally turns out to be true—a suicide is found to have been murder. As Holmes declares in "The Resident Patient," "This is no suicide. . . . It is a very deeply planned and cold-blooded murder." There is, however, one notable exception. It is, eerily enough, in one of the last Holmes mysteries, "The Problem of Thor Bridge," a story that Green once cited in an essay. A wife is found lying dead on a bridge, shot in the head at point-blank range. All the evidence points to one suspect: the governess, with whom the husband had been flirting. Yet Holmes shows that the wife had not been killed by anyone; rather, enraged by jealousy over her husband's illicit overtures to the governess, she had killed herself and framed the woman whom she blamed for her misery. Of all Conan Doyle's stories, it digs deepest into the human psyche and its criminal motivations. As the governess tells Holmes, "When I reached the bridge she was waiting for me. Never did I realize till that moment how this poor creature hated me. She was like a mad woman— indeed, I think she was a mad woman, subtly mad with the deep power of deception which insane people may have."

I wondered if Green could have been so enraged with the loss of the archive that he might have done something similar, and even tried to frame the American, whom he blamed for ruining his relationship with Dame Jean and for the sale of the archive. I wondered if he could have tried, in one last desperate attempt, to create order out of the chaos around him. I wondered if this theory, however improbable, was in fact the least "impossible."

I shared with Gibson some other clues I had uncovered: the call that Green had made to the reporter days before his death, saying that "something" might happen to him; a reference in a Holmes story to one of Moriarty's main henchmen as a "garroter by trade";

and a statement to the coroner by Green's sister, who said that the note with the three phone numbers had reminded her of "the beginning of a thriller."

After a while, Gibson looked up at me, his face ghastly white. "Don't you see?" he exclaimed. "He staged the whole thing. He created the perfect mystery."

BEFORE I WENT back to America, I went to see Green's sister, Priscilla West. She lives near Oxford, in a three-story eighteenth-century brick house with a walled garden. She had long, wavy brown hair, an attractive round face, and small oval glasses. She invited me inside with a reticent voice, saying, "Are you a drawing-room person or a kitchen person?"

I shrugged uncertainly, and she led me into the drawing room, which had antique furniture and her father's children's books on the shelves. As we sat down, I explained to her that I had been struggling to write her brother's story. The American had told me, "There is no such thing as a definitive biography," and Green seemed particularly resistant to explication.

"Richard compartmentalized his life," his sister said. "There are a lot of things we've only found out since he died." At the inquest, his family, and most of his friends, had been startled when Lawrence Keen, who was nearly half Green's age, announced that he had been Richard's lover years ago. "No one in the family knew" that Green was gay, his sister explained. "It wasn't something he ever talked about."

As West recalled other surprising fragments of Green's biography (travels to Tibet, a brief attempt at writing a novel), I tried to picture him as best I could with his glasses, his plastic bag in hand, and his wry smile. West had seen her brother's body lying on the bed, and several times she told me, "I just wish . . ." before falling silent. She handed me copies of the eulogies that Green's friends had delivered at the memorial service, which was held on May 22, the day Conan

Doyle was born. On the back of the program from the service were several quotes from Sherlock Holmes stories:

> I caught a glimpse of a great heart as well as of a great brain.
> He appears to have a passion for definite and exact knowledge.
> His career has been an extraordinary one.

After a while, she got up to pour herself a cup of tea. When she sat down again, she said that her brother had willed his collection to a library in Portsmouth, near where Conan Doyle wrote the first two Holmes stories, so that other scholars could have access to it. The collection was so large that it had taken two weeks, and required twelve truckloads, to cart it all away. It was estimated to be worth several million dollars—far more, in all likelihood, than the treasured archive. "He really did not like the idea of scholarship being put second to greed," West said. "He lived and died by this."

She then told me something about the archive which had only recently come to light, and which her brother had never learned: Dame Jean Conan Doyle, while dying of cancer, had made a last-minute deed of apportionment, splitting the archive between herself and the three heirs of her former sister-in-law, Anna Conan Doyle. What was being auctioned off, therefore, belonged to the three heirs, and not to Dame Jean, and, though some people still questioned the morality of the sale, the British Library had reached the conclusion that it was legal.

Green also could not know that after the auction, on May 19, the most important papers ended up at the British Library. Dame Jean had not allotted those documents to the other heirs, and had willed many of them to the library; at the same time, the library had purchased much of the remaining material at the auction. As Gibson later told me, "The tragedy is that Richard could have still written his biography. He would have had everything he needed."

Two questions, however, remained unclear. How, I asked West, did an American voice wind up on her brother's answering machine?

"I'm afraid it's not that complicated," she said. The machine, she continued, was made in the United States and had a built-in recorded message; when her brother took off his personal message, a prerecorded American voice appeared.

I then asked about the phone numbers in the note. She shook her head in dismay. They added up to nothing, she said. They were merely those of two reporters her brother had spoken to, and the number of someone at Christie's.

Finally, I asked what she thought had happened to her brother. At one point, Scirard Lancelyn Green had told the *London Observer* that he thought murder was "entirely possible"; and, for all my attempts to build a case that transcended doubt, there were still questions. Hadn't the police told the coroner that an intruder could have locked Green's apartment door while slipping out, thus giving the illusion that his victim had died alone? Wasn't it possible that Green had known the murderer and simply let him in? And how could someone, even in a fit of madness, garrote himself with merely a shoelace and the help of a spoon?

His sister glanced away, as if trying one last time to arrange all the pieces. Then she said, "I don't think we'll ever know for sure what really happened. Unlike in detective stories, we have to live without answers."

DAVID GRANN *is a staff writer at* The New Yorker. *His stories have appeared in the* New York Times Magazine, *the* Atlantic Monthly, *and the* New Republic, *where he previously served as managing editor. His work has also been excerpted in several collections, including* The Best American Sports Writing 2003 *and* The Best American Crime Writing 2004.

Coda

Ever since I was a boy, I have read the Holmes stories, enthralled by them. Critics have long tried to determine the source of their hold on the popular imagination. Some have argued that it is because of the spell of their logic, or the dialogue between Holmes and Watson, or the Victorian mood they evoke. But for me it was simply the thrill of the chase—that the game was indeed afoot, as Holmes always put it with delight.

When I started this story, I inevitably found myself approaching it in the same fashion. Here at last, I thought, was a mystery worthy of Holmes. And initially as I went about my reporting, piecing together each clue, I could feel that same sense of wonder I had as a boy when, say, I discovered, in "The Adventure of the Speckled Band," that the suspect had killed his stepdaughter with "the deadliest snake in India." But the more I spoke with Richard Lancelyn Green's family and friends, the more I was reminded of another sensation, one that rarely intrudes in the Sherlockian game: grief. Indeed, by the end it occurred to me that I had never been investigating a mystery, but a tragedy.

Clive Thompson

THE VIRUS
UNDERGROUND

FROM THE *New York Times Magazine*

THIS IS HOW EASY it has become.

Mario stubs out his cigarette and sits down at the desk in his bedroom. He pops into his laptop the CD of Iron Maiden's *Number of the Beast*, his latest favorite album. "I really like it," he says. "My girlfriend bought it for me." He gestures to the fifteen-year-old girl with straight dark hair lounging on his neatly made bed, and she throws back a shy smile. Mario, sixteen, is a secondary-school student in a small town in the foothills of southern Austria. (He didn't want me to use his last name.) His shiny shoulder-length hair covers half his face and his sleepy green eyes, making him look like a very young, languid Mick Jagger. On his wall he has an enormous poster of Anna Kournikova—which, he admits sheepishly, his girlfriend is not thrilled about. Downstairs, his mother is cleaning up after dinner. She isn't thrilled these days, either, But what bothers her isn't Mario's poster. It's his hobby.

When Mario is bored—and out here in the countryside, surrounded by soaring snowcapped mountains and little else, he's bored a lot—he likes to sit at his laptop and create computer viruses and worms. Online, he goes by the name Second Part to Hell, and he has written more than one hundred and fifty examples of what computer experts call "malware": tiny programs that exist solely to self-replicate, infecting computers hooked up to the Internet. Sometimes these programs cause damage, and sometimes they don't. Mario says he prefers to create viruses that don't intentionally wreck data, because simple destruction is too easy. "Anyone can rewrite a hard drive with one or two lines of code," he says. "It makes no sense. It's really lame." Besides which, it's mean, he says, and he likes to be friendly.

But still—just to see if he could do it—a year ago he created a rather dangerous tool: a program that autogenerates viruses. It's called a Batch Trojan Generator, and anyone can download it freely from Mario's Web site. With a few simple mouse clicks, you can use the tool to create your own malicious "Trojan horse." Like its ancient namesake, a Trojan virus arrives in someone's e-mail looking like a gift, a JPEG picture, or a video, for example, but actually bearing dangerous cargo.

Mario starts up the tool to show me how it works. A little box appears on his laptop screen, politely asking me to name my Trojan. I call it the "Clive" virus. Then it asks me what I'd like the virus to do. *Shall the Trojan Horse format drive C:?* Yes, I click. *Shall the Trojan Horse overwrite every file?* Yes. It asks me if I'd like to have the virus activate the next time the computer is restarted, and I say yes again.

Then it's done. The generator spits out the virus onto Mario's hard drive, a tiny 3k file. Mario's generator also displays a stern notice warning that spreading your creation is illegal. The generator, he says, is just for educational purposes, a way to help curious programmers learn how Trojans work.

But of course I could ignore that advice. I could give this virus an enticing name, like "britney_spears_wedding_clip.mpeg," to fool people into thinking it's a video. If I were to e-mail it to a victim, and if he clicked on it—and didn't have up-to-date antivirus software, which many people don't—then disaster would strike his computer. The virus would activate. It would quietly reach into the victim's Microsoft Windows operating system and insert new commands telling the computer to erase its own hard drive. The next time the victim started up his computer, the machine would find those new commands, assume they were part of the normal Windows operating system and guilelessly follow them. Poof: everything on his hard drive would vanish—e-mail, pictures, documents, games.

I've never contemplated writing a virus before. Even if I had, I wouldn't have known how to do it. But thanks to a teenager in Austria, it took me less than a minute to master the art.

Mario drags the virus over to the trash bin on his computer's desktop and discards it. "I don't think we should touch that," he says hastily.

COMPUTER EXPERTS called 2003 "the Year of the Worm." For twelve months, digital infections swarmed across the Internet with the intensity of a biblical plague. It began in January, when the Slammer worm infected nearly 75,000 servers in ten minutes, clogging Bank of America's ATM network and causing sporadic flight delays. In the summer, the Blaster worm struck, spreading by exploiting a flaw in Windows; it carried taunting messages directed at Bill Gates, infected hundreds of thousands of computers, and tried to use them to bombard a Microsoft Web site with data. Then in August, a worm called Sobig.F exploded with even more force, spreading via e-mail that it generated by stealing addresses from victims' computers. It propagated so rapidly that at one point, one out of every seventeen e-mail messages traveling through the Internet was a copy of Sobig.F. The computer-security firm mi2g estimated that the worldwide cost of these attacks in 2003, including clean-up and lost productivity, was at least $82 billion (though such estimates have been criticized for being inflated).

The pace of contagion seems to be escalating. When the

Mydoom.A e-mail virus struck in late January, it spread even faster than Sobig.F; at its peak, experts estimated, one out of every five e-mail messages was a copy of Mydoom.A. It also carried a nasty payload: it reprogrammed victim computers to attack the Web site of SCO, a software firm vilified by geeks in the "open source" software community.

You might assume that the blame—and the legal repercussions— for the destruction would land directly at the feet of people like Mario. But as the police around the globe have cracked down on cybercrime in the past few years, virus writers have become more cautious, or at least more crafty. These days, many elite writers do not spread their works at all. Instead, they "publish" them, posting their code on Web sites, often with detailed descriptions of how the program works. Essentially, they leave their viruses lying around for anyone to use.

Invariably, someone does. The people who release the viruses are often anonymous mischief-makers, or "script kiddies." That's a derisive term for aspiring young hackers, usually teenagers or curious college students, who don't yet have the skill to program computers but like to pretend they do. They download the viruses, claim to have written them themselves, and then set them free in an attempt to assume the role of a fearsome digital menace. Script kiddies often have only a dim idea of how the code works and little concern for how a digital plague can rage out of control.

Our modern virus epidemic is thus born of a symbiotic relationship between the people smart enough to write a virus and the people dumb enough—or malicious enough—to spread it. Without these two groups of people, many viruses would never see the light of day. Script kiddies, for example, were responsible for some of the damage the Blaster worm caused. The original version of Blaster, which struck on August 11, was clearly written by a skilled programmer (who is still unknown and at large). Three days later, a second version of Blaster circulated online, infecting an estimated seven thousand computers. This time the FBI tracked the release to Jeffrey Lee

Parson, an eighteen-year-old in Minnesota who had found, slightly altered, and rereleased the Blaster code, prosecutors claim. Parson may have been seeking notoriety, or he may have had no clue how much damage the worm could cause: he did nothing to hide his identity and even included a reference to his personal Web site in the code. (He was arrested and charged with intentionally causing damage to computers; when his trial begins, probably this spring, he faces up to ten years in jail.) A few weeks later, a similar scene unfolded: another variant of Blaster was found in the wild. This time it was traced to a college student in Romania who had also left obvious clues to his identity in the code.

This development worries security experts, because it means that virus-writing is no longer exclusively a high-skill profession. By so freely sharing their work, the elite virus writers have made it easy for almost anyone to wreak havoc online. When the damage occurs, as it inevitably does, the original authors just shrug. *We may have created the monster,* they'll say, *but we didn't set it loose.* This dodge infuriates security professionals and the police, who say it is legally precise but morally corrupt. "When they publish a virus online, they *know* someone's going to release it," says Eugene Spafford, a computer-science professor and security expert at Purdue University. Like a collection of young Dr. Frankensteins, the virus writers are increasingly creating forces they cannot control—and for which they explicitly refuse to take responsibility.

"WHERE'S THE BEER?" PhiletOast3r wondered.

An hour earlier, he had dispatched three friends to pick up another case, but they were nowhere in sight. He looked out over the controlled chaos of his tiny one-bedroom apartment in small-town Bavaria. (Most of the virus writers I visited live in Europe; there have been very few active in the United States since 9/11, because of fears of prosecution.) PhiletOast3r's party was crammed with twenty friends who were blasting the punk band Deftones, playing cards, smoking furiously, and arguing about politics. It was a Saturday night. Three girls sat on the floor, rolling another girl's hair into thick dreadlocks, the hairstyle of choice among the crowd. PhiletOast3r himself—a twenty-one-year-old with a small silver hoop piercing his lower lip—wears his brown hair in thick dreads. (PhiletOast3r is an online handle; he didn't want me to use his name.)

PhiletOast3r's friends finally arrived with a fresh case of ale, and his blue eyes lit up. He flicked open a bottle using the edge of his cigarette lighter and toasted the others. A tall blond friend in a jacket festooned with anti-Nike logos put his arm around PhiletOast3r and beamed.

"This guy," he proclaimed, "is the *best* at Visual Basic."

In the virus underground, that's love. Visual Basic is a computer language popular among malware authors for its simplicity; PhiletOast3r has used it to create several of the two dozen viruses he's written. From this tiny tourist town, he works as an assistant in a home for the mentally disabled and in his spare time runs an international virus-writers' group called the "Ready Rangers Liberation Front." He founded the group three years ago with a few bored high school friends in his even tinier hometown nearby. I met him, like everyone profiled in this article, online, first e-mailing him, then chatting in an Internet Relay Chat channel where virus writers meet and trade tips and war stories.

PhiletOast3r got interested in malware the same way most virus authors do: his own computer was hit by a virus. He wanted to know how it worked and began hunting down virus-writers' Web sites. He discovered years' worth of viruses online, all easily downloadable, as well as primers full of coding tricks. He spent long evenings hanging out in online chat rooms, asking questions, and soon began writing his own worms.

One might assume PhiletOast3r would favor destructive viruses, given the fact that his apartment is decorated top-to-bottom with anticorporate stickers. But PhiletOast3r's viruses, like those of many malware writers, are often surprisingly mild things carrying goofy payloads. One worm does nothing but display a picture of a raised middle finger on your computer screen, then sheepishly apologize for the gesture. ("Hey, this is not meant to you! I just wanted to show my payload.") Another one he is currently developing will install two artificial intelligence chat-agents on your computer; they appear in a pop-up window, talking to each other nervously about whether your antivirus software is going to catch and delete them. PhiletOast3r said he was also working on something sneakier: a "keylogger." It's a Trojan virus that monitors every keystroke its victim types—including passwords and confidential e-mail messages—then secretly mails out copies to whoever planted the virus. Anyone who spreads this Trojan would be able to quickly harvest huge amounts of sensitive personal information.

Technically, "viruses" and "worms" are slightly different things. When a virus arrives on your computer, it disguises itself. It might look like an Out-Kast song ("hey_ya.mp3"), but if you look more closely, you'll see it has an unusual suffix, like "hey_ya.mp3.exe." That's because it isn't an MP3 file at all. It's a tiny program, and when you click on it, it will reprogram parts of your computer to do something new, like display a message. A virus cannot kick-start itself; a human needs to be fooled into clicking on it. This turns virus writers into armchair psychologists, always hunting for new tricks to dupe someone into activating a virus. ("All virus-spreading," one virus writer said caustically, "is based on the idiotic behavior of the users.")

Worms, in contrast, usually do not require any human intervention to spread. That means they can travel at the breakneck pace of computers themselves. Unlike a virus, a worm generally does not alter or destroy data on a computer. Its danger lies in its speed: when a worm multiplies, it often generates enough traffic to brown out Internet servers, like air conditioners bringing down the power grid on a hot summer day. The most popular worms today are "mass mailers," which attack a victim's computer, swipe the addresses out of Microsoft Outlook (the world's most common e-mail program), and send a copy of the worm to everyone in the victim's address book. These days, the distinction between worm and virus is breaking down. A worm will carry a virus with it, dropping it onto the victim's hard drive to do its work, then e-mailing itself off to a new target.

The most ferocious threats today are "network worms," which exploit a particular flaw in a software product (often one by Microsoft). The author of Slammer, for example, noticed a flaw in Microsoft's SQL Server, an online database commonly used by businesses and governments. The Slammer worm would find an unprotected SQL server, then would fire bursts of information at it, flooding the server's data "buffer," like a cup filled to the brim with water. Once its buffer was full, the server could be tricked into sending out thousands of new copies of the worm to other servers. Normally, a server should not allow an outside agent to control it that way, but Microsoft had neglected to defend against such an attack. Using that flaw, Slammer flooded the Internet with fifty-five million blasts of data per second and in only ten minutes colonized almost all vulnerable machines. The attacks slowed the 911 system in Bellevue, Washington, a Seattle suburb, to such a degree that operators had to resort to a manual method of tracking calls.

PhiletOast3r said he isn't interested in producing a network worm, but he said it wouldn't be hard if he wanted to do it. He would scour the Web sites where computer-security professionals report any new software vulnerabilities they discover. Often, these security white papers will explain the flaw in such detail that they practically provide a road map on how to write a worm that exploits it. "Then I would use it," he concluded. "It's that simple."

Computer-science experts have a phrase for that type of fast-spreading epidemic: "a Warhol worm," in honor of Andy Warhol's prediction that everyone would be famous for fifteen minutes. "In computer terms, fifteen minutes is a really long time," says Nicholas Weaver, a researcher at the International Computer Science Institute in Berkeley, who coined the Warhol term. "The worm moves faster than humans can respond." He suspects that even more damaging worms are on the way. All a worm writer needs to do is find a significant new flaw in a Microsoft product, then write some code that exploits it. Even Microsoft admits that there are flaws the company doesn't yet know about.

Virus writers are especially hostile toward Microsoft, the perennial whipping boy of the geek world. From their (somewhat self-serving) point of view, Microsoft is to blame for the worm epidemic, because the company frequently leaves flaws in its products that allow malware to spread. Microsoft markets its products to less expert computer users, cultivating precisely the sort of gullible victims who click on disguised virus attachments. But it is Microsoft's success that really makes it such an attractive target: since more than 90 percent of desktop computers run Windows, worm writers target Microsoft in order to hit the largest possible number of victims. (By relying so exclusively on Microsoft products, virus authors say, we have created a digital monoculture, a dangerous thinning of the Internet's gene pool.

Microsoft officials disagree that their programs are poor quality, of course. And it is also possible that their products are targeted because it has become cool to do so. "There's sort of a natural tendency to go after the biggest dog," says Phil Reitinger, senior security strategist for Microsoft. Reitinger says that the company is working to make its products more secure. But Microsoft is now so angry that it has launched a counterattack. Last fall, Microsoft set up a $5 million fund to pay for information leading to the capture of writers who target Windows machines. So far, the company has announced $250,000 bounties for the creators of Blaster, Sobig.F and Mydoom.B.

THE MOTIVATIONS of the top virus writers can often seem paradoxical. They spend hours dreaming up new strategies to infect computers, then hours more bringing them to reality. Yet when they're done, most of them say they have little interest in turning their creations free. (In fact, 99 percent of all malware never successfully spreads in the wild, either because it expressly wasn't designed to do so or because the author was inept and misprogrammed his virus.) Though PhiletOast3r is proud of his keylogger, he said he does not intend to release it into the wild. His reason is partly one of self-protection; he wouldn't want the police to trace it back to him. But he also said he does not ethically believe in damaging someone else's computer.

So why write a worm, if you're not going to spread it?

For the sheer intellectual challenge, PhiletOast3r replied, the fun of producing something "really cool." For the top worm writers, the goal is to make something that's brand-new, never seen before. Replicating an existing virus is "lame," the worst of all possible insults. A truly innovative worm, PhiletOast3r said, "is like art." To allow his malware to travel swiftly online, the virus writer must keep its code short and efficient, like a poet elegantly packing as much creativity as possible into the tight format of a sonnet. "One condition of art," he noted, "is doing good things with less."

When he gets stuck on a particularly thorny problem, PhiletOast3r will sometimes call for help from other members of the Ready Rangers Liberation Front (which includes Mario). Another friend in another country, whom PhiletOast3r has never actually met, is helping him complete his keylogger by writing a few crucial bits of code that will hide the tool from its victim's view. When they're done, they'll publish their invention in their group's zine, a semiannual anthology of the members' best work.

The virus scene is oddly gentlemanly, almost like the amateur scientist societies of Victorian Britain, where colleagues presented papers in an attempt to win that most elusive of social currencies: street cred. In fact, I didn't meet anyone who gloated about his own talent until I met Benny. He is a member of 29A, a superelite cadre within the virus underground, a handful of coders around the world whose malware is so innovative that even antivirus experts grudgingly admit they're impressed. Based in the Czech Republic, Benny, clean-cut and wide-eyed, has been writing viruses for five years, making him a veteran in the field at age twenty-one. "The main thing that I'm most proud of, and that no one else can say, is that I always come up with a new idea," he said, ushering me into a bedroom so neat that it looked as if he'd stacked his magazines using a ruler and level.

"Each worm shows something different, something new that hadn't been done before by anyone."

Benny—that's his handle, not his real name—is most famous for having written a virus that infected Windows 2000 two weeks before Windows 2000 was released. He'd met a Microsoft employee months earlier who boasted that the new operating system would be "more secure than ever"; Benny wrote (but says he didn't release) the virus specifically to humiliate the company. "Microsoft," he said with a laugh, "wasn't enthusiastic." He also wrote Leviathan, the first virus to use "multithreading," a technique that makes the computer execute several commands at once, like a juggler handling multiple balls. It greatly speeds up the pace at which viruses can spread. Benny published that invention in his group's zine, and now many of the most virulent bugs have adopted the technique, including last summers infamous Sobig.F.

For a virus author, a successful worm brings the sort of fame that a particularly daring piece of graffiti used to produce: the author's name, automatically replicating itself in cyberspace. When antivirus companies post on their Web sites a new "alert" warning of a fresh menace, the thrill for the author is like getting a great book review: something to crow about and e-mail around to your friends. Writing malware, as one author e-mailed me, is like creating artificial life. A virus, he wrote, is "a humble little creature with only the intention to avoid extinction and survive."

Quite apart from the intellectual fun of programming, though, the virus scene is attractive partly because it's very social. When PhiletOast3r drops by a virus-writers chat channel late at night after work, the conversation is as likely to be about music, politics, or girls as the latest in worm technology. "They're not talking about viruses—they're talking about relationships or ordering pizza," says Sarah Gordon, a senior research fellow at Symantec, an antivirus company, who is one of the only researchers in the world who has interviewed hundreds of virus writers about their motivations. Very occasionally, malware authors even meet up face-to-face for a party; PhiletOast3r once took a road trip for a beer-addled weekend of coding, and when I visited Mario, we met up with another Austrian virus writer and discussed code for hours at a bar.

The virus community attracts a lot of smart but alienated young men, libertarian types who are often flummoxed by the social nuances of life. While the virus scene isn't dominated by those characters, it certainly has its share—and they are often the ones with a genuine chip on their shoulder.

"I am a social reject," admitted Vorgon (as he called himself), a virus writer in Toronto with whom I exchanged messages one night in an online chat channel. He studied computer science in college but couldn't find a computer job after sending out four hundred résumés. With "no friends, not much family," and no girlfriend for years, he became depressed. He attempted suicide, he said, by walking out one frigid winter night into a nearby forest for five hours with no jacket on. But then he got into the virus-writing scene and found a community. "I met a lot of cool people who were interested in what I did," he wrote. "They made me feel good again." He called his first virus FirstBorn to celebrate his new identity. Later, he saw that one of his worms had been written up as an alert on an antivirus site, and it thrilled him. "Kinda like when I got my first girlfriend," he wrote. "I was god for a couple days." He began work on another worm, trying to recapture the feeling. "I spent three months working on it just so I could have those couple of days of godliness."

Vorgon is still angry about life. His next worm, he wrote, will try to specifically target the people who wouldn't hire him. It will have a "spidering" engine that crawls Web-page links, trying to find likely e-mail addresses for human-resource managers, "like careers@microsoft.com, for example." Then it will send them a fake résumé infected with the worm. (He hasn't yet decided on a payload, and he hasn't ruled out a destructive one.) "This is a revenge worm," he explained—for "not hiring me, and hiring some loser is not even half the programmer I am."

MANY PEOPLE might wonder why virus writers aren't simply rounded up and arrested for producing their creations. But in most countries, writing viruses is not illegal. Indeed, in the United States some legal scholars argue that it is protected as free speech. Software is a type of language, and writing a program is akin to writing a recipe for beef stew. It is merely a bunch of instructions for the computer to follow, in the same way that a recipe is a set of instructions for a cook to follow.

A virus or worm becomes illegal only when it is activated— when someone sends it to a victim and starts it spreading in the wild, and it does measurable damage to computer systems. The top malware authors are acutely aware of this distinction. Most every virus-writer Web site includes a disclaimer stating that it exists purely for educational purposes, and that if a visitor downloads a virus to spread, the responsibility is entirely the visitor's. Benny's main virus-writing computer at home has no Internet connection at all; he has walled it off like an airlocked biological-weapons lab, so that nothing can escape, even by accident.

Virus writers argue that they shouldn't be held accountable for other people's actions. They are merely pursuing an interest in writing self-replicating computer code. "I'm not responsible for people who do silly things and distribute them among their friends," Benny said defiantly. "I'm not responsible for those. What I like to do is programming, and I like to show it to people—who may then do something with it." A young woman who goes by the handle Gigabyte told me in an online chat room that if the authorities wanted to arrest her and other virus writers, then "they should arrest the creators of guns as well."

One of the youngest virus writers I visited was Stephen Mathieson, a sixteen-year-old in Detroit whose screen name is Kefi. He also belongs to PhiletOast3r's Ready Rangers Liberation Front. A year ago, Mathieson became annoyed when he found members of another virus-writers group called Catfish_VX plagiarizing his code. So he wrote Evion, a worm specifically designed to taunt the Catfish guys. He put it up on his Web site for everyone to see. Like most of Mathieson's work, the worm had no destructive intent. It merely popped up a few cocky messages, including: *Catfish_VX are lamers. This virus was constructed for them to steal.*

Someone did in fact steal it, because pretty soon Mathieson heard reports of it being spotted in the wild. To this day, he does not know who circulated Evion. But he suspects it was probably a random troublemaker, a script kiddie who swiped it from his site. "The kids," he said, shaking his head, "just cut and paste."

Quite aside from the strangeness of listening to a sixteen-year-old complain about "the kids," Mathieson's rhetoric glosses over a charged ethical and legal debate. It is tempting to wonder if the leading malware authors are lying—whether they do in fact circulate their worms on the sly, obsessed with a desire to see whether they will really work. While security officials say that may occasionally happen, they also say the top virus writers are quite likely telling the truth. "If you're writing important virus code, you're probably well trained," says David Perry, global director of education for Trend Micro, an antivirus company. "You know a number of tricks to write good code, but you don't want to go to prison. You have an income and stuff. It takes someone unaware of the consequences to release a virus."

But worm authors are hardly absolved of blame. By putting their code freely on the Web, virus writers essentially dangle temptation in front of every disgruntled teenager who goes online looking for a way to rebel. A cynic might say that malware authors rely on clueless script kiddies the same way that a drug dealer uses thirteen-year-olds to carry illegal goods—passing the liability off to a hapless mule.

"You've got several levels here," says Marc Rogers, a former police officer who now researches computer forensics at Purdue University. "You've got the guys who write it, and they know they shouldn't release it because it's illegal. So they put it out there knowing that some script kiddie who wants to feel like a big shot in the virus underground will put it out. They know these neophytes will jump on it. So they're grinning ear to ear, because their baby, their creation, is out there. But they didn't officially release it, so they don't get in trouble." He says he thinks that the original authors are just as blameworthy as the spreaders.

Sarah Gordon of Symantec also says the authors are ethically naive. "If you're going to say it's an artistic statement, there are more responsible ways to be artistic than to create code that costs people millions," she says. Critics like Reitinger, the Microsoft security chief, are even harsher. "To me, it's online arson," he says. "Launching a virus is no different from burning down a building. There are people who would never toss a Molotov cocktail into a warehouse, but they wouldn't think for a second about launching a virus."

What makes this issue particularly fuzzy is the nature of computer code. It skews the traditional intellectual question about studying dangerous topics. Academics who research nuclear-fission techniques, for example, worry that their research could help a terrorist make a weapon. Many publish their findings anyway, believing that the mere knowledge of how fission works won't help Al Qaeda get access to uranium or rocket parts.

But computer code is a different type of knowledge. The code for a virus is itself the weapon. You could read it in the same way you read a book, to help educate yourself about malware. Or you could set it running, turning it instantly into an active agent. Computer code blurs the line between speech and act. "It's like taking a gun and sticking bullets in it and sitting it on the counter and say-ing, 'Hey, free gun!' " Rogers says.

Some academics have pondered whether virus authors could be charged under conspiracy laws. Creating a virus, they theorize, might be considered a form of abetting a crime by providing mate-rials. Ken Dunham, the head of "malicious code intelligence" for iDefense, a computer security company, notes that there are cer-tainly many examples of virus authors assisting newcomers. He has been in chat rooms, he says, "where I can see people saying, 'How can I find vulnerable hosts?' And another guy says, 'Oh, go here, you can use this tool.' They're helping each other out."

There are virus writers who appreciate these complexities. But they are certain that the viruses they write count as protected speech. They insist they have a right to explore their interests. In-deed, a number of them say they are making the world a better place, because they openly expose the weaknesses of computer sys-tems. When PhiletOast3r or Mario or Mathieson finishes a new virus, they say, they will immediately e-mail a copy of it to antivirus companies. That way, they explained, the companies can program their software to recognize and delete the virus should some script kiddie ever release it into the wild. This is further proof that they mean no harm with their hobby, as Mathieson pointed out. On the contrary, he said, their virus-writing strengthens the "immune sys-tem" of the Internet.

These moral nuances fall apart in the case of virus authors who are themselves willing to release worms into the wild. They're more rare, for obvious reasons. Usually they are overseas, in coun-tries where the police are less concerned with software crimes. One such author is Melhacker, a young man who reportedly lives in Malaysia and has expressed sympathy for Osama bin Laden. Anti-virus companies have linked him to the development of several worms, including one that claims to come from the "Al Qaeda net-work." Before the Iraq war, he told a computer magazine that he would release a virulent worm if the United States attacked Iraq—

a threat that proved hollow. When I e-mailed him, he described his favorite type of worm payload: "Stolen information from other people." He won't say which of his viruses he has himself spread and refuses to comment on his connection to the Qaeda worm. But in December on Indovirus.net, a discussion board for virus writers, Melhacker urged other writers to "try to make it in the wild" and to release their viruses in cybercafes, presumably to avoid detection. He also told them to stop sending in their work to anti-virus companies.

Mathieson wrote a critical post in response, arguing that a good virus writer shouldn't need to spread his work. Virus authors are, in fact, sometimes quite chagrined when someone puts a dangerous worm into circulation, because it can cause a public backlash that hurts the entire virus community. When the Melissa virus raged out of control in 1999, many Internet service providers immediately shut down the Web sites of malware creators. Virus writers stormed online to pillory the Melissa author for turning his creation loose. "We don't need any more grief," one wrote.

IF YOU ask cyberpolice and security experts about their greatest fears, they are not the traditional virus writers, like Mario or Phile-tOast3r or Benny. For better or worse, those authors are a known quantity. What keeps antivirus people awake at night these days is an entirely new threat: worms created for explicit criminal purposes.

These began to emerge last year. Sobig in particular alarmed virus researchers. It was released six separate times throughout 2003, and each time, the worm was programmed to shut itself off permanently after a few days or weeks. Every time the worm appeared anew, it had been altered in a way that suggested a single author had been tinkering with it, observing its behavior in the wild, then killing off his creation to prepare a new and more insidious version. "It was a set of very well-controlled experiments," says

Mikko Hypponen, the director of antivirus research at F-Secure, a computer security company. "The code is high quality. It's been tested well. It really works in the real world." By the time the latest variant, Sobig.F, appeared in August, the worm was programmed to install a back door that would allow the author to assume control of the victim's computer. To what purpose? Experts say its author has used the captured machines to send spam and might also be stealing financial information from the victims' computers.

No one has any clue who wrote Sobig. The writers of this new class of worm leave none of the traces of their identities that malware authors traditionally include in their code, like their screen names or "greetz," shout-out hellos to their cyberfriends. Because criminal authors actively spread their creations, they are cautious about tipping their hand. "The FBI is out for the Sobig guy with both claws, and they want to make an example of him," David Perry notes. "He's not going to mouth off." Dunham of iDefense says his online research has turned up "anecdotal evidence" that the Sobig author comes from Russia or elsewhere in Europe. Others suspect China or other parts of Asia. It seems unlikely that Sobig came from the United States, because American police forces have been the most proactive of any worldwide in hunting those who spread malware. Many experts believe the Sobig author will release a new variant sometime this year.

Sobig was not alone. A variant of the Mimail worm, which appeared last spring, would install a fake popup screen on a computer pretending to be from PayPal, an online e-commerce firm. It would claim that PayPal had lost the victim's credit card or banking details and ask him to type it in again. When he did, the worm would forward the information to the worm's still-unknown author. Another worm, called Bugbear.B, was programmed to employ sophisticated password-guessing strategies at banks and brokerages to steal personal information. "It was specifically designed to target financial institutions," said Vincent Weafer, senior director of Symantec.

The era of the stealth worm is upon us. None of these pieces of malware were destructive or designed to cripple the Internet with too much traffic. On the contrary, they were designed to be unobtrusive, to slip into the background, the better to secretly harvest data. Five years ago, the biggest danger was the "Chernobyl" virus, which deleted your hard drive. But the prevalence of hard-drive-destroying viruses has steadily declined to almost zero. Malware authors have learned a lesson that biologists have long known: the best way for a virus to spread is to ensure its host remains alive.

"It's like comparing Ebola to AIDS," says Joe Wells, an antivirus researcher and founder of Wild-Lists, a long-established virus-tracking group. "They both do the same thing. Except one does it in three days, and the other lingers and lingers and lingers. But which is worse? The ones that linger are the ones that spread the most." In essence, the long years of experimentation have served as a sort of Darwinian evolutionary contest in which virus writers have gradually figured out the best strategies for survival.

Given the pace of virus development, we are probably going to see even nastier criminal attacks in the future. Some academics have predicted the rise of "cryptoviruses"—malware that invades your computer and encrypts all your files, making them unreadable. "The only way to get the data back will be to pay a ransom," says Stuart Schechter, a doctoral candidate in computer security at Harvard. (One night on a discussion board I stumbled across a few virus writers casually discussing this very concept.) Antivirus companies are writing research papers that worry about the rising threat of "metamorphic" worms—ones that can shift their shapes so radically that antivirus companies cannot recognize they're a piece of malware. Some experimental metamorphic code has been published by ZOmbie, a reclusive Russian member of the 29A virus-writing group. And mobile-phone viruses are probably also only a few years away. A phone virus could secretly place 3 a.m. calls to a toll number, sticking you with thousand-dollar charges that the virus's author would collect. Or it could drown 911 in phantom calls. As Marty Lindner, a cybersecurity expert at CERT/CC, a federally financed computer research center, puts it, "The sky's the limit."

The profusion of viruses has even become a national-security issue. Government officials worry that terrorists could easily launch viruses that cripple American telecommunications, sowing confusion in advance of a physical 9/11-style attack. Paula Scalingi, the former director of the Department of Energy's Office of Critical Infrastructure Protection, now works as a consultant running disaster-preparedness exercises. Last year she helped organize "Purple Crescent" in New Orleans, an exercise that modeled a terrorist strike against the city's annual Jazz and Heritage Festival. The simulation includes a physical attack but also uses a worm unleashed by the terrorists designed to cripple communications and sow confusion nationwide. The physical attack winds up flooding New Orleans; the cyberattack makes hospital care chaotic. "They have trouble communicating, they can't get staff in, it's hard for them to order supplies," she says. "The impact of worms and viruses can be prodigious."

THIS NEW age of criminal viruses puts traditional malware authors in a politically precarious spot. Police forces are under more pressure than ever to take any worm seriously, regardless of the motivations of the author.

A young Spaniard named Antonio discovered that last fall. He is a quiet twenty-three-year-old computer professional who lives near Madrid. Last August, he read about the Blaster worm and how it exploited a Microsoft flaw. He became intrigued, and after poking around on a few virus sites, found some sample code that worked the same way. He downloaded it and began tinkering to see how it worked.

Then on November 14, as he left to go to work, Spanish police met him at his door. They told him the antivirus company Panda Software had discovered his worm had spread to 120,000 computers.

When Panda analyzed the worm code, it quickly discovered that the program pointed to a site Antonio had developed. Panda forwarded the information to the police, who hunted Antonio down via his Internet service provider. The police stripped his house of every computer—including his roommate's—and threw Antonio in jail. After two days, they let him out, upon which Antonio's employer immediately fired him. "I have very little money," he said when I met him in December. "If I don't have a job in a little time, in a few months I can't pay the rent. I will have to go to my parents."

The Spanish court is currently considering what charges to press. Antonio's lawyer, Javier Maestre, argued that the worm had no dangerous payload and did no damage to any of the computers it infected. He suspects Antonio is being targeted by the police, who want to pretend they've made an important cyberbust, and by an antivirus company seeking publicity.

Artificial life can spin out of control—and when it does, it can take real life with it. Antonio says he did not actually intend to release his worm at all. The worm spreads by scanning computers for the Blaster vulnerability, then sending a copy of itself to any open target. Antonio maintains he thought he was playing it safe, because his computer was not directly connected to the Internet. His roommate's computer had the Internet connection, and a local network—a set of cables connecting their computers together—allowed Antonio to share the signal.

But what Antonio didn't realize, he says, was that his worm would regard his friend's computer as a foreign target. It spawned a copy of itself in his friend's machine. From there it leapfrogged onto the Internet—and out into the wild. His creation had come to life and, like Frankenstein's monster, decided upon a path of its own.

CLIVE THOMPSON *lives in New York City. He is a contributing writer for the* New York Times Magazine. *He is also a columnist for the online magazine* Slate*, and writes regularly for* Wired, Details, Discover, *and* New York magazine. *In his spare time, he publishes www.collisiondetection.net a blog about science and technology.*

Coda

The thing that surprised me most about the "virus scene" is how much it was like a scientific society: All these teenagers worldwide, staying up all night researching new programming techniques, then writing long reports they gave away for free, just to prove they could bust a hard problem. (One sixteen-year-old in Austria showed me a meticulous article he'd written on a programming technique—and it was five thousand words, ten times longer than any paper he's required to write for school.) This is partly why it'll likely be impossible for authorities to ever extinguish virus writing. That's not for a lack of trying; in fact, since I published the article, two authors of the most virulent worms of 2003 have been caught: Jeffrey Lee Parsons, an American eighteen-year-old who released a "Blaster" worm, received one and a half years in jail, while a German of the same age. Sven Jaschan, was charged for releasing the infamous Sasser worm. New worms are still appearing every week—and now they're starting to invade mobile phones, the next great frontier of Internet-connected devices.

Jonathan Miles

Punch Drunk Love

FROM *Men's Journal*

THE BEST BAR FIGHT I ever witnessed took place in a tiny shit-kicky bar in Wyoming, somewhere along the road between Sheridan and Gillette. Outside there was a faint skein of April snow on the ground. Inside it was Hawaiian night. The bar was festooned with tropical knickknackery and paper palm trees, grass skirts were free for the taking, and the owners—a salty-mouthed blonde and her mother—were forcing everyone to wear leis, including me. I was in the company of a Canadian poet and a Wyoming painter, fellow artists-in-residence at a foundation down the highway; we'd been snowbound for a few weeks, and, like loggers emerging from a long stint in a lumber camp, we were itchy for a bit of fun. Some hot whiskey, some social chainsmoking, a smile from a hard-faced girl, perhaps a clumsy two-step, and maybe—you never know—the spectacle of a good-natured late-night fistfight.

It was a perfect place for all that. A singer-guitarist with a drum machine mixed Merle Haggard and Joan Jett into his sets. An old Indian in new blue Wranglers and a belt buckle the size of a 45-rpm record tore up the dance floor with all seven of the women present, with the exception of the owner-mother, who chose to dance solo with an oversize chef's knife raised above her head, as if baiting criticism or suitors or both. Besides us, the only other nonlocals in the bar were three itinerant sheepshearers from New Zealand—two drunk louts and a girl.

I got the full story only later. Allegedly, one of the Kiwi sheepshearers—a short, stout, vinegary guy—took to throwing roasted peanuts at the head of a local boy, one peanut after the other. The local boy had some tragic name—I swear, everyone pronounced it "Art Fart," though it must surely have been Art Vart. In any case, skinny Art Fart—clad in a grass skirt with an impromptu bikini top made from coconut shells and twine over his shirt— finally tired of being pelted with bar peanuts, said words to that effect to the Kiwi sheepshearer (who was also, I should note, wearing a grass skirt), and, like that, the fight was on.

Smart money was on the Kiwi. He'd started it, had some solid farm muscle on him, appeared to have piss for brains, and, unlike Art Fart, wasn't sporting coconut titties. But chalk one up for the U.S. of A.: After the typical cuss-and-shove windup, Art Fart threw a lanky-armed punch that sent the Kiwi buckling to the floor, hula skirt and all. There may have been some subsequent tussling—a crowd swiftly circled them, blocking my view—but the decisive blow had been struck. The fight officially ended, as I recall, when the salty blonde charged from behind the bar with a pistol, though I wouldn't swear to that in a court of law; maybe she just threatened gunplay.

"We have to get out of here," said my poet companion. With a smile I refused, and there in that bar, as the Kiwis hustled their frothy countryman outside and into the giant RV that was their home during sheepshearing season, and as Art Fart ordered a victory round, I tried to explain to him, knuckleheadedly, what I'm about to attempt to explain, just as knuckleheadedly, to you: The spectacle of a good bar fight, properly executed and healthily ended, is not merely annoying boorishness. The best of them—an admittedly minor slice—are shaded with the elements of high art. Think ballet, with its orchestrated stepwork, and opera, with its epic, heart-on-the-sleeve passions, or any kind of gladiatorial drama. Naturally, these overlofty comparisons apply to boxing matches and run-of-the-mill fistfights, too, but the bar fight has a sublimity all its own. Because it's fueled by alcohol, it's usually a rank amateur's game, with all the unpredictability this implies, and unlike boxing and most angry fistfights, it's sometimes lacquered with a gloss of comedy. Flying peanuts, grass skirts—that sort of thing. For millennia, saloons have served as comfortable petri dishes for sex and violence. I am either too honest or too unsophisticated to suggest that one can exist without the other. There is a mammalian side to all of us; on occasion it rears its head, snarls, makes a mess, acts the fool, howls at the moon, gives or gets a black eye.

BEFORE WE get rolling here, though, I feel it necessary to clarify my terms and to set a few ground rules. When I say bar fight, I mean this: one-on-one, hand-to-hand combat that occurs inside a saloon, or just outside its door. Except in those rare instances when a life is at stake, weapons have absolutely no place in a proper bar fight. In short: no knives, chairs, bottles, derringers, swords, or mounted billfish (a possible urban myth I once heard in Australia had a man attacking another with a marlin yanked off the wall), and absolutely no throwing opponents through plate-glass windows. (Let's call this last one the Charles Barkley rule, to dishonor Barkley's throwing of a man through the window of an Orlando bar in 1997 after the man had thrown a glass of ice at the NBA star. It's hard not to secretly admire Barkley, however, for his reply when asked if he had any regrets: "I regret," he said, "that we weren't on a higher floor.")

A proper bar fight pits one man (or woman—but wow are those fights scary) against another, with the only outside involvement coming from pals or patrons attempting to stop the fight. Holding a guy down while your friend pummels him is evil bullshit; pummeling a guy while your friend holds him down is evil bullshit squared. The proper bar fight ends quickly, though there are exceptions (like John Wayne's epic brawl in *The Quiet Man*, but then that's a movie), but when it's over it's over. Injuries—broken noses, fingers, hands, ribs, and jaws, along with assorted bruises and the famed cauliflower ear—are an obvious and common consequence, but their seriousness should never be dismissed. The rallying cry that a friend reported hearing a fighter bellow in a Tennessee roadhouse—"C'mon, I'll cripple ye!"—is okay to utter, but forbidden to enact. "The casualties in barroom fights are staggering," William Burroughs wrote in *Naked Lunch*, and it's true. Type "bar fight" into Google and the results are sobering: "Bar Fight Leaves 10 Dead in Guatemala," "Student Dies Trying to Stop Bar Fight," "Bar Fight Ends in Stabbing Outside Local Club," "Five Men Shot After Bar Fight in Michigan." For the record, these grim variations and extensions fall far outside this essay's beery scope. However faint and friable it may be, I prefer to maintain a line in the sand between behavior that is merely bad and that which is sociopathic.

THE HISTORY of bar fighting is, as far as I can discern, almost wholly undocumented, though a few historical tidbits can be found glittering amid the archival dust. The origins of the phrase "the real McCoy," for instance, are said, perhaps apocryphally, to be traceable to a turn-of-the-century saloon fight. As the story goes, an obnoxious drunk accused then-welterweight boxing champ Norman Selby, a.k.a. "Kid McCoy," of being a fraud. McCoy, inventor of the notorious "corkscrew punch" that Muhammad Ali later claimed as his own, promptly and definitively beat the stuffing out of his accuser, who weakly admitted, as he clambered back upright, that he'd been laid out by "the real McCoy." Without bar fights, too, the history of the American west would be one very long episode of *Little House on the Prairie*. One of the enduring Western myths is that gunfights were staged, quite formally, as cowpoke variations on European duels. More often, if not always, they were standard-issue saloon brawls that spilled out onto the street and resulted in the snap-crackle-pop of gunfire. Beyond that, however, the history of bar fighting remains locked among the men, young and old, who trade their smoky stories in private, twisting the fights' origins and outcomes to suit their egos and/or bleary memories. ("The guys who get beat up always deny they started anything," an ex-bouncer from Maine told me. "And if they got beat up by two guys, it's ten in the retelling.")

Despite this hazy history, however, I think it's fair to make a few assumptions. The first is that the original bar fight surely happened within hours or days of the appearance of the first bar. (The scientific basis for this will be explored shortly.)

The second is that no culture in which alcohol is publicly served is immune to them. Even Tibetan Buddhists—widely, if perhaps inaccurately, considered to be more violence-averse than we hayseed Americans—have their share of bar brawls. In Tibet's Kham province, fights between Tibetan and Chinese drinkers are said to be commonplace; several years ago, in the Tibetan capital of Lhasa, a fingernail discovered in a dish in a Chinese restaurant sparked a giant brawl, during which wine bottles were hurled at policemen trying to restore order. Stray fingernails are not typically fuel for fights in the United States but then we do not suffer from the sorts of geopolitical tensions that would cause one to suspect a restaurant of serving human flesh. In a similar vein, we are also not prone to bar fights caused by soccer club rivalries, as in Europe, though college football rivalries seem to take up a little of that slack. Suffice it to say that bar fights are not a product of globalization. When it comes to late-night scraps, we are the world.

The third assumption is that the unwritten chronicle of bar fights features a cast of mostly men, though women of a certain flinty temperament are also prone to bar fighting. In my lifetime I've witnessed two girl-on-girl brawls and both scared the bejesus out of me. Girls are not indoctrinated, by pop culture or society, with the vague code of fighting that usually—and I stress the word usually—keeps boys from pulling hair or gouging eyes. The term *catfight* is popularly applied to these fights, and it's an apt analogy; as with battling cats, there is rarely anything you can do to stop these fights, and it's best, from my experience, to simply run for cover when one breaks out. This isn't to suggest that such fights aren't worth witnessing. If you're accustomed to ladies of a genteel sort, there's a world-upside-down element to them, and they can sometimes have the frightening appeal of Shark Week on the Discovery Channel. I'm told that many men take pleasure in the spectacle of females fighting. Though this fetish falls outside my sphere of kinks, some overly red-blooded men also get turned on by car wrecks or Christina Aguilera. Disaster, I guess, can have a certain pervy allure.

Young men are the predominant combatants in any saloon fight, since the tempers of older men take much longer to come to a boil. (Regarding alcohol and youth, Plato warned, "It is wrong to add fire to fire.") Tim Sylvia, the former heavyweight champ of the Ultimate Fighting Championship league, told me that he used to pick fights in Maine bars when he was nineteen or twenty "just to prove my masculinity." Young men feel they have much to prove; older men, as a very general rule, tend to feel more comfortable in their skins.

This is not to suggest, however, that old men are immune to beer tempers. Many years ago, in a Deep South beer joint, a white-haired man of about seventy threatened to kick my ass because he suspected I was a "beer spy." The full story emerged after I'd denied the charge and was able to calm him down: He claimed he'd found a condom floating in a capped bottle of Budweiser. He'd notified Anheuser-Busch, he said, and they'd agreed to ship him a free case of Bud if he would just send them back the bottle in question. "I told 'em that'd be fine so long as either Mr. Anheuser or Mr. Busch called me to apologize," he said. "And, lookit, I told 'em they'd have to call me at night because I ain't about to sit by the phone all damn day." Because I'd been alone at the bar, scribbling away at some piece of writing or other, he'd assumed I was a spy dispatched by Anheuser-Busch to find and reclaim that dread bottle. I'm not sure what I would have done if the old man had actually attacked me—hard to envision a happy outcome there. In the end, though, he apologized and fetched me some homegrown beef-steak tomatoes from his truck, which, to this day, are the best tomatoes I've ever eaten.

IF YOU ASK a bartender the cause of a just-fought brawl, during that excited hush that settles upon a saloon in the moments after the combatants have been tossed, chances are he'll answer, "They were just drunk." And chances are he'll be right. (Bartenders, I've found, usually are.) The science behind this is rather simple: By depressing the central nervous system, alcohol acts as a disinhibitor, making us feel more freewheeling and incautious. This is why, after four of five drinks, you have the courage to approach the laughing blonde in the dizzyingly see-through blouse, but also why you might feel sturdy enough to take on the six-foot-six meathead who won't stop wagging his tongue through his fingers at your girlfriend. "We call that 'beer muscles,'" says Sylvia, the UFC champ.

Recent scientific research has added an interesting wrinkle to the alcohol-violence connection. According to a study published in the January 2003 issue of the medical journal *Alcoholism: Clinical and Experimental Research,* acute administration of alcohol can induce a rapid increase in testosterone—four times the normal amount, in some cases—in the brains of rodents. The implications for human behavioral and endocrine pathology seem clear: The more you drink, the more your social inhibitions dissolve, but also the more your testosterone amounts—the dipstick level of your co-jones, so to speak—may rise. A chalkboard equation, then, might look something like this: C_2H_5OH (ethyl alcohol) = negative inhibitor neurotransmitter abilities + 4× testosterone levels = Popeye, on a shore leave bender, giving Bluto a big black shiner for goosing Olive Oyl's skinny little rump. Argh argh argh.

Scientific evidence notwithstanding, that bartender would be only half right. If mere drunkenness were the cause of barroom brawls, happy hour at T.G.I. Friday's would be the most dangerous sixty minutes on the planet; you'd have to step over bodies just to order a Tom Collins. If you liken a bar fight to, say, an exploding can of gasoline, then bloodstream alcohol is surely the gasoline; there's no disputing that. But for every such explosion there's a spark that makes it go boom. As Seneca wrote, "Drunkenness does not create vice. It merely brings it into view."

What's the most common spark? To answer that we have to first divide bar fights into two distinct categories. One we'll call Psycho Fights. Plainly put, these are fights that happen because someone in a saloon is a psychotic asshole, and they include fights prompted by out-of-the-blue utterances like *Whatthefuckyoulookinat?* or *Yougotaproblemwithme?* Psycho Fights don't actually require a cause; the presence of the psycho is cause enough. "A lot of guys go out looking for fights," says Sylvia. "They're pissed off at something their wife or girlfriend did, or about something that happened at work. When that guy is looking for a fight, he can't be talked out of it." Bullies are bullies, and they're always uninteresting. Our interest here lies more in the causes of the second category of bar fights, which I hesitate to call Rational Fights, since, of course, no violence is rational, especially after seven Coors Lights and two shots of Cuervo. Let's just call them Non-Psycho Fights.

In order to gauge the top three causes of Non-Psycho Fights, I surveyed a wide swath of bartenders, barflies, bouncers, lawmen, and other folks with some connection to saloon life. Some of the answers were too local for my purposes ("Him," one upstate New York bartender said, cocking a thumb at a surly solo drinker), while others, like the top-three list I received from a retired Mississippi lawman, had a ring of poetry to them: "Women, property lines, and dogs." (The other list that could double as a country music album title went like this: "Drunks, women, and drunk women.") Fully tabulated, nonetheless, my survey results broke down as follows. Cause Number One: women who are present in the bar. Cause Number Two: women who are not present but vividly remembered. Cause Number Three: old grudges that don't officially involve women but might involve them if you scratch down deep enough.

Cause One includes acts of "chivalry"—protecting a woman's safety or honor—but also encompasses acts of rabid jealousy, e.g., pummeling your ex-girlfriend's date. Cause Two is so closely related to Cause One that an argument could be made to merge them, but there is a distinction: In the first case the fights start suddenly, with the attacks unplanned. A lout insults your date; you take a swing. Your ex strolls in with a bumblefuck insurance salesman; you take a swing. Or, conversely: you, an insurance salesman but certainly no bumblefuck, walk into a bar with a hot divorcée on your arm, only to find yourself sucker-punched by her red-eyed ex. But Cause Two produces a slightly different kind of fight, one generated by unhealed romantic wounds, by conflicts that have simmered for a while. To the unschooled observer, a fight that breaks out in a bar because some guy took offense at the song another guy played on the jukebox might seem random and ridiculous. If you'd known that the guy who played the song had stolen the other guy's girlfriend a half-decade before, and that the song he'd played was the Aerosmith ballad that had been on the radio when the poor fella first unsnapped her bra that night by the lake, it might make more sense. "The season of love is that of battle," Darwin wrote. The roots of these fights run deep.

Which leads us smoothly into Cause Three: old grudges. You see this less in big cities than you do in small towns, where the tight confines of the county limits mean that you're forced to come face-to-face, on a regular basis, with the dickhead who fouled you in that high school district finals game way back when, a foul that, though the referee didn't call it, caused you to (a) miss the game-winning shot, (b) lose your chances for a college scholarship, (c) lose your cheerleader girlfriend, and (d) go to work for your father at the grain mill and marry ol' Brenda who got fat as a house after the kids were born and never does nothing but watch *Dr. Phil* and complain about the way your boots smell. Years later that same dickhead beats you in a casual game of pool, and it's all too much to take. You snap. (Pool tables, by the way, were a popular survey answer; notable also-rans included politics, athletic allegiances, and, yep, jukeboxes.)

Not long ago, at the Dunes Saloon in Michigan's Upper Peninsula, I ran into the novelist Jim Harrison, who offered me this theory: "Most bar fights can be traced back to someone's dog getting shot twenty years before." Some urbanites among you might cry bullshit—it's difficult, though amusing, to imagine two fellows tussling over a dead bird dog in Manhattan's '21' Club—but I can attest to its limited accuracy. Several years back, in Mississippi, a man shot and killed my German shorthair pointer—long story, not worth rehashing. But if I ever come across that bastard in a saloon . . . well, I swear I'll knock him halfway to next Tuesday. I have warned my wife and lawyer of this pledge, along with the owner of the bar where this knocking is most likely to occur. None of them approves, but the bar owner is a dog lover, so I suspect he'll overlook any damages.

A DIRTY TRUTH: Most bar fights are just noisy nonevents. The average barroom brawl lasts about two to five seconds, according to Peyton Quinn, a former bouncer in "problem bars" who now operates Rocky Mountain Combat Applications Training in Lake George, Colorado, where he instructs bouncers and other security types in the finer points of fistfighting. (Literally, it's the school of hard knocks.) "Bar fights are generally very sloppy affairs," says Quinn. "Once that adrenaline rush hits, people tend to lose fine motor control and just flail at each other—often ineffectually."

UFC champ Sylvia seconds that judgment: "In bar fights you don't see strategic fighting at all," he says. "Just a lot of haymaking. Usually the guy who gets in the first punch is the winner."

The typical bar fight, then, can be easily choreographed: It's a sucker punch that may or may not be followed by a second punch, but rarely a third. A number of fights go quickly to the floor and become dusty wrestling matches. This often happens when the victim of a sucker punch, dazed and weakened, tries to ward off any further blows by tackling his opponent. Punches thrown in close quarters don't have much oomph to them, so the tackler attempts to give himself a respite via sloppy grappling. This isn't a recommended tack, however. "Personally, I hate to fight on the ground," Quinn wrote in *A Bouncer's Guide to Barroom Brawling,* his 1990 primer on bar fighting. "For one thing, if a guy has any buddies or you have some enemies around, they will often start kicking your head and ribs while you're on the floor and otherwise preoccupied." By and large, however, bar fights are settled by a single punch, one angry whap to the head that defines and decides the evening.

Which is not to suggest, of course, that there aren't variations. Smart bar fighters, says Sylvia, hit their opponents smack in the nuts. "Best place to strike," he counsels. Goofy types who are destined to fail attempt intricate martial-arts moves, something Quinn strenuously discourages. Some guys pull hair and bite: Mike Tyson's chomping of Evander Holyfield's ear may have been a freakish anomaly in the boxing ring, but in a particularly rabid bar fight, *c'est la vie.* I might also add two intriguing variants on bar fighting tactics that I've come across in my readings. During America's frontier days a noteworthy fighting technique was to get your opponent's bottom lip between your thumb and fingers and then yank it down like a stuck window shade, half-severing the lip from the face. This is obviously an abomination and has no place here except as a gruesome point of interest. A description of the other tactic appears in Raleigh Trevelyan's recent biography of Sir Walter Raleigh. As a young rakehell, Raleigh grew tired of a "bold, impertinent fellow" in a tavern and, after popping him one, "sealed up his mustache and beard with wax." To my mind this facial-hair waxing clearly violates bar fight decorum, but it is kind of funny.

I LIKE TO think that I was once involved in the perfect bar fight. This was about eight years ago, in Mississippi, back when I was spending nine or ten hours a day in a second-story saloon on the town square, a time in my life for which I bear a certain hungover nostalgia. My opponent, in this case, was my best drinking pal, a longhaired South Carolinian a year or two my junior. The cause of the fight was, naturally, a woman—in this case, one present in the bar. For a while she'd been my girlfriend, and then she wasn't, a change in status that I seemed unable to reconcile in my head. No one else had much liked her, and the judgment of pals was that, by splitting with her, I'd escaped a grim future—a judgment endorsed, adamantly, by the South Carolinian. Yet I was drunk, moony, unsure, second-guessing my fate as old Tom Waits songs crackled on the bar's hi-fi. An hour shy of last call, the ex approached me in the bar, and, forgive me, I thought this might be my one thump-hearted chance to woo her back. That's when the South Carolinian appeared, butting into the conversation in a way that I might liken to a circus clown crashing a Middle East peace conference. Scram, I told him. He scrunched up his face and made nonsensical noises. The ex-girlfriend, who'd long lamented my lack of maturity as well as my choice in friends, rolled her eyes and made motions to leave. I mean it, I told him. He crossed his eyes and stuck his tongue out to one side. I grabbed him by the neck. He grabbed me by the neck. We began throttling each other, muttering mean curses. No punches—just throttling, growling, bared teeth. I don't recollect how long this went on, but at some point we looked up, simultaneously, to see the entire bar population frozen in a baffled stare, watching us choking each other. And the ex? Nowhere to be seen.

We looked at each other, sighed, shrugged, dropped our choke-
holds, took two stools at the bar, and bought each other beers.
We've pledged to finish that fight, and perhaps someday we will. In
the meantime, though, we drink in peace.

JONATHAN MILES *is a contributing editor to* Men's Journal *and*
Field & Stream, *and writes regularly for the* New York Times Book
Review. *His work has twice been included in* The Best American
Sports Writing *anthologies. A longtime resident of Oxford, Mississippi,
he now lives in Warwick, New York, and is at work on a novel.*

Coda

This essay was actually assigned as punishment for punching a *Men's
Journal* editor at a staff party at an East Village saloon—the magazine journalism equivalent, I suppose, of having to write "I will not
punch my editors" one hundred times on the blackboard. I won't
bore you with the details of the scuffle though I will note the following: (a) tequila was involved, and (b) truth to tell, the editor had
it coming. Let me add that this is strenuously unusual behavior for
me. I am a happy drinker more prone to sloppy hugs than frothy
fist-throwing, but, again: When you mix tequila with a blowhard
editor, things can sometimes fall apart. My starkest memory of the
evening is the sound of the locks clicking shut on the door after I'd
been ejected from the bar; they seemed to go on forever. As a fresh
transplant to New York from the South, I didn't know a door could
have that many locks.

Naturally there were consequences: For one thing, I had to write
this essay. Bad behavior has always fascinated me, though the subject
of bar brawling arrived with its own set of difficulties. The line between bad behavior and sociopathic behavior, in this case, is terribly
thin. I have zero interest in the kinds of fights bullies engage in to

puff up their frail sense of machismo; that's just violence for vio-lence's sake, and it happens all too frequently and odiously around the world. What interested me, instead, were the kinds of amateur bar fights ignited by overdoses of passion plus liquor. That is to say, bar fights fought by otherwise reasonable (or semireasonable) peo-ple for concrete (or semiconcrete) reasons. Broken hearts, political differences, grudges, and slights, that sort of thing. Obviousness aside, I wondered: Why *does* liquor—and a bar setting—prompt people to violence? What exactly causes people to snap? And why do so many of them rip off their shirts before fighting?

As to my essay's happy presence in these pages, I must confess that it rarely occurred to me to think of bar fighting—at least of the amateur, one- or two-punch, black eye–resulting variety I tried to focus on—as a *crime*, though I suppose it certainly is. The ideal bar fight should be quick and for the most part painless enough to never require police attention but, true, it's assault and battery, no matter how loose and saggy the punches. I'm reminded of the time, ten years or so ago, when I was fired as a reporter for a small Mis-sissippi daily for listing a man's legendary bootlegging past in his obituary. Huffily, the publisher informed me that the paper was not in the habit of noting people's crimes in their obituary. "But boot-legging isn't a *crime*," I protested. "It's a . . . service." I believe my newspapering career ended at that very precise moment.

I no longer touch tequila, by the way. (A pal of mine smartly calls it "felony juice.") Nor do I punch people. I am, however, still inexorably drawn to saloons where folks do both. As they say: One thing at a time.

Lawrence Wright

THE TERROR
WEB

FROM *The New Yorker*

FOR MUCH OF SPAIN'S modern history, the organization that
has defined its experience with terror is ETA, which stands for
Euzkadi Ta Azkatasuna (Basque Homeland and Liberty). ETA, which
was founded in 1959, has a clear political goal: It wants to set up a
separate nation, comprising the Basque provinces, in northern
Spain, and parts of southern France. Although ETA has killed some
eight hundred people, it has developed a reputation for targeting, almost exclusively, politicians, security officials, and journalists. Over
the years, the terrorists and the Spanish police have come to a rough
understanding about the rules of engagement. "They don't commit attacks on the working class, and they always call us before an
explosion, telling us where the bomb is situated," an intelligence
official in the Spanish National Police told me recently in Madrid.
"If they place a bomb in a backpack on a train, there will be a cassette tape saying, 'This bag is going to explode. Please leave the
train.'" And so on March 11, when the first reports arrived of mass
casualties resulting from explosions on commuter trains, Spanish

intelligence officials assumed that ETA had made an appalling mistake.

At 7:37 a.m., as a train was about to enter Madrid's Atocha station, three bombs blasted open the steel cars, sending body parts through the windows of nearby apartments. The station is in Madrid's center, a few blocks from the Prado Museum. Within seconds, four bombs exploded on another train, five hundred and fifty yards from the station. The bombs killed nearly a hundred people. Had the explosions occurred when the trains were inside the station, the fatalities might have tallied in the thousands; a quarter of a million people pass through Atocha every workday. The trains at that hour were filled with students and young office workers who live in public housing and in modest apartment complexes east of the city. Many were immigrants, who had been drawn by the Spanish economic boom.

As emergency crews rushed to the scene, two more bombs demolished a train at the El Pozo del Tío Raimundo station, three miles away. By then, José María Aznar, the prime minister, had learned of the attacks, which were taking place at the end of an uneventful political campaign. The conservative Popular Party, which Aznar headed, was leading the Socialists by four and a half points in the polls, despite the overwhelming opposition of the Spanish population to the country's participation in the war in Iraq. It was Thursday morning; the election would take place on Sunday.

At 7:42 a.m., one minute after the El Pozo bomb, a final bomb went off, on a train at the suburban Santa Eugenia station. Emergency workers arrived to find mangled bodies littering the tracks. The Spanish had never seen anything like this—the worst ETA atrocity, in 1987, killed twenty-one shoppers in a Barcelona grocery store. At Santa Eugenia, there were so many wounded that rescue crews ripped up the benches in the waiting area to use as stretchers. In all, there were a hundred and ninety-one fatalities and sixteen hundred injuries. It was the most devastating act of terrorism in

European history, except for the 1988 bombing of Pan Am Flight 103 over Lockerbie, Scotland.

Aznar, who survived an ETA car bomb in 1995, had made the elimination of the group his biggest priority. His security forces had decimated ETA's ranks, but they were aware that remnants of the organization were attempting to stage a retaliatory attack in Madrid. The previous Christmas Eve, police had arrested two ETA commanders who had planted backpack bombs on trains, and in February the Civil Guard intercepted an ETA van that was headed to the capital carrying eleven hundred pounds of explosives. A top Spanish police official, a political appointee, told me that authorities had planned a major strike against ETA for March 12, the last official day of campaigning. Such a blow might have boosted Aznar's party at the polls. ETA, however, had seemingly struck first.

At 10:50 a.m., police in Alcalá de Henares received a call from a witness who pointed them to a boxy white Renault van that had been left that morning at the train station. "At the beginning, we didn't pay too much attention to it," an investigator told me. "Then we saw that the license plate didn't correspond to the van." Even that clue, though, struck a false note. When ETA operatives steal a car, they match it with license plates from the same model car. It had been years since ETA had made such an elementary mistake.

The lack of warning, the many casualties, the proletarian background of many of the victims, and ETA's quick disavowal of the crime all suggested that there was reason to question the assignment of blame. The police no longer considered ETA capable of carrying off such an elaborate attack. Moreover, the telephones of known ETA collaborators were bugged. "The bad guys were calling each other, saying, 'Was it us? It's craziness!'" a senior intelligence official said.

That afternoon, detectives looked more carefully at the white van. They collected fingerprints, and under the passenger seat they found a plastic bag with seven detonators matching the type used in the bombings. There were cigarette butts, a woman's wig, and a Plácido Domingo cassette. In the tape player was a different recording—it bore Arabic inscriptions, and turned out to be Koranic recitations for religious novices. By that time, police had learned that the explosive used in the bombings was Goma-2, which ETA no longer used. "We told the government that there was something odd, that it was possibly not ETA," the intelligence official told me.

That evening, however, Aznar called the editors of Spain's newspapers. "ETA is behind the attacks," he assured them. Then he called José Luis Rodríguez Zapatero, his Socialist opponent, to tell him about the van with the Arabic tape; at the same time, he insisted that "there is no doubt who did the attacks."

The case broke open in the middle of the night, when a young police officer, sorting through belongings recovered from the trains, opened a sports bag and discovered twenty-two pounds of Goma-2, surrounded by nails and screws. Two wires ran from a blue mobile phone to a detonator. It wasn't clear why the bomb had failed to explode.

Police officers realized that a chip inside the phone would contain a record of recently dialed numbers. By tracing these calls, they were quickly able to map out a network of young Arab immigrants, many of whom were known to Spanish intelligence. Data stored on the chip revealed that a calling plan had been set up at a small telephone and copy shop in Lavapiés, a working-class neighborhood near the Atocha station. The store was owned by Jamal Zougam, a Moroccan who had previously been under surveillance because of alleged connections to Al Qaeda. He was soon arrested.

Information began leaking to the public about the direction of the investigation. By Friday afternoon, demonstrators were standing in front of the Atocha station, holding signs that linked the tragedy to the war in Iraq. It was clear that the election would swing on the question of whether Islamists or ETA terrorists were responsible for the bombings. That day, the interior minister, Ángel

Acebes, insisted publicly that ETA was the prime suspect—even trough the police were now certain that ETA was not directly involved.

At twilight, some eleven million Spaniards assembled around the country to protest the violence. In rainy Madrid, the umbrellas stretched for miles down the Paseo del Prado. The anger and grief of the marchers were compounded by confusion about the investigation. "I walked with a million people in Madrid's streets," Diego López Garrido, a Socialist deputy in the Spanish congress, told me. "Many people were saying, 'Who is the author of these attacks?' And they wondered, 'Why is the government lying to us?'"

THE DAY of the bombings, analysts at the Forsvarets Forsknings-institutt, a Norwegian think tank near Oslo, retrieved a document that they had noticed on an Islamist Web site the previous December. At the time, the document had not made a big impression, but now, in light of the events in Madrid, it read like a terrorist road map. Titled "Jihadi Iraq: Hopes and Dangers," it had been prepared by a previously unknown entity called the Media Committee for the Victory of the Iraqi People (Mujahideen Services Center).

The document, which is forty-two pages long and appears to be the work of several anonymous authors, begins with the proposition that although Coalition forces in Iraq, led by America, could not be defeated by a guerrilla insurgency, individual partners of the Coalition could be persuaded to depart, leaving America more vulnerable and discouraged as casualties increased and the expenses became insupportable. Three countries—Britain, Spain, and Poland—formed the European backbone of the Coalition. Poland appeared to be the most resolute, because the populace largely agreed with the government's decision to enter Iraq. In Britain, the war was generally deplored. "Before the war, in February, about a million people went out on a huge march filling the streets of London," the document notes. "This was the biggest march of political protest in the history of Britain." But the authors suggest that the British would not withdraw unless the casualty count sharply increased.

Spain, however, presented a striking opportunity. The war was almost universally unpopular. Aznar had plunged his country into Iraq without seeking a consensus, unlike other Coalition leaders. "If the disparity between the government and the people were at the same percentage rate in Britain, then the Blair government would fall," the author of this section observes. The reason Aznar had not yet been ousted, the author claims, was that Spain is an immature democracy and does not have a firm tradition of holding its rulers accountable. Right-wing Spanish voters also tended to be more loyal and organized than their leftist counterparts. Moreover, the number of Spanish casualties in Iraq was less than a dozen. "In order to force the Spanish government to withdrawn from Iraq, the resistance should deal painful blows to its forces," the writer proposes. "It is necessary to make utmost use of the upcoming general election in Spain in March next year. We think that the Spanish government could not tolerate more than two, maximum three blows, after which it will have to withdraw as a result of popular pressure. If its troops still remain in Iraq after these blows, the victory of the Socialist Party is almost secured, and the withdrawal of the Spanish forces will be on its electoral program." Once Spain pulled out of Iraq, the author theorizes, the pressure on Tony Blair, the British Prime Minister, to do the same might be unbearable—"and hence the domino tiles would fall quickly."

The document specifies that the attacks would be aimed at Spanish forces within Iraq—there is no call for action in Spain. Nonetheless, the authors' reading of the Western political calendar struck the Norwegian researchers as particularly keen. "The relation between the text and the bombings is unclear," Thomas Hegghammer, a researcher at Forsvarets Forskningsinstitutt, told me. "But, without the text, we would still be asking, 'Is this a coincidence?'"

That day, Hegghammer forwarded a copy of the document to

Haizam Amirah Fernández, a colleague at Madrid's Real Instituto Elcano. Amirah was shocked. Until now, the announced goals of Al Qaeda had been mainly parochial, directed at purging the Islamic world, especially Saudi Arabia, of Western influences; overturning the established Arabic governments and restoring the clerical rule of the ancient caliphate, and purifying Islam by returning it to the idealized time of the Prophet. In an audiotape aired on the Arabic satellite channel Al Jazeera in February 2003, Osama bin Laden, the leader of Al Qaeda, had identified Jordan, Morocco, Nigeria, Pakistan, Saudi Arabia, and Yemen as "the most qualified regions for liberation." (Iraq was notably absent from his list.) And yet he offered no political platform—no plan, for instance, for governing Saudi Arabia on the morning after the revolution. As for the rest of the world, bin Laden's goals seemed to be motivated mainly by revenge. In 1998, he had decreed that it was the "duty of every Muslim" to kill Americans and their allies. The spectacular violence that characterized Al Qaeda's attacks was not a means to a goal—it was the goal. Success was measured by the body count, not by political change.

The Internet document suggested that a new intelligence was at work, a rationality not seen in Al Qaeda documents before. The Mujahideen Services Center, whatever that was, appeared to operate as a kind of Islamist think tank. "The person who put together those chapters had a clear strategic vision, realistic and well thought out," Amirah says. He told Hegghammer, "This is political science applied to jihad."

Although the document was posted on the Internet in December 2003, the authors note that a draft had been written in September. In October, assassins shot a Spanish military attaché in Iraq, José Antonio Bernal Gómez, near his residence; in November, seven Spanish intelligence agents were ambushed and murdered south of Baghdad. Photographs of the killers standing on the agents' bodies circulated on Islamist Web sites. Another Internet document soon appeared, titled "Message to the Spanish People," signed by the Information Commission for the Help of the Iraqi People (Department of Foreign Propaganda), which threatened more attacks. "Return to your country and live peacefully," it demands, or else "the battalions of the Iraqi resistance and its supporters outside of Iraq are able to increase the dosage and will eclipse your memory of the rotten spies."

Variations in the Arabic transcriptions of English words in the "Jihadi Iraq" document suggested to Amirah that writers of various nationalities had drafted it. For instance, in some cases the *T* in Tony Blair's name was transcribed with the Arabic *ta*, but in the section about Spain the author used the *dha*, which is more typical of the Moroccan dialect. Also characteristic of Morocco is the use of Arabic numerals (the style used in the West) in place of the numbering system that is common from Egypt to the Persian Gulf. Those clues, plus certain particularly Moroccan political concerns expressed in the document, such as the independence movement in Western Sahara, suggested that at least some of the authors were diaspora Moroccans, probably living in Spain.

The link between the Internet document and the bombings soon became clearer. There is a reference early in the document to Abu Dujana, a companion of the Prophet who was known for his ferocity in battle. His name had been invoked by other jihadis, notably in the suicide bombings at the J. W. Marriott hotel in Jakarta in August 2003. On Saturday evening, a television station in Madrid received a call from a man speaking Spanish with a Moroccan accent, who said that a videotape had been placed in a trash bin near the city's main mosque. "We declare our responsibility for what has occurred in Madrid, exactly two and a half years after the attacks on New York and Washington," a masked speaker on the videotape said. He identified himself as Abu Dujan al-Afghani, "the military spokesman for Al Qaeda in Europe." He continued, "It is a response to your collaboration with the criminal Bush and his allies. You love life and we love death, which gives an example of what the Prophet

Muhammad said. If you don't stop your injustices, more and more blood will flow."

Until this tape appeared, even those investigators who were arguing that the train bombings were perpetrated by Islamic terrorists, not ETA, had been troubled by the fact that there were no "martyrs" in the attacks. It is a trademark of Al Qaeda to sacrifice its killers; this practice has provided a scanty moral cover for what would otherwise be seen simply as mass murder. But, when the investigators saw that the man calling himself Abu Dujan al-Afghani was dressed in white funeral robes, they realized that suicide was on the horizon.

THE AL QAEDA cell in Spain is old and well established. Mohamed Atta, the commander of the September 11 attacks, came to Spain twice in 2001. The second time was in July, for a meeting in the coastal resort of Salou, which appears to have been arranged as a final go-ahead for the attacks. After September 11, Spanish police estimated that there were three hundred Islamic radicals in the country who might be affiliated with Al Qaeda. Even before then, members of the Spanish cell had been monitored by police agencies, as is evident from the abundant use of wiretaps and surveillance information in indictments that were issued in November 2001, when eleven suspects were charged with being Al Qaeda members—the first of several terrorist roundups. And yet, according to Spanish police officials, at the time of the Madrid attacks there was not a single Arabic-speaking intelligence agent in the country. Al Qaeda was simply not seen as a threat to Spain. "We never believed we were a real target," a senior police official said. "That's the reality."

At four o'clock on Saturday afternoon, sixty hours after the attacks and the day before the elections, Interior Minister Acebes announced the arrest of Jamal Zougam and two other Moroccans.

Still, he continued to point at ETA. But by now the Socialists were publicly accusing the government of lying about the investigation in order to stay in power.

Polls opened the next morning at nine. Thirty-five million people voted, more than 77 percent of the electorate, 8 percent more than expected. Many were young, first-time voters, and their votes put the Socialists over the top. As José Luis Rodríguez Zapatero declared victory, he again condemned the war in Iraq and reiterated his intention to withdraw troops.

Four days later, the Abu Hafs al-Masri Brigades, a group claiming affiliation with Al Qaeda, sent a bombastic message to the London newspaper *Al-Quds al-Arabi*, avowing responsibility for the train bombings. "Whose turn will it be next?" the authors taunt. "Is it Japan, America, Italy, Britain, Saudi Arabia, or Australia?" The message also addressed the speculation that the terrorists would try to replicate their political success in Spain by disrupting the November U.S. elections. "We are very keen that Bush does not lose the upcoming elections," the authors write. Bush's "idiocy and religious fanaticism" are useful, the authors contend, for they stir the Islamic world to action.

On April 2, two weeks after the election, a security guard for the AVE, Spain's high-speed train line, discovered a blue plastic bag beside the tracks forty miles south of Madrid. Inside the bag were twenty-six pounds of Goma-2. Four hundred and fifty feet of cable had been draped across the security fence and attached, incorrectly, to the detonator. Had the bomb gone off when the AVE passed by—at a hundred and eighty m.p.h., carrying twelve hundred passengers— the results could have been far more catastrophic than those of March 11. Spanish citizens asked themselves: If the bombings of March 11 had accomplished the goals set by Al Qaeda, what was the point of April 2?

GUSTAVO DE ARISTEGUI is one of the leaders of the Popular Party in Spain's Basque country. For years, he represented Donostio-San Sebastián, the region's capital, in the Spanish congress. A lawyer and former diplomat, Aristegui has been preoccupied for many years with the rise of Islamic terror. His father was Spain's Ambassador to Lebanon and was killed in Beirut in 1989, when Syrian forces shelled his diplomatic residence.

"Al Qaeda has four different networks," Aristegui told me in Madrid, the day after the Socialists took power. "First, there is the original network, the one that committed 9/11, which uses its own resources and people it has recruited and trained. Then, there is the ad-hoc terrorist network, consisting of franchise organizations that Al Qaeda created—often to replace ones that weren't bloody enough—in countries such as the Philippines, Jordan, and Algeria." The third network, Aristegui said, is more subtle, "a strategic union of like-minded companies." Since February 1998, when Osama bin Laden announced the creation of the World Islamic Front for Jihad Against Crusaders and Jews—an umbrella organization for Islamist groups from Morocco to China—Al Qaeda has expanded its dominion by making alliances and offering funds. "Hamas is in, or almost in," Aristegui said. "Bin Laden is trying to tempt Hezbollah to join, but they are Shia, and many Sunnis are opposed to them." Finally, there is the fourth network—"imitators, emulators," who are ideologically aligned with Al Qaeda but are less tied to it financially. "These are the ones who committed Madrid," Aristegui said.

Until the Madrid attacks, the Al Qaeda operations—in Dhahran, Nairobi, Dar es Salaam, Aden, New York, Washington, Jerba, Karachi, Bali, Mombasa, Riyadh, Casablanca, Jakarta, and Istanbul—had been political failures. These massacres committed in the name of jihad had achieved little except anger, grief, and the deaths of thousands. Soon after September 11, Al Qaeda lost its base in Afghanistan and, along with that, its singular role in the coordination of international terror. New groups, such as the bombers in

Madrid, were acting in the name of Al Qaeda, and although they may well have had the blessings of its leaders, they did not have the training, resources, or international contacts that had bolstered the previous generation of terrorists. Some operations, such as the 2003 attack on Western compounds in Riyadh, which killed mainly Muslims, were such fiascos that it appeared that Al Qaeda was no longer able to exercise control.

"Al Qaeda is not a hierarchical organization, and never was," Marc Sageman, a psychiatrist, a former CIA case officer, and the author of *Understanding Terror Networks*, told me. "It was always a social movement." The latest converts to the cause didn't train in Afghanistan, and they approach jihad differently. "These local guys are reckless and less well trained, but they are willing to kill themselves, whereas the previous leaders were not," Sageman said. Moreover, as the Spanish attacks showed, the new generation was more interested in committing violence for the sake of immediate political gain.

The kind of short-term tactical thinking displayed in the "Jihadi Iraq" document and the March 11 bombings is decidedly out of step with Al Qaeda's traditional world view, in which history is seen as an endless struggle between believers and infidels. It is the mind-set of fundamentalists of all religions. This war is eternal, and is never finally won until the longed-for Day of Judgment. In this contest, the first goal is to provoke conflict. Bold, violent deeds draw the lines and arouse ancient resentments, and are useful even if they have unsought consequences. Polarization is to be encouraged, radical simplicity being essential for religious warfare. An Al Qaeda statement posted on the Internet after the March 11 bombings declared, "Being targeted by an enemy is what will wake us from our slumber." Seen in this light, terrorism plays a sacramental role, dramatizing a religious conflict by giving it an apocalyptic backdrop. And Madrid was just another step in the relentless march of radical Islam against the modern, secular world.

Had the Madrid cell rested on its accomplishment after March 11,

Al Qaeda would properly be seen as an organization now being guided by political strategists—as an entity closer in spirit to ETA, with clear tactical objectives. April 2 throws doubt on that perspective. There was little to be gained politically from striking an opponent who was complying with the stated demand: the government had agreed to withdraw troops from Iraq. If the point was merely humiliation or revenge, then April 2 makes more sense; the terrorists wanted more blood, even if a second attack backfired politically. (The Socialists could hardly continue to follow the terrorist agenda with a thousand new corpses along the tracks.) April 2 is comprehensible only if the real goal of the bombers was not Iraq but Spain, where the Islamic empire began its retreat five hundred years ago. "Spain is a target because we are the historic turning point," Aristegui said. "After this, they are going to try to hit Rome, London, Paris, and the United States harder than they did before."

Juan Áviles, a history professor at Madrid's Autonomous University and an adviser to the Civil Guard, told me, "From our Western point of view, it doesn't make sense that the killings of Atocha are meaningless. In Spain, we expect ETA to behave in certain ways. With Al Qaeda, the real dimensions of the threat are not known. And that produces uneasiness."

IN THE weeks after the March 11 attacks, Spanish police combed the immigrant neighborhoods outside Madrid, carrying photographs of suspects. "We didn't have them perfectly located, but we knew they were in Leganés," a police official told me. Leganés is a bland suburb of five-story red brick apartment complexes. The wide streets are lined with evenly spaced, adolescent oaks. In the mornings, the sidewalks are full of commuters rushing for the trains; then the place is vacant, except for grandmothers and strollers. In the evenings, the commuters return and close their doors.

At three o'clock on the afternoon of April 3, the day after the discovery of the bomb on the AVE tracks, police approached an apartment building on Calle Carmen Martín Gaite. They saw a young Moroccan man with a baseball cap on backward who was taking out trash. He yelled something in Arabic, then ran away at an impressive pace. (He turned out to be a track champion; the police did not catch him, and he remains at large.) A moment later, voices cried out, "*Allabu Akhbar*," and machine-gun fire from the second floor of the apartment house raked the street, scattering the cops. Over the next few hours, the police tactical unit, Grupo Especial de Operaciones, evacuated the residents of nearby apartments. Tanks and helicopters moved in, and the siege of Leganés began.

Inside the apartment were seven young men. Most of them were Moroccan immigrants who had come to Europe seeking economic opportunity. They had gone through a period of becoming "Westernized"—that is to say, they had been drinkers, drug dealers, womanizers. They hung out in cybercafes. They folded into the ethnic mix of urban Madrid. But they also lived in the European underground of Islamic radicalism, whose members were recruited more often in prison than in the training camps of Afghanistan.

Their leader was Sarhane Ben Abdelmajid Fakhet, who was thirty-five years old and had a round, fleshy face and a patchy beard. He was a real-estate agent who had come to Madrid eight years earlier on a scholarship to study economics. His boss told the Spanish press that Fakhet was "a wonderful salesman," who held the record for the number of apartments sold in a month. Yet he did not talk to his coworkers or make friends with other Spaniards; he remained sequestered in his Muslim world.

"He was very soft and well educated," Moneir Mahmoud Aly el-Messery, the imam at the principal mosque in Madrid, told me. The mosque—a massive marble structure, built with Saudi money—is the center of Muslim cultural life in the Spanish capital. It overlooks the M-30, one of the main freeways feeding into Madrid. When Fakhet was a student, he worked in the restaurant that is attached to the mosque, and he sometimes came to Messery's weekly religion class. In the beginning, the imam noticed that

Fakhet spoke familiarly to women as well as to men. "Then, for three or four years, I sensed that he had some extremist thoughts," Messery recalled. After class, Fakhet would ask telling questions, such as whether the imam believed that the leaders of the Arab countries were true believers, or if Islam authorized the use of force to spread the religion. Last year, he married a sixteen-year-old Moroccan girl who veiled her face and dressed entirely in black, including gloves. His performance at work declined, and he eventually stopped showing up altogether. According to police, he attended meetings with a small group of fellow Muslims at a barbershop in Madrid, where the men would drink holy water from Mecca. Police believe that this ritual was aimed at absolving the men of the sin of suicide, which is condemned by Islam.

Soon after the attacks of September 11, the imam had a dream about Fakhet. "Sarhane was in his kitchen, cooking on the stove," he recalled. "I saw what he was cooking was a big pot of worms. He tried to give me a plate of the food to eat. I said no. I said, 'Please clean the kitchen!'" Days later, the imam confronted Fakhet. "This is a message from God!" the imam said to him. "The kitchen is the thought, and the thought is dirty." Fakhet didn't respond. "He's a very cold person," the imam told me.

Fakhet was not the only young man in the M-30 mosque who had taken a turn toward extremism. Amer Azizi, a thirty-six-year-old Moroccan who was a veteran of jihad in Bosnia and Afghanistan, had been indicted in Spain for helping to plan the September 11 attacks. (He was accused of setting up the July 2001 meeting between Atta and other conspirators in Salou.) Among people who frequented the mosque, Azizi had the reputation of being a drug addict, although he attended some classes on Islam along with Fakhet. In June 2000, when the Arab countries' ambassadors to Spain came to the mosque to mourn the death of the Syrian dictator Hafez al-Assad, Azizi insulted them, yelling, "Why do you come to pray for an infidel?" Police charge him with being a senior member of Al Qaeda and the leader of the Moroccan Islamic Combat Group, which was responsible for five bombings in Casablanca in May 2003. He fled Spain just before his indictment.

Another of Fakhet's friends was Jamal Ahmidan, a drug dealer who police say financed the March 11 bombings with seventy pounds of hashish. Messery blamed an Islamist cleric in London, Abu Qatada, a radical Palestinian from Jordan who emigrated to Britain as a refugee in 1994. After September 11, police in Hamburg found eighteen tapes of Abu Qatada's sermons in Mohamed Atta's apartment there. British authorities arrested him in October 2002, but he still wields great authority among Islamists around the world. The imam told me, "It was as if there were black hands behind a curtain pushing these young men."

AT SIX O'CLOCK in the evening on April 3, three hours after the start of the Leganés siege, a handwritten fax in Arabic, signed by Abu Dujan al-Afghani, arrived at *ABC*, a conservative daily in Madrid. Referring to the bomb found beside the AVE tracks the day before, the author argues that it failed to explode because "our objective was only to warn you and show you that we have the power and capacity, with the permission of Allah, to attack you when and how we want." The letter demanded that Spain withdraw its troops from both Iraq and Afghanistan by the following Sunday. Otherwise, "we will turn Spain into an inferno and make your blood flow like rivers." On the surface, the fax represented another turn toward tactical political thinking; more likely, it was an attempt to salvage a bungled operation.

Outside the Leganés apartment, the police attempted to negotiate, but the cornered terrorists cried out, "We will die killing!" Phone calls that they made to relatives during the siege confirmed their intentions. They also attempted to call Abu Qatada in London's Belmarsh Prison, apparently seeking a fatwa that would morally sanction their suicide.

Instead of turning off the electricity and waiting them out, the police decided to storm the apartment. They ordered the terrorists to come out "naked and with your hands up." One of the occupants responded, "Come in and we'll talk." At 9:05 p.m., the police blew the lock on the door and fired tear gas into the room. Almost immediately, an explosion shattered the apartment, killing the terrorists and a police officer. The blast was so intense that it took days before the authorities could determine how many people had been in the apartment. The body of Jamal Ahmidan was hurled through the walls and into a swimming pool. One of the seven bodies still has not been identified.

In the ruins, police found twenty-two pounds of Goma-2 and two hundred copper detonators that were similar to those used in the train bombings. They also found the shredded remains of a videotape. These fragments were painstakingly reassembled, to the point where police could view the final statement of Fakhet and two other members of the cell, which called itself "the brigade situated in Al Andalus." Unless Spanish troops left Iraq within a week, the men had declared, "we will continue our jihad until martyrdom in the land of Tariq ibn Ziyad."

Al Andalus is the Arabic name for the portion of Spain that fell to Muslim armies after the invasion by the Berber general Tariq ibn Ziyad in 711. It includes not only the southern region of Andalusia, but most of the Iberian Peninsula. For the next eight hundred years, Al Andalus remained in Islamic hands. "You know of the Spanish crusade against Muslims, and that not much time has passed since the expulsion from Al Andalus and the tribunals of the Inquisition," Fakhet says on the tape. He is referring to 1492, when Ferdinand and Isabella completed the reconquest of Spain, forcing Jews and Muslims to convert to Catholicism or leave the Iberian Peninsula. "Blood for blood!" he shouts. "Destruction for destruction!"

Were these the true goals of Al Qaeda? Were the besieged terrorists in Leganés simply struggling to get Spain out of Iraq, or were they also battling to regain the lost colonies of Islam? In other words, were these terrorists who might respond to negotiation or appeasement, or were they soldiers in a religious fight to the finish that had merely been paused for five hundred years?

Less than a month after 9/11, Osama bin Laden and his chief lieutenant, Dr. Ayman al-Zawahiri, had appeared on Al Jazeera. "We will not accept that the tragedy of Al Andalus will be repeated in Palestine," Zawahiri said, drawing an analogy between the expulsion of the Moors from Iberia and the present-day plight of the Palestinians. The use of the archaic name Al Andalus left most Spaniards nonplussed. "We took it as a folkloric thing," Ramón Pérez-Maura, an editor at *ABC*, told me. "We probably actually laughed." This January, bin Laden issued a "Message to the Muslim People," which was broadcast on Al Jazeera. He lamented the decline of the Islamic world: "It is enough to know that the economy of all Arab countries is weaker than the economy of one country that had once been part of our world when we used to truly adhere to Islam. That country is the lost Al Andalus."

THE MUSLIMS who were expelled from Al Andalus took refuge mainly in Morocco, Algeria, and Tunisia. Some families, it is said, still have the keys to their houses in Córdoba and Seville. But the legacy of Al Andalus persisted in Spain as well. Up until the Victorian era, the country was considered to be more a part of the Orient than of Europe. The language, the food, and the architecture were all deeply influenced by the Islamic experience—a rival past that Catholic Spain, in all its splendor, could never bury. "In modern Arabic literature, Al Andalus is seen as the lost paradise," Manuela Marín, a professor at the Consejo Superior de Investigaciones Científicas, in Madrid, told me. "For Spain, the history of Al Andalus has a totally different meaning. After all, what we know as Spain was made in opposition to the Islamic presence on the peninsula. Only recently have people begun to accept that Islam was a part of Spain."

Although many Spanish historians have painted Moorish Spain as something other than paradise for Jews and Christians, for Muslims it remains not only a symbol of vanished greatness but a kind of alternative vision of Islam—one in which all the ills of present-day Islamic societies are reversed. Muslim tourists, including many heads of state, come to Spain to imagine a time when Islam was at the center of art and learning, not on the fringes. "The Alhambra is the number one Islamic monument," Malik A. Ruíz Callejas, the emir of the Islamic community in Spain and the president of Granada's new mosque, told me recently. "Back when in Paris and London people were being eaten alive by rats, in Córdoba everyone could read and write. The civilization of Al Andalus was probably the most just, most unified, and most tolerant in history, providing the greatest level of security and the highest standard of living."

Imams sometimes invoke the glory of Al Andalus in Friday prayers as a reminder of the price that Muslims paid for turning away from the true faith. When I asked Moneir el-Messery, of the M-30 mosque, if the Madrid bombers could have been motivated by the desire to recapture Al Andalus, he looked up sharply and said, "I can speak of the feeling of all Muslims. It was a part of history. We were here for eight centuries. You can't forget it, ever."

The fear that the "Moors" would one day return and reclaim their lost paradise—through either conquest or immigration—has created a certain paranoia in Spanish politics. Construction of the mosque in Granada was delayed for twenty-two years because of the intense anxiety surrounding the growing Islamic presence. In 1986, Spain joined the European Union; generous EU subsidies ignited an economic boom, drawing thousands of young men from North Africa. "The Muslims are young, and male, and they come by themselves," Mohammed el-Afifi, the director of press relations at the M-30 mosque, told me two years ago, when I visited him. "They don't speak Spanish, and they don't have much information about Spain. And they arrive with a different religion." At the time, Afifi placed the number of Arab immigrants in Spain at three hundred thousand. Now the number of Arabic-speaking immigrants is five hundred thousand, not including half a million illegals. The

Spanish government has encouraged official immigration from South America at the expense of North Africa, but smugglers in high-speed power boats make nightly drop-offs on the ragged Spanish coastline, and the frequent discovery of corpses washing up on the beaches testifies to the desperation of those who did not quite get to shore.

Muslim immigration is transforming all of Europe. Nearly twenty million people in the European Union identify themselves as Muslim. This population is disproportionately young, male, and unemployed. The societies these men have left are typically poor, religious, conservative, and dictatorial; the ones they enter are rich, secular, liberal, and free. For many, the exchange is invigorating, but for others Europe becomes a prison of alienation. A Muslim's experience of immigration can be explained in part by how he views his adopted homeland. Islamic thought broadly divides civilization into *dar al-Islam*, the land of the believers, and *dar al-Kufr*, the land of impiety. France, for instance, is a secular country, largely Catholic, but it is now home to five million Muslims. Should it therefore be considered part of the Islamic world? This question is central to the debate about whether Muslims in Europe can integrate into their new communities or must stand apart from them. If France can be considered part of *dar al-Islam*, then Muslims can form alliances and participate in politics; they should have the right to institute Islamic law, and they can send their children to French schools. If it is a part of *dar al-Kufr*, then strict Muslims must not only keep their distance; they must fight against their adopted country.

The Internet provides confused young Muslims in Europe with a virtual community. Those who cannot adapt to their new homes discover on the Internet a responsive and compassionate forum. "The Internet stands in for the idea of the *ummah*, the mythologized Muslim community," Marc Sageman, the psychiatrist and former CIA officer, said. "The Internet makes this ideal community concrete, because one can interact with it." He compares this virtual *ummah* to romantic conceptions of nationhood, which in-spire people not only to love their country but to die for it.

"The Internet is the key issue," Gilles Kepel, a prominent Arabist and a professor at the Institut d'Études Politiques, in Paris, told me recently. "It erases the frontiers between the *dar al-Islam* and the *dar al-Kufr*. It allows the propagation of a universal norm, with an In-ternet Sharia and fatwa system." Kepel was speaking of the Islamic legal code, which is administered by the clergy. Now one doesn't have to be in Saudi Arabia or Egypt to live under the rule of Islamic law. "Anyone can seek a ruling from his favorite sheikh in Mecca," Kepel said. "In the old days, one sought a fatwa from the sheikh who had the best knowledge. Now it is sought from the one with the best Web site."

To a large extent, Kepel argues, the Internet has replaced the Arabic satellite channels as a conduit of information and communi-cation. "One can say that this war against the West started on tele-vision," he said, "but, for instance, with the decapitation of the poor hostages in Iraq and Saudi Arabia, those images were propagated via Webcams and the Internet. A jihadi subculture has been created that didn't exist before 9/11."

Because the Internet is anonymous, Islamist dissidents are less susceptible to government pressure. "There is no signature," Kepel said. "To some of us who have been trained as classicists, the cyber-world appears very much like the time before Gutenberg. Copyists used to add their own notes into a text, so you never know who was the real author."

Gabriel Weimann, a senior fellow at the United States Institute of Peace, has been monitoring terrorist Web sites for seven years. "When we started, there were only twelve sites," he told me. "Now there are more than four thousand." Every known terrorist group maintains more than one Web site, and often the sites are in differ-ent languages. "You can download music, videos, donate money, re-ceive training," Weimann said. "It's a virtual training camp." There are two online magazines associated with Al Qaeda, *Sawt al-Jihad* (Voice of Jihad) and *Muaskar al-Battar* (Camp al-Battar), which feature how-to articles on kidnapping, poisoning, and murdering hostages. Specific targets, such as the Centers for Disease Control, in Atlanta, or FedWire, the money-clearing system operated by the Federal Reserve Board, are openly discussed. "We do see a rising focus on the U.S.," Weimann told me. "But some of this talk may be fake—a scare campaign."

One of the sites has been linked directly to terrorist acts. An editor of *Sawt al-Jihad*, Issa bin Saad al-Oshan, died in a gun battle with Saudi police on July 21, during a raid on a villa in Riyadh, where the head of Paul M. Johnson, Jr., the American hostage, was discovered in the freezer.

The importance of the Internet in the case of Madrid is disputed among experts. "Yes, the Internet has created a virtual *ummah*," Olivier Roy, an expert on political Islam at the French Centre National de la Recherche Scientifique, wrote to me recently. "The Web sites seem to attract the lonely Muslim cybernaut, who does remain in a virtual world. But Madrid's bombers used the Internet as a tool of communication. Their leaders had personal links with other Al Qaeda members, not virtual ones."

Thomas Hegghammer, the Norwegian investigator, divides the jihadi Internet community into three categories. "First, you have the message boards," he explained in a recent e-mail. "There you find the political and religious discussions among the sympathizers and potential recruits. The most important message boards for Al Qaeda sympathizers are Al Qal'ah (The Fortress), Al Sahat (The Fields), and Al Islah (Reform)." These boards, Hegghammer wrote, provide links to the "information hubs," where new radical-Islamist texts, declarations, and recordings are posted. "You often find these among the 'communities' at Yahoo, Lycos, and so on," Hegghammer continued. "There are many such sites, but the main one is Global Islamic Media." It was at this site that Hegghammer discovered the "Jihadi Iraq" document. "Finally, you have the 'mother sites,' which are run by people who get their material directly from the ideologues or operatives. They must not be confused with the myriad amateur sites (usually in English) set up by random sympathizers or bored kids."

Hegghammer pointed to several key sites associated with Al Qaeda, including Al Faruq (He Who Distinguishes Truth from Falsehood) and Markaz al-Dirasat wal-Buhuth al-Islamiyyah (Center for Islamic Study and Research). "Al Faruq is difficult to place geographically and organizationally, but it seems closer to the Afghanistan-based elements of Al Qaeda," Hegghammer wrote. Markaz al-Dirasat concentrates on Saudi Arabia. These sites move continuously, Hegghammer wrote, sometimes several times a day, to avoid being hacked by intelligence agencies or freelance Internet vigilantes. One of Al Qaeda's first sites, Al Neda, was operating until July 2002, when it was captured by an American who operates pornography sites. The Internet jihadis now cover themselves by stealing unguarded server space. Jihad videos have recently been discovered on servers belonging to George Washington University and the Arkansas Department of Highways and Transportation.

Last March, in Pakistan, Jamal Ismail, a reporter for Abu Dhabi TV, showed me how he monitors the Al Faruq site. Each day, he receives an e-mail with a link, which leads him to the new address. Like several other jihadi sites, the Al Faruq site announces itself with a white stallion racing across the screen, which is the Al Qaeda logo. "Every few days, it announces a new name, but it is the same Web site with a new look," he told me. "It concentrates on Iraq, Saudi Arabia, and Afghanistan." In mid-July, I asked Ismail via e-mail if there was any discussion of the upcoming American Presidential election; the Department of Homeland Security had just announced contingency plans to postpone the election in the event that Al Qaeda attempts to disrupt it. "There is no new article like the Spanish one, but we are all expecting people to talk about it," Ismail said. Sageman said that he had seen "vague statements along the lines of 'We'll do to the U.S. the same as we did to Spain,'" but nothing specific or authoritative.

I went to Yahoo Groups and typed in "jihad." There were a hundred and ninety-two chat groups registered under that category. With my Arabic-speaking assistant, Nidal Daraiseh, I checked out qa13ah.net, which had 7,939 members. On March 12, the day after the train bombings, a message titled "The Goals of Al Qaeda in Attacking Madrid" had been posted by a writer calling himself Gallant Warrior. Echoing a theme that is frequently repeated on these sites, the writer noted that by carrying out its threat to Spain, Al Qaeda proved that its words were matched by actions: "Al Qaeda has sent a message to the crusading people: do not think that death and fear are only for the weak Muslims. . . . Aznar, the American tail, has lost. And great fear has spread among the people of the countries in alliance with America. They will all be vanquished. Thank God for letting us live this long to see the jihad battalions in Europe. If anyone had predicted this three years ago, one would have said he was dreaming."

Another site I visited, ikhwan.net, was unusual in having a number of female correspondents. A writer named Murad chastised those who condemned the Madrid bombings. "You pity the deaths of those non-Muslims so quickly! If Muslims had died in their lands in the manner the writer discusses, would he have cried for them?" A woman named Bint al-Dawa responded, "Brother Murad, Islam does not allow the killing of innocent people." A man who called himself "Salahuddeen2" entered the discussion: "We have said that we are against the killing of civilians anywhere, but the enemies of God kill Muslim civilians every day and do not feel shame. They should drink from the same bitter cup."

Though these sites have become an ideological home for many Muslims, for most Arab immigrants Europe has provided comfort and support, while at the same time allowing them the freedom to maintain their Islamic identities. Three Moroccan immigrants died on the trains on March 11. One was a devout thirteen-year-old girl, Sanae Ben Salah, for whom the M-30 mosque was said to have been her "second home." Another, Mohamed Itabien, twenty-seven, was an illegal immigrant who taught Arabic classes at a mosque in Guadalajara. He was the sole source of support for his family, including eleven siblings, most of whom lived in a tiny town in Morocco where there were no telephones. The third, Osama el-Amrati, was a builder who was engaged to a Spanish woman. "Europe has given us opportunities our own countries didn't give us," Mustapha el-M'Rabet, the head of the Moroccan Workers and Immigrants Association, told me in Madrid. "Our children are in school, and we are working. Thousands of families in Morocco can live with the money we get here." When I asked M'Rabet if Al Andalus was part of the lure for Moroccan immigrants, he said, "Nobody with common sense could talk about going back to that. It's madness. It's a disease."

Under Aznar, relations with Morocco deteriorated to the point where, in 2002, the countries broke off diplomatic relations over various problems, including territory disputes, immigration, and the flow of drugs into Europe through Spain (according to the United Nations, Morocco exports twelve billion dollars' worth of marijuana each year). Eventually, the governments returned their ambassadors, without resolving the disputes that had led to the rupture. When twelve suicide bombers struck in Casablanca in May 2003, killing forty-five people, one of their targets was a restaurant called Casa de España.

"Spain is the bridge between the Islamic world and the West," Haizam Amirah Fernández said, when we met in a conference room at Madrid's Real Instituto Elcano shortly after the train bombings. "Think of that other bridge to the east, Turkey. Both have been hit by jihadist terrorists—in the same week." In Istanbul, on March 9, two suicide bombers attacked a Jewish club, killing one person and injuring five others. "The whole idea is to cut off these bridges," Amirah said. "If the goal is to polarize people, Muslims and infidels, that is a way of doing it. Jihadists are the most fervent defenders of the notion of a clash of civilizations." ·

One evening, I went to a pub with some Spanish cops. "There is this legend that Spain and the Arab world were friends," a senior investigator said. He nodded toward the waitress and the customers at several nearby tables. "Here in the bar are five Arabs sitting next to you. Nobody used to think it was strange. Now people are reacting differently." He paused and said, "They want to smell the jasmine of Al Andalus and pray again in the Granada mosque. Can you imagine the mentality these SOBs have?"

ON A SPLENDID April day in Paris, I went to lunch with Gilles Kepel, the Arabist scholar, and Jean-Louis Bruguière, the doughty French counterterrorism judge. Despite the beautiful weather, the men were in a gloomy frame of mind. "I am seriously concerned about the future," Bruguière said, as we sat at a corner table under an arbor of lilacs that shed blossoms onto his jacket. His armor-plated Peugeot was parked on the street and his bodyguards were discreetly arrayed in the restaurant. "I began work on this in 1991, against the Popular Front for the Liberation of Palestine, the Armed Islamic Group of Algeria. These groups were well known and each had an understandable structure. The majority were sponsored by states—Syria, Libya, Iraq. Now we have to face a new and largely unknown organization, with a loose system and hidden connections, so it is not easy to understand its internal functioning. It appears to be composed of cells and networks that are scattered all over the world and changing shape constantly."

Bruguière pointed to the Istanbul bombings in November 2003, and the March 11 bombings in Madrid as being the opening salvos in a new attack on Europe. "They have struck in the east and in the south," he said. "I think the next stop will be in the north."

"London or Paris," Kepel suggested.

"The principal target is London," Bruguière declared.

Chechnya is playing a larger and more disturbing role in the worldwide jihad, Bruguière said. At present, Al Qaeda and its affiliates operate on a rather low-tech level, but in Chechnya many recruits are being trained to exploit the technical advantages of developed countries. "Some of these groups have the capacity for hijacking satellites," he told me. Capturing signals beamed from space, terrorists could devastate the communications industry, shut down power grids, and paralyze the ability of developed countries to defend themselves.

"In 2001, all the Islamist actors in Madrid were identified," Bruguière said. His own investigations had led him to the Spanish capital that June. He quickly informed the Spanish police that Jamal Zougam, the owner of the phone shop, was a major contact for jihad recruits in Europe and Morocco. But Zougam was not apprehended. French and Spanish authorities have a long history of disagreement over the handling of terrorism, with the Spanish accusing the French of giving sanctuary to ETA terrorists. Bruguière said that when he arrived in Madrid he found that "the Islamic threat was underassessed." The Spanish police had made him wait a year before allowing him to interview Zougam. After Bruguière went back to Paris, the Spanish police put Zougam under surveillance and searched his apartment, finding jihadi tapes and videos. The authorities briefly renewed their interest in him after the 2003 Casablanca bombings, but once again there was insufficient evidence to arrest him.

I asked Bruguière if he thought that the Madrid attacks represented an evolution in Al Qaeda's operational ability, or suggested that the organization had lost control. He said that Al Qaeda was now little more than "a brand, a trademark," but he admitted that he had been surprised. "It was a good example of the capacity and the will of these groups to adopt a political agenda. The defeat of the late government and the agreement of the new government to withdraw troops—it was a terrorist success, the first time we have had such a result."

Later, Kepel and I discussed the reason that Europe was under attack. "The future of Islam is in Europe," he said. "It has a huge Muslim population. Either we train our Muslims to become modern global citizens, who live in a democratic, pluralistic society, or, on the contrary, the Islamists win, and take over those Muslim European constituencies. Then we're in serious trouble."

"I DOUBT WHETHER anyone can seriously suggest that Spain has not acted in a way that suggests appeasement," Ramón Pérez-Maura, the editor at *ABC*, told me shortly after Zapatero had announced plans to withdraw Spanish troops from Iraq in May, without waiting to see if U.N. peacekeeping troops would become involved. Pérez-Maura recalled a recent lunch he had had with the Iranian ambassador to Spain, Mortez Alviri. According to Pérez-Maura, Alviri said that Miguel Angel Moratinos—Zapatero's pick for foreign minister—had approached the Iranians to negotiate with Moqtada al-Sadr, the radical Shiite cleric, whose militia was engaged in savage urban warfare with Coalition troops. (Moratinos has denied this.) According to Pérez-Maura, Alviri passed Moratinos's message along, and, less than a day after Zapatero announced the withdrawal, Sadr said from Najaf that Spanish troops would be allowed to leave Iraq unmolested. That was a false promise. American and Spanish forces had to shoot a path through Sadr's militia in Najaf, which repeatedly attacked them.

On April 15, the voice of Osama bin Laden spoke again. "This is a message to our neighbors north of the Mediterranean, containing a reconciliation initiative as a response to their positive reactions," bin Laden said on the Arab satellite channel Al Arabiya. Now it was the Al Qaeda leader who cast himself in the role of a rational political actor. "It is in both sides' interest to curb the plans of those who shed the blood of peoples for their narrow personal interest and subservience to the White House gang." He proposed a European committee to study "the justice" of the Islamic causes, especially Palestine. "The reconciliation will start with the departure of its last soldier from our country," bin Laden said—not indicating if he was referring to Iraq, Afghanistan, or the entire Muslim world. "The door of reconciliation is open for three months from the date of announcing this statement. . . . For those who want reconciliation, we have given them a chance. Stop shedding our blood so as to preserve your blood. It is in your hands to apply this easy, yet difficult, formula. You know that the situation will expand and increase if you delay things. . . . .Peace be upon those who follow guidance."

From bin Laden's perspective, he was offering to bring Europe into an unsettled middle ground called the *dar al-Sulh*. This is the land of the treaty, where Muslims live as a peaceful minority. European leaders rejected bin Laden's proposal almost immediately, seeing it as a ploy to aggravate the tensions in the Western alliance. "It's the weirdest thing in the world," a senior FBI official told me. "It shows he's on the ropes, desperate."

Bin Laden's truce offer immediately became a topic of discussion on the Islamist Web sites. "This initiative should be considered a golden opportunity to the people of Europe," read a posting by Global Islamic Media on qal3ah.net. "Do not find it strange if after a while, a year or so, you will hear about secret negotiations by one country and representatives of Al Qaeda. . . . The organization has come to represent the Islamic *ummah* and speaks in its name. It appears that we are returning to the days of the caliphate."

On another site, islah.tv, a writer calling himself "Ya Rab Shahada" (Oh God, Martyrdom) picked up on the theme: "The Sheikh speaks these words as the Caliph of the Muslims and not as a wanted man. . . . This is the sign to begin the big strike on America." Another writer said, "Here we have the lands of Al Andalus where the trains were struck. The Sheikh is isolating America now . . . and it will be seen who will choose peace from those who chose suicide." A writer calling himself "@adlomari@" added, "The Sheikh has . . . proved to the world that Europe does not want peace with Muslims, and that it wants to be a partner in the Crusader crimes against Muslims. The coming days will show that events in Europe are coming if it does not respond to the Sheikh's initiative. Tomorrow is near."

The fact that bin Laden was addressing nations as an equal showed a new confidence in Al Qaeda's ability to manipulate the political future. Exploiting this power will depend, in part, on convincing the West that Al Qaeda and bin Laden remain in control of the worldwide Islamist jihad. As long as Al Qaeda is seen as being an irrational, unyielding death cult, the only response is to destroy it. But if Al Qaeda—amorphous as that entity has become—has evolved into something like a virtual Islamist state that is trying to find a permanent place for itself in the actual world, then the prospect of future negotiations is not out of the question, however unlikely or repellent that may sound to Americans. After all, the Spanish government has brokered truces with ETA, which has killed four times as many people in Spain as Al Qaeda has, and the accelerated withdrawal of Spanish troops from Iraq following the train bombings has already set a precedent for accommodation, which was quickly followed by the Dominican Republic, Honduras, and Nicaragua. Last year, Germany paid a six-million-dollar ransom to Algerian terrorists, and the Philippines recently pulled its fifty troops out of Iraq in order to save a hostage from being beheaded.

On July 21, immediately after the Philippine hostage was freed, new warnings appeared on the Internet, from a body called the Tawhid Islamic Group, promising terror attacks against Poland and Bulgaria unless they withdrew their troops from Iraq. Although leaders of both countries immediately rejected the demands, opinion polls showed that popular sentiment was turning against the countries' presence in Iraq. Another threat, allegedly from Abu Musab al-Zarqawi's group, Tawhid and Jihad, warned Japan that "queues of cars laden with explosives" were waiting, unless Japanese humanitarian troops left Iraq. Also in July, the Abu Hafs al-Masri Brigades posted a communiqué on the Internet ordering Italians to overthrow their Prime Minister, Silvio Berlusconi. "We are in Italy, and not one of you is safe so long as you refuse our Sheikh's offer," the message said. "Get rid of the incompetent

Berlusconi or we will truly burn Italy." The Internet warriors have been emboldened, although it is impossible to know how seriously to take their threats.

Appeasement is a foolish strategy for dealing with Al Qaeda. Last year, many Saudis were stunned when the terrorist group struck Western compounds in Riyadh—shortly after the United States had announced that it would withdraw troops from Saudi Arabia, fulfilling one of bin Laden's primary demands. The Saudis now realize that Al Qaeda won't be assuaged until all foreigners are expelled from the Arabian Peninsula and a rigid theocracy has been imposed. Yet some of the countries on Al Qaeda's hit list will no doubt seek to appease terrorists as a quick solution to a crisis.

Intelligence officials are now trying to determine who is the next target, and are sifting through "chatter" in search of a genuine threat. "We see people getting on the Internet and then they get on their phones and talk about it," a senior FBI official told me. "We are now responding to the threat to the U.S. elections." The idea of attacking before Election Day, the official said, "was born out of Madrid." Earlier this year, an international task force dubbed Operation Crevice arrested members of a bomb-making ring in London. During the investigation, officials overheard statements that there were jihadis in Mexico awaiting entry into the United States. That coincided with vague warnings from European imams about attacks before the elections. As a result of this intelligence, surveillance of border traffic from Mexico has been increased.

Even though Al Qaeda has been weakened by the capture of key operatives, such as Khalid Sheikh Mohammed, the architect of the 9/11 attacks, it is hardly defunct. "There is a replacement for Mohammed named Abu Faraj," the FBI official said. "If there is an attack on the United States, his deputy, Hamza Rabia, will be responsible. He's head of external operations for Al Qaeda—an arrogant, nasty guy." The official continued, "The most dangerous thing now is that no one is in control. These guys don't have to go back to bin Laden or Zawahiri for approval."

ONE OF the most sobering pieces of information to come out of the investigation of the March 11 bombings is that the planning for the attacks may have begun nearly a year before 9/11. In October 2000, several of the suspects met in Istanbul with Amer Azizi, who had taken the nom de guerre Othman Al Andalusi—Othman of Al Andalus. Azizi later gave the conspirators permission to act in the name of Al Qaeda, although it is unclear whether he authorized money or other assistance—or, indeed, whether Al Qaeda had much support to offer. In June, Italian police released a surveillance tape of one of the alleged planners of the train bombings, an Egyptian housepainter named Rabei Osman Sayed Ahmed, who said that the operation "took me two and a half years." Ahmed had served as an explosives expert in the Egyptian Army. It appears that some kind of attack would have happened even if Spain had not joined the Coalition—or if the invasion of Iraq had never occurred.

"The real problem of Spain for Al Qaeda is that we are a neighbor of Arab countries—Morocco and Algeria—and we are a model of economy, democracy, and secularism," Florentino Portero, a political analyst at the Grupo de Estudios Estratégicos, in Madrid, told me. "We support the transformation and Westernization of the Middle East. We defend the transition of Morocco from a monarchy to a constitutional monarchy. We are allies of the enemies of Al Qaeda in the Arab world. This point is not clearly understood by the Spanish people. We are a menace to Al Qaeda just because of who we are."

LAWRENCE WRIGHT *is the author of five books of nonfiction (most recently,* Twins*) and one novel (*God's Favorite*). He is also a screenwriter (*The Siege *and* Noriega: God's Favorite*). He has been a staff writer for* The New Yorker *since 1992.*

Coda

Since 9/11, I have been working on a history of Al Qaeda, so I was in Afghanistan when the bombs went off in Madrid on March 11, 2004. One of the fascinating details that did not get published in the article concerned the origin of the legend of Al Andulus, the Islamic Camelot. Washington Irving, America's first internationally famous author, arrived in Spain in 1826, to write a biography of Christopher Columbus. While he was in the country, he befriended the Gypsies who were living in the ruins of the Alhambra, and he drew from them stories of the Moorish reign. Published in 1832, Irving's book *The Alhambra* was an immediate international success, capturing, as it did, the splendid sense of decay and lost glory that so animated the nineteenth-century romantic sensibility. The myth of Al Andalus, that of an Islamic empire of tolerance and justice, encompassed by a superb appreciation of beauty in all its manifestations in art and nature, was created in part by the same man who had drawn so imaginatively upon the ghost stories and fairy legends of upstate New York. Irving was so associated with the boom in Spanish tourism that followed that he returned ten years later as the American ambassador. He eventually published a two-volume biography of the prophet Mohammed.

Craig Horowitz

ANATOMY OF A
FOILED PLOT

FROM *New York* MAGAZINE

ON A RAIN-SOAKED SATURDAY morning, nine days before
the start of the Republican convention at Madison Square Garden,
an Egyptian known as Dawadi left his house on Staten Island to
pick up two friends. They had plans to spend the day together and
to take care of a little business.

Dawadi wore a baseball cap pulled down over his eyes. He
looked as if he were heading out to do some weekend errands. He
drove to Rossville, a middle-class Staten Island neighborhood,
where he picked up James Elshafay, an unemployed nineteen-year-
old Tottenville High School dropout. The two men greeted each
other warmly. Though they had known each other for less than a
year, Dawadi had become a mentor to the naive, sometimes confused younger man. Mature, well-educated, and religious, Dawadi
was, some would say, even a father figure for Elshafay, who had
grown up in a house with just his mother and an aunt.

Driving cautiously toward Queens in the heavy rain, the two
men passed the time discussing the best way to handle the day's pri-

mary activity—a careful examination of the Herald Square subway station in preparation for planting a bomb.

After considering a variety of targets, they had decided on the subway station. Now they needed detailed information to put together a plan. They wanted to know the number and location of cops on the platforms at different times of the day. Which areas were covered by video cameras? Since the likeliest place to hide a bomb was a garbage can, they needed to know how many there were, where they were located, and when they got emptied. And they needed to find the best path to go in and then get out quickly after planting the device.

When they reached Thirty-fourth Avenue in Astoria, Shahawar Matin Siraj, a twenty-two-year-old Pakistani national, came down from his apartment and got in the car. Siraj, who entered the United States illegally nearly six years ago, was wearing a do-rag and baggy jeans. He had said when they planned their recon maneuvers that he wanted to disguise himself. He didn't want to "look Arabic." In English so thickly accented it can make him difficult to understand, he said he wanted to "look hip-hop, like a Puerto Rican."

On the way to midtown, the three men made small talk, and then the conversation shifted to the Verrazano-Narrows Bridge. Though they had already decided that blowing up the Verrazano would be better left for some time in the future—it would be very difficult, they believed, to put a bomb on the bridge without being seen—they nevertheless passed the time in a lively back-and-forth about the best place to plant explosives on the bridge to ensure the destruction of the entire span.

Finally, the trio parked on Madison Avenue and Thirtieth Street. To make sure they didn't attract attention, they decided to split up, do what they needed to do, and meet back near the car when they finished. They went their separate ways, and each man descended into the Thirty-fourth Street subway station using a different entrance.

SIX DAYS later, two of the three were arrested for plotting to blow up the Thirty-fourth Street subway station. Siraj was quietly picked up a couple of blocks from Islamic Books and Tapes, the shop on Fifth Avenue in Bay Ridge where he worked. Elshafay was sitting on the steps of the Noor Al mosque on Richmond Terrace when he was taken into custody with nary a voice raised.

Dawadi, as it turned out, was a confidential informant working for the NYPD. He had spent more than a year on the case, first building a relationship with Siraj and then with Elshafay. With his identity now revealed, he disappeared from the Arab Muslim community in Bay Ridge (the largest one in the city, with some thirty thousand members) as abruptly as he had become a part of it.

Identifying, getting close to, and ultimately arresting Siraj and Elshafay, two lone terrorists with no connections to Al Qaeda or any other international organization, who were motivated by all of the jihad chatter crackling in the air, was a direct result of much of the work that has been done by the NYPD since 9/11. "These kinds of homegrown, lone-wolf incidents start way below the level the federal government would focus on," says David Cohen, the NYPD's deputy commissioner for intelligence. "If we weren't doing it, nobody would be."

Cohen, who was once the number four spook at the CIA, is sitting with his back to a brick wall in the Half King, a funky, out-of-the-way pub on the far West Side in the twenties. It's afternoon and the place is library-quiet. But Cohen's routine level of suspicion is so highly evolved that when I ask if he'd like to sit out back in the pub's garden, he shakes his head. "Gardens have ears," he says cryptically.

Police Commissioner Ray Kelly, Cohen, and other high-ranking members of the department like to talk about the international intelligence-gathering capabilities that have been developed since 9/11. NYPD detectives are now posted in cities around Europe and the Middle East. But the listening posts that have been established in neighborhoods throughout the city, while decidedly less glamorous, are probably of greater value. A crudely planned, locally developed attack—like the one cops believe they thwarted with the arrests of Siraj and Elshafay—could still cause plenty of death, destruction, and panic, and may now be what keeps Kelly and his inner circle awake at night.

Kelly says the arrests of Siraj and Elshafay are proof that the investment made in the NYPD's Intelligence Division has paid off. "Yes, we want to work with other agencies, and yes, we have detectives placed overseas," he says. "But in New York City, we're on our own. We have to protect our own turf."

Global events, he argues, give people like Elshafay and Siraj permission to think the way they think. "We have an overarching concern about the lone wolf, the unaffiliated terrorist," he says. "That's why this case is so important to me."

According to several sources close to the investigation, Elshafay is in the process of pleading guilty and making a deal with the U.S. Attorney's office in Brooklyn. It is still unclear whether Siraj will plead or fight the charges. (Neither defendant's lawyer responded to repeated requests for comment.)

SHAHAWAR MATIN SIRAJ first came to the attention of the Police Department's Intelligence Division nearly a year and a half ago. Someone in Bay Ridge phoned in a report to a terrorist hotline the NYPD had set up after 9/11 that there was a young man who regularly engaged in virulent anti-American tirades. He worked at a Muslim bookstore located next to the Islamic Society of Bay Ridge, which encompasses a thriving community center, a nursery school, and one of the most active mosques in the city. The turnout for Friday-afternoon prayers regularly exceeds one thousand men, filling the mosque and forcing many others to participate, via loudspeakers, out on the street.

Siraj was worth keeping an eye on, intelligence officers believed, because of the tenor of his rhetoric and because he was apparently careful about when he spoke his mind. He wasn't some hothead who shot his mouth off to whoever came into the bookstore; Siraj vented only in front of people he believed he could trust.

After getting reports about Siraj for months, the cops decided, as Cohen puts it, "to send assets to that location." Specifically, they assigned Dawadi, their informant, to develop a relationship with Siraj, to become his friend and gain his confidence.

The odd seduction began last year during Ramadan. Dawadi started going to the bookstore and the mosque, occasionally talking to Siraj but always careful not to push things and scare his target away. Slowly, over four or five months, Siraj began to open up to his new friend.

At the same time, detectives investigated Siraj and his family, and a picture began to emerge. A native of Karachi, Pakistan, Siraj entered the United States illegally in 1999. Though the cops aren't certain, they believe he came across the border from Canada. His mother, father (who also works at the bookstore, which is owned by an uncle), and eighteen-year-old sister were already here legally.

Not long after sneaking across the border, Siraj was arrested for assault. The charges were eventually dropped, but he was arrested again for assault this past June, in a case involving an altercation in front of a store. He worked hard to present himself as a tough guy, telling Dawadi and others that he'd left Pakistan after killing two people. He also claimed that he'd been shot by one of his victims before killing him. Though cops have been unable to verify his story, Siraj was easy to anger and often lost his temper during his months with Dawadi.

"It was critical for us to determine if Siraj was connected to anyone overseas," says one detective who worked the case. "It's an interactive process. We watch who he hangs around with, how he deals with people, and in particular we look at his general level of sophistication. Things like whether he takes his own countersurveillance measures."

During the first six or seven months of the operation, Dawadi would hang around the bookstore, he'd occasionally drive Siraj home after work, and they would have long conversations about Islam. There was some radical talk, but nothing beyond banal, mostly boilerplate hostility. But the urgency of the rhetoric and the momentum for acting on it picked up dramatically when Siraj introduced Dawadi to his friend James Elshafay in April.

Only nineteen, Elshafay is the American-born product of an Irish-American mother and an Egyptian father, who split up when he was very young. Overweight, sloppy-looking, and on medication for anxiety, Elshafay has been treated for psychological problems. (A comic moment on police-surveillance video, taken the day the suspects conducted their reconnaissance of the subway, shows him standing in the rain after emerging from the station, eating a falafel with the filling oozing out the sides and onto his hands.)

Cops describe him as lost: not in school, not working, and in some state of turmoil about his identity. His only friend other than Siraj seemed to be his mother, who, cops say, coddled him and drove him everywhere.

September 11 was a turning point for Elshafay. "After 9/11, there was a lot of anti-Arab sentiment being expressed around the city," one detective says. "James saw people he grew up with and went to school with on Staten Island carrying signs that said on the front GOD BLESS AMERICA and on the back KILL ARAB BABIES, and he felt the police didn't do anything about it."

When he was introduced to Dawadi in April, he had an extraordinarily ambitious, handwritten wish list of possible targets to attack. In addition to the Thirty-fourth Street subway station, the list included the station at Fifty-ninth and Lexington, a Forty-second Street station, the Verrazano Bridge, a Staten Island jail, and three police precincts on Staten Island—the 123rd in Tottenville, the 120th in St. George, and the 122nd in New Dorp.

Elshafay also had a crudely drawn map of the targets that he gave to Siraj, who then showed it to Dawadi. "Are you crazy?" Dawadi said when Siraj unfolded the map. "You'd better get rid of that." Siraj stuck it between some volumes on a shelf in the bookstore.

Elshafay had begun to develop a vague interest in his Islamic heritage about a year and a half ago, growing a beard and starting to pray regularly. After their meeting, Dawadi nourished his growing piety. It was an easy way for them to bond. They went to the mosque and prayed together. Dawadi took him to a shop on Atlantic Avenue to buy his first kufi. He bought him an English translation of the Koran. He recommended books for Elshafay to read, like those by Abu Hanifah, a seminal Islamic scholar who died in 767 and is considered one of the greatest imams in Muslim history.

Soon Siraj began discussing the merits of various kinds of explosives and showed Dawadi some CDs he had that contained bomb-making instructions. He also talked more heatedly about blowing things up and doing harm to U.S. military personnel and law-enforcement officers.

"I want at least one thousand to two thousand to die in one day," Siraj said at one point.

In June, NYPD intelligence officers decided that the suspects had crossed a boundary. To make sure they got what they needed to make a case, and to prevent an attack, Dawadi began to wear a wire to record his conversations with the two. Detectives also instructed Dawadi to tell Siraj and Elshafay that he was a member of a Muslim brotherhood, which would support them and offer whatever assistance they needed to pull off an attack.

As July approached, Siraj talked about his "willingness to do jihad." "I'm going to fuck this country very bad," he said.

FIFTH AVENUE in Bay Ridge, between Sixty-fifth and Ninety-second Streets, is one of those colorful New York commercial strips that exist as a kind of taken-for-granted testament to the extraordinary diversity of the city. On one short stretch, there is the Chinese

Pagoda, a restaurant whose sign also features large Arabic script. The Killarney Pub is right next to an Arabic boutique, which is down the street from Musab Bin Omayer, a grocery store celebrating a renovation. And in every window recently, not just those of the Cleopatra Restaurant and the Jerusalem Hair Stylist, were signs marking the end of Ramadan.

Across from the Baraka restaurant is a five-story white-brick building that houses the Islamic Society of Bay Ridge. I met Zein Rimawi, one of the society's founders and a current board member, on the street in front of the building. The society is a multipurpose community organization that includes what is now one of four mosques in Bay Ridge.

A Palestinian with six brothers, who comes from a small town about twenty-five miles northwest of Jerusalem, Rimawi has a round, pleasant face covered by a close-cropped beard. He owns an aquarium store and is the only one in his family to have moved to the United States. "Why did I come to America?" he asks, without pausing for an answer. We'd moved inside to a meeting room on the third floor. "Every one of my brothers has his own house, his own car, and he can send his kids to college. I don't have a house. I don't have a car. I came here for justice, for freedom. These were the most important things. But now I don't see it. So what did I accomplish? What do I have?"

Rimawi speaks calmly, in modulated tones, but his anger and disappointment are palpable. As he talks, the spirited singing voices of a pre-K class rise to fill the room from one floor below us. "Of course we are angry; we have been targeted," he continues as he takes off his jacket.

"Put on the TV and you get sick from it. You see Afghanistan, and it's a war against the Muslims. Iraq, it's a war against the Muslims. Palestine, it's a war against the Muslims. Chechnya, a war against the Muslims. Everywhere you look, it's the same thing. Now even in the Sudan."

But the deeper hurt has come closer to home. He knows Shahawar

Matin Siraj and his family. The imam asked him to help when Siraj was arrested, and Rimawi spent some time checking the reputations of the lawyers being considered. He was instrumental in their decision to stay with the court-appointed counsel.

Rimawi reflects the general feeling in the community when he argues that the case against Siraj and Elshafay is simply one more example of law-enforcement officials' unjustly arresting Muslims for public-relations value. "The Bush administration needs to keep arresting Muslims," he says. "They must be able to say 'See, we stopped another terrorist, we found another sleeping [sic] cell. We are protecting you from the terrorists.'"

An affable man with generally moderate views, Rimawi believes that as long as the government keeps telling people over and over that the terrorists are going to strike again soon, the arrests will continue. "If later it turns out they're not guilty, who cares? It's the idea of it. I believe in that. We are being targeted. The first cell they arrested in Detroit, they are free now. In Albany, free now. They said there was a mistake in the translation. Gimme a break."

Rimawi's passion is not diminished at all when I tell him Elshafay has apparently pleaded guilty. "Innocent or not is not the point," he says.

"If you take a young man like that and tell him you are religious and you are experienced and clever, and you work him for a year and you keep talking to him and telling him 'We have to do this,' it's easy for that young man to say, 'Yes, let's do it.' Of course that would happen. Doing this, they could arrest most young Muslim people."

The cops, however, are adamant that this was not, as Cohen puts it, "in any way about leading a horse to water. Our CI was very careful to let the suspects take the lead and do the talking."

From the beginning, Rimawi watched as Dawadi tried to ingratiate himself in the community. He says the informant came to the mosque and introduced himself as a religious man. He told everyone his father was a well-known author of Islamic books in Egypt.

"When he heard the call for prayer, he would start to cry," Rimawi says, shaking his head almost in disbelief. "When someone would read the Koran, he would start to cry. He was a very good actor."

Though the cops dismiss the notion out of hand, Rimawi believes that Dawadi's original target was the imam, not Siraj. He says Dawadi tried to get close to the sheik. He told the religious leader he was a real-estate developer, but because he was new to the community people didn't trust him. He asked the sheik to be his partner. He told him he wouldn't have to do anything other than let Dawadi use his name and he would split the profits.

When the imam turned him down for the second time, Rimawi says, and told Dawadi not to come see him anymore, he turned his attention to Siraj.

No doubt part of Rimawi's frustration over the case is the bitter irony that for years, the board members of the Islamic Society of Bay Ridge have worked enthusiastically and energetically to be good neighbors, to become an integral part of the community.

Though Rimawi says he has not personally experienced any hostility or hate, he compares the situation for American Arabs now to that of blacks in the fifties and sixties. "I wish I could leave," he says finally, turning out the lights.

"My wife and children went to Palestine and Jordan recently. I told them, 'Find a place you like and we'll move back.' But my kids were born here; they don't want to go."

ON MONDAY, AUGUST 23, two days after Siraj, Elshafay, and Dawadi conducted their reconnaissance of the Thirty-fourth Street subway station, the men got together in Brooklyn to give real shape to their attack plan. Playing out his role, Dawadi said the brotherhood had approved their mission and directed them to conceal the bombs— which Dawadi would get from the brotherhood—in backpacks.

In the midst of the session, Siraj, who had from the beginning been the most vocal about his desire to commit an act of terror and had tried to project the façade of a tough guy, seemed to get cold feet. Suddenly, he told his companions he didn't want to handle the bombs. He would help with the planning, he would go with them to Thirty-fourth Street, but he didn't want to actually go down into the subway with the explosives. "I am not ready to die," he said.

"There was silence for a bit when Siraj finished talking," one of the detectives says. "Then, very calmly, James says, 'I'll do it. I'll place the bombs in the subway.' "

Energized by his decision to be the pivotal player in the plot, Elshafay then said he had an idea. He'd dress like an Orthodox Jew to put the explosives in place. He'd put on side curls and a long black coat. He would go in the Thiry-third Street entrance and come out on Thirty-fourth, and they could pick him up there. Warming to this image, Siraj suggested putting the bombs in a Macy's bag. "Jews shop at Macy's," he offered.

By this time, days before the start of the Republican convention, the cops were taking every precaution. They had the suspects under twenty-four-hour surveillance and were working closely with the U.S. Attorney's office to make sure they were getting all the elements they needed for an airtight case.

Then, early in the morning on August 27, one of the lead detectives got a call at home to get to the NYPD's counterterrorism bureau in Brooklyn as quickly as possible. The decision had been made to move on the suspects.

Since Siraj had an assault case pending against him, the cops used it as a lure. They called and asked him to come to the 68th Precinct in Bay Ridge at three o'clock to get the case closed out. He said fine. But when he left work at Islamic Books and Tapes that Friday afternoon, he was headed in the opposite direction.

Not taking any chances, the cops grabbed him. In his pocket was the original hand-drawn map of targets that Elshafay had first given him back in April—the one he had hidden among the volumes in the bookstore.

Elshafay was also called by the cops and told there was a traffic accident they needed to talk to him about. His mother dropped him at the mosque on Staten Island, where the cops arrested him. Before they put him in the patrol car, he asked if he could have a cigarette.

"There's no question in our mind that they would have played this out completely," says Cohen. "If they couldn't get the explosives or if they just got frustrated, they had other options. All it takes is an AK–47 and a desire to become a martyr. Well, they have no options now."

CRAIG HOROWITZ *has covered politics, crime, and the New York Police Department for more than a decade as a contributing editor at* New York *magazine. Horowitz, who has written more than forty cover stories for* New York *magazine, is at work on his first novel.*

Coda

The arrest of the would-be subway bombers took place barely forty-eight hours before the opening of the Republican convention in New York. As a result, it was, for the most part, a one-day news event. While under different circumstances the successful undercover police operation might have been a significant ongoing story, given the timing, it was swallowed up by convention coverage.

Consequently, police department brass couldn't have been more eager when I approached them about doing a piece that examined the undercover operation. They were so eager, in fact, they did something they never do—they gave me access and details against the wishes of the U.S. Attorney's office. The accused terrorists hadn't even been indicted yet and the U.S. Attorney's office was taking great pains to insure that nothing interfered with the successful prosecution of the suspects. This included a ban on talking to the media.

But the cops desperately wanted this story told. Three years ago, when Ray Kelly became New York City's Police Commissioner, he revamped the NYPD to deal with the dangers of a post–9/11 world. He created a counterterrorism unit, he hired talent from the CIA and the military, and he vowed that fighting terrorism would be just as important as fighting street crime.

However, when you're battling street crime, success and failure are easy to measure. Murder goes up or goes down. Rapes increase or they decrease. But how do you effectively measure the terrorist acts that didn't happen? The ones all the painstaking work may have prevented? In fact, most of the successes will never be made public.

Telling the story of the arrests of James Elshafay and Shahawar Matin Siraj gave the NYPD an unusual opportunity to get the word out.

Justin Kane and Jason Felch

To Catch
an Oligarch

FROM *San Francisco* MAGAZINE

THE STRANGE AND EPIC CASE of the United States of America versus
Pavel Ivanovich Lazarenko, which this spring asked twelve Bay Area
residents to decide whether the former prime minister of a country
six thousand miles away had broken the nation's laws more than a decade ago, actually began one cool night in January 1998 when FBI
special agent Bryan Earl paid a visit to a small Dumpster in Sausalito.

Earl is not the type to skulk under cover of darkness. A smooth-
faced man with hints of gray at his temples, gentle blue eyes, and a
profound sincerity, he looks more like a tax accountant than one of
Louis Freeh's or Robert Mueller's blue-suited special agents. His pious demeanor hints at his Mormon upbringing on the quiet side of
Las Vegas, and it's easy to picture him wandering around Mexico in
a suit and tie, with a small black name tag on his chest and the Book
of Mormon under his arm, as he did twenty years ago. Not the first
man you would imagine in the FBI, he is the first man you would
want working there—the embodiment of God, family, and country.

At age thirty-two, tired of practicing corporate law in D.C., he
had sent an application to the FBI on a whim and then surprised

himself by joining up. A year later, as a rookie fresh out of Quantico, he found himself in San Francisco, eventually part of the FBI's local ten-member Eurasian Organized Crime Squad, investigating financial fraud and money-laundering schemes linked to the former Soviet Union and, in some cases, the infamous Red Mafiya. Earl enjoyed being part cop, part missionary, spreading the gospel of the American legal system among former communists for whom the distinction between politics, business, and crime had fallen with the Berlin Wall.

In late 1997, Earl had been handed the name of Peter Nikolayevich Kiritchenko, a Sausalito businessman whom Ukrainian authorities had asked the FBI to check out. It was a routine foreign police request, the kind, Earl's supervisor would later say, that most FBI agents would fulfill and forget. According to the Ukrainians, Kiritchenko had come up in the early stages of a Ukrainian investigation into the just-deposed prime minister, Pavel Lazarenko. At the time, Ukraine was a new ally of the United States, helping reduce the dangerous stockpile of nuclear weapons in the former Soviet Union, and nobody wanted to endanger the fragile relationship that had been forged with Ukraine's autocratic president, Leonid Kuchma. Lazarenko was Kuchma's biggest political rival. Many Ukrainians considered the investigation into the upstart presidential challenger to be a politically motivated ploy.

But Earl pushed on. By January 1998, he had pieced together an outline of Peter Kiritchenko's story. Three years earlier, Kiritchenko had uprooted his life as a middle-aged Ukrainian commodities trader in Warsaw to move his wife, daughter, and business to the Bay Area. A compact man with sandy blond hair, cheeks ruddy from vodka, and a taste for excess, Kiritchenko stuck out in San Francisco's Russian-speaking community. He drove a burgundy Bentley and, on a two-acre lot high atop Tiburon, was building a Mediterranean-style mansion with a 360-degree view of three bridges that he dubbed Shangri-la. His neighbors knew him from his petition asking the city to let him install a shooting range in the basement. Meanwhile, he had invested about $25 million in local real estate, snapping up a Sausalito condo, two small San Francisco apartment buildings, and over eighty undeveloped acres in Tiburon. The Ukrainian, Earl thought, was worth a closer look.

At 10:00 p.m. one weeknight that January, Earl tucked his young child into bed, kissed his wife good night, and slipped into jeans and a sweatshirt. From his home in the city, he drove north across the Golden Gate Bridge into the hulking darkness of the Marin Headlands, following the necklace of lights to the Sausalito shoreline. From Bridgeway he turned onto Harbor Drive and pulled his standard-issue domestic sedan into the empty parking lot of the brown three-story office building at One Harbor Drive. In a Dumpster at the back of the lot, he found a single trash bag with the day's detritus from Kiritchenko's office. He tossed it in his trunk and drove away. No search warrant needed. By eleven, Earl was home in bed.

The "trash cover," as agents call it, became Earl's nightly routine. Every weekday morning for eighteen months he would bring the bag thirteen floors up the elevator of the Phillip Burton Federal Building on Golden Gate Avenue and dump its contents on his desk. Occasionally Earl felt silly taking off his suit jacket to sift through garbage like a Tenderloin hobo. His colleagues ribbed the rookie for the mess he made. But it was fruitful. The trash yielded clues—envelopes from something called European Federal Credit Bank; a Post-it note with the word *Dugsbery* scrawled on it; envelopes bearing the return addresses of some of San Francisco's most respected banks. All of it suggested to Earl that the Ukrainians could be right—there appeared to be a multimillion-dollar pipeline between Ukraine and the Bay Area.

AMONG SAN FRANCISCO's thirty thousand Russian-speaking émigrés—many of whom are Jews and political refuseniks who arrived as refugees over the past thirty years and congregate in the bakeries, churches, and restaurants along Geary Boulevard—only a small number have attracted the attention of the Eurasian Organized

Crime Squad. In the 1970s, the KGB released thousands of hard-core prisoners from the Soviet gulags, where they had formed tight-knit criminal clans, and allowed them to emigrate across the globe. Over time these clans evolved into the sophisticated Russian Mafiya, operating multinational drug, prostitution, and insurance and welfare fraud rings, among other enterprises. The California Department of Justice has reported that Russian criminal groups are operating in California, including "approximately three hundred former Soviet Union crime figures and associates in the San Francisco Bay Area." Many are from the Ukraine, members of an offshoot of the Odessa Mafiya.

The Bay Area, one of the world's banking hubs as well as home to many Russian-speakers, has become a favorite place for the Mafiya to launder some of its global take. Much of the EOC squad's work involved tracking that money down. For example, as Earl staked out Kiritchenko's Dumpster by night, by day he was helping investigate a young Russian émigré, Alexander Lushtak, who had bilked the local Russian community out of millions with an elaborate Ponzi scheme that promised tax-free returns of up to 25 percent. Lushtak pleaded guilty in June 2000 to money launder-ing. During his trial, according to one published report, an FBI memo emerged claiming Lushtak had laundered as much as half a billion dollars of Russian organized-crime money through his bank account in New York.

But not all the Russian loot that has flooded into San Francisco comes from the Mafiya. As the Soviet Union collapsed, state-owned industries were divvied up among politicians, crooks, and entre-preneurs. These new oligarchs built a Wild West capitalist economy in which pay-to-play was the rule. Government contracts, interna-tional trade deals, the rights to natural resources—every potential profit came at a price. Later, as the young countries tried to impose the rule of law on the chaotic system, the oligarchs responded by spiriting their politically embarrassing fortunes out of the country and into banking systems where they couldn't be touched.

It was an influx for which Earl was prepared. His course work in international and Soviet law at Columbia University Law School and experience in financial litigation made him an immediate asset to the squad, and he began taking Russian classes. Earl knew that investigations into complex financial crimes—considered among the FBI's most challenging—hew to a single axiom: follow the money. The scraps from Kiritchenko's office that Earl riffled through each day were threads in a dense web of holding companies, off-shore corporations, and beneficial trusts. It looked designed to disguise something, but what was this small-time trader hiding?

It was no secret that Kiritchenko advertised his ties to Pavel Lazarenko, handing out gold-embossed business cards reading: ADVISER TO THE PRIME MINISTER. In photos, Lazarenko—who was said to have accumulated up to a billion dollars, despite earning about five thousand dollars a year in government salary—towered over the crowds gathered to see him, an unnerving glare on his fleshy face. He was a bear of a man, about six-foot-three, counting his full, starchy head of hair.

The prime minister had begun his career driving a tractor on a collective farm, but by age twenty-four, "Pasha," as his friends called him, had already become the powerful director of a state farm in the Soviet Republic of Ukraine. By thirty-three, he headed all agriculture in his home region of Dnepropetrovsk. Even the fall of the Soviet Union in 1989 did not slow Lazarenko's rise. A year after Ukraine declared its independence, he was appointed governor of Dnepropetrovsk, and by 1996, Lazarenko had moved to Kiev to accept the premiership, the second most powerful man in a nation of fifty million. He was forty-three.

"He had an aura," recalls Olena Prytula, a leading Ukrainian journalist. Prytula came to Stanford University on a fellowship this year and was one of the few Ukrainians to cover Lazarenko's trial. She first met Lazarenko in 1996 at a ceremony outside of Kiev commemorating the Soviet victory over Germany. "He looked like the devil to me. I thought, 'This man is capable of killing someone,'" she says. "He would say something, and everyone would do it immediately. All of the journalists called him *haziain*, master."

Kiritchenko always called Lazarenko not Pasha but *Pavel Ivanovich*. The use of the formal patronymic made it clear who held the power. But Kiritchenko's connection to the Ukrainian leader wasn't just business. At the same time Earl began investigating, Lazarenko had flown from Ukraine to San Francisco to attend the christening of Kiritchenko's first granddaughter. During a simple ceremony at St. Nicholas Cathedral, a cozy Russian Orthodox Church on Fifteenth and Church Streets, Pavel Lazarenko was named the child's godfather.

Afterward, at a party Kiritchenko hosted at the now-defunct Mediterranean restaurant Splendido in Embarcadero Center, the two men traded toasts, thanking each other for years of business success. After the toasts, Lazarenko and Kiritchenko began singing together. There had been much wine and vodka, but the song was not a drunken one. It was an old Ukrainian song, soft and heartfelt, a song about never-ending loyalty. "More than best friends, they were brothers," says a Ukrainian who was there.

Yet as Earl spent the summer investigating Kiritchenko, Lazarenko, safely outside U.S. jurisdiction, remained in the background. That changed, however, when an obscure company called Dugsbery Incorporated closed a deal with Marin County real estate agent Nan Allen to purchase a $6.75 million Novato estate once occupied by comedian Eddie Murphy. Rumor had the buyers as Russians.

DUGSBERY—Earl had seen the word scrawled on a Post-it note in Kiritchenko's trash. From the public record, he'd discovered it was a shell company owned by Kiritchenko with a single account at WestAmerica Bank. Kiritchenko was already building his Shangri-la. Why would he need an even bigger mansion, with twenty rooms, five swimming pools, two helicopter landing pads, a full-sized ballroom, gold-plated doorknobs, and a master bedroom larger than entire Nob Hill apartments?

The answer was in the news. Back in Ukraine, the godfather was in a fight for his life. Now he had a hideout, just in case.

EARL WAS eager to explore the Ukrainian connection himself. In December 1998, he boarded a commercial flight to Kiev with Martha Boersch, an assistant U.S. attorney with the San Francisco Organized Crime Strike Force, who had been assigned to work with him just days earlier. Like Earl, Boersch was well suited to the case, and a lot less green. A graduate of Berkeley's Boalt law school, she had been a government prosecutor for six years, had already won a number of complex fraud cases, and was lead attorney on Lushtak's Ponzi-scheme prosecution. She also spoke Russian.

On the flight, Earl updated Boersch. A month earlier his findings had been included in an FBI memo requesting help from Swiss authorities who were investigating Lazarenko's and Kiritchenko's numbered Swiss bank accounts. It was titled simply "Re: Peter Kiritchenko, Russian Organized Crime" and laid out the FBI's ideas: While living in Warsaw, Kiritchenko had been "involved in myriad criminal schemes," including moving millions in "stolen Ukrainian government funds." He disguised the money as trade in ferrous metals, wheat, and sunflower seeds. He was also suspected of selling prefabricated houses made in Elk Grove, California, to the Ukrainian government at almost a 200 percent markup using falsified invoices.

Earl's most intriguing find, however, came from a discarded FedEx envelope from European Federal Credit Bank. The offshore bank based in Antigua had been cofounded by someone Earl and Boersch knew well, Ponzi schemer Alexander Lushtak. It was now chaired by Alex Liverant, a Ukrainian Jew who had immigrated to San Francisco in 1979. When EuroFed needed capital, Earl had learned, Kiritchenko became its primary investor and was now sharing a business address with Liverant. Under Kiritchenko's watch, EuroFed began opening U.S. dollar correspondent and investment accounts in San Francisco financial institutions big and small: Merrill Lynch, Bank Boston Robertson Stephens, Hambrecht and Quist, Pacific Bank, and Commercial Bank of San Francisco. The memo concluded that "millions of dollars have been obtained illegally" and that Kiritchenko was using EuroFed to "minimize his tax exposure in the U.S."

It was a classic money-laundering case, Boersch thought—moving the proceeds of certain illegal activities through U.S. financial institutions with the intent to conceal their origins. But there was one huge twist: the money wasn't the proceeds of crimes committed here. The alleged frauds all had taken place in Ukraine.

That didn't matter, Boersch argued. Read liberally, the criminal code implied that anyone in the world who committed fraud or extorted money could be charged with money laundering if they ever brought that money here. This was a daring approach—so daring it had never been tried in U.S. courts.

ARMED WITH their novel legal theory, Boersch and Earl arrived jet-lagged at the Kiev airport for what they thought would be a low-profile trip to meet with Ukraine's government investigators and confirm their ideas about Kiritchenko. They were greeted by a crowd of people waving signs and chanting, "Free Lazarenko!"

Boersch and Earl were stunned when their hosts explained that while they had been in the air, the Swiss investigators tracking Lazarenko's assets had charged the presidential challenger with money laundering in Switzerland. Since Lazarenko had left office the previous year under a haze of allegations, the Swiss and a team of about fifty Ukrainian investigators had dogged him even as his opposition party won a bloc of seats in Parliament. The Swiss were expected in Kiev any moment.

The turn of events transformed the fact-finding trip into a multinational swap meet, with the Swiss, Ukrainian, and American investigators exchanging leads in their overlapping investigations. Boersch and Earl spent their days bundled in winter clothes in an unheated interrogation room interviewing potential witnesses. The witnesses explained how Lazarenko used his political power to direct government contracts for housing to Kiritchenko. From the

Swiss, the pair soon learned that before Kiritchenko had invested close to $100 million in EuroFed, Lazarenko had asked for $96 million in cash from his Swiss accounts before settling on withdrawing two $48 million bearer checks.

Earl is a family man through and through, and he missed his kids—he'd just had his second—during his trip. But he was picking up Russian and also enforcing criminal law in an exotic foreign locale, which he loved. "It was snowy and there were beautiful parks, big trees," he says. "In Dnepropetrovsk I'd go run in the mornings, freezing cold. My Ukrainian people thought I was crazy." On the drive back from the provincial capital to Kiev, he says, "everybody was out ice fishing, and we'd stop by these little markets and look at all these big fish. It was an experience."

At night, the Ukrainians hosted elaborate six-hour banquets to celebrate the historic cooperation. For a country whose criminal corruption makes it "the epicenter for global badness," in the words of a former State Department official, teaming up with the FBI was a sign of acceptance. The vodka toasts continued to midnight, and Earl, who doesn't smoke or drink, was obliged to attend. His fascination with two things Russian began to wane. "It's a game—let's see who can outdrink who—but I don't think they enjoy it," he says. "And the pickled food! It's their history, how they preserved stuff. But it's horrible."

Soon after Earl returned home, he found his investigation turned on its head. Lazarenko's wife, Tamara; son, Oleksandr; and twin daughters, Katya and Lessia, had moved into the Novato mansion. With the Ukrainians' legal vise closing in, the oligarch was feathering his nest. Earl put Lazarenko's name on an FBI watch list that would alert him the moment the former prime minister stepped on a plane to the United States.

The call came just a month later. As Kuchma's "anticorruption" campaign came to fruition, Ukraine's parliament voted to revoke Lazarenko's immunity from prosecution. The politician fled to Athens and on February 19, 1999, boarded a plane bound for JFK

International Airport. Earl knew he was coming before Lazarenko had fastened his seat belt.

Suddenly the routine police request had exploded into the biggest case in the Eurasian Organized Crime Squad's history and one of the highest-profile cases within the FBI.

When INS agents briefed by Earl greeted Lazarenko at the arrival gate, the imperious Ukrainian immediately requested political asylum. He would take his chances on America's legal system rather than Ukraine's or Switzerland's.

On the face of it, Lazarenko's application for political asylum had some validity. He had been running for president as a reformer against a brutal autocrat who wanted him in jail or dead. Some Ukrainians suspected Lazarenko's only crimes were failing to share his "profits" with Kuchma, and then having the audacity to use that money to run against him for president. In audiotapes secretly recorded by a bodyguard of the president and first released in November 2000, Kuchma can be heard mentioning Lazarenko as an oligarch whose demise might conveniently satisfy the American government, which was pushing him to do something about the country's rampant corruption. "Who from the oligarchs?" an aide asks. "Who embarrasses you most of all? Whom can I give to the American intelligence?" (The same tapes revealed Kuchma authorizing the sale of stealth radar to Saddam Hussein and allegedly ordering the death of a top Ukrainian journalist—the cofounder of Olena Prytula's publication—who was later found beheaded in a forest outside Kiev.) Lazarenko was no saint, but some observers wondered if the United States had been conned into doing Kuchma's dirty work.

Lazarenko's arrival, meanwhile, threw the U.S. government into a tizzy. Ukraine was calling for his head, and the Swiss were preparing to file for his extradition. While the State Department madly debated the options, Lazarenko was detained until his asylum petition was considered. At his own request, he was transferred to Marin County Jail so he could be closer to his family. He was eventually moved to the Camp Parks Federal Correctional Institution in the Contra Costa County town of Dublin.

For Earl and Boersch, Lazarenko's surprising appearance was also problematic. He had always been a secondary concern in the investigation. Most of the evidence Earl had accumulated against Kiritchenko implicated Lazarenko, but there was not enough for an indictment against either of them.

Still, the endgame was on. Earl's Swiss colleagues had gathered enough evidence to include Kiritchenko in their case against Lazarenko and asked the agent to present the extradition warrant. One morning at 6:00 a.m., Earl knocked on the door of Shangri-la, finally coming face-to-face with a bleary-eyed Kiritchenko. After eighteen months, his covert investigation had just become overt.

EARL'S VICTORY was tempered by a decision by the Bureau of Prisons, which, over the objections of Earl and Boersch, put Peter Kiritchenko and Pavel Lazarenko in the same jail cell at Camp Parks, two miles from downtown Dublin and thirty long miles from Shangri-la. For six months, the two men would spend all day together plotting a defense.

Their confinement was a classic example of what game theory calls, with good reason, the prisoner's dilemma. Given two prisoners, both implicated heavily in a case, the best group outcome is achieved if they refuse to cooperate with the prosecution. But while sticking together may save them both, each prisoner knows the surest ticket to freedom—or a favorable plea bargain—is to betray the other.

Under these psychologically grueling conditions, paranoia set in. Though the available evidence indicates that Lazarenko had not met with Earl or Boersch to discuss cooperating, Kiritchenko believed he was about to be betrayed and did the only rational thing. He asked for a meeting with Earl and Boersch. Earl did not want to give up on prosecuting Kiritchenko, whom the FBI not only suspected of masterminding the money laundering but was investigating for deeper connections to Russian Mafiya. But Kiritchenko was what the case against the bigger fish needed: an eyewitness who could put a human face on the complex financial transactions for a jury.

The government's ultimate offer hinted at just how badly it needed him. He would cop to one felony count of interstate transportation of stolen property, for which he would be allowed to appeal any sentence over thirty-seven months. But when it was all over, he and his wife and daughter would go back to their enviable lives unscathed and with guaranteed green cards to boot. Apart from a $3 million "voluntary restitution," he'd be allowed to keep everything he owned: his $11 million Shangri-la, all his businesses and other properties—including a $3 million condo in Los Angeles—and his yacht. After accepting the offer, Kiritchenko packed up his belongings and walked out of the cell with Lazarenko watching. He had won his freedom—and broken his brotherhood—by telling Earl where the money had come from and gone.

IT WAS quite a tale. As the Soviet Union crumbled, Kiritchenko, a low-level Communist functionary, had rushed into the void left by the central government, hoping to set up a small import-export company to trade in the resource-rich Dnepropetrovsk region. He learned that the regional governor, Lazarenko, controlled everything and demanded a cut of the business done on his turf. On January 13, 1993, Kiritchenko met with Lazarenko in a Warsaw hotel. The two walked to a nearby financial institution called American Bank in Poland, and the trader gave the governor $40,000 to open a dollar account. It was a down payment, Kiritchenko said. As they left the bank, Lazarenko told him, "I work with everyone fifty-fifty." For the next five years, Kiritchenko faithfully sent half of his profits to Lazarenko, who in return made Kiritchenko a very rich man.

When Earl and Boersch heard that story, they saw the potential underlying crime under Ukrainian law. As long as they could convince a jury that the lowly commodities trader had been, in that moment, victimized by the all-powerful politician's scheme, it was extortion. Alone, that seemed enough to pursue the money-laundering charge.

Yet the rest of Kiritchenko's story complicated matters, for it was not a victim's tale. He quickly became Lazarenko's partner, often traveling between Marin County and Europe to serve as bagman. Well acquainted with European banking, he opened Swiss bank accounts, making sure money from Lazarenko's rapidly growing wealth was flowing smoothly out of Ukraine. The two men flew together to Panama to purchase Panamanian passports for $100,000 (to allow them to travel on the down-low), to Switzerland to meet with their bankers, and to Hawaii and Canada to vacation with their families. It was a deal so sweet that Kiritchenko forgot to stop paying Lazarenko when he was booted out of office.

When Lazarenko became a political hot potato, Kiritchenko's importance to his patron only grew, he told Earl and Boersch. Now the safety of Lazarenko's wealth depended on him. With investigators breathing down Lazarenko's neck, Switzerland was no longer a haven. That's when Kiritchenko approached Liverant, the co-owner of EuroFed, and bought a discreet place to stash money. After a quick trip to Antigua to check out EuroFed's books, Kiritchenko paid $1.1 million for two-thirds of the bank. Soon the two $48 million checks withdrawn from the Swiss accounts poured through the Bahamas and into EuroFed.

Earl and Boersch thought they had more than enough. They approached Robert Mueller, who was then head of the U.S. attorney's office in San Francisco, and presented their case.

Mueller's reply: "Go ahead. Indict."

THE GRAND JURY indictment of Pavel Lazarenko came down in May 2000, charging him in a sweeping conspiracy to launder what eventually became $114 million through San Francisco financial institutions. It would be an international prosecution the likes of which had never been seen. The last time the government had put a former head of state on trial, armed forces had invaded Panama in Operation Just Cause to capture General Manuel Noriega. This time, the government enlisted a Bay Area jury to call a former prime minister to account.

Even so, the prosecution's case shared elements of a foreign invasion. It represented a zealous expansion of American jurisdiction across the world. If Lazarenko was convicted, it would give U.S. attorneys the authority to judge whether anyone anywhere had committed fraud or extortion under their own nation's legal code, and then to hold them accountable in U.S. courts, as long as their money had moved through ubiquitous dollar accounts.

The world's crooks and their cronies weren't the only ones watching Lazarenko's case. Anyone in America who moves large, sometimes mysterious sums for a living, including investment bankers and real-estate brokers, had a stake in the outcome. It's illegal to deliberately ignore the tainted source of a deposit. So far the FBI and IRS have worn kid gloves on such "willful blindness" cases, never once criminally charging a U.S. bank in a money-laundering case. Still, finance watchers have wondered if the winds could shift. (In this case, the city's bankers were never called to testify. Yet in August the Justice Department launched a criminal probe into a Washington, D.C., bank's possible role in laundering money for former Chilean dictator Augusto Pinochet and other foreign officials.)

Lazarenko would not go down without a brawl. The millions in his EuroFed accounts had been frozen in Antigua, but he still had hundreds of millions hidden out of the United States' reach and spent it freely. From jail, he hired a string of the Bay Area's top defense attorneys to argue the United States was overstepping its bounds, craftily dragging out the trial's approach each time he changed horses. Over the course of three and a half years, University of San Francisco Law School dean Joseph Russoniello, East Bay defense attorney Cristina Arguedas, who assisted on the O. J. Simpson case, and Harold Rosenthal, who handled the Billionaire Boys Club case, all came and went.

Eventually Lazarenko assembled a dream team. Dennis Riordan, Rosenthal's partner and ranked among the nation's best appellate lawyers, was in charge of motions and legal arguments. From behind thick, oversized glasses, Daniel Horowitz, a death-penalty lawyer and occasional TV commentator, conducted depositions of foreign witnesses in Ukraine and across Europe. Then, three months before the trial began, Doron Weinberg, a tough and preeningly confident civil rights attorney turned white-collar defense attorney, came on to argue the case in court.

Yet center stage belonged to Lazarenko. During opening statements this past March, the twelve Bay Area jurors—initially ten women and two men—often glanced furtively at him, trying to figure him out. Lazarenko, sitting perfectly upright on the other side of the court, was dressed impeccably in an understated black suit. During recesses, he stood outside in the hall, chest thrust forward and hands clasped behind his back, drawing his linebacker's frame over his gaggle of supporters, with whom he consulted in Russian. Lazarenko's wife had returned to Ukraine, and his twin daughters appeared rarely, but his two aides and translators, both named Yuriy, one fat, the other skinny, were there. So was his son, Oleksandr, a thuggish-looking twenty-something with slick black hair who was often mistaken for a bodyguard. But no member of Lazarenko's posse drew more whispers than Oksana Tsykova, a blonde with striking Russian features and a growing belly who translated for Lazarenko at the defense table. A family friend of Lazarenko's who'd migrated from Ukraine to the Bay Area, she was in her third trimester when the trial began and gave birth days before the verdict. She would not confirm or deny that they were lovers.

Lazarenko looked like a free man, and in a way he was. Nine months earlier, he'd been allowed to post his frozen EuroFed accounts—though he no longer had control of them—as an essen-

tially illusory $86 million bail so he could be released into house ar-
rest in a two-bedroom San Francisco apartment at an undisclosed
location.

If Lazarenko appeared commanding, Earl was tired and nervous.
He'd spent six of the previous twelve months overseas, away from
his kids, missing much of his youngest child's kindergarten year in
preparation for the trial. Now he would work seven long days a
week until it ended. Six years of digging were at stake.

WARY OF LEGAL PROCEEDINGS that turn into personal dra-
mas, the prosecution approached the trial with dry factuality. Their
opening was simple and straightforward. Boersch stood behind a
podium and recited the spare tale of how $114 million made it
from Ukraine to the United States. All she asked the jurors to do
was follow the money.

In Doron Weinberg's opening argument, he conceded many of
the facts—the bank records, the account balances, the Elk Grove
prefabs. What he offered was an alternate story. The money wasn't
criminal proceeds. It came from deals made by people unfamiliar
with capitalism's rules. Lazarenko wasn't laundering money. He
was protecting it from a rival who would do anything to keep a
Western-minded reformer from impeding his reelection. And
when Lazarenko fled to the United States, Earl and Boersch were
waiting with a case handed to them by Kuchma and reliant on the
testimony of a betrayer—Kiritchenko.

This story of foreign intrigue was no stretch. Testimony was
given in Russian, Ukrainian, Greek, Macedonian, French, and
Dutch. Witnesses testified via videotape recorded at foreign dispo-
sitions that were often not under oath under U.S. law. Tens of
thousands of pages of foreign documents were introduced into evidence.

From their war room, a rented two-level apartment in Opera
Plaza on Van Ness Avenue, Lazarenko and his defense team had

formulated a three-pronged strategy: attack the political roots of the case, attack the worrisome precedent, and attack Peter Kiritchenko. They worked eighteen-hour days, sandwiching five hours in the courtroom with long stretches spent poring over transcripts and motions.

The effort was paying off. Just days into the trial, Earl and Boersch seemed listless, wearied by Weinberg's relentless cross-examinations and, it seemed at times, by their own stultifying task. Earl sat at the foot of the prosecution table, running the computer that displayed exhibits. Boersch and her team of attorneys reviewed transcripts while the videotaped depositions they had taken earlier played on the big screen.

Almost every day Earl and Boersch tangled with the sprawl of the trial. Trials had featured foreign records and witnesses before, but never to the extent this one did. Earl had interviewed potential witnesses during five separate trips to Ukraine, but many simply refused to appear. "If we say to somebody, 'Will you come to the United States?' and they say, 'No,' then we're SOL [shit out of luck]," Earl said, showing uncharacteristic frustration.

Fortunately for the prosecution, its star witness lived on the other side of the Golden Gate Bridge. Three weeks into the trial, the man Lazarenko once called "brother" climbed the steps of the witness box reluctantly. He scanned the packed gallery, nervously avoiding Lazarenko's cold gaze. For the next five days, Kiritchenko dutifully told in Russian the story he had given Earl and Boersch more than four years ago. At times he stumbled into the traps Weinberg set to impeach his credibility, and he even refused to concede that the deals he and Lazarenko did in Ukraine were wrong. But Earl thought the defense failed to turn Kiritchenko into a liar.

"It might have appeared to be begrudging and it probably was, but it was who he is. He didn't pretend to be something he wasn't."

Yet the chinks in the prosecution were growing. Their star witness's penchant for blurting out the unflattering truth came to a head as he described the day after he'd cut his deal with the government, when he was released from prison. Kiritchenko packed his belongings and turned to Lazarenko to say good-bye. He embraced his friend and gave him a kiss on the cheek.

"And you *hugged* him and *kissed* him on the cheek?" Weinberg asked softly during his cross-examination.

"I kissed him. That was a *Judas* kiss!" Kiritchenko burst out in reply.

The crowded courtroom let out a collective gasp. The defense had turned the tide.

THE FINAL WEEK of the prosecution's case was a parade of disappointment. Reticent witnesses had left Earl and Boersch holding a weak hand, and the droning of the videotaped depositions reduced what was initially a capacity crowd to a few hardy souls. It was Dali on downers, the courtroom clock dripping off the wall and into a horizonless tedium.

The coup de grâce came at the hands of a motion to dismiss, written by the silver-maned Riordan. On May 7, Judge Martin J. Jenkins threw out twenty-four of the fifty-three counts in the indictment, coming down hard on the prosecution for overreaching the scope of the limited Ukrainian law that existed at the time. "It is simply inconceivable to try someone for something that wasn't criminal at the time and place it was committed," Jenkins told Boersch.

Lazarenko's victory was imminent. Nearly seven weeks into the trial, Martha Boersch and Bryan Earl appeared ready for the trial to end.

Earl's hopes for a conviction were tied precariously to the tangled paper trail he'd accumulated. The defense, meanwhile, hammered away at Kiritchenko's credibility, their three-pronged strategy narrowed to a single-minded smear campaign. Lazarenko's team trotted out Ukrainian after Ukrainian to testify to the heartfelt friendship between the partners, painting Kiritchenko as a traitor and liar who had every incentive to turn on Lazarenko. In the end, Weinberg argued to the jury, "It all comes down to this: Do you believe Peter Kiritchenko beyond a reasonable doubt?"

The answer came at 11:30 a.m. on Thursday, June 3. After deliberating for about twenty-four hours over four days, the jurors filed into the packed courtroom.

The foreman handed the verdict to a U.S. marshal, who passed it to Judge Jenkins. He examined it without expression and gave it to his courtroom deputy. She stood and read. Guilty. Guilty. Guilty. She said it again and again, twenty-nine times in all. Guilty on all counts and all underlying crimes—the jurors had checked every box on the verdict form.

Lazarenko did not flinch as the verdict was read. When the deputy had finished, he turned to Weinberg and asked, "Where shall I go now?" Weinberg wasn't sure.

THE VERDICT LEFT confusion in its wake. Though Earl, Boersch, and the rest of the prosecution team quietly accepted congratulations from colleagues who had crowded the courtroom to hear the jury's decision, they knew enough to downplay the results. By checking every box on the verdict form, the jurors had affirmed what appeared to be incompatible theories about what crimes had been committed in Ukraine. Their subsequent refusal to talk to anyone, rare in legal circles, left everyone wondering what—beyond exhausted sighs—went on during deliberations. "I don't think this jury had any idea what it was charged with deciding," says Weinberg, and the speed with which the jurors returned the verdict made it hard to disagree. "And I don't think the United States should be able to impose its view [of financial law] on the world."

The defense attorney wasn't alone. The precedent, if upheld, "invites a jury to say, 'This just generally looks sleazy,'" says Robert Weisberg, a Stanford law professor and expert in white-collar law. "It makes prosecutors the moral arbiters of world capitalism."

But Bryan Earl was characteristically clear-eyed in defending what the government had done. "We weren't out fishing; he came to us. And he brought his money, and he brought himself, and he bought a big house and tried to set up his hiding place in the United States," Earl says with sincerity. "That doesn't strike me as us trying to impose our will on somebody else."

In Earl's mind, he was just doing his duty to his country: enforcing the laws on the books, never mind the precedent or the political fallout. But the agent's priorities were back in evidence when Mueller, now head of the FBI, phoned Earl to congratulate him on securing one of the FBI's top convictions ever. Mueller spoke to a colleague of Earl's, complimented their work, and asked to talk to Earl. But the agent was at his daughter's kindergarten graduation, where he'd asked not to be bothered.

Epilogue

Pavel Lazarenko is still under house arrest in a San Francisco apartment; government arguments that he should return to jail were rejected. He will be sentenced this fall and could face as many as fifteen years. Doron Weinberg and Dennis Riordan will have many avenues to appeal the conviction—the appeal will begin in 2006—and are confident they will make him a free man.

Lazarenko's Novato mansion was put on the market for $12 million.

Peter Kiritchenko lives in the $3 million condo he owns in Beverly Hills. He will also be sentenced this fall but, according to the terms of his plea agreement, should face a sentence of no more than thirty-seven months.

The Ukrainian presidential election will take place October 31. President Leonid Kuchma will not run for reelection, but his handpicked successor is expected to square off with a young and popular Western-style reformer. The opposition has promised a revolution if Kuchma does not deliver a fair election.

Martha Boersch announced she was leaving the U.S. attorney's office. She will join the San Francisco offices of Jones Day, where she will specialize in white-collar defense.

U.S. attorney Kevin V. Ryan, a successor of Robert Mueller in San Francisco, vowed to prosecute other "corrupt public officials at home and abroad" using Boersch's legal theory and tougher money-laundering laws passed as part of the Patriot Act.

Bryan Earl still lives in San Francisco and works on the Eurasian Organized Crime Squad but is interested in joining the FBI's international programs to help fellow agents coordinate and assemble similar transnational investigations.

JUSTIN KANE *is now a freelance writer in Washington, D.C. He wrote and reported "To Catch an Oligarch" with the support of the Center for Investigative Reporting, where he was an intern and an associate. His work has also appeared in the* Financial Times, *the* San Francisco Chronicle, *and* Radio Free Europe. *He is a 2002 graduate of Swarthmore College.*

JASON FELCH *wrote and reported this story as fellow at the Center for Investigative Reporting in San Francisco. He has written for the* New York Times Magazine, *the* Washington Post, *and* Legal Affairs. *He is a staff writer at the* Los Angeles Times.

Coda

Shortly after this story was published in October 2004, the dioxin-scarred reformer Viktor Yuschenko rode a wave of popular support to triumph. Pavel Lazarenko watched the Orange Revolution unfold on satellite television from his undisclosed Bay Area apartment where, under house arrest, he still awaits sentencing.

The Western media portrayed the bloodless revolution as the victory of democracy over the thuggish post-Soviet regime of Leonid Kuchma and his lackey Viktor Yanukovych. But there are no angels in Ukraine. Yuschenko's first act as president was to appoint a former Lazarenko crony, Yulia Tymoshenko, as his prime minister.

In the months after the first, fraudulent election, Tymoshenko's movie-star looks and firebrand speeches in Kiev's Independence Square had made her a hero of the Orange Revolution. Yet only nine months earlier, Lazarenko's U.S. prosecutors had cast her as Ukraine's Kenneth Lay. They argued that she had paid Lazarenko an $86 million bribe in exchange for state natural-gas concessions. The deal had made Tymoshenko at least $400 million, with estimates running into the billions, and earned her the moniker *hazova princessa*, "The Gas Princess."

The U.S. charges connected to the bribe were dismissed because no harm to the Ukrainian state could be proved, but there is no denying the two were close partners. During Lazarenko's war with Kuchma, Tymoshenko's capital helped fund Lazarenko's opposition party. When Lazarenko fled Ukraine, she faced the wrath of Kuchma, who opened a corruption probe into her business activities. Allegations of bribery, money laundering, corruption, and abuse of power briefly landed her in jail, though formal charges were never filed. As recently as 2003, Russian officials issued international arrest warrants for her, accusing her of bribing Russian defense ministry officials in the mid-1990s.

Like Lazarenko, Tymoshenko has dismissed the allegations as political moves by a rival bent on her destruction. But even Yuschenko, who first hired her five years ago to help fight corruption in the energy industry, admitted then, "You need a crook to catch a crook."

Today, she is almost equally beloved and despised by Ukrainians, 44 percent of whom backed Yanukovych. To supporters, she is Ukraine's Joan of Arc; to critics, she is the devil in Dolce & Gabbana. Her appointment suggests that, despite the revolution, dismantling Ukraine's entrenched oligarchy—particularly one created by state-sanctioned corruption—will take more than merely dethroning Kuchma.

For Lazarenko, however, Tymoshenko's appointment to the office he once held may be his salvation. As this book went to press, his defense team had submitted a motion for a new trial, arguing that key documents and witnesses suppressed by Kuchma's government during the trial may now be available.

They may be right. In her new role, Tymoshenko will oversee the Ukrainian investigators that once hounded her and Lazarenko. Ukraine's general prosecutor, who provided much of the evidence against Lazarenko, recently said he embraces the arrival of the Orange Revolution and closed an investigation into Tymoshenko days after she was named prime minister.

Lazarenko's attorneys believe that if their client is given a new trial, he almost certainly would go free, aided by the glowing publicity of Ukraine's electoral saga. Instead of the cast of ex-communists who filled the witness box, jurors would see Lazarenko's old allies in a new light, fresh from the victorious battle for democracy.

That may be optimistic, but the story of Pavel Lazarenko isn't over yet.

Bruce Porter

A Long Way
Down

FROM THE *New York Times Magazine*

You could hear the corrections officer jingle his chain and turn his heavy Folger Adam key in the lock before the door swung open and Jay Jones came walking into the visiting room. It's a big space with a lot of chairs but no exterior windows, so Jones had no way of knowing the sun shone brightly outside and high-up clouds were drifting over the grassland west of Oklahoma City. Dressed in forest-green pants and shirt, with white socks and black shoes, he looked more like the guy who comes to fix your dishwasher than an inmate of a federal institution. This was the Transfer Center of the United States Bureau of Prisons, the transportation hub for thousands of state and federal convicts passing through each year on their way from one prison to another. Jones was part of the "cadre," or group of inmates who dish up the meals, cut the grass, and generally keep the facility running. I had last seen him six months before, on June 30, 2003, in an upscale subdivision south of Tulsa where he wished good-bye to his wife and his daughter and his son-in-law standing on the steps of their house. He had changed considerably since then. His ruddy face had acquired the proverbial jailhouse pallor; he was down about twenty pounds, owing to his distaste for prison food. And he wasn't as quick to smile as he had been the previous spring.

Jones, who is sixty-two, was starting a five-year sentence for conspiracy in what amounted to corporate fraud. His former company, Commercial Financial Services, or CFS, had occupied fifty-one floors of the Cityplex Towers on the outskirts of Tulsa, which vied with the Bank of Oklahoma headquarters as the tallest building in the city. Its business involved buying bad credit-card loans from commercial banks, like Chase, Citibank, and MBNA, then chasing down cardholders and getting them to pay the money they owed. The idea was to collect more money than CFS paid the banks for the debt. CFS also bundled the loans into securities and sold these as bonds to raise the cash to buy more accounts. The crime Jones pleaded guilty to involved devising a scheme to make it appear as if the company was doing a better job collecting on the bad loans than it actually was, which would encourage investors to keep buying the bonds. When the truth came out, bond sales evaporated, the company went bankrupt, its four-thousand-odd employees lost their jobs and bondholders were left with more than $1 billion in near-worthless paper.

At his sentencing, Jones stood before the judge in Federal District Court in Tulsa, looking solemn and contrite, and said that he was sorry for what he had done. He apologized to the investors, apologized to his former employees, to the members of his family and to any others whom he had harmed, "either emotionally or financially." And, for sure, there is no argument that Jones was sorry for getting caught. In private moments, however, he betrays a bitterness over his treatment by the government, the veiled conviction that his transgression wasn't serious enough to deserve prison. "I did what I did, and there's a certain punishment that goes along with that; whether I realized it at the moment or not is kind of immaterial," he said a few months before going to jail, speaking in the tight, hurried-up twang characteristic of rural Oklahoma. "I certainly knew it was nefarious, a little wormy, unethical, make no mistake about that. But criminal? Whether I thought that or not, I can't remember; but I was certainly willing to take the risk. Fraud? Honestly, the first time I ever looked at that squarely in the face, in that light, was when the government brought it up. Here, it seemed like I was being a good soldier, saving the company. But when I was talking to the government about that, they said, 'No, you did it because of greed.' They said, 'No, you continued the deception, the fraud, to be able to continue selling the securitizations.' "

What happened to Jones and CFS received little play outside Tulsa and the financial trade press, but this kind of story has certainly become a familiar narrative on the American business scene. Bright prospect starts off in career, works hard to build successful enterprise, then one day, as if contracting a moral virus, turns from solid corporate citizen into closet criminal. And the startling thing about it is that until that news photo showing him being led away by federal marshals, the telltale overcoat draped over his handcuffs, not even the people who counted themselves as his most intimate acquaintances would have suspected a thing. Some of these defendants, of course, are coldblooded criminals underneath—psychopaths with MBAs. "As a white-collar criminal-defense lawyer, you occasionally meet people who just spend their lives going from one fraud to another and essentially rip people off whenever they can and don't care how many people they hurt," says Benjamin Brafman, a defense lawyer in Manhattan whose client list has ranged from doctors, lawyers, and corporate executives to Michael Jackson and associates of the Gambino crime family of Brooklyn. Other kinds of business-class fraudsters, he says, become so successful and powerful that they can't imagine that the laws applying to others are also meant for them. "I've met people in different professions who are simply stunned by the suggestions that they are subject to prosecution, that they could end up in jail and the government would have the temerity to take them on."

In most of the cases he has handled, though, neither of the

characterizations apply: "It's my experience that the preponderance of individuals caught up in criminal investigations in the white-collar arena are not what people would call evil. They do not get up that morning and decide, Today I'm going to commit a crime. Most of these are normal people who end up just getting caught in something that spins out of control."

As a rule, he has noticed, the more unassailable a person's background, the harder it is for him to take the fall. The boiler-room shark, the Mafia interloper in the business world—they seem capable of accepting punishment as just a disagreeable cost of doing business. But, Brafman says, "when a person with an impeccable history, with no prior experience in the criminal-justice system, suddenly finds himself under investigation or under indictment, his world completely collapses around him. It's much worse than being told you have a terminal illness, because when you're told you have a terminal illness, everyone who loves you rallies around you, and all of your friends and family offer support and compassion and help because they recognize they might soon lose you. But if you're suddenly indicted, you're a pariah. You bring embarrassment and shame into your home and into your extended family. You lose your business; you lose your money; you have the possibility of going to prison. The life support you counted on for your entire existence begins to disappear. It's a terrible, terrible thing. I've seen middle-aged people in my office grow old in front of my eyes. And I don't think anyone ever recovers from the experience."

I met Jay Jones in late January 2003, several months before he had to report to prison, and that winter and into the spring we spent a lot of time talking and driving around rural Oklahoma in his 1975 powder blue Cadillac Deville. He liked the Deville for the wide expanse it gave him behind the wheel, and we drove in it to visit some of the mile-markers in his life—down to Shawnee, where he and his wife, Jennifer, began their marriage; to Muskogee, where he had started up the company with his business partner, Bill Bartmann. The driving helped distract him from thinking about what lay ahead. Trying to be helpful, a friend had given him a handbook called *Down Time: A Guide to Federal Incarceration*, written by an ex-inmate who counsels white-collar defendants. It told about a $175 monthly spending limit at the commissary, the three hundred monthly phone minutes and the rules on visitation. But it said little to ease the anxieties that ranked uppermost in Jones's mind. He had seen the prison movies. Would the guards down there be nasty to him? What about the other inmates? Would he be safe?

One morning we headed up to Blackwell, in the wheat-growing area near the Kansas line, where Jones spent his boyhood and where he hadn't visited in several decades. A thick wet snow was falling, so you couldn't tell where prairie left off and sky began. Blackwell loomed in the distance by virtue of its grain elevators shooting up at the south end of town. Driving onto Main Street, Jones was taken by how many of the old brick-front stores had gone out of business or had been replaced by curio shops offering up relics of the town's past. No more Sears, no more JC Penney. "A single Wal-Mart can pretty much clean out half of one of these little towns," he said. Jones came from humble origins and started out in the workaday world while still in his teens. His father spent most of his adult life as a route man for Wilson foods, taking meat orders from small-town butchers. He died of a heart attack at age fifty-seven while fixing up the camper truck he planned to take on fishing trips during retirement. To earn extra money, the whole family would go out on weekends picking pecans at local orchards. Jones's younger brother, Joe, about half his size, climbed up to shake down the nuts so the others could scrabble for them on the ground. Unlike his straight-arrow brother, Jay admits to taking a few financial shortcuts as a boy—stealing change out of the newspaper racks on Main Street, charging a carton of cigarettes at the corner store supposedly for his mother, then selling them to his friends. "Jay was more the adventurous one, more willing to go the route, take the risk," said Joe, now a preacher who teaches physical education at a college in Lawton,

Oklahoma. "I was more 'One in the hand is worth two in the bush.' His was 'Let's shake the bush and see what comes out.'"

Their boyhood differences persisted into later life. "Our folks grew up in the Depression and raised both of us that the object of life was to find a big company, a stable environment, find something that is solid and stay with it," said Jay, whose cheerful, jokey personality tends to mask the real thoughts churning around in his head. "Joe pretty much has done that, and I did for a long time, too, worked for Wilson foods for thirteen years and had a pretty decent job. But I just came to the conclusion one day that people who did well financially were those who had their own business, and I figured if I was ever going to do anything, I'd better get on with it. And so I did, and it's been a roller coaster ever since."

After failing at several different ventures, Jones ran into Bartmann, a lawyer who had moved to Oklahoma from Des Moines and had gone bankrupt selling oil pipes. Together they started CFS in 1986 and in the next decade made it into a huge financial success. In addition to his regular salary of $1 million—and that was tax free, since every April the company also covered whatever he owed the IRS—Jones took an annual distribution from company profits to the tune of several millions more. And since CFS was a partnership and Jones owned 20 percent of the company, on paper his net worth added up to between $500 million and $1 billion.

In those months before prison, when he wasn't sleeping well and his eyes would blink open at two or three in the morning, Jones would sometimes kill the time until dawn by taking a sorry inventory of the material riches in his life that were now lost. He would think about the $5 million, fourteen-thousand-square-foot dream house that he and his wife had started building south of Tulsa. As conceived, it had granite walls and huge gables, a main staircase inspired by the one in Tara from *Gone with the Wind* and two artificial ponds connected by a waterfall. To people driving past, it would have looked as if someone had managed to airlift in a full-blown château from one of the wine regions of France. It didn't look that way at the moment, to be sure. Right then it sat forlornly in a field of mud, its siding wrapped in tar paper and its windows open to the rain and the snow. Around it was a chain-link fence with a big padlock on the gate and a sign advising people that the U.S. government had a lien on the property.

He also thought about those trips in the company's $25 million, fifteen-passenger Gulfstream G-IV, which he ordered up for spur-of-the-moment vacations for his wife and two grown daughters and their husbands and two or three other couples as well. Fly to Paris and the Caribbean, to Bulls games in Chicago, front-row-center seats, put it all on the company tab as a business expense. Give all that money to the government, it would only waste it. Most frequently, he and Jennifer flew to Las Vegas, where they both gambled heavily. Jones's game of choice was craps, and he could easily drop $30,000 in a weekend. Her husband playing craps is a picture that Jennifer still keeps in her head; she loved the way he would try to make a point, bent out over the table, his fist shaking with the dice and a foot flailing loose in the air. "I find it hard to describe what it was like," Jones said about being so suddenly so rich. "It was the realization when you walked into a store, no matter what kind of store it was, not that you could just buy anything you wanted but that you could buy the whole store! It was a feeling, I don't know if 'power' is the right word. More, I'd say, 'awe.'"

Another thing feeding on his mind those nights was how he might have provided his life story with a more positive ending. Aside from the criminality involved, the downfall of CFS had its roots in the company's very success. In the late nineties it grew so fast—from fewer than two hundred employees in 1995 to twenty times that number just three years later—that it lost the personal touch on the telephone that had produced such a high rate of return. Back in the early days when he and Bartmann were calling debtors, they developed a patter that was "sweet as peaches," Jones recalled. "First you get into their minds, let them know you're there and you're not going away. Then you get into their hearts, create a friend: 'I'm here to help you, not hurt you, harass you. We don't want to see you suffer. I been there myself; I know how it feels.' Then, after you get into their minds and their hearts, you get into their pocketbooks."

The ability CFS developed to wheedle money out of former deadbeats had generated an A rating for the bonds it sold to investors. That meant more money so CFS could buy more loans. But with collections beginning to flag in early 1997, it needed the bond money even more, not only for new loans but also to pay the interest and principal on previous bond issues that could no longer be covered by loan collections. In essence, CFS embarked on a garden-variety Ponzi scheme, borrowing hundreds of millions from new investors to pay off old ones, hoping somehow that collections would pick up in time to cover the difference. As a stopgap measure, CFS started selling off some of its loans to a firm in Chicago to make it appear to investors that its collectors were still reaching their monthly goals. That September, however, the Chicago company announced that it would buy no more loans, and CFS suddenly faced disaster.

What happened next is the thing Jones now regards with deepest regret. Although he founded the company with Bartmann, his main task as vice president had been to devise the computer program that rated the collectability of the loans; once that was done, he largely stayed on the sidelines, came into work when he wanted, practiced his guitar in the office. He recalled: "Here I am, sitting out there, fat and happy. I've got millions in the bank and many more millions in the company, and a gazillion dollars as far as net worth, I mean cash, unencumbered. When I was worrying about the cost of the house we were planning, the accountants told me, 'You fool, you're worth so much money you don't have to worry!'

"So in late September of ninety-seven, somehow I became aware the Chicago company is not going to buy any loans this month. Bill had this amazing ability to convince you to do something before you—I have a hard time describing this—but he could in some manner plant a thought in your mind to make it your idea before he proposed the idea or even brought it up. He's a great thinker, and somehow I became aware we are not going to reach our goals in September, and if we don't, I thought at the time, in all probability it's going to destroy our bond rating. So I said, 'Hell, I got the money in the bank, I'll buy 'em.' And Bill says, 'You can't do that, you're an insider.' And I said, 'What if I find somebody to do it for me?' And he said, 'Maybe.' " (Bartmann's attorney did not return calls.)

That very day, Jones recalls, he phoned a lawyer friend down in Shawnee and got him to set up a straw corporation called Dimat, into which Jones fed money from his share of CFS profits so that the company could begin purchasing loans from CFS as a replacement for the firm in Chicago. The scheme provided camouflage for a year, to the tune of $63 million in bogus loan purchases. Then in October 1998, an anonymous letter arrived at Standard and Poor's, one of the rating firms that had been giving CFS bonds their A rating. The letter revealed that Dimat was really a sham corporation and that all its "purchases" of CFS loans were a ruse, paid for by money from CFS itself, to give investors a false picture of the company's financial health. Virtually instantly, the market for CFS bonds dried up; with no cash coming in, the company defaulted on payments to previous bondholders. Bankruptcy ensued, and by the following July, CFS was no more.

Needless to say, this was not the way Jones thought things would turn out. In his mind, the Dimat scheme was only a temporary arrangement, to give CFS managers time to get collections up to their previously high level. "The choice was certainly mine, whether I fully realized it or not at the time," Jones told me. "That first time, when it started, the company wasn't in that bad trouble. But as it got further, I should have recognized that if we'd quit after the first two times, if we did that, there would still have been no harm, no foul. We could have simply said, 'Guys, we've missed the projections here.' We could have said, 'We're going home, and you've got to figure out what to do.' I wouldn't have liked that, it wouldn't have been great for investors, but certainly there would have been no criminal activity."

A blizzard of investor suits rained down on Jones and Bartmann—as well as its white-shoe law firm, Mayer Brown and Platt in Chicago, which had advised CFS on how to sell bonds based on nothing but deadbeat debt, and also Chase Securities, which had vouched for and sold many of those bonds. The workings of the fraud, however, proved so complicated that it took the U.S. attorney's office in Tulsa three more years, until the end of 2002, to sort things out. At that point, Bartmann—who owned 80 percent of the company and insisted that he knew nothing about the Dimat scam, that it was Jones's idea alone—was indicted on fifty-eight counts, including conspiracy, bank fraud, mail fraud, wire fraud, and money laundering, all of which added up to a possible seven hundred years in prison. Jones, on the other hand, was allowed to plead guilty to a single count of conspiracy as part of his agreement to testify against Bartmann, whose trial was set for the fall of 2003.

In Jones's mind, it was Bartmann's fault anyway that the company had ended up selling more bonds than it had the capacity to pay off. A take-no-prisoners entrepreneur and a mesmerizing salesman, Bartmann harbored a streak of grandiosity remarkable even given the brash and bold style of Oklahoma's business world. On out-of-town trips, he traveled with an entourage of armed security men who talked in code words over Secret Service–style radiophones. And for one company outing, he chartered a fleet of Boeing 747s to fly some three thousand CFS employees and their spouses to Las Vegas for the weekend, gave them each $500 to spend at the tables, and then strode onstage for a pep rally at the Thomas and Mack arena dressed as Julius Caesar. "Instead of selling a bond issue for, say, $200 million, if we had sold it for $100 million, the company would still have prospered and grown, not as dynamically, but the collection goals would have been achievable," Jones said. "But 'Nooo, we can't do that.' Bartmann had bought and sold stuff his whole life, and if he could sell something for ten, you'd be a fool to take five. My former partner, if I had to describe him in three or four words, it would be, 'He always tended to take a bridge too far.'"

If Bartmann was the one who steered the company into choppy water, it was Jones who proposed breaking the law to get it out, an action the government insisted came out of pure avarice. When it comes to looking out for himself, Jones seems to allow a degree of moral wiggle. After he had to stop construction of his dream house, he bought a Gothic stone structure in South Tulsa for $750,000 in cash and then put it in his wife's name. Should any of those angry investors persist in coming after him for recompense after he gets out of prison, he also shielded himself by making Jennifer go through a divorce of convenience last spring and asked the judge to set alimony at $7,500 a month. If a court ruled that the alimony took precedence over Jones's enormous debts, the first $7,500 he might someday make each month could effectively be his.

His daughter Holly, thirty-six, a graduate of Oklahoma State University who for a while worked as a midlevel manager at CFS, says that she thinks there was also a psychological dimension to why her father did what he did, something deeper than avarice. "What he did was totally plausible to me," said Holly, who lives in Dallas with her husband and who gave birth to Jones's first grand-daughter shortly after he went to prison. "I had seen some of the fights Dad and Bill had had. Dad ended up doing nothing. They excluded him from everything, future planning. He sat there and watched TV and played his guitar. As humble as he is, he's just like any other person who likes to think he's important. I can see my dad would do this for Bill by virtue of the fact that here was his chance to say: 'Hey, I'm doing something. I'm making a difference. I'm helping to save the company.'"

Maybe some of that's true. But Jones also admits that along with saving the company, he had this other idea of taking over those $63 million in CFS loans himself—the ones that he had bought surreptitiously through Dimat—and setting up a junior version of CFS in Nevada as his own company, handy to the gambling casinos.

He even formed a shell corporation for this purpose called Card Services of Nevada. "The plan was that I'd leave CFS, and it pretty much stayed as that throughout the whole period. Then one day that anonymous letter bubbles up."

Winter passed into spring, a lushly green period in eastern Oklahoma, and Jones was trying to keep himself busy. He bought a smoker, which he used for practice in barbecuing great slabs of meat, thinking that maybe he would open a rib-and-country-music place after he got out of prison. He also worked on a list of things he had long wanted to do but had never found the time for—seeing the Chicago Cubs play at Wrigley Field, taking a rafting trip down the Snake River in Idaho. Jennifer, meanwhile, often sat alone at home, not holding up so well. For one thing, she had acquired a bad case of paranoia, imagining that out of anger over her husband's coming testimony, Bartmann was devising ways to harm the Jones family. She feared that people hired by Bartmann were following her while she was out on shopping trips. Returning home, she was sure a Bartmann intruder had been in the house and had moved things around in the kitchen to frighten her. Her doctor put her on Klonopin and Paxil, and she took Ambien so she could sleep. She was also drinking more than her daughters thought was useful, and she began to see a psychotherapist. "I'm still feeling numb, so I can't tell sometimes if I have any feelings at all," she said. "Dr. Ferraro says I need to make more concrete plans about what my life is going to be like after Jay's gone. He says, 'What I want you to do for us is to think of ways you're going to live.' But sometimes I just get to crying—like I missed an appointment with Dr. Ferraro because all I did that day was I didn't get out of bed, just spent the day crying."

Whatever its ups and downs, her married life ranked as a definite improvement over what she had been through as a child growing up in Shawnee. The family lived next door to the Sinclair filling station run by her father, who was a fearsome drinker and a womanizer and had wreaked havoc on the family, right until he committed suicide in his garage via carbon monoxide fumes. A brother she had been close to died in an automobile accident; her sister was murdered by her husband with a shotgun. At the end, her family had dwindled down to just her mother and her. "I went from my mother's house when I was eighteen to marry Jay Jones, and I have never been alone my whole life," she said that spring. "I don't want to live in this house by myself. It's just so big, and I'm terrified of being alone. There are so many places for people to hide."

Along with her fears of being alone, Jennifer nurses a deep and growing anger at her husband—not quite so much for how he wrecked their lives as for not telling her about his crime until the day after he made his plea bargain with the government and knew he was going to prison. "When this first unfolded for me, I didn't understand a lot about what happened, because I couldn't really understand what CFS did in the first place," said Jennifer, who talks in a little-girl voice that is sometimes hard to hear. The three of us sat in their family room. Forsythia bloomed all over their yard, and Miss Celie, their fluffy Maltese, pranced around the inch-thick white carpet in front of a giant TV set. "Really, I don't know what you did, Jay," she said, gazing at her husband across the room. "If I had to tell people what my husband did for a living, this is what I would say: he bought loans at a certain percentage and sold them for more. That's all I could tell you. And Jay did not tell me about what happened until the night before he had an appointment with his lawyer, who was going to tell me about it the next day. But somehow Jay blurted it out that night, that he was in trouble. He told me the details, but all I can remember taking from that is he did something wrong. I always told him, when he went with Bill Bartmann: 'You've got to tell me. I've got to be in on the decisions.' And he never told me, because if he had told me, if anything had been suggested that was improper, in any way, I would have said, 'No!' I really believe that's why I was always left out. Of everything. I know it was the reason."

After his case hit the front page of the *Tulsa World*, Jay more or less went directly to ground. He stopped attending services, for instance, at the Harvard Avenue Christian Church, a modern brick edifice where his younger daughter, Terri, taught preschool and where he usually sat front and center with his wife on Sundays, singing loud enough for everyone to distinguish his voice. "It's kind of like someone dies," he said. "What do you say? 'Sorry for your loss'? I just didn't want the people I would come into contact with to have to come up with some kind of statement like that."

His minister, the Rev. Stephen Wallace, was one of the few people the U.S. attorney allowed Jones to talk to about details of his plea bargain, and Jones went to see him right after he knew it was all going to be made public. "Mainly what I did was listen and ask, How can we be helpful to Jennifer and the daughters?" Wallace told me. The Jones family was also on the church's "telecare" list, which meant they would get called every now and then to see if they wanted a prayer said for them in absentia. Jones wasn't his first congregant to run afoul of the law by any means, but Wallace found this sort of counseling somewhat challenging. "How do you show mercy on the one hand—'You're a cared-for person; you're an important person in God's eyes; God sees us all as precious'—but at the same time say that what they did was wrong, it was hurtful to a lot of people? Sometimes people are willing to accept that kind of thing and sometimes not. They say, 'I didn't do anything,' and a lot of times you don't know what really did happen. But since Jay's consistently said, 'I messed up here,' it made it easier. We could move on to a message of forgiveness and grace and then repentance."

As the reporting date closed in, Jay and Jennifer began to peel away their early hopes that some kind of miracle would keep him from going away. On May 9 of last year, when the federal judge put his imprimatur on the sentencing deal, Jennifer relinquished her illusion that maybe he would get some sort of house-arrest arrangement. Quite to the contrary, she learned, unlike the state variety, federal sentences are served in full, with no possibility of parole.

The most Jones could hope for was a 15 percent reduction for good behavior, which meant the earliest he would be out was the end of September 2007. In a letter sent to his lawyer, Jones's doctor tried to get him special consideration, saying he was deeply concerned about what prison might do to his health. He had suffered two heart attacks, after all, in 1986 and 1998, the last around the time he learned of the anonymous letter to the rating agencies, and was taking three different medications for high blood pressure. Jones's lawyer, Robert Nigh, a former public defender who represented Timothy McVeigh in the unsuccessful appeal of his death sentence, recommended against sending the letter on to the Bureau of Prisons. Their likely response would be to assign Jones to a special medical facility out of state, which would make family visits difficult.

Neither was Jones getting any comfort from his prison handbook, which suggested that his agreement to testify for the government at the Bartmann trial in September would not exactly endear him to the other inmates. "The only—I guess 'disturbing' would be the right word—thing out of the whole book that I saw would be, and it's just something I'll have to deal with, I guess, is they don't like rats," he said early in June as we drove the Deville down to check out a barbecue place outside of Shawnee. "One thing the author seems to focus on is keep to yourself, mind your own business, leave everything alone and don't rat anyone out, which is understandable. But I guess I'll just have to risk that, and I could justify that by saying I guess I'd rather get the [expletive] beat out of me four or five times than I would spending another fifteen or twenty years in jail."

On Friday, June 27, with just three more days to go before prison, Jones announced that he would like to put on his special electric blue Porter Wagoner suit and his high-crown white cowboy hat—his Tom Mix hat, he calls it—and drive up to play country music that night in Chelsea, fifty miles north of Tulsa. Jones has played the guitar ever since he was a boy, mostly songs from the fifties and sixties dealing with loss, heartbreak and premature death of girlfriends and close relatives. His suit had been tailor-made by the famous Manuel of Nashville, sewn with thousands of sequins in a gambling motif, with cards and dice and dollar signs. It cost $10,000 and was in the style of the one Manuel had made for Wagoner to wear at Grand Ole Opry shows. He had worn it only three or four times since he bought it in 1997, which was obvious that night from the difficulty he had buckling his trousers.

Jones would play country music anywhere they allowed him to, but he particularly liked going up to Chelsea because hardly anyone knew him there. The gig was at the civic center near the Burlington Northern railroad tracks, where every Friday night thirty or forty farm couples, many in their seventies and eighties, gather for potluck supper and to push and pull one another around the dance floor. Jones usually plays backup rhythm, but this time he stepped up to the mike to employ his thin, reedy voice in service of a bluegrass song that started off "There's a cabin in the pines in the hills of Caroline/and a blue-eyed girl is waiting there for me." During a smoking break outside, he took some ribbing about how Porter Wagoner must be missing his suit by now, when the lead guitarist in the group, who hits more than seven feet in his boots and cowboy hat, slipped Jones a piece of paper with his name and address on it and said quietly, out of anyone's hearing, "You write me a letter, and I'll write ya' back."

June 30 started with a blinding rainstorm that for half an hour forced cars on the freeways encircling Tulsa to pull off to the side. Jennifer had taken two Ambiens the night before, but still didn't manage to sleep. Jones was awakened at 4:00 a.m. by the cat pouncing on his chest. The prison wanted him there by noon, and I volunteered to drive him the two hours down to Oklahoma City because friends had advised it would be too wrenching for the family to drop Jones off. Holly wasn't there because the doctor said that she was too close to her delivery date to travel up from Dallas. Jay's younger daughter Terri, twenty-nine, arrived with her husband, Jay Q., and a dozen Krispy Kreme doughnuts, while Jones attended to a list of last things to do. Yes, he fitted a fresh propane tank onto the cooker out on the deck. Yes, he canceled his cell phone, and he told Jennifer where to go in case of a tornado. Get down into that little closet in the basement, where she keeps Miss Celie's dog food, he says. The whole house can blow away, and that room will still be standing.

Terri started reading out of the prison manual. "Daddy, it says to take your eyeglasses and a lot of change for the vending machine."

"Sweetheart, they don't let you have money."

"Yes, they do, and you can take your wedding ring and—" Jennifer cut in to tell him not to forget his medicine.

"Mom, I don't know if you can take your medicine," Terri said. This made Jennifer start to cry.

"He has to take his medicine."

"No, he can take his eyeglasses, he can take his Bible or a religious medal and he can take his wedding ring, as long as it doesn't have any stones, and that's it."

As it neared 9 a.m., Jones wanted to get going, get it over with. He hates good-byes. "Jennifer, if it comes down to it, and you have a choice to make between taking the advice of some psychologist or your daughters, take your daughters' advice. They know you better."

Jennifer wasn't hearing much because she was sobbing uncontrollably. "Oh, Jay," she said. "You know, this is the first time I haven't had to pack for you when you're going somewhere."

They hugged for two or three minutes at the front door, and then Jones broke off and got in the car and waved.

HOME FOR JONES now is an eight-foot-by-fourteen-foot room in F pod on the seventh floor of the Transfer Center, a newly constructed high-rise near the Will Rogers World Airport. It has orange brick walls and tall slit windows, eight inches wide, that from a distance look like the loopholes in a medieval castle. He sleeps in the top bunk and shares a toilet and writing desk with his cellmate, a fifty-six-year-old white-collar offender also from Tulsa. (Following the advice in his handbook, Jones doesn't want to say what crime he committed.) Like Jones, permanent members of the service cadre are doing time mostly for nonviolent offenses—parole violators on drug charges, counterfeiters, child pornographers—and no fighting is tolerated. The only major fight on Jones's pod so far occurred one morning when he was awakened by two inmates trading blows just outside his door, spattering blood all over the day-room floor. From what Jones heard, it was over a piece of chicken smuggled in from the kitchen. Both men were taken immediately to the special housing unit, or "hole," and shortly thereafter transferred to a higher-level institution.

For a time, Jones's job was in the prison library, where he photocopied pages for inmates' law cases and wheeled around the book cart. He regarded it as the highlight of his day, taken up otherwise by watching TV and playing endless rounds of bridge and pinochle with three of the older inmates. Recently, he was reassigned as an orderly on the "smoke deck," an outdoor area covered with razor wire where he picks up butts and wipes down tables. His family sends him books, but he never got much pleasure out of reading. "Weekends are the hardest because of the utter boredom," he says. "You don't work, but you get up at the same time because you can only sleep for so long, and then there's nothing to do."

His spirits rose considerably last August when the chaplain issued him an old guitar to practice with in his room so he could play along with the hymns during the Thursday and Sunday services. He lost the guitar, though, when he was transferred to the Tulsa County Jail for the Bartmann trial and it was given to someone else. Adding to his disappointment was the fact that unlike Jones, Bartmann ended up getting off without any punishment. The government put up fifty-three witnesses and spent thirty-eight trial days laying out its case, but besides what Jones had to say, its evidence was all circumstantial. After a week of deliberation, the jury decided that the U.S. attorney had not proved beyond a reasonable doubt that Bartmann knew anything about the Dimat scam. They voted to acquit.

Jones's testimony for the government was covered heavily in the Tulsa paper, which meant it got all over the prison. A few of the inmates now snub him in the cafeteria. But not many, he says. "The rat issue is one that doesn't bother me," he says. "There is a certain population, very small, maybe ten percent, that that would bother. But the people who have a problem with it are generally not the people I would care very much about anyway."

Jones's visits from family members—spread among Jennifer and his daughters and his brother Joe, they average one every weekend—also come with a certain amount of discomfort. Depending on the guard's mood of the day, Jones may or may not be required to strip naked after the visit and bend over in a duck squat so that anything secreted in his anal cavity would drop out onto the floor. The one plus side of prison is that he is now getting a full night's sleep, "better than I have for four years," he says. "After all, I've got no worries anymore. The only worries you have are the ones you create, and it's hard to create one in here. It's a very controlled, very organized environment. Anticipation of the unknown was a factor before, and now that that's been realized, there's nothing left. It is what it is, and you learn to live with it."

As for Jennifer, to the general surprise of her family, she seems to be doing just fine. "I've enjoyed myself, going to movies, out to dinner," she said last December, as Miss Celie still pranced about on the plush carpet. Outside there was a for-sale sign on the lawn, and Jennifer had been looking for a smaller place near Holly's in Dallas. "I wondered what it would be like, being without a man, but it's kind of fun," she said. "Do you know every strong relationship that I had with another woman Jay has always made fun of?" She now sees Dr. Ferraro only every other Thursday and misses no more appointments because she is in bed crying. "Right now we're going through my hate for my husband," she said. "I love him, but I get so mad at him—thinking what he did just boggles my mind sometimes. Dr. Ferraro suggested that when the time is right I write Jay a letter and tell him how I feel. Sometimes when I go see him, I want to tell him: 'Yes, it's hugs and kisses and love right here, but I can't tell you how I feel in front of the inmate population and the guards. Sometime we've got to discuss that.'

"This is a big and brand-new experience for me. I don't have as much animosity toward Bill as I did. When you get down to it, Jay has to accept responsibility for his actions, and he can't blame it on somebody else. He says, 'I'm sorry; I don't know why I did it.' He can say that all he wants, but I think he thinks everything is hunky-dory, which it isn't. You know I love him, and I'm not going to leave him. It's just that saying 'I'm sorry' sometimes is not enough."

BRUCE PORTER *is the author of* Blow, *a story about the rise and fall of a cocaine smuggler that was made into the movie starring Johnny Depp and Penelope Cruz. He writes frequently about guns, drugs, and prisons for the* New York Times Magazine *and on different subjects for* Gourmet *and other magazines. He teaches at the Columbia University Graduate School of Journalism, where he is special assistant to the dean, and he lives with his wife and daughter in the Cobble Hill section of Brooklyn.*

Coda

My editor thought that hanging out with a corporate miscreant in the months before he goes off to prison would make for a good story, and one that no one had written yet. The reason no one had, as I quickly found out, was that none of these guys would talk to a journalist. Lawyers warned their clients that for an executive to talk openly about his crime would not sit well with his soon-to-be fellow inmates. And their wives and children had faced humiliation enough at school and the country club to now have the story spread all over the *New York Times Magazine*.

Then one day in January 2003, I got a call from Jay Jones down in Tulsa, Oklahoma. He'd heard I was looking for a corporate

crook to follow and said that he might fill the bill, in that he'd perpetrated a fraud at his company that had cost investors more than
$1 billion. The story had been all over local papers, so he had noth-
ing left to hide. And it was six months before he had to report to
the Federal prison in Oklahoma City to begin his five-year stretch.
Being gregarious, as well as the sort who couldn't abide sitting
around doing nothing, he felt that talking to me might at least do to
fill up his remaining time.

When he picked me up at the Tulsa airport in his 1975 Cadillac
Deville, I knew right away we'd get along fine, one old-car freak to
another. So for two or three days every month, I'd fly down and we'd
drive that Deville around rural Oklahoma, visiting the little towns
where he had spent a threadbare childhood. We'd eat at out-of-the-
way barbecue places, and Jay would fantasize that after finishing his
sentence—he'd be sixty-seven by then—he was going to open up a
rib joint of his own, talked about a special rub he thought might
bring in the crowd. And he played country guitar at Friday night
dances, where I'd push old ladies around the floor as Jay sang win-
some songs in his high-pitched voice about the simple life that had
long disappeared.

I also drove Jay down to the prison on the final day, his wife and
two grown daughters having been advised that wishing good-bye at
the gates would be too filled with pain. The last I saw him was
when the correction officer rolled open the chain-link fence at the
inmate entrance and put his hand on Jay's arm and said to me, "You
can go now, sir," and they disappeared behind the walls.

A little while ago I got word from Jay's daughter Holly that he's
getting along okay, except for the bland food and the tremendous
lack of activity. And recently they gave him back the prison guitar
for accompanying the hymns sung at weekly chapel services. The
deal was he could keep the instrument in his cell to practice on;
and, if sound could travel all the way up to New York City, I'm sure
right now that, along with the church music, I'd be hearing him
sneaking in a few of those sad songs about the days gone by.

Jeff Tietz

FINE
DISTURBANCES

FROM *The New Yorker*

UNITED STATES BORDER PATROL operations above the Texas stretch of the Rio Grande often begin with a single tracker on foot, staring at the earth. In the Border Patrol, tracking is called cutting sign. "Cutting" is looking; "sign" is evidence. No technology is involved. Trackers look for tread designs printed in the soil and any incidental turbulence from a footfall or moving body. They notice the scuff insignia of milling hesitation at a fence and the sudden absence of spiderwebs between mesquite branches and the lugubrious residue of leaked moisture at the base of broken cactus spines. (The dry time is a stopwatch.) The best trackers know whether scatterings of limestone pebbles have come off human feet or deer hooves. They particularly value shininess—a foot compresses the earth in one direction, which makes it shine, and wind quickly unsettles this uniformity, so high-shining groups are irresistible.

Low-light cameras and night-vision goggles and thermal-imaging scopes and seismic sensors are useful along the river, but in the brushland north of it pretty much the only thing to do is follow illegal immigrants on foot. Nearly every southern Border Patrol station maintains a network of footprint traps called drags—twelve-foot-wide swaths of dirt that are combed every day with bolted-together tractor tires ball-hitched to the back of an SUV. Agents monitor drags endlessly and follow foreign prints into the brush.

One morning just after dawn, I was out with an agent named Mike McCarson. He was driving a customized Ford F-250 down a ranch road, cutting a drag that ran alongside it. The Rio Grande was close; the sky was unusually congested. The drag and the ranch road extended out of sight through mesquite and prickly-pear cactus and purple sage and huisache and whitehorn, all semiaridly dwarfish: the horizon was visible everywhere. Driving about eight mph, McCarson leaned out the window a bit, his hinged sideview mirror folded flush with the door.

McCarson is forty-three; he has been tracking illegal immigrants for eighteen years. He works out of the Border Patrol's Brackett-ville station, which is about twenty miles northeast of the Rio Grande and thirty miles east of the town of Del Rio. Brackettville's hundred and twenty agents are responsible for a twenty-five-hundred-square-mile rectangle of mesquite flat and limestone breaks. No more than forty agents are ever in the field at once—one per ninety square miles.

Federal guidelines recommend that undocumented aliens be apprehended at least five times before they're charged with illegal entry and held for trial, but Brackettville's agents rarely detain people unless they've been caught more than fifteen times. On any given trip, an illegal immigrant's odds of eluding Brackettville's defenses are extremely good. Immigrants can angle in from anywhere along a fifty-mile stretch of the Rio Grande, and overpowering numbers of people often cross the river simultaneously. Brackettville doesn't have the personnel to track more than five groups at once.

"It's just the luck of the draw which ones we chase," McCarson told me as we drove. "We generally don't even work groups as small as three, four people, or groups that happen to have crossed real early the night before."

I spent many days with McCarson, cutting drags and trails and meandering through mesquite in the F-250. He is a big, sauntering, freewheelingly mouthy guy who says "tars" for "towers" and "BOO-COO" for "beaucoup," a word he uses a lot, sometimes as a noun ("There's boo-coos of trails through there"). McCarson instinctively registers the happenstance, ambient comedy of ordinary life, sometimes with a falsetto, arc-of-joy cackle. He likes to stop for lunch on hillsides and in old Seminole cemeteries, and he can be precipitately melodramatic. ("Now, the seasoned journeyman agent will see the totality of circumstances in his area and know precisely what's normal activity and what's not.") McCarson is married but doesn't have kids, which may partly explain his widely entrepreneurial imagination: he owns a scuba business on Lake Amistad; he's a partner in a San Angelo real-estate venture; he's a successful self-taught stock picker.

On the drag, we were seeing a lot of overlapping cloven-hoof sign, like combinations of the alphabet's last four letters. Agents have found sign of people crawling across drags on their hands and knees (long, chutelike impressions), and sign of people tiptoeing across drags (shoe-tip abbreviations), and sign of people walking across drags backward in socks (blunted images, kicked soil revealing the true direction of travel). Someone once walked across a drag on his hands (profound, torqued handprints); the man was followed from the drag to a railroad siding, where the prints transformed themselves into elongate gouges in the embankment stones: running hard, he'd jumped a freight. Sometimes, illegal immigrants will survey drags until they find a particularly rocky stretch and cross there, stepping only on stable rocks, as if they were fording a stream. If yielding terrain frames the rocks, they leave almost no sign.

Ideally, a tracker will find fresh prints on a drag, follow them until he can establish a line of travel, and radio in the group's drag coordinates, its heading, and its tread profile. Then another agent will cut the group on a drag some miles north or northeast—all the sheltering towns and safe houses and freight tracks and pickup points lie that way—and either catch it or radio in a revised line, allowing a third agent to leap up to the group. In practice, it's often impossible to categorically identify a group, establish a line, or get a forward cut.

Because the surest way to identify a group is by its distinct assembly of tread patterns, trackers use a lexicon of soles: super chevron, racetrack, wishbone eight ball, propeller, Tetris, basket weave, Kmart special, rifle sights, Flintstones, hourglass, running W, matchstick. When I was out with McCarson, the radio regularly issued sole descriptions: a "diamond-within-a-diamond heel with an instep logo," an "island running W with a slash in the middle and a fine line," a "beetle pincer in the toe." The increasing complexity of sneaker-sole designs frequently creates neologisms. Regions, and sometimes stations, have their own dialects: a sole dominated by lugs in the shape of a Z is a "zebar" in Brackettville and a "zorro" in Del Rio.

We cut a blank stretch for a while. "It's gonna be a little quiet," McCarson said. "We haven't had much moon." The moon is a prime instrument of navigation, because it illuminates without stark exposure. (Illegal immigrants also use the sun, stars, and diverse landmarks.) A few minutes later, McCarson stopped the truck. "Well, we got some crossers," he said.

The prints were shallow and had been scrambled by superimposition; it took McCarson about thirty seconds to disentangle the tread designs and stride lengths and foot sizes. I couldn't find a discrete print. "Group of five," he said: running W, matchstick, heavy-lug boot, fine wire mesh, star-in-the-heel waffle. "They were here last night. They're fresh, but they're not smokin'-hot fresh. When the ground is retaining moisture like this, and you don't have much wind, the sign can hold its shape for a long time. But I see a little better color in our prints than in theirs." Foot pressure, con-

centrating moisture in the soil, darkens prints; the clock of evapora-
tion steadily lightens them. I couldn't see any color difference.
"They could be anytime last night," McCarson said. "And we've
had the correct amount of moisture over the correct amount of
time to make the ground about like concrete, so they're not leavin'
much sign."

If drag prints aren't decisive, trackers examine a group's sign
along the first stretch of trail, wary of the corrosive or stabilizing
effects of weather and terrain—hilltop wind withers prints; damp
arroyos embalm them—and noticing things like insect crossings
and preservative soil composition and raindrop cratering. Every
left-behind object is a potential timekeeper. There are rare, unam-
biguous tokens: jettisoned cans of beans that ants haven't yet noticed, sunlit Kleenex still clammy with mucus, fresh bread crusts on
a hot, clear day. But most often agents encounter noncommittal
objects—desiccated bread crusts in full sun which could be two or
ten hours old.

Swinging the shepherd's cane he uses as a tracking aid, Mc-
Carson started cutting. Just beyond the drag was a strip of mesquite
scrub, and then freight tracks on a high gravel embankment. In the
scrub, the prints disappeared abruptly, as if the group had been
chopped out. But McCarson read a carnival of sign through the
scrub and followed a sequential displacement of gravel up the
embankment. He pointed to a railroad tie and kept going. Possessed
by the live trail, he couldn't pause to explain.

I sat down and studied the tie. It looked like every other tie. I
began shifting position relative to the obfuscated sun. Eventually,
three stacked Ws of discoloration, collectively the size of a half-
dollar, shimmied into view.

On the other side of the tracks, McCarson was standing in front
of a fence, methodically locating the crossing point with his cane.
Beyond the fence, the mesquite gave way to scrofulous pastureland.
The wind picked up and a stop-start drizzle began. Any moderately
heavy rain melts sign, toughens vegetation, and hardens the arid

earth. McCarson walked along the edge of the scattershot grasses for a while, hesitant, and then accelerated.

He was mainly scrutinizing stalks of buffalo grass and curly mesquite grass and king ranch bluestem. The group had pressed the grasses forward. Now at a vestigial angle, the stalks reflected the light more directly, like opened compact mirrors, whitening it. McCarson described this effect later; for the moment, my experience remained completely secondhand—even after he had amplified the sign by walking right over it, my glances fell nowhere.

I could see that moisture had strengthened and limbered up the grasses: instead of breaking and lying inert after receiving their foot-blows, which makes for the brightest reflection, they had been rebounding in slow motion for many hours, and had nearly regained their posture, although adhering rain droplets now pulled them down like sinkers and a jittery wind ceaselessly repositioned them. Under the dingy, dropped-down clouds, the reflective power of the grass was negligible, and the rainy light shrank the color differences.

The mesquite thickened; the grasses faded out; the static of drizzle hardened the ground and corroded the sign. "This is some tough cuttin'," McCarson said, neutrally. The terrain was too stingy for prints, but the walkers had scored the earth with the soles of their shoes, and McCarson was following the scuff marks, which were often the size of fingernail clippings and about as much lighter than the surrounding earth as a No. 2 pencil is lighter than a No. 1.

In cow shit or ant-processed dirt or hoof-crushed earth, McCarson found fractional footprints. Largely dismantled by drizzle and generally separated by a quarter mile, they were about the size of suit buttons. For retracing purposes, he marked them by scraping a line in the adjacent dirt with his cane. He kept moving and held the silence of his concentration, but there was satisfaction in the absoluteness of the stroke and the granular conclusive sound itself: *shhhick!*

The ground was still hardening; the rain-erosion got worse. McCarson slowed, occasionally bending down a little and poking something diagnostically with his cane, but he never crouched and almost never came to a full stop.

"Well, we're just suckin' on the hind teat on this one," he said. A minute later he said, "Oh, by God, that's them!" and accelerated down an alley of spectral sign. Five minutes later, he slowed again. "The odds of following these five are pretty slim in these ground conditions," he said. "We're losin' so much time just tryin' to stay on the sign, we won't really catch 'em unless we take a risk."

So we held their line and walked fast down numberless, seemingly uninstructive trails. McCarson's trail choices appeared to be random, but he was sensing the path of least resistance, relating it to the group's hypothetical line of travel and behavioral tendencies, and occasionally seeing candidate sign. A few times, where the ground turned permissive, we swept perpendicularly back and forth, hoping for trapped sign. After fifteen minutes, McCarson said he was beginning to doubt the trueness of the line.

We walked windingly for maybe a mile. Suddenly McCarson stopped, reached down, and picked something up. All the quick walking had reminded me that we were operating in undifferentiated wilderness the size of two Rhode Islands. McCarson stood and opened his palm. In it was an aspirin-size mud clot distinguished by a sole-honed ridge with a strict curvature. He handed it to me and kept going. A ludicrously deteriorated trail of disturbance had nonetheless held its integrity, in McCarson's eyes, for about five miles. The clot seemed talismanic. But we never got a forward cut, the weather didn't improve, and the trail died.

"We never know who we're gonna catch," McCarson told me on the way back to the station. "The weather plays a tremendous role. You get into drought conditions and you can run groups until you lose daylight and never stall out. A hard rain and you lose all your sign. It's just shithouse luck if we catch 'em.

"Our real effectiveness is in actin' as a screenin' mechanism—

we're a deterrent, which is not something you can really see out in the field, and some agents that might not love tracking get really hung up on that. They can't get over it, and they turn into sorry, disgruntled agents. What this job boils down to is desire—you started with a hundred sets of tracks on your drags, and you're trying to get ten. It's not a factory job—there's no boss, you're not stamping out *x* number of product. What determines that you should try to catch those ten when ninety are already gone? I know what you really wanna ask, which you haven't asked it yet, is how many get away. Well, they all get away. That's the answer. Eventually, they all get away."

McCARSON GREW UP working on his grandfather's ranch, outside Comstock, which is about fifty miles northwest of Brackettville. The ranch didn't keep him entirely busy; as soon as he was old enough, he began hiring himself out to bigger local ranches, where he worked through the daylight hours and then traded money at cards and dice in bunkhouses until he could spend it in town on his day off. He never felt a desire to leave southwest Texas. He studied government at Angelo State University, but by the time he graduated livestock-raising in the region had lost most of its commercial viability.

McCarson had always liked the gun-slinging look of Comstock's Border Patrol agents, and noticed that they often worked without supervision. "That's what really did it," McCarson told me. "Because I liked to hunt and fish, and it looked more like huntin' and fishin' than workin'—they'd give you a vehicle and you were on your own."

When he began tracking, he saw immediately that his hunting skills were almost useless for following people. Border Patrol trainees learn to track informally and opportunistically, tailing journeymen on live trails and asking questions as circumstances permit. McCarson augmented the process by walking exhausted, still-legible trails whenever he could, as far as he could, which is generally encouraged but not frequently undertaken because agents have to do it on their own time.

"Everything you need to know about tracking I can explain in about two sentences," he told me. "You're evaluating the ground for the difference between the disturbance made by humans and the disturbance made by any other force. After that, it's all practice. It's all just looking."

A planetary difference in vision separates great trackers from ordinary trackers. At Brackettville, McCarson and about a dozen other trackers occupy a paramount plane. "There's just a certain level you get to, where you can't say who's better," McCarson says. "And I can't even tell you what that level is as far as particular sign—it's just, if there's something there, we'll see it."

ONE SLOW DAY, after driving the length of a blank drag, McCarson gave me a concentrated lesson. We parked at the edge of a ranch road. In the adjacent dirt, day-old prints held faintly for a while and then disappeared into mesquite. McCarson checked the angle of the sign and pointed at the horizon, toward the group's destination. Then he pointed at a deer trail. "I can see all *kinda* sign through there," he said, and strolled off to make a cell-phone call.

But there was nothing to see: vacant inflexible earth, sparse mesquite-branch detritus, mesquite leaves in inconsistent profusion, various and occasional flat square-inch plants—beggar's-lice, horehound, hedge parsley—and rare tufts of short grasses. All color fell along a drastically shortened mustard-olive-ash continuum. The longer I went without seeing anything, the harder I looked at tiny things close by, and the more obdurately flawless they seemed.

McCarson ambled back. "You wanna see more but you ain't," he said. "That's the maximum the earth's gonna give you." He aimed his cane at some beggar's-lice. I got close and saw that several stalks had been nudged forward and now leaned at a slight angle, maybe thirty degrees from their natural posture. McCarson pointed to two seedpods the size of ball bearings which had exploded under downward pressure. He pointed to a half-inch mesquite twig that listed a little; its bark at the contact point was a fine-particulate smear. He pointed to a piece of ground the size of a playing card: half the stalks in a tuft of buffalo grass were stabbing ardently forward, and the adjoining earth had also been compressed—once spherical granules and clods of soil urged down toward two dimensions—and this compression was continuous and equivalent in degree through the two mediums of grass and earth.

These pygmy symbols were all within six feet, but they were isolated, camouflaged, and enclosed by a lot of pristine terrain—they didn't relate to one another directionally. McCarson waited for a moment while my eyes struggled to absorb them, and then strolled off. My eyes didn't absorb anything. I was afraid to move and contaminate the sign: I'd been immobilized by tininess. From somewhere in the brush, McCarson said into his cell phone, "Did those spearguns come in yet?"

After a while, he came back and pointed to a small area in a patch of mesquite leaves, which are very thin. I couldn't see anything; the leaves appeared to be flush with the ground. Then I got to within a few inches and noticed that they hovered microns above it, as if they'd been levitated by some exceptionally weak force—static electricity raising arm hairs or surface tension holding water above a glass rim. McCarson's area—he kept his cane trained on it—was composed of undamaged leaves that were truly flush with or partially embedded in the earth. The compacted region was a few inches long and about the width of a shoe sole.

"See those dingleberry bushes?" McCarson said. They were the size of Ping-Pong balls, and from a distance I couldn't tell that they'd been crushed: in two dimensions, they retained their fundamental color and some unbroken seeds and a remnant network infrastructure, the way road-killed toads can look like living toads minus a dimension. Up close, I saw fine fragmentation and a uniformity of flattening—a broad pad of compression—that only a shoe, not an angular hoof or a puncturing paw, could have made.

SIGN CUTTING is overwhelmingly hushed and uneventful, but the screen of the ground shows action. Trackers find bits of skin and sock on the fishhook spines of horse-crippler cactus and watch the stride transformation and inexorable decline in mobility as the injury worsens. They watch as groups exhaust themselves and start resting more frequently, and as disoriented or fractious groups splinter. The day after a moonless night, the ground shows walkers equivocally chafing their way through mesquite thickets.

Agents watch as weak people stop so that everyone else can go on, and as they later stand up and try to keep going or give up and try to get caught. Very occasionally, in summer, the ground leads Brackettville agents to corpses. Death in the brush is notable for the attempts that dying people make to undress: a dehydrated, overheated body swells as death approaches, so the dying remove their shirts and shoes and socks, and unbuckle their belts. They seem to find comfort in order, folding items of clothing and arranging their belongings. They prefer to die under the boughs of trees, on their backs.

After a few nights sleeping in the brush, people emanate an odor of campfire smoke and sweat that can float for hours over an abandoned campsite. In wetter weather, the smell of canned sardines persists for a day. Cutting trails, agents step over shit and piss and blood and spit. They find handkerchiefs, pocket Bibles, bottles of Pert Plus, and photographs of daughters with notes on the back (*"Te extraño. Regresa a casa pronto. Te Amo, Isela"*). They find messageboard graffiti on water tanks ("23/2/03 *Por Aquí Pasó Costa Chelo Felipe L. Miguel*"), and the roasted remains of emus, doves, jackrabbits, and javelinas. The great majority of illegal immigrants are adult men, but sometimes agents find diapers and tampons and tiny shoes.

As trackers move through diffuse fields of abandoned objects, fixing the age of the sign, they assure themselves that they're walking through a group's recent past. They want to walk right into its present. They want the sign to turn into its authors. On live trails, the metamorphosis feels imminent, because it always could be. Groups stop unpredictably; if your group lays up at the right time, you'll find yourself disconcertingly deep in a marginal trail yet two minutes from an arroyo filled with snoring. The people you're chasing might appear on the other side of every rise you crest.

Because sign is so shifty and strongly insinuating, it's hard to avoid equating the trail with the people it evokes. Trackers say they're "running" or "chasing" a trail; they say they just "caught" a trail; they say, "That trail got away." The language of tracking treats the sign at the leading edge of a trail as the group itself. After cutting a trail's frontier, trackers say things like: "They're in this pasture," or "They're right there trying to find a good spot to jump the fence," or, simply, "They're here."

WHEN YOU start to see sign, everything unrelated to the trail vacates your mind. Sign cutting is a vigil with no clear object: the sign mediums continuously reconstitute themselves. You often find valuable dominant indicators, but you have to will yourself to remain receptively nonpartisan; otherwise you'll steadily grow blind to divergent marks, and terrain changes will instantly cloak the trail.

Eventually, the microworld entrances: every plant has distinct attitudes and behaviors beyond the obvious—the way it holds its berries; carries and orients and discards its leaves; shrivels and responds to wind; bends with the weight of raindrops. Soil classes reorganize themselves uniquely after a rain. Rocks erode and array themselves in singular patterns. And color and form at that scale are infinitely variable: a cluster of scrub-oak leaves is a thousand shades.

But every medium has, beneath its variability, a composite architecture and a native range of hues, and this is what you have to see, because divergence from it is sign. If you remain rigidly zoomed in, you pick up the endless variations and they hypnotize you and veil the composite. You can't memorize precise schemes of coloration and structure—although the best trackers hold in their heads very good approximations of the hybrid aesthetics of scores of terrain types—but you can learn to see how particular facets of unadulterated landscape acquire a range of colors and shapes over time, so that when you look at a pasture or stream bank or anthill you grasp its physical essence and all its natural deviations, and interloping shapes and colors quickly declare themselves to you. When rain liquefies the ground beneath branch litter, the twigs sink and the liquid soil adheres to the million unique contours of wood and bark and stiffens into a perfect seal. Later, running the trail after the ground has hardened almost beyond compressibility, you'll unconsciously seek out broken seals: millimeter-wide earthworks of shattered crust.

After about an hour and a hundred confirmed sightings, the trail's autonomous sign began to cohere. First it was a stirring paraphrase of recent movement, and then an expression of willfulness pressed into the ground: the overarching intent of a journey. This filled me with an almost violent exultation whose energy was instantly focussed on the next span of information. I couldn't help experiencing sympathetic sensations: I'd see a sneaker-cracked branch and feel it breaking underfoot; I'd see a recently embedded rock and feel my sole bending over it.

McCarson gradually taught me to look for the identifying rhythm of the trail. Group size and behavior correspond to a certain frequency of potential sign; the potential is realized according to the receptivity of the terrain. If two people walk fast and abreast of each other over hard ground while concealing their sign, they'll leave transparent traces; if fifteen people ingenuously plod single-file over impressionable earth, they'll basically plow a new road. Our linear group of five was mainly concerned with speed; they didn't brush out on drags or attempt to walk along the hard edges of animal trails; they didn't bother to avoid print-trapping sandy soil. They didn't stop, and they left nothing behind. Without quite realizing it, I began to think of them as professionals, moving wordlessly in a kind of improvisational accord.

Ultimately, I began to see disturbance before I'd identified any evidence. A piece of ground would appear oddly distressed, but I couldn't point to any explicit transformation. Even up close, I couldn't really tell, so I didn't say anything. But I kept seeing a kind of sorcerous disturbance. It didn't seem entirely related to vision— it was more like a perceptual unquiet. After a while, I pointed to a little region that seemed to exude unease and asked McCarson if it was sign. "Yup," he said. "Really?" I said. "Really?" "Yup," McCarson said.

McCarson experienced this phenomenon at several additional orders of subtlety. In recalcitrant terrain, after a long absence of sign, he'd say, "There's somethin' gone wrong there." I'd ask what, and he'd say, "I don't know—just disturbance." But he knew it was human disturbance, and his divinations almost always led to clearer sign. Once, we were cutting a cattle trail—grazing cows had ripped up the sign, which had been laid down with extreme faintness— and McCarson pointed to a spot and said, "I'm likin' the way this looks here. I'm likin' everything about this." He perceived some human quality in a series of superficial pressings no wider than toadstools, set amid many hoof-compressions of powerfully similar sizes and colors and depths. I could see no aberration at all, from five inches or five feet: it was a cow path. But McCarson liked some physical attribute, and the relative arrangement and general positioning of the impressions. Maybe he could have stood there and parsed the factors—probably, although you never stop on live trails—but he wouldn't have had any words to describe them, because there are no words.

A FEW DAYS LATER, some agents were chasing a group of twelve who had crossed the river well after midnight. They had incised their tread marks on many powdered-up roads and drags—the chief identifier was "a motion wave with lugs around it in a horse-shoe in the heel"—and tracking conditions in the brush were good, so at all points the line of travel was easy to establish and forward cuts came quickly.

As McCarson drove fast down ranch roads in quest of cuts, the radio transmitted updates: "I got 'em here at this deer blind—they got a real good shine on 'em." "They're crossing another road right here—hold on, there's some fresh toilet paper." "I got 'em laid up here in a real new jacal"—a branch shelter that illegal immigrants sometimes make—"and I got their campfire, still real warm." Around the fire were slick peach pits and cans with sardine juice in them—a scene so vibrant it was like seeing the group disappear around a corner. "This is lookin' like one of those rare story-book-endin' trails," McCarson said. "Just *click-click-click-click*."

Two cuts later, we were at the trail's apex, where six Border Patrol SUVs and about ten agents had converged. The sign described a sudden dispersal into opaque brush: the group had heard its pursuers and taken off. The agents were staring contentedly into meshes of mesquite. A green-and-gold Border Patrol helicopter appeared and dropped to about twelve feet above the thicket, raucously rotor-washing everything; it nosed around the mesquite for about three minutes, and then the pilot's voice came stereophonically out of everyone's radio, saying the group was thirty yards away, prone beneath an absurdly undersized camouflage tarp. The junior agents surrounded the hiding place and yelled instructions; twelve depleted men crawled out. The agents told them to sit in a row, perfunctorily searched them, and began discussing transportation arrangements. The captives were all young men; without speaking, they moved from vigilance to dejection to resignation. They received permission to eat, and pulled out Cokes and canned corn and tuna and slices of Wonder Bread and plastic jugs of biologically tinted water.

When I was in southwest Texas, I watched Brackettville agents catch twenty-six people in five groups—all, except this one, by sensor or routine observation or accident. Every capture was quiet: no running, no resistance. In eighteen years, McCarson has drawn his gun two times. He has never fired it. The captured groups were representative: no one had drugs or warrants or enough previous captures to justify detention and criminal charges. The illegal immigrants were all adult men seeking work, tired and disinclined to flee: the chances of escaping after visual contact are slim, and the turnaround time is fast—the Del Rio sector runs a daily shuttle back to Ciudad Acuña. After the capture and pat-down, agents and immigrants, in a momentary common languor, stood around and talked sparingly about the weather or the river level or noteworthy episodes from the immigrants' voyage.

"We just got lost," an older man with a bronchial cough told me one cold dawn, after he and his four underdressed companions, loitering at a highway intersection, had been searched and ushered into a Border Patrol SUV. "The stars—the stars were our map at night, but look at the clouds. Look at the sky." It was impervious, and had been for the past two nights.

Once, I lay on my stomach in a mesquite thicket, waiting with two agents for a group of four that had tripped a sensor. The agents yelled and leaped forward only when the men were within ten feet; the group seized up and went submissively slack in a single motion. After the pat-down, one man began ruefully emptying from his pockets a collection of pretty rocks; for some reason, the agents and I looked away. Walking back to the truck, the men began heedlessly climbing a barbed-wire fence; one of the agents gave them a patient lesson in how to scale it. Another time, a guy whose group had been spotted from the air sociably handed an agent a big rattle and said he'd killed a six-foot snake. The agent examined the rattle deferentially, shook it, said, "That's a big snake," returned the rattle, walked the group of men to his truck, and locked them in the back.

Now McCarson and a few other senior agents were leaning against an SUV, watching the junior agents, who were watching the detainees finish their food. I was thinking that as trackers follow illegal immigrants, often right at the mesmerizing limit of what they can detect, they're mustering up the emotions and sensations of mercurial imaginary travelers, and then the imaginary is suddenly, alienatingly replaced by the real: men physically homogenized by days in the brush, all with the same propulsive need. It's a need no Border Patrol tracker will ever be able to identify with. Before the twelve men finished eating, McCarson walked back to his truck and radioed Brackettville to see if anything else was pending.

JEFF TIETZ *is a contributing writer at* Rolling Stone. *His work has appeared in* The New Yorker, Harper's, *and the* Atlantic Monthly.

Coda

One day a friend of mine called and told me to read an essay on tracking that had incongruously appeared on the op-ed page of a newspaper. It was a very short essay, but its author had fit in many of the elements that make tracking wondrous. I saw that the craft was ancient and sophisticated and beautiful; I also recognized the possibility that its tiny mechanics could be shown *in action*: as smugglers ran south, shooting over their shoulders; as trails led to corpses; as trackers, racing after guides, repeatedly overcame improvised subterfuges.

The facts I learned in Brackettville were dispiriting. Chasing live trails usually involved a mute guy hurrying randomly through the middle of nowhere. He would be, understandably, very hard-pressed to explain what he was doing. He would also be very unlikely to catch anybody himself, because many widely dispersed agents collaborated on apprehensions. Apprehensions tended to be sedate and perfunctory. Real-time chases between smugglers and trackers almost never occurred. The chance of discovering a dead body in terrain with shade and seasonal streams and windmill wells was basically zero.

I went out with Border Patrol agents for probably ten full shifts, asking questions all the time. I learned a lot about strategy and logistics, but systematic instruction in sign cutting is a foreign idea in the Border Patrol, and incompatible with chasing people. I took my besides-the-point notes home and began working hard to make myself believe in them.

After a few weeks of extracting staged action and pretend insights from my notebooks, I was forced to admit that I hadn't actually seen anything. I needed to go back and get lessons. Ten days, however, was right at the limit of bureaucratic tolerance. It also seemed improbable that the Border Patrol would pull its best trackers off live trails and/or give away many hours of senior-agent manpower in order to provide me with intensive training. The only thing I could think of was to try and get permission to go out with McCarson again, perhaps by claiming that I needed just a few more facts for my story, and then pester him for special instruction on slow days. It worked, and before long came the moment when, for no knowable reason, multiple pieces of sign appeared to me as a single constellation.

Stephen J. Dubner

THE SILVER
THIEF

FROM *The New Yorker*

SOMETIME DURING THE EARLY hours of January 29, 2002, a great deal of sterling silver vanished from a mansion near Rhinebeck, New York. The mansion, known as Edgewater, was built in 1823 and for decades was the home of a family named Donaldson. Its current owner is Richard Jenrette, a retired financier whose hobby is preserving historic homes. Jenrette takes his hobby seriously. He once tracked down the last living Donaldson descendant, who had moved to the south of Spain, and persuaded her to repatriate the family's original silver to Edgewater. This included a flatware set decorated with the Donaldson crest (a raven perched on rocks) and a dozen teaspoons, each engraved with a sign of the zodiac (a bow to the Victorian interest in astrology, and a playful means of marking the seating arrangement). All of these items were stolen, as were a toddy ladle and a fish server, luncheon knives and demitasse spoons, a chocolate pot, and a six-piece tea set—many of which were designed by such fine silver makers as Tiffany, Gorham, and Martin-Guillaume Biennais.

The mansion also had Gilbert Stuart paintings and antique

porcelain, but these had not been taken, and some of the lesser silver was left behind. Furthermore, the alarm had not been tripped. The burglar had gingerly pried the wooden molding from the glass panes of an exterior door, removed the glass, and shimmied inside, thereby failing to break the alarm contacts on the door. Jenrette, who was at his winter home in St. Croix when his caretaker phoned with the news, speculated that the burglar had some kind of inside connection, or had at least visited the mansion. Edgewater was occasionally open to tour groups, and Jenrette had recently held a fund-raising party for Hillary Clinton that drew several hundred people. He wondered if perhaps one of the guests—or, more likely, some guest's hard-up nephew or brother-in-law who had been told of the party—had broken into the grand, remote house along the Hudson River.

That night, there was another burglary, ten miles south of Edgewater, at Wilderstein, the former home of Daisy Suckley, who was a distant cousin and close companion of Franklin D. Roosevelt. (Suckley gave the president his famous Scottish terrier, Fala.) Again, the haul was silver, and the job was equally meticulous. The method of entry was the same. Wilderstein had an interior motion detector, which somehow had been evaded.

The state troopers in Rhinebeck realized that they were dealing with a specialist. The burglar left no fingerprints or clues. There wasn't much to do except alert the antiques publications, the auction houses, and the *Times*, which ran a brief article about the burglaries.

Nearly two weeks later, Cornell Abruzzini, a police detective in Greenwich, Connecticut, was having his morning coffee when a colleague stopped by with the *Times* article. "Doesn't this sound like the silver guy you nailed?" he asked. Abruzzini read the article, then called Rhinebeck and said, with barely an introduction, "I know the guy who's doing your burglaries."

Abruzzini told Tom Fort, the trooper who was handling the case, the name of the thief: Blane Nordahl. But Nordahl had in recent years used various aliases, which included David Price and Robert Demiani. Abruzzini advised Fort to check the local motels for all three names. On his tenth try, at a Super 8 several miles south of Rhinebeck, the trooper got lucky. A man called David Price had paid cash for a room. Miraculously, the clerk had done what motel clerks are supposed to do with a cash customer: taken down information on his car—a Cadillac Seville—and photocopied his driver's license. The picture on David Price's license was of Blane Nordahl. He had checked out more than a week earlier.

SEVERAL MONTHS AGO, I drove out to Greenwich to talk with Cornell Abruzzini about Nordahl. Abruzzini is a well-spoken forty-five-year-old who pronounces his last name with brio, as if it were an exotic dessert. Trim, with deep-set eyes, he is bald on top but has dark hair on the sides and a thick beard, which has an auburn tinge. That night, he wore jeans, a black sweatshirt, and black Reeboks. He was working a freelance job as a night watchman for an antiques show at Greenwich's aging civic center.

I arrived after midnight, and we sat in the lobby at a card table, shivering a bit, the pipes clanking, as we paged through fastidiously organized three-ring binders that Abruzzini has devoted to Nordahl's case: police reports, crime-scene photographs, silver inventories, copies of phony driver's licenses. Abruzzini is considered the ranking expert on Nordahl, a fact that both pleases and irritates him. He is proud of the investigative work he did that led to Nordahl's arrest, in 1996, for six burglaries in Greenwich. Yet Nordahl seems impossible to stop: after completing a prison term, he inevitably returns to stealing. (He has been arrested more than a dozen times for burglary.) "It's like watching the same bad movie again and again," Abruzzini told me.

Abruzzini had interviewed Nordahl extensively after the arrest for the Greenwich burglaries. The silver thief, I learned, was thought to have stolen at least ten million dollars' worth of silver in more than fifteen states. Though Abruzzini is not the sort of policeman who thinks it fitting to compliment a criminal, he eventually allowed that Nordahl was the most accomplished burglar he had encountered (which, in Greenwich, is not empty praise), and easily the most distinctive.

Nordahl, who is forty-three, had a standard method. He scouted his locales through *Architectural Digest* or the *Robb Report*, or by calling real-estate agents. He'd tell them that he was hoping to buy a big old home in a settled neighborhood, and ask where he should look. During a daytime drive, he took note of houses that were set back from the road. After a nap at his motel and a light dinner, he set out at about midnight.

He parked in unremarkable locations. As Nordahl once told Abruzzini during an interview, "You have to park where it fits in. If it doesn't fit in, then you can't park there." He often walked several miles through forest or back yards, and considered several dozen houses before choosing one.

Nordahl carried two nylon duffelbags: an empty one for the silver and a smaller one filled with screwdrivers, a carpet knife, wire cutters, a wood chisel, nail pullers, a flashlight, a white cotton rag, duct tape, and a Wonder Bar—a piece of thin black steel that can pry open almost anything. Nordahl was good with his tools, Abruzzini told me, and he was patient. One night in Greenwich, he said, Nordahl spent two hours creating a hole in the door. His reward: flatware for a hundred and ten people, and an exquisite tea service.

All the while, Nordahl wore nipple-tipped cotton gardening gloves to avoid leaving fingerprints. After collecting the silver, he passed the two duffelbags through the door opening, then climbed out. He examined the silver for maker's marks, discarded anything that wasn't worth carrying, and hid the bags near a road—under a bush, if possible—on his way back to his car. "One job he did here, he parked four or five miles away," Abruzzini said. "How he finds his way to and back, it's amazing. If I gave the same task to seven-eighths of the cops in town, they couldn't do it."

Within hours of a burglary, the silver was on its way to Nordahl's fence, in New York. He preferred to deliver it himself, to insure top dollar, but whenever he was beyond driving distance of New York he sent it by UPS.

Malcolm X, who as a young man was a burglar in Boston, offered an account of his former trade in his autobiography. "I had learned from some of the pros, and from my own experience, how important it was to be careful and plan," he wrote. "Burglary, properly executed, though it had its dangers, offered the maximum chances of success with the minimum risk. If you did your job so that you never met any of your victims, it first lessened your chances of having to attack or perhaps kill someone. And if through some slipup you were caught, later, by the police, there was never a positive eyewitness."

The average burglar, however, is lazy, sloppy, haphazard, unimaginative, and thus unsuccessful. Nordahl was none of these, but over time his methodology had become as distinctive as a signature. That's why Nordahl became the prime suspect in the Rhinebeck burglaries the moment Abruzzini read about them.

No thief was born as good as Nordahl, Abruzzini told me. A thief had to evolve—and foul up—along the way. If I wanted Nordahl's complete history, Abruzzini said, I should speak with a retired detective in central New Jersey named Lonnie Mason. He had known Nordahl for twenty years, Abruzzini added, and he still lived a few miles from where Nordahl began his career.

LONNIE AND MARY MASON, their four children, and a stout German shepherd named Lexy live in a yellow clapboard house in Avon-by-the-Sea, New Jersey. Mary is an accountant with the United States Treasury Department; Lonnie, fifty, is now a stay-at-home dad. He keeps his old police files upstairs in dog-eared brown folders. He has a thick neck, a bulky chest, and a bristly brush cut, and he wears steel aviator glasses. While we spoke in the living room, Mason's ten-year-old son, Chris, sat worshipfully at his father's feet. Mason, sunk deep in a big corduroy recliner, occasionally yanked the lever, a nervous habit.

Mason was a cop for twenty-eight years, the last fourteen of which were spent as an investigator in the Monmouth County prosecutor's office. Monmouth is a pastoral coastal area known for horses, old money, and colonial tastes: perfect for a silver thief. Mason has arrested Blane Nordahl twice. He spoke of him the way someone might speak of a roguish relative—general disapproval moderated by grudging admiration, mixed with a sense that you can never be rid of him. The first thing Mason told me about Nordahl was that he had once tried to help him reform: "I said, 'Blane, if you ever want to use your knowledge in a positive way, I'd work with you.' I said, 'You could work in the insurance industry in the area of silver. You could work with alarm systems. If you want to team up, go into a business, we could turn this into a crime-prevention program.'"

"What did he say?" I asked.

"He said, 'I don't think so.'"

Nordahl grew up in Minnesota and Wisconsin, Mason told me, and his parents divorced when he was young. His father, David, became a successful artist who moved to Santa Fe, painting realist Apache scenes. (His work has been collected by Steven Spielberg and Michael Jackson.) His mother, Sharon, held waitressing and office jobs, and now lives in Indiana. As a boy, Blane was shuttled between the two of them.

Initially, he was a good student—his family thought that he might become an architect—but sometime in high school he lost interest. He began cutting class and smoking pot. More than anything, he was in a hurry to make money. So he quit school during the eleventh grade, in 1978, to take a construction job. But he couldn't stay out of trouble. His family gave him two choices: become a cop or join the navy.

In his early naval training, Nordahl won a series of awards, and spoke of becoming a navy SEAL. He was eventually posted to Earle Naval Weapons Station, in Colts Neck, New Jersey. But in

1983 he was arrested for his first burglary. The navy later charged him with desertion, and he was discharged.

Nordahl's first crimes were undisciplined, Mason told me, and bore little resemblance to his mature work. He was a common house thief, taking whatever was available. He usually worked during the afternoon, and he visited the same towns repeatedly. Worse yet, he had partners. "He tied up with a group of guys and started doing jobs," Mason said. "After he did the jobs and they rolled over on him when they got caught, he decided to go solo."

Nordahl came to consider burglary both a profession and an art. He once told a detective that an alleged accomplice "doesn't have the brains or the talent or the ambition" to be a good burglar. Taking crime seriously had a bracing effect on Nordahl. He stopped using drugs and gave up alcohol, cigarettes, and even caffeine. He tried to eat well, and he worked out constantly. Only five feet four inches tall, he built himself a gymnast's body: strong shoulders, skinny hips, muscular legs.

He began to focus on sterling silver. This was perhaps Nordahl's smartest move, Mason told me. In terms of risk versus reward, breaking into a home to steal a television set is foolish. Stealing jewelry requires venturing upstairs, into the bedroom. But silver is kept downstairs, in the dining room or in a butler's pantry, far from sleeping homeowners. Nordahl started spending hours in the library, studying the makers, vintages, and hallmarks of antique silver.

Like a baseball scout, Lonnie Mason liked to keep track of emerging criminal talent. When Nordahl was arrested in 1985 for some burglaries a few towns over, Mason tried to interview him, but Nordahl wouldn't talk. So Mason began to investigate him, and learned that the closest thing Nordahl had to a fixed address was Camden, New Jersey, a ragged city across the river from Philadelphia, and an hour's drive from Monmouth County.

In the spring of 1991, there was a rash of silver burglaries in Rumson, New Jersey, and Mason was called in to consult with the local police. At the time, most of Nordahl's robberies took place on

Thursday nights. So on the following Thursday evening Mason had sixteen men assigned to him for an overnight stakeout. They blanketed a two-block area of Rumson. By Friday morning, with no sign of Nordahl, Mason was relieved. "I thought, Thank God," Mason told me. "Maybe he saw one of our guys and called it off." Just after Mason got home and went to bed, his boss phoned. "He said, 'Can you tell me why I authorized all this overtime? Because he hit three houses last night.' And I said, 'Well, what section? Because I know one section he didn't hit.' My boss gave me the addresses, and it was the two-block radius we were in."

Mason learned to recognize the signs of Nordahl's presence. If someone climbed a telephone pole and snipped the alarm wires, that was Nordahl. (Later, when he got better at evading alarms, he abandoned this method.) If a burglar had somehow stolen the silver without disturbing the pair of Rottweilers inside, that was Nordahl. (It is the whiff of a person's sweat, triggered by adrenaline, that agitates a dog, but Nordahl—whose mother had bred Alaskan malamutes—was oddly affectless.) From soil samples taken outside victims' homes, Mason learned that Nordahl sometimes used a chemical solution to determine whether the stolen silver was sterling or plate.

Several months after the failed stakeout in Rumson, Mason was sent to investigate a burglary in the town of Little Silver. The burglar had entered an unlocked kitchen window, and taken only the sterling. Mason called for a tracking dog and his forensics man, even though he had little hope of finding anything. But beneath the open window lay a soft garden bed. The burglar had stepped in the dirt, climbed through the window, and landed on the kitchen counter. The result was a muddy sneaker print on the counter. "I know you can't lift it," Mason told the forensics man. "But I want you to photograph that thing for the next three hours until you get a good picture."

An arrest warrant for Nordahl was issued. Thanks to Mason's earlier legwork, he knew that Nordahl was staying at a motel in Camden. "We went down there that night, found out what room he was in, then called and pretended we were the manager—you know, 'Are you checking out tomorrow?'" Mason told me. "We knew he was in there. I had the Camden County Fugitive Unit with me, and they look like the front line for the Eagles. We went and we hit the door—*and he wasn't in the room.* Finally, I see Blane hiding behind the door. So I reach around with my left hand—I have my gun out—and I grab him. I go to holster my weapon, he comes out from behind the door. He grabs my arm, and now we're wrestling. Well, we flipped, and we went over the TV. It looked like something out of a cartoon. He went skidding across the rug with me on his back—he got this big rug burn on his cheek. And we came to rest on a pair of sneakers. I said, 'Nah, couldn't be.' We rolled over the sneaker, and it had the same tread.'"

Persuaded by the sneaker print, Nordahl accepted a plea bargain. He served two and a half years of a five-year sentence. When he was released, he returned to stealing, but he added an important precaution to his routine. After each night's work, he would take his sneakers, his clothes, his gloves, and his tools and toss them into a lake or a Dumpster. Mason told me that Nordahl had made him a better cop; Mason had clearly made Nordahl a better burglar. Sometimes he now wore shoes two sizes too large, with extra socks, so the police couldn't even match his size.

IN DECEMBER 1994, Nordahl stole nearly a quarter of a million dollars' worth of silver from four homes in Essex Fells, New Jersey, a tiny town about twenty-five miles west of Manhattan. In the coming months, he continued to work in New Jersey, the old-money fringes of Philadelphia, and Westchester County, in New York. But according to Lonnie Mason, and to police in various jurisdictions, he also began to travel more extensively: the outskirts of Boston and Baltimore (much of the loveliest colonial silver is in those areas); Grosse Pointe, Michigan; Kennebunkport, Maine; New Castle, Delaware; and Winnetka, Illinois. In the winter, he could be found in Miami and Palm Beach.

He couldn't help boasting about his abilities, and spoke openly of the wonderful movie his life could make, starring Bobby (never Robert) De Niro. Mason had tried to warn Nordahl that he wouldn't be so quick and nimble forever. "He said he didn't have to be quick anymore, because he was so good," Mason told me. "He said, 'By the time you get to the scene, I'm out of the state.'" Nordahl continued to rob homes in Monmouth County; on one job, he took the silver but left behind a thousand dollars in cash that lay on the dining-room table. Mason took this as a taunt.

If an economist were to analyze Nordahl's operation, he might well be impressed. Economics is, at root, the study of incentives, and Nordahl had rationally concluded that the incentives for stealing silver easily trumped the incentives to stop. He was essentially a one-man economy, and he had pinpointed a valuable yet abundant commodity. Perhaps most important, Nordahl had found a weakness in the criminal-justice system. Robbery was a shrinking discipline—burglary rates have fallen by half since the early nineteen-eighties—and the jail sentences were light.

A psychiatrist, however, might argue that Nordahl was driven by an irrational compulsion. One former girlfriend of Nordahl's told me that he was fixated on stealing every night. "He got high off it," she said. "He *liked* going into houses when people were sleeping. He said it's more exciting to go into a house when people are there and get away with it." Lonnie Mason also described Nordahl's behavior as an addiction: "This is what he exists for, and it's all about his infatuation with money." Mason argues that silver was particularly appealing to Nordahl because it connotes the sort of family that passes along precious things from one generation to the next— a family that was distinctly unlike Nordahl's own. As Mason sees it, Nordahl remained embittered by his parents' divorce; he resented his father and became extraordinarily close to his mother. (When Mason got hold of Nordahl's phone records, he was astonished by the number of calls between the two.) Nothing gave Nordahl greater pleasure, Mason believes, than stealing a rich man's silver and turning it into cash that he could shower on his mother—who, while unhappy about her son's calling, appreciated his devotion.

Converting silver into money was the most inefficient part of Nordahl's scheme. According to Mason, Nordahl once revealed that his fence paid him between 10 and 20 percent of the silver's book value. For many years, he fenced his silver to a man who lived in Weehawken, New Jersey, and kept a small jewelry shop in the diamond district of Manhattan. The former girlfriend I spoke with said that Nordahl earned "about seven thousand dollars a day," which seems high until one considers that he rarely took a night off.

The size of Nordahl's assets is unknown. A proper assessment would require help from the IRS, which Mason once tried to enlist, unsuccessfully. Nordahl is clearly not a miser: a 1995 receipt trail constructed by the FBI showed that he once spent nearly twenty-five thousand dollars in just three months. And this was only a fractional report, covering some of Nordahl's credit cards, but no cash.

In *To Catch a Thief*, Cary Grant plays a retired cat burglar who lives in a mountainside French villa. While serving an elegant lunch to an insurance agent, he explains why he stole: "Oh, to live better; to own things I couldn't afford; to acquire this good taste, which you now enjoy." To judge by his receipts, Nordahl's spending was more prosaic. Much of his discretionary spending took place at Wal-Mart and Walgreen's; during one six-week stretch, he spent $2,462.51 at Wal-Mart alone. His clothing came from Men's Wearhouse and Today's Man; there were charges of $79.34 and $132.24 for adult-video rentals; and a bill for $47.40 from Al's Pawn-a-Rama, in Lake Park, Florida.

The ex-girlfriend told me that Nordahl could be remarkably generous. She had lost custody of her young son, and Nordahl paid her legal fees to try to get the boy back. Nordahl tended to take up with junkies from the Camden area—women who had children but no job, someone who could travel with him. According to Lonnie Mason, Nordahl often supplied a woman with drugs to keep her compliant. She never accompanied him on his late-night work, but the next day he might drive her past the grand gated houses that he had robbed.

Early one Sunday morning in May 1996, silver valued at $151,399 was stolen from Ivana Trump's house on Vista Drive in Greenwich. A few nights later, a house on Pecksland Road, several miles to the north, lost $202,829 in silver, most of it Francis I by Reed & Barton. The community was rattled by these burglaries, and the police felt pressed to catch the thief. Cornell Abruzzini, who had been on the Greenwich burglary squad for two years by this time, was placed on the case. He immediately recognized these break-ins as the work of the thief who had committed three other robberies in Greenwich the previous summer. Abruzzini had never seen such clean crime scenes. At one house, the burglar made a tidy stack of the door molding he had pried off to gain entry.

Abruzzini learned that similar burglaries had recently taken place in East Hampton; the police there put him in touch with Lonnie Mason, who told the story of Blane Nordahl and guessed that the Greenwich jobs were his work. The stack of door molding was classic Nordahl, Mason told Abruzzini: he was a neat freak, and kept his socks arranged perfectly in their drawer. Mason was eager to help Abruzzini catch Nordahl, but warned that it would be difficult to gather sufficient evidence to arrest him. Nordahl was so practiced that he was virtually untouchable, unless he was caught in the act.

A week after the Ivana Trump burglary, Mason called back. Nordahl was staying at a Super 8 in Stamford, he told Abruzzini, with a longtime on-and-off girlfriend from New Jersey named Luanne. Mason knew this because, after years of chasing Nordahl, he had managed to turn Luanne into a confidential informant. She was not always a reliable informant—at the time, she was a drug addict who regularly went back on her word—and she had returned to living in motels with her cat-burglar boyfriend. But at least she had checked in with Mason. Now Mason suggested that it was time to scare her into submission.

The Greenwich police staked out the Super 8 in Stamford. One night, they saw Nordahl and Luanne packing up the car. Although they didn't have enough evidence to arrest Nordahl, they confronted the pair, and handed Luanne a cell phone. Lonnie Mason was on the other end.

"Oh, shit," she said.

"Luanne, you have two choices here," Mason told her. "You can either stay on tour with Blane and get indicted down the road, or you can go with these cops and cooperate."

Luanne started to cry. Nordahl glared at her. Mason knew that Luanne had a ten-year-old son back in New Jersey, and he told her to think about him, not Nordahl. She cried some more, then ended the phone call and climbed into the police car.

"What are you doing?" Nordahl said. He warned her that she'd be in trouble without him, Luanne told me, since he had her heroin.

"I'll get it from the police," Luanne said.

A few months later, on August 24, Nordahl did one more silver burglary in Greenwich—just for spite, he later admitted to Abruzzini. Luanne, meanwhile, had started to talk. Mason used a clever ploy to cement her cooperation: he drove to her house and showed her a photograph that had been in Nordahl's possession—a picture of a blond woman in a white dress posing in front of the Manhattan skyline.

"That son of a bitch!" Luanne said. She dug out a picture and showed it to Mason: an identical image, except with Luanne in it. Both photographs were taken on a promenade in Weehawken, she told Mason, just down the street from the home of Nordahl's fence. Now Luanne began to provide the Greenwich police with many details about Nordahl: how he obtained fake IDs, for example, by placing counterfeit documents in a toaster oven to artificially age them. With the promise of Luanne's testimony, Cornell Abruzzini was able to get a warrant to arrest Nordahl for six Greenwich burglaries.

Nordahl must have realized that he was being aggressively pursued, because Mason couldn't track him anywhere in New Jersey.

He wondered if perhaps Nordahl had sought safe haven with his mother, in Indiana. He asked the FBI to put her home under surveillance. Mason soon got word that Nordahl had been spotted driving toward his mother's home, his truck full of drywall. Apparently, he was renovating her house. FBI agents told Mason that they would take Nordahl into custody, and Mason tried to warn them that they were dealing with an escape artist.

"I'll never forget it," Mason recalled. "It was a rainy, nasty day. They said, 'We chased him in the front door of his mom's house and out the back, and he's in a wooded area. We have him cordoned off. We have helicopters up, we got dogs here. It's nineteen degrees, and it's going to snow. He cannot survive in the woods for any length of time.' I said, 'How long have you been out there?' He said, 'Oh, about forty-five minutes.' I said, 'I'm telling you right now: Blane is gone. Blane is probably ten miles away right now. Call me back when you find out I was right.' Next day, I get a call: 'You're not going to believe this. He was at a bank withdrawing money by the time we were talking to you on the phone.'"

The FBI flagged the credit card that Nordahl had used to buy the drywall—it was issued to one of his aliases—and began tracing his movements. He made it to Wisconsin and did some shopping in Sparta, the town where he went to junior high school, and the last place where he'd lived within the law. The police issued a teletype describing Nordahl's vehicle, which an off-duty officer spotted at a Wal-Mart. Inside, Nordahl was buying fourteen Sterilite storage containers and two boxes of trash bags. More police officers arrived in the parking lot, and they arrested him as soon as he stepped outside.

The police inventoried Nordahl's belongings in his vehicle and in his motel room, and found, among other items, nationwide motel directories, a video titled *How to Create a New Birth Certificate*, a rubber stamp that read ORIGINAL DOCUMENT, and a book called *How to Launder Money*. He had been traveling with two cats, one white and one black, named Romeo and Juliet; a series of receipts from various animal clinics suggested that he was a devoted pet owner. Not surprisingly, he had no sterling silver and no piles of cash.

Nordahl spent only three months in a Wisconsin jail before his extradition back East, but it was long enough for him to earn a bad reputation. He was always shouting for the TV to be turned up louder, and other inmates complained that he kept the water in his cell running all night. This was because he was trying to escape. At night, he used a spoon to try to dig through his cell wall, then patched the growing hole with toothpaste. He told a prisoner named Dennis that he had three or four million dollars waiting for him in various banks, and promised to pay Dennis fifty thousand dollars if he'd help him break out. Nordahl explained that he planned to make his move on a Sunday afternoon, because the Green Bay Packers were on a playoff run and the guards might be distracted by the game. He also said he would kill Dennis if he tried to stop him. Instead, Dennis ratted him out, and Nordahl was moved to a new cell.

NORDAHL'S ARREST WAS BIG NEWS in the towns that he'd visited during his most recent spree. Ivana Trump had not been the only high-profile victim: in Palm Beach, Nordahl had robbed the home of Curt Gowdy, the retired sportscaster. In East Hampton, police suspected that he had made a run at Steven Spielberg's house but was put off by a motion detector. (It was also widely reported, erroneously, that he had burgled Bruce Springsteen's home in Monmouth County.) Some newspapers began calling Nordahl "the burglar to the stars," although Nordahl never knew or cared whose home he was entering. He discovered that he had stolen from Trump only when he got back to his motel and found her last name stamped on two dinner plates—which turned out to be pewter.

It soon became evident that, despite the efforts of Lonnie Mason and Cornell Abruzzini, Nordahl wasn't going to be spending much time in prison. None of the cases against him were strong. The police had no forensic evidence, no silver, no record of his cash proceeds. Nor was any prosecutor eager to go to trial with a heroin addict as the star witness. Nordahl also knew that some three dozen police departments in nine states were anxious to shift their un-solved burglaries from open- to closed-case files. Robert Eisler, a criminal attorney in Deal, New Jersey, represented Nordahl at the time. "If you're in law enforcement and you've got some cold cases," Eisler told me, "you'll give your kidney just to get somebody to say, 'I did that.' "

Eisler, whose clients are typically biker-gang members, armed robbers, and sexual predators, saw an opportunity to craft a deal that would make everyone happy. "Blane harms nobody, aside from the fact you'll never see your great-great-great-grandfather's knife and fork again," Eisler said. The people who lost their silver felt vio-lated, but most of them were adequately reimbursed. It was really the insurance companies that suffered most—and who can work up much sympathy for them?

In September 1997, Eisler and Nordahl signed off on a deal with federal prosecutors that encompassed, according to Abruzzini, a hundred and forty-four recent burglaries. Nordahl agreed to hold proffer sessions with police officers from the various jurisdictions and describe his burglaries so that they could officially clear their cases. In exchange, Nordahl pleaded guilty only to the interstate transport of stolen property.

Nordahl's plea agreement called for him to help the FBI trap his fence—who, Nordahl hinted, might have Mafia ties. Nordahl, now free on ball, was supposed to visit the fence in New York while wearing a wire. But he could not get the FBI's attention, nor could Eisler, Mason, or Abruzzini. "I'm getting collect calls from Blane saying, 'These guys ain't using me, what's the deal?' " Abruzzini told me. "Meanwhile, Blane goes back to his old tricks, and starts clob-bering them in Baltimore. He may have been working for the feds during the day, but he was doing his own work at night."

In November 1998, Nordahl was arrested again, in Baltimore (with burglary tools but no silver), and was finally sent to prison.

He was released in April 2001, and placed under federal probation. Abruzzini and Mason assumed that Nordahl would resume his burglaries, but there wasn't much they could do about it.

It was only in February 2002, after Abruzzini learned of the Rhinebeck burglaries, that he suspected Nordahl was active again. He began helping the Rhinebeck troopers track Nordahl. As it turned out, the United States Marshals in Camden, Nordahl's home base, were also looking for him, because he had failed to report to his probation officer. The Marshals soon captured Nordahl outside a Dunkin' Donuts shop in Mount Laurel, driving a green Cadillac Seville, and he was sent to a federal prison in Elkton, Ohio. He intimated to the authorities that he had intentionally violated his probation: a man like him could hardly be expected to take a nine-to-five job and report regularly to a probation officer. Now he would max out his prison term and be set free with no constraints.

LAST NOVEMBER, after nearly two years of refusals, Nordahl agreed to be interviewed. He was due to be released from the Elkton prison in ten days, but he had recently received some bad news: a grand jury in Poughkeepsie, New York, had indicted him for the two Rhinebeck burglaries. A helpful document had been found in the Cadillac: handwritten directions to one of the Rhinebeck mansions. That document, along with the photocopy of Nordahl's fake driver's license from the Super 8, had given the police enough information to move forward. Still, there was no forensic evidence. Tom Fort, the state trooper in Rhinebeck, told me to expect a "signature crime" prosecution. "One of our arguments is the fact that Blane and only Blane could have committed these burglaries," he said.

Nordahl seemed to view the indictment as more of a nuisance than a threat. "They're grabbing at straws, hoping to make a bale of hay," he told me. "My belief is that, basically, I've been charged based on my past." We were sitting on blue office chairs in a concrete-block conference room. Nordahl was not handcuffed—Elkton is a minimum-security prison—and he wore all khaki, including an insulated jacket several sizes too large. His hair was thinning, but otherwise he looked surprisingly boyish: he was buff and trim, with good color, smooth skin, clear blue-green eyes. But he sat stiffly, hands in his pockets, and didn't smile once during our conversation.

As Nordahl sees things, the police are as deceptive as criminals. "Society as a whole always thinks that cops are being honest, and the truth is they're very dishonest," he said. "Police say things to cover their own ass. Or they'll say things to go ahead and establish something if that's the piece that they need. They won't lie about everything—just about one thing or two things."

When I mentioned Cornell Abruzzini, Nordahl said, "This fucking guy's a clown." He had surmised that it was Abruzzini's grand-jury testimony that resulted in the Rhinebeck "signature crimes" indictment. Nordahl reminded me that his 1997 guilty plea was for the transportation of stolen property, not for the hundred-plus burglaries he had spoken about in his proffer sessions. In his view, it was improper for Abruzzini to establish his "signature" by citing those discussions. "Those negotiations, that process, is not a public record, but they've made it a public record," Nordahl said. "It's very illegal to do that. These guys don't know that I understand the law as well as I do."

He wasn't interested in discussing the details of his burglaries. "I don't want to give something, inadvertently or otherwise, and somehow it comes back to bite me in my ass," he said. I passed along a message from Richard Jenrette, the owner of the Edgewater mansion. Jenrette had said that if I ever interviewed Nordahl I should tell him that Jenrette had traveled across the Atlantic to obtain the mansion's silver, and wondered if there was any chance that Nordahl might locate it. He responded with a stony glare.

I asked him about his childhood. "When I was really young, I was basically athletic," he said. "But then once my parents got divorced my mom kind of moved around a bunch. That kind of stopped everything." He added, "I learned to work with my hands in school. I took drafting and sheet metal and carpentry and things like that, and I built great big tree forts. . . . If you learn at a young age, then you have an ability to visualize things, you have a natural ability—a natural balance, you know, a coordination."

He said that he had never been afraid during a burglary. "To be honest with you, I don't think anybody who breaks the law, no matter what it is, is really thinking about the other side of the coin," he said. I asked Nordahl if he took particular pleasure in stealing from the wealthy. "A lot of this stuff they don't even use," he said. "It's more of a trophy, almost. Not trying to rationalize it, but I can see feeling sorry for somebody who gets robbed of their paycheck, and that paycheck was necessary to pay for food." He added, "I don't commit crimes where someone walks up to an old lady who collects welfare and she's getting twenty dollars out of her ATM. That's absurd." He said of his crimes, "There certainly have been times probably I felt guilty, and there have been other times I probably didn't."

I wanted to know what became of the silver he stole. I told him that, as I understood it, the better pieces were exported to Europe for resale, but lesser pieces were melted down. "Well, that would be speculation," he said. "I wouldn't know."

Lonnie Mason had told me that Nordahl would sometimes lose himself, eyes bugged out, when he discussed his burglaries in detail. But the story that made his eyes bulge on this day wasn't really about his skill as a thief. It was something that happened in Monmouth County in 1984.

"This was in my younger days of doing things differently—in the daytime," he told me. He had robbed two homes but had found little of value. As he was approaching another house, he was spotted by a police car; Nordahl ran a few blocks and jumped into a thick row of hedges. He took off his white shirt, curled up, and covered himself with dirt. Police officers swarmed the area; Nordahl could hear them close by. "The one thing you never do is look at somebody if you know they're coming by," he said. "I close my eyes, and I don't think about them." The police finally left several hours later, at 9:00 p.m. Nordahl broke into a few more houses, but came up empty. "So I'm, like, 'Well, fuck this. I'm going to make some money still.'" He found a big house on the edge of a marsh and decided to camp out until everyone was asleep—but Nordahl dozed off. When he woke up in the morning, he decided to break in anyway. But, as soon as he came out into the open, police cars arrived. He doubled back toward the marsh and could hear police officers chasing him, and a helicopter in the near distance. The ground was mucky and flat, but he found a small ridge and burrowed underneath it. Policemen were stomping all around him, and the helicopter was overhead. "I'm thinking, They've got to be able to see me. Time goes by and nothing happens." One cop stepped on Nordahl's leg. "I thought, Now he's going to say, 'All right, buddy, get up.' Nothing happened." Nordahl stayed hidden until it was dark again, and the police left. "At that point, I decided, well, I'm not going to do anything more tonight. I went to the train station and caught a train to New York."

He leaned back and sighed. I began to think that perhaps it wasn't the stealing that was the thrill for Nordahl so much as the escaping. He said, "If you were being chased by a bear, your adrenaline's going to be pumping, you know what I mean? Later, you might not really say, 'Gee, that was fun.' But, at the same time, if nothing else really was going on, it might have added flavor to the day. As long as you got away from the bear. But, of course, if you got caught by the bear, you know, it's another story."

Nordahl later said that he was tired of living on the run. "My whole plan was to go on with a real life now," he said. "I have no visions of being some criminal for my life. That's not cool. My whole thing is I want to get into real estate, remodelling homes, things like that." He added, "Of course, I want to be married. Of course, I want to have kids of my own someday. I've been distant from my own family, and I need to reconnect. You need to be a part of their lives and so forth. And this doesn't let you be a part of someone's life." Earlier, I asked if anyone visited him in prison. "No," he said.

Mason and Abruzzini had warned me that Nordahl always talked about changing his ways. "Blane couldn't go straight if you snapped a chalk line for him," Abruzzini said. Luanne, his ex-girlfriend, had also told me that he would never stop. "He'll be seventy-eight with a goddam cane, walking down the street stealing silver," she said.

Nordahl insisted that if he could leave jail tomorrow he would not return to burglary. "I really don't think so," he said. "I think I've got to put all that behind me. I guess when you're young and so forth, if your life is mundane, a burglary can throw something in there. But then you start to realize that the mundaneness of life sometimes has value."

THREE WEEKS LATER, Nordahl did walk out of jail, the beneficiary of bureaucratic oversight. He had been moved from the federal prison to a nearby Ohio county jail to await extradition to New York for the Rhinebeck burglaries. But before the extradition was arranged a judge allowed him to post bond. The Ohio authorities apparently had not been informed of his recidivist history, or of his propensity for flight.

In Rhinebeck, Tom Fort sent a sheepish e-mail to the Dutchess County assistant district attorney who was prosecuting the case: "On 12/06/03 at 12:09 a.m., Nordahl posted a $50k bond and was released from the Columbiana County Jail in Ohio. He is scheduled for a 12/17/03 hearing at the Ohio court, but I think we can probably forget about him appearing." Fort's guess was right.

Abruzzini and Mason were both furious at how sloppily the case had been handled. The bail bondsman tried calling the phone number that Nordahl had given him, but it was a fake. Nordahl's mother—who had wired the cash required for bail—swore to the bondsman that she was as shocked as he was by her son's disappearance.

Robert Eisler, the lawyer, suggested to me that Nordahl would tap into his savings and disappear, perhaps to a tropical island. Mason and Abruzzini predicted that he would go looking for silver immediately. "My gut feeling is he's back in Camden," Mason told me. "He's got a number of safe houses there, criminals and junkies. He throws them money when he's around so they can buy their stuff, and they let him stay." He added, "Blane is a creature of habit. In my opinion, he'll have done a job by this weekend."

On a Friday morning less than two weeks after Nordahl jumped bail, the police in Princeton Borough, New Jersey, were called to investigate a meticulous burglary of sterling silver. A week later, several similar thefts were reported in Bergen County, just across the river from Manhattan. These were followed by burglaries in Concord and Wellesley, Massachusetts.

Neither Mason nor Abruzzini had any reason to get involved. Abruzzini had no more Greenwich cases to clear; Mason was no longer a cop. But, just as Nordahl left his signature on his crimes, Mason and Abruzzini wanted to leave their signatures on the Nordahl case, and the detectives went back to work.

Their collaboration had not always been easy. Abruzzini, as smooth and fastidious as Greenwich itself, approaches his job like a clinician. He likes to draw diagrams and flow charts depicting a criminal's activity. Mason is more intuitive, a believer in street smarts and grunt work. But now the two men combined their strengths: Mason became the lead general in the Nordahl manhunt, while Abruzzini coordinated the efforts of various detectives. Police officers in several states went looking for any paper trail that Nordahl might have generated—a rental car, parking tickets, motel check-ins. They studied surveillance tapes from motels near the various silver burglaries; they watched the homes of his girlfriends around Camden.

Mason suggested a replay of the flip-the-girlfriend trick. The police caught up with Lisa, the blond woman in the photograph that Mason had shown Luanne back in 1996. Lisa had recently violated probation herself, so the police picked her up in Camden for questioning. The manhunt had by now yielded a motel surveillance video of Nordahl with another woman. When the police showed a photo still of the video to Lisa, she cursed: the woman was her best friend. Lisa began to talk. Nordahl had stayed with her after jumping bail in Ohio, and he had gone back to stealing and was flush with cash. She told the police that Nordahl was now fencing his silver with some Russian mobsters on Canal Street.

"Once we have that exact location, we'll go in there, show Blane's picture," Mason told me in mid-January. "We'll say, 'We know he's fencing here, and when we arrest him he's facing a life term and he'll turn on you.' Within a week, we'll find Blane in a drum in the East River, because that's how these guys play." Mason said he would be comfortable with that outcome. "I'm cold and calloused," he said. "The bottom line is, Blane's gotten away too many times. Maybe this would be the fitting end to a life in crime."

Mason's reply stunned me: he had never struck me as remotely hard-hearted. I knew that he had grown tired of pursuing Nordahl. I began to think, too, that Mason, who had offered to help Nordahl turn straight, was disappointed in him. Months earlier, I had asked Mason what other kind of work Nordahl might be suited for. "With his mind?" Mason said. "I honestly don't think there's anything Blane *can't* do."

If Mason was right about the Russian mobsters, then it was the police who saved Blane Nordahl's life. Lisa told them that Nordahl had occasionally stayed in Philadelphia with her sister and her brother-in-law. The police had Lisa and her sister set Nordahl up— call him, tell him everything was okay there, and invite him to come by.

Nordahl drove up that night in a black Ford Explorer and circled the block. He parked, approached the house, and once inside was set upon by three cops. A dozen more waited outside. He fought hard, and wound up in a Philadelphia jail cell with a face like a smashed tomato and the sour knowledge that the police had been helped by his close friends.

In the coming weeks, various police jurisdictions began to fight over the right to prosecute Nordahl. He entered his jailhouse-lawyer mode, hoping once again to roll up the assorted charges into a single light plea. But on March 23, he was finally extradited to Poughkeepsie. At his arraignment, the Dutchess County prosecutor said he planned to argue that Nordahl should serve twenty-five years to life if convicted for the Rhinebeck burglaries. Nordahl flushed when he heard this. Later, after he was photographed and fingerprinted at the trooper barracks, I tried to ask him a few questions. "Now is not a good time for me" was all he would say.

For months, I had put off calling Nordahl's mother, Sharon Fitzsimmons, who now works as an accountant in a state prison in Indiana. The police warned me that if Nordahl found out that I had called her he would stop talking to me—and that Fitzsimmons would never talk anyway. But now I tried her.

"He's not a completely bad person," she told me. "He's a very likable person. I think his big problem was intelligence and no common sense. I just wish this would all come to an end. The last time I talked to him about what he was doing—this was a few years back—his response was that it's an excitement thing. He said he got bored. So I said, 'Well, why don't you take up skydiving?' I said, 'We're not wealthy people, but we'll back you up. We'll support you morally, we'll be there for you.'"

Lonnie Mason once told me about his hunch that Nordahl had walled up his savings inside his mother's house when he renovated it, and I asked Fitzsimmons if this was true. She laughed hard. "I've heard it all. 'You've probably got cans of money buried in your backyard!' You think with six dogs they wouldn't have dug something up?"

She told me what a good and smart and interesting kid Blane had been, but mostly she talked about how disappointed she was. "What I've had to do is basically realize these are his decisions," she said. "I've told him I can't help him anymore. He's over forty now, and his decisions are his own."

Although Blane had always written to her regularly, Fitzsimmons said, he rarely discussed his troubles. But his recent letters "have a different edge to them," she told me. "He's concerned that it's going to be a life thing. I think basically he's scared. He's saying he wants to get on the right path now, for good."

Then she opened a recent letter and read me a bit: "I don't want to die in jail, and I don't want you or dad to pass away without seeing my life change." She paused, then said, "I've never heard that from him before." The letter was only a slightly different version of the story that Nordahl had pitched to me recently—and to Cornell Abruzzini, and to his lawyer, and probably to half a dozen others. But I didn't need to tell that to his mother. She sounded as if she didn't believe him, either.

STEPHEN J. DUBNER *is the author of the* New York Times *best-selling* Freakonomics *(2005, with Steven D. Levitt),* Turbulent Souls: A Catholic Son's Return to His Jewish Family *(1998),* and Con-fessions of a Hero-Worshiper *(2003). He is now working on a book about the psychology of money, and another book about Jewish ethics. Most of his journalism has appeared in the* New York Times Maga-zine *but also in* The New Yorker, Time, New York, *and elsewhere.*

Coda

It only took two years to write this article. I made my first phone calls in March of 2002. I was finishing up a book that concerned Pittsburgh, so I was in the habit of reading the Pittsburgh papers every morning. In the *Post-Gazette* one day was an article about some silver burglaries that, if pattern held, were likely committed by a certain Blane Nordahl, who had just been arrested outside of Philadelphia. A quick search of the Philly papers yielded a few more articles. So my first conscious act in writing this story about burglary was to burgle the work of those journalists in Pittsburgh and Philly. To them: apologies, and thanks.

I got to work, trying to reconstruct the past few years of Nordahl's life. I was happy to save string, see how things turned out. What I really wanted was an interview with Nordahl himself, which took forever to arrange. Finally he agreed. Then he changed his mind. Then he changed his mind again, but with conditions. By the time I finally sat down with him at a federal prison in Ohio, I knew more about Nordahl than I know about some of my own siblings. (This isn't as strange as you might think; there are eight of us, and some of the facts are pretty murky.) Nordahl was, without question, one of the dullest interviews I've ever conducted. His story was terrific, but he wasn't the guy to tell it. He was too arrogant, too paranoid, too controlling. The story came from Lonnie Mason and Cornell Abruzzini, from Bobby Eisler and Tom Fort, generous gentlemen each of them, and a small army of others.

Early one morning, soon after Nordahl jumped bail, went on a burglary tear, and got busted again, Lonnie Mason called me. He said that two of Nordahl's friends—the people he was staying with when he was arrested, and who had in fact set him up—were killed in a one-car crash. Police suspected the brake line was cut. Mason thought that Nordahl had arranged from jail to have them killed, to eliminate potential witnesses. He couldn't ever prove it; knowing Lonnie, he's probably still trying.

A few months after this article was published, *Law & Order: Criminal Intent* ran an episode based on Nordahl. Lonnie and I both happened to be watching. During commercials, we chatted on the phone. We couldn't believe how thoroughly they had lifted the story: every detail, every twist, every idiosyncrasy. It made sense, of course. A story about a thief, which began in thievery, should surely end in thievery. It was a good episode, one of my favorites.

Philip Weiss

STALKING
HER KILLER

FROM *New York* MAGAZINE

AT 4:30 ON A TUESDAY AFTERNOON, I stood on the south side of Montague Street in Brooklyn watching the Social Security offices, waiting for Dennis to come out. I wasn't sure what he looked like. I had a number of photographs of him at age twenty-four, a thickly built blond guy with thinning hair and broad heavy planes in an intelligent face. Bearded, introverted. But what use were the pictures? They were from 1976. Dennis had lately turned fifty.

Having gotten a primer from a private-eye friend about tailing people, I followed a few fiftyish Dennises down the street. None of them seemed right. Then it got to be 5:20 and I was heading home myself when a man came out of the office door and everyone else on the rush-hour block seemed to vanish. Most of his hair was now gone, but the beard was still there, and so was the inward intensity, the determined anonymity. Dennis's oddball spirit was so distinct and strong that it had passed unchanged from the old pictures I carried. He wore jeans and a T-shirt, carried a knapsack, wore photo-gray glasses, as he had worn jeans and a T-shirt and carried a knapsack and worn photogray glasses twenty-six years before, on the night that Deb in one of her last acts had knocked his glasses off, breaking them. He had left them in the blood on the floor of her hut, got on his bike, bicycled off into the darkness.

He looked like what he had been then: a Peace Corps volunteer. I followed him down the street and into the subway, then lost him.

I'D FIRST HEARD of Dennis more than twenty-five years ago. In 1978, I was twenty-two and backpacking around the world when I'd crashed with a Peace Corps volunteer in Samoa named Bruce McKenzie. He said that a year or so back in the Kingdom of Tonga, a tiny island nation in a crook of the dateline, a male Peace Corps volunteer had killed a female volunteer. There had been some kind of triangle. He was a spurned or jealous lover. He had stabbed her many times. The American government had moved heaven and earth to get him out of Tonga. Bruce didn't know any names, but he said the case had caused considerable friction between the Peace Crops and Pacific-island governments, and hearing this by the light of a kerosene lamp, with the heavy rain clattering on the roof, I formed a romantic idea of a story out of Maugham or Conrad, of something terribly wrong that had unfolded in an out-of-the-way place. A true idea, as things would turn out.

I returned to the story several times in the intervening years, learning the killer's name, Dennis Priven, and something of the government machinations that had given him his freedom. It became an occasional obsession, something that nagged at me all my adult life.

The victim's name was Deborah Gardner. She was twenty-three, a natural girl in a seventies way, with a laid-back Pacific Northwest vibe. In Tonga, in 1976, she rode her bicycle everywhere by herself at night, even when people told her she shouldn't, she didn't wear makeup, she put her thick dark hair up in a rubber band at night and took it down in the morning, washed her clothes by stamping

on them barefoot in a basin with a Jethro Tull tape going. She decorated her one-room hut with tapa cloth and native weavings, and
lay on her bed all afternoon reading Heinlein or Hesse.

Her hut was on the outskirts of Nuku'alofa, Tonga's capital city,
alongside the home of a gangling, humorous Californian named
Emile Hons, who was friendly with Dennis. Deb taught science
and home economics at the leading educational institution in the
country, Tonga High School.

People said she was the prettiest girl in the Peace Corps. She
dressed modestly, in denim skirts and men's button-down shirts, but
men still noticed her big laugh and the way her body moved. There
were seventy other volunteers in the country, and sometimes it
seemed like every guy in the capital wanted to go out with her. She
had dated two New Yorkers, ethnic exotics to her own western-
mixed Lutheran background; and then a third New Yorker had
wanted to date her, too.

She was polite to Dennis Priven. He lived a mile or so away
from her and taught chemistry and math at the leading Methodist
high school. Most volunteers were wary of him. He was the best
poker player on the island, and took everyone's money, and they did
not understand why he didn't look anyone in the eye and carried a
large Seahorse dive knife with him everywhere.

Still, he had a few close friends, drawn to him by his humor and
intelligence. "[He] succeeds at what he wishes to do," volunteer
Barbara Williams wrote home about Dennis. "Since he has a beard
and usually wears cut-off blue jeans, the Tongans think he's sloppy—
which he isn't. Keeps his desk, bookshelves, home very nearly neat as
a pin. The students are scared of him, not knowing that beneath
that gruff exterior lies a tender heart of the sort that rescues fair
damsels in distress. He'd hate to think so, though, disliking senti-
mentality. All in all he's too good to waste—I keep wanting to
match him up with some fluffy little wisp of a girl with a will of
iron. They'd live happily ever after."

Dennis pined for the voluptuous girl with the Kelty backpack from Washington State. One night, he awkwardly invited Deb to come over to his house for dinner, and she accepted. His friends helped him put the meal together. Emile thought of it as a high-school gambit, and other friends of Dennis also saw the date in high-school terms. Perhaps implicit in the planning was a judgment of Deb—Dennis was a serious soul, Deb was a party person. He'd be good for her.

The dinner went badly. Dennis had high expectations and had gotten Deb a gift, spending real money. He was full of awkward feeling, and the situation became unpleasant. She ran out of his house, got on her bicycle, rode into the night.

When Deb saw a former boyfriend, Frank Bevacqua, later, she was upset. "He must have spent one hundred dollars on this dinner. Doesn't he know I don't want to go out with him?"

"You have to tell him that."

Over the next few months, Dennis's thoughts about Deb became more sinister. It upset him that she skinny-dipped in violation of *tapu*, or taboo (the word is originally Tongan), and did not thank him enough after he had put in a sink for her. She found it impossible to escape him. He came to her school on his bike every day to visit, even after her vice-principal had told him that he was not welcome there. And though his behavior—the knife he always carried, some bizarre and menacing statements—drew the official attention of the small Peace Corps staff, he somehow managed to hang on into the last months of his two-year service.

In part to escape him, Deb applied for a transfer to another island. Then in October 1976, the Peace Corps held a dance for a new group of volunteers, and that night seemed to unhinge Dennis. Deb got drunk, and fell twice on the dance floor, and then Emile took her home, accompanied her into her hut.

Five nights later, Dennis arrived there himself. He had his dive knife with him, and also a syringe, a metal pipe, and two jars containing cyanide. Later his friends would learn that he intended a surgical murder, in which he would club Deb with the pipe and make her unconscious, then destroy her. But Deb started fighting him, fending off his knife with her hands, leaving horrible wounds; ultimately, Dennis stabbed her twenty-two times. Her Tongan neighbors discovered him dragging her out the front door. He jumped on his bicycle and fled into the dark, and the neighbors brought her to the hospital in the back of an old green truck. Doctors worked valiantly, but the damage to her aorta and carotid artery was so severe she would have died if Vaiola Hospital had been the Mayo Clinic.

Dennis's plan called for him to kill himself, as he told friends later, but he changed his mind about that part. At midnight, he bicycled to the house of a friend, Paul Boucher, and the two of them went to the police station. Why have you come here? asked the Tongan detectives. I have tried to kill myself, he said. He had taken an overdose of Darvon, and feebly cut his wrists.

"Do you know Miss Deborah Gardner?" asked Chief Inspector Faka'ilo Penitani.

"No."

"Was she a friend of yours?"

"I have nothing to say."

TWO DAYS LATER, Emile brought Deb's body home to the United States. Deb's parents were divorced, her mother living in Tacoma, her father in Anchorage. They came together at the funeral for the first time in years, and though they were disturbed when a Peace Corps official said that the government would have to pay for Dennis's defense, they accepted the policy. Dennis had done it; he was locked up, and was going to be for a long time.

In the weeks to come, the Peace Corps threw itself completely behind Dennis. A volunteer was in a primitive jail, facing hanging. The future of the Tongan program was at risk. The woman's shell-shocked parents did not show up in the country, and no one in the United States knew about the case. The Peace Corps was careful to keep it that way. Even when it reported the case to Vice President

Nelson Rockefeller so that he could send condolence letters to the Gardners, the message was oblique. "She died shortly after her arrival at the hospital." Nothing about a murder. And though policy called for immediate announcement of volunteer deaths, the Peace Corps waited nineteen days, till November 2, 1976, the day of the presidential election, Carter over Ford. The story was buried.

Over the next three months, the Peace Corps did all it could to make the nightmare in Tonga go away. It brought in Tonga's most famous lawyer from New Zealand to represent him. It summoned a psychiatrist from Hawaii who testified that Dennis was a paranoid schizophrenic. Dr. Kosta Stojanovich's words were translated into Tongan as "double-minded" for a jury of seven Tongan farmers, none of whom had graduated from high school.

There was no counterexpert. There wasn't a psychiatrist in all the kingdom, and the Tongan government could not afford to bring one in. And though the prosecution tried to demonstrate that the murder grew out of a jealous triangle, Peace Corps witnesses proved elusive on this score. Even Emile said that his relationship with Deb was "brother-sister." The jury went out for twenty-six minutes before rendering an insanity verdict, and Crown solicitor Tevita Tupou complained bitterly to the king: "It appeared to me that all pity was with Priven and none was shown to the dead girl. The Peace Corps effort may have been made to try and save the name of the movement from the embarrassment of one of their members being convicted of murder. I find this very strange justice if this was the case."

The worst was yet to come. The Tongan police minister was for keeping Dennis at the Tongan prison farm. But the king and other members of the cabinet deferred to the Americans. The State Department gave a letter to the prime minister promising that Dennis would be hospitalized involuntarily in Washington till he was no longer a danger to himself or others, and that if he made any effort to escape his fate, he would be arrested. These were misrepresentations. Sibley, the hospital the State Department cited, only accepted voluntary commitments, and when he got back to Washington in January 1977, Dennis refused to go in. Peace Corps lawyers then desperately called the Washington police, who said that they had no power to arrest Dennis.

At last, under pressure from the Peace Corps, his parents, and the two friends who had brought him back, Dennis agreed to see a psychiatrist at Sibley. Zigmond Lebensohn reached an opposite conclusion to Stojanovich's back in Tonga. Dennis wasn't psychotic, he was shy and sexually inexperienced and had suffered a "situational psychosis." He had been led on by a pretty girl who then slammed the door. "For this kind of guy, that triggered everything. Everything went kaflooey," Lebensohn later told me. He could not commit him.

After the case ended in 1977, a story went out among teachers and doctors and policemen and schoolchildren back in Tonga: Dennis Priven was dead. He stepped off the plane in the United States, and someone from the girl's family, her uncle or brother, came up and shot him on the tarmac. The story went around like wildfire. People wanted to believe it. The story satisfied a deep social understanding, that if somebody killed someone, it would catch up with him, he would die.

But Dennis didn't die. He was free. He went home, moved into his parents' co-op in Sheepshead Bay. He got a clean discharge from the Peace Corps—Completion of Service—and a month later applied for a new passport, and reportedly got it. He rejoined his Brooklyn College fraternity poker game, though the frat brothers joked that you should keep sharp objects away from him. Once, a group of buddies confronted him about Tonga—Did that really happen? Dennis shrugged. He said it had happened, it was a long story.

His family came apart. Miriam, his sickly mother, died a year after his return. Sidney, his printer father, moved to Florida with a new wife.

Dennis and his older brother, Jay, a coach at Boys and Girls High, stopped speaking. He was the eternal Peace Corps volunteer. He wore his beard heavy and rode his bicycle everywhere. He didn't look people in the eye.

He married a Hispanic woman in the early nineties. By 1996, he was divorced, still living in the apartment he had grown up in. He worked at Social Security, as a top computer manager: area systems coordinator. He made $78,000 a year.

I'd spent years thinking about Dennis, even dreaming about him. It had become more than a writing project—one that I'd started several times over the decades. It was something approaching a mission. Deb Gardner was alive in me, in a sense. I was surprised at how much anger I felt over the injustice done to her by Priven and her own government. In the late nineties, I'd taken the story up in earnest, going to Tonga several times. And finally, toward the end of my reporting, I approached him. I wrote him a letter, saying I was writing a book about the events in Tonga in 1976 and wanted his help. A few days later, I was standing outside the Sheepshead Bay subway station, trying to chart his movements, when I got a call on my cell phone. It was Dennis; he wanted to meet me. "This will be short," he said.

WORKMEN WERE eviscerating Broadway at Prince. The jackhammers were going, girls walked by in their slip dresses. From the coffee bar at the front of Dean and DeLuca, I saw a girl whose lace underwear showed above her wrap skirt and thought about how these women would have seemed to the kids in Deb's Peace Corps group, Tonga sixteen, with their long dresses to wear in a conservative, Christian society.

I'd spent years preparing to meet Dennis. In my knapsack I had documents from New Zealand, the analyses the government had done for the Tongans on Deb and Dennis's clothing twenty-six years before. I wanted to be ready if he said he was innocent.

Dennis arrived promptly at noon. He was the man I'd seen in

Brooklyn a few days before, with dark glasses and a fixed, lowered, oxlike expression.

We shook hands, and Dean and DeLuca suddenly felt tight as a closet. He gave a tilt of his head, and we went out.

"Do you go by the standard journalistic ethics?" he said, turning onto Prince.

"Yes, why?"

"So . . . everything I tell you is going to be off the record."

"Okay."

And I interpreted that in the strictest way. "Everything I tell you." Not anything he asked me, or showed me.

We spent the afternoon together. As we talked, we walked up and down lower Manhattan, sticking to the big avenues. In some ways he was the most important person in the story, and I didn't understand who he was.

There were two theories about him. One was the anybody-can-snap theory that an old colleague of his, Gay Roberts, had told me in New Zealand. In his second year in Tonga, Dennis was isolated and unhappy, and one bad thing after another had happened, till he'd snapped, Gay said—it might happen to anyone. Then there was the evil-genius theory that the Tongan police minister, 'Akau'ola, and Deb's former boyfriend Frank Bevacqua, subscribed to. Dennis was a poker player. He'd planned this to a fare-thee-well, playing lawyers and governments and shrinks off each other.

Dennis walked beside me, now and then giving the faintest smile. The same untelling mug that people had watched during his nine-day trial. He stared straight ahead through dark-brown Armani glasses, but now and then I got a glimpse of his eyes: deep-set, dark, big, liquid holes. I couldn't say what he was thinking, though when I told him the Gay Roberts theory he went to a plate-glass window and traced a big circle on it with his finger and then stuck his finger in the middle of the circle.

His beard was shaved neatly around his mouth and cheeks, but his shoulders in a cutoff Champion T-shirt were hairy, and he had a funny walk in his jeans shorts. His manner was so sensitive that it sometimes seemed feminine. There was that tenderness Barbara Williams had seen. Now and then he reached out and grabbed me, to stop me from walking into traffic, and the sense his friends had had in Tonga, that he would do anything for you, was mine. A couple of times he stopped me in a brotherly way to tug the zipper up on my knapsack. It was his mind that was most interesting. It was strange, and it could go anywhere. And he was funny.

When we hit Union Square, he pulled out a folded piece of paper and read me a proposal. He said I could convey his terms to my editors, so I will report its fuzzy outline here: Dennis had no interest in my book coming out, but if I waited a few years to publish he would tell me everything.

I should have anticipated such a gambit. Emile had described to me a chilling visit to Dennis in jail after the murder when Dennis had unfolded a grand double-jeopardy scheme in which Emile would come forward at the last minute of the trial and take the rap, freeing Dennis—after which Dennis would come forward during Emile's trial. In this way, Dennis had theorized, they would both go free.

What I told Dennis was that he should come forward because of the havoc the case had left in the minds of a hundred or so people who knew about it, the idea that a person could kill someone and walk away from it. I reminded him of what Tongans had said to him many times, that he must apologize to the girl's family and ask their forgiveness. I reminded him of the scene in *Crime and Punishment* where Raskolnikov confesses to Sonya the prostitute and says, What should I do? and Sonya says, Go to the crossroads and kiss the ground in four directions and say I have sinned, and God will give you life again.

It was my own form of bluff. The Gardners didn't want to talk to Dennis. If Dennis went to Deborah's mother in Idaho on bended knee, Wayne would know what to do with him and it wasn't listen. Wayne wanted Dennis imprisoned, or hanged back in Tonga. He wanted justice.

I didn't tell Dennis that. What was his idea of justice, anyway? I'd learned that he was too interior a person to believe in justice, his imagination too crazy and elaborate. He lacked any superego. This was just some misunderstanding that had happened between a couple of people. "She deserved it," he had said in Tonga, and maybe he still believed that, and in that sense he seemed to me evil. He had treated the murder and his release as a form of accomplishment, not something to be regretted.

He'd maintained a poker face for three months in Tonga. He had almost killed himself with hunger strikes two or three times so as to be kept in the jail in downtown Nuku'alofa, near his friends, rather than at the isolated prison farm. And while Emile had refused to play the double-jeopardy game, other friends had helped him. He'd made a kind of confession to Barbara Williams, in order to gain admission back into the human family, but Barbara's loving expectation that he would be incarcerated in a mental hospital meant nothing to him. Another friend had given him a Bible that he had read thoroughly in jail, and he had then told Dr. Stojanovich that he was Deb's Jesus Christ and savior and she was possessed by the devil—or he had allowed Stojanovich to say as much on the stand. Then, in the States, Dennis had told Dr. Lebensohn that Deb had led him on and crushed him. Two different stories, each the key to its respective legal doorway.

Believing it pointless to cite a larger social good, I appealed to Dennis's grandiosity. I said that what he had pulled off was actually a stunning addition to the annals of crime. There was a brilliance to it, a negative brilliance, for sure, but most surprisingly, the story was unsung.

I was going to change that; didn't he want to help?

"Okay, if I'm as smart as you say I am, then how come it's not me with the big house by the lake in Seattle?"

"You're as smart as Bill Gates, you just care about different things," I said.

I'd pictured this encounter for years, and always with explosive scenes. He did get angry a couple of times, and I had the underlying sense that he was deeply dissociated, but all in all it was a civilized meeting. He was a free man in Soho. We were two middle-aged cerebral New Yorkers, lost in conversation, tied together by intense feelings about a beautiful loner of a woman whom he had prevented from ever growing old, and whose crystalline girlhood had trapped me, too, in seventies amber.

We went back to Dean and DeLuca. I got a bottle of juice and he got a lemonade, and we walked south. "I want to show you my pictures," I said.

We sat on a rusted iron stoop on Grand Street and I showed him one hundred or so of the images I'd collected. He flipped impassively through the pictures of Deb, broke down when he saw a picture of his old friend Paul Boucher, lost it for a few minutes, had to walk off down the street. The narcissistic monster, only thinking about his own bloody life.

Then he carefully drew something from his knapsack he'd brought along, a stiff card with a blue edge, his membership in the Royal Nuku'alofa Martini Club, a group founded by expatriates in 1975. It was an artifact from before Deborah, before his life had fallen apart.

In the months that followed our meeting, Dennis was to quit his job at Social Security and change his phone number again. Having gotten away with murder twenty-eight years ago, he was condemned to preserve that terrible achievement. He was still on his bicycle, rushing into the dark forever. He could put the thing away in a box, but the box never went away. For the time being, though, Dennis put away his card, and I put away my pictures of Deb. We got our knapsacks on, had a moment's small talk, then he headed toward Broadway, I headed toward Lafayette. He didn't look back, I'm sure of that, but then neither did I.

PHILIP WEISS *is a New York author. This piece is drawn from his book,* American Taboo: A Murder in the Peace Corps. *He has worked for many years as a journalist, writing a column in the* New York Observer. *He has been a contributing writer to the* New York Times Magazine, Harper's, *and* Esquire. *He is at work on a book about the army in Australia and New Guinea during the Second World War.*

Coda

Investigating the murder of Deborah Gardner took me four years, 2000–2004. For those years it was the most important thing in my life, as it had to be if I were going to dig out the facts in the case. I was willing to go anywhere to talk to anyone who had information about what had happened in Tonga in 1976. I visited Tonga ten times, New Zealand half a dozen times, Australia three times, in addition to half the States. The book that came out of that reporting ended an oral legend that had eaten at people in the South Pacific and the United States by documenting a shady and shameful episode of politicized murder, in which the Peace Corps and State Department worked to free a disturbed young American Peace Corps volunteer who had stalked and then killed another volunteer on a remote island.

It was a great story. And I'm embarrassed to say that it took me a long time to get around to it.

The Peace Corps volunteer who told me about the murder, so long ago, in 1978, didn't know Deborah's name, nor the name of her killer, Dennis Priven, but he conveyed an awareness of a distant drama and justice that I could never get out of my head. Over the years I made halfhearted efforts to learn more. I found out that the government had suppressed the case and that the killer had been freed in the United States not four months after the murder. I found out that Deb Gardner was a spirited and generous person. Poe said that the death of a beautiful young woman was the most poetical topic in the world and I was not about to disagree. In April 2000, I finally saw her photograph, and I stopped wondering about what had happened and committed myself to investigating the case.

That project caused pain to a number of people, even Deb's family, whom the Peace Corps had lied to about the case. But it was worth it. A burden was lifted from people who were close to the matter and had always needed to say something, including a number of Tongans who had fought for Deb.

It appears now that there will be some official action in the case. Norm Dicks, the congressman from Deb Gardner's home district in Washington State, has called for an investigation. The U.S. Attorney's office in Seattle is looking into the matter, though he has indicated that it may be too late for an indictment, to which Deb's father, Wayne, at last fully engaged by the case, has responded, "So—I have to stomp my own snakes?" The Peace Corps has continued to circle the wagons. It meets all inquiries about the Gardner matter with bromides about how much it "mourns" Deborah Gardner. It has made no real effort to look at the facts and recommend changes in policy, or maybe even offer an apology to the Gardner family.

Dennis Priven continues to live in Brooklyn, New York. He has made no statement about the case.

Debra Miller Landau

Social
Disgraces

FROM *Atlanta* MAGAZINE

HE WORE HIS DEAD uncle's underwear so he wouldn't have to buy his own, then spent freely on tailored suits. He'd tell his wife to keep the air-conditioning off to keep the bills at bay, and would tightly budget groceries, then turn around and throw luxurious dinner parties. His former in-laws say he'd tell new acquaintances his father worked in the Hearst publishing empire, then deny it when the truth came out that his dad was a typesetter who struggled to make ends meet.

A South Boston kid who grew up playing stickball in his blue-collar neighborhood, James Sullivan made it his life's mission to become something, or someone, else.

Eager to shed his working-class roots, Sullivan, a onetime Macon liquor distributor, married an Atlanta socialite, made millions and began grasping at the rungs of whatever social ladder he could reach.

In 1998, the Fulton County District Attorney's Office indicted James Sullivan for his alleged role in the shooting death of his wife, Lita. At the time of the indictment, Sullivan simply vanished. For four years he led authorities on an international manhunt that went from Atlanta to Florida, Costa Rica, Panama, Venezuela, and finally Thailand. At the top of the FBI's Most Wanted list, Sullivan's photo flashed around the world. His biographical sketch portrayed a man who loved the good life, who frequented fancy resorts and restaurants, most likely with an attractive woman on his arm.

The FBI also noted that Sullivan was likely to be spotted swiping condiments from restaurants he visited.

What drove a man who buried his fortune in complex offshore accounts to burrow away sugar packets and swipe saltshakers? Fear he'd lose everything? Or was his penurious personality ingrained, reflecting a hardscrabble upbringing?

The conflict between Sullivan's social aspirations and his scabrous persona will be front and center early next year when he stands trial—again—for allegedly masterminding and financing Lita's death. As the facts of Lita's death and her tumultuous relationship with James are examined once more, it is certain that her onetime husband—and the man sitting at the defense table—will be scrutinized just as hard.

MACON

Growing up in the Irish Catholic, rough-and-tumble streets of Dorchester, a South Boston neighborhood, Sullivan learned early that if he ever wanted out, he'd have to be shrewd, smart, and different. Despite his working-class roots, young Sullivan gained an impressive education. He went to high school at the academically challenging Boston Latin School and won an academic scholarship to College of the Holy Cross in Worcester, Massachusetts. He graduated with an economics degree in 1962 and later studied finance at Boston University. Three years after completing school, he married Catherine Murray and the couple had four children in short order. Sullivan worked in the comptroller's department at Jordan

Marsh, a Boston department store, and later at Peat, Marwick and Mitchell accounting firm.

Sullivan moved to Macon in 1973 when his childless uncle, Frank Bienert, asked him to help run Crown Beverages, a successful wholesale liquor distribution company Bienert founded in 1962.

In Macon, Sullivan's swagger, charm, and ambition helped him carve a niche among the city's movers and shakers. Although many Maconites found his brashness offensive to their old-boy approach to business, Sullivan gained headway in the community by working with the Chamber of Commerce and charitable organizations.

When Bienert died in 1975, Sullivan became the sole heir to the distributorship. Less than a year later, he and Catherine divorced, citing irreconcilable differences. She got custody of the kids, one thousand dollars a month in child support, and moved back to their home near Boston.

James Vincent Sullivan and Lita LaVaughn McClinton met in early 1976 when she was working as an assistant manager at T. Edward's, an upscale clothing boutique in Lenox Square. He wore polyester pants, thick horn-rimmed glasses, and a mop of curly hair, but he was charming and affable, with a thick New England accent.

To Lita's friends and family, it seemed an odd union. Jim was white, an outsider, rough around the edges. She was from a prominent, politically active African-American family in Atlanta. A former debutante, polished and trim, Lita went to private schools and cotillions, a social girl who made friends easily. She had recently graduated with a degree in political science from Spelman College. He was thirty-four and she ten years younger.

Always impeccably dressed and passionate about fashion, Lita set to work updating Sullivan's wardrobe, teaching him how to fix his hair and convincing him to ditch the glasses for contact lenses. Though Sullivan lived in Macon and Lita in her hometown Atlanta, they began dating. He brought her gifts, took her to dinner and dancing, movies and basketball games. The relationship blossomed and a few months later, Sullivan proposed.

Jo Ann and Emory McClinton, Lita's parents, had misgivings about Sullivan from the start. "Jim was not readily accepted by members of our family," says Jo Ann, who has been a member of the Georgia legislature since 1992. "But Lita wanted to marry him and, as a parent, well, you can't see into the future, you can't see what's going to happen."

Emory, a retired regional civil rights compliance director for the Federal Highway Administration and now on the board of the Georgia Department of Transportation, says he was immediately suspicious of Sullivan's arrogance and self-aggrandizing. He worried about the ten-year age difference, and the stress a mixed-race couple had to endure.

Lita had already accepted James's proposal when she found out about his ex-wife and children. "Of course we were shocked," recalls Jo Ann. "That's just the beginning of his deceit, his lies," adds Emory.

On December 29, 1976, Lita and Sullivan married in a small ceremony in Macon. Not long before, Sullivan surprised Lita, over drinks and dinner, with a prenuptial agreement. Lita's divorce lawyer Richard Schiffman Jr. would later describe the agreement as "rather one-sided." He said, "in essence, Mr. Sullivan receives everything and Mrs. Sullivan receives virtually nothing." She was in love and naive; without reading the details, she signed.

Lita worked as a buyer for Rich's in Atlanta, commuting back and forth to Macon on weekends. She later quit her job and moved permanently to Macon. The Sullivans moved into a spacious, columned mansion overlooking the Ocmulgee River at 1276 Nottingham Drive, in the mostly white, affluent neighborhood of Shirley Hills. They filled the home with Louis XVI furniture, Gorham silver, and Baccarat crystal. Although he was making a decent living as the owner of Crown Beverages, the couple lived beyond their means, spending to keep up with the society in which they both aspired to belong.

The interracial marriage provoked mixed reactions in Macon,

even prompting disapprovers to throw garbage on the Sullivans' lawn. Lita knew how to persevere. No stranger to racial tension, she grew up in the thick of the civil rights movement. Born in Atlanta in 1952, she was the eldest of three children. Along with her siblings, Valencia and Emory Jr., Lita was one of the first black students to attend St. Pius X High School.

Even though he was a Northerner and she a black woman, the Sullivans attended fund-raisers and charitable events and became embedded in Macon's upper echelons. Lita worked with the American Heart Association, counseled unwed mothers, and helped in the Macon beauty pageants. Under Lita's tutelage, Georgia Court of Appeals Judge Yvette Miller was the first African-American woman to be crowned "Miss Macon" in 1979.

To outsiders, the marriage seemed happy, but inside that house on Nottingham, things were starting to fall apart. The generosity Sullivan first showed Lita began to wane.

In December 1982, six years into their marriage, Lita found a Christmas card sent to Jim from a woman signed, "missing your kisses at Christmas." Jim was away in Florida and Lita was distraught; she hadn't wanted to believe the rumors that he'd been seeing other women, but she couldn't deny this overt confirmation. Lita later testified that she drove to the return address on the envelope, and waited for the woman to come home. Her worst fears were realized when the woman confirmed she'd been having an affair with Sullivan since the summer.

Devastated, Lita went to Atlanta and met with lawyer John Taylor, an acquaintance and friend of the Sullivans. He suggested she confront Sullivan and when she did, he denied the allegations, even getting angry that she'd ever accuse him of infidelity. She wanted to trust Sullivan, wanted to make the marriage work, and Sullivan agreed that he did, too. Taylor suggested the couple sign a postnuptial agreement, one that would supersede the prenup and supposedly give Lita more financial security should the marriage dissolve. The postnup gave her $300 a week, plus $30,000 for three years if they ever divorced. Again, without examining the details, Lita signed the agreement. Its validity, and whether she was coerced into signing, would become a contested topic later.

Despite her instincts to leave, she'd come from a home where family values and loyalty meant everything. She stuck with the marriage.

WEST PALM BEACH

In 1983, Sullivan sold Crown Beverages for $5 million. The working-class kid from Boston had hit the big time. Now free of the distributorship, James Sullivan was eager to get out of Macon, and he purchased a beachfront mansion for $2 million. Built in the 1920s by Swiss architect Maurice Fatio, the home was considered "historic" and sat, overlooking the ocean, like a beacon of wealth.

Lita never even saw the house before they moved. She later said, "I did not intend ever to make Palm Beach my home as I was not accepted in the social community there. I stated to my husband on many occasions that I did not want to live in Palm Beach. When my husband purchased the Palm Beach home, he did so over my objections and I told him I would never make it my permanent residence."

During the move from Macon to West Palm Beach, Sullivan met truck driver Tony Harwood, an event that would later change the course of both their lives. At first, they were just two guys shooting the breeze while movers packed the truck. A lady's man who wore tight jeans, cowboy boots, and a pack of Lucky Strikes rolled in his T-shirt sleeve, Harwood had been around the block. He'd done time in a North Carolina prison, first for burglary, later for escape. Something about him got Sullivan talking.

"He told me he had a problem with an ex-wife and she was going to take him through the hoop," Harwood later told the Georgia Bureau of Investigation (GBI). "He said he really needed somebody to take care of her. Get her out of the way. I said, 'I'll take care of her for you for $25,000.' He kind of looked at me and said, 'You have somebody that can do it?' And I just winked at him." Sullivan later mailed Harwood a certified check for $14,000 to Harwood's home, a double-wide trailer, in Finger, North Carolina. Sullivan told him the rest would come later. Harwood waited.

In West Palm, Sullivan, then forty-two, focused intently on climbing the fickle and complex social ladder. Although his red brick and coquina mansion's address at 920 South Ocean Boulevard gave Sullivan clout, he realized acceptance in the Palm Beach social sphere would require cunning. He played tennis, took flying lessons, hobnobbed over cocktails, and hosted extravagant parties. He won a coveted appointment on the city's Landmark Preservation Commission and thought he'd secured a first-class ticket to the jet set, but what he didn't realize is that the Palm Beach elite mistrusted a man with new money, especially, it seemed, one with a black wife. Sullivan frequently went out alone or, ever more frequently, with other women.

Lita began finding clues of Sullivan's ongoing affairs. When she'd confront him, he'd respond by cutting off her finances. They had vicious fights, so bad sometimes that the police were called to break it up. Sullivan became increasingly cheap with Lita, telling her to keep the air-conditioning turned off, giving her a pittance for groceries or gas.

Lita grew depressed and reclusive. She saw a psychologist to figure out ways to save her marriage, but by then it seemed hopeless. In 1984, she convinced Sullivan to buy a second home in Atlanta, so Lita could go back when she wanted to. They bought a four-bedroom townhouse on Slaton Drive in Buckhead in the mid-$400s.

On August 12, 1985, as their ten-year anniversary approached, Lita gathered her gumption. While Sullivan was out, she rented a U-Haul trailer, hitched it to the back of her 1973 Mercedes 450 SL, and packed it full of her belongings. The Sullivans' maid would later testify that Lita packed "canned goods, paper products, household items, antiques, plus more than twenty cartons of crystal, porcelain and sterling silver."

A few days later, she filed for divorce.

ATLANTA

Once free of Palm Beach, Lita enjoyed her life in Atlanta. She cherished close friends, having her family near. She dated some men and entertained at her townhouse. She worked for different charities, and was heavily involved in arranging decorations and entertainment for the 1986 New Year's Crescendo Ball for Cystic Fibrosis, held at The Ritz-Carlton, Buckhead.

The only constantly hovering cloud was her divorce. New lawyers, new motions, new court dates, new fears. Though she had almost no contact with Sullivan, their lawyers volleyed back and forth. Sullivan had attacked her character, alleging that she was an adulteress, a thief, and a drug addict. He said he found dollar bills with cocaine residue sitting in the curve of a shoehorn in her medicine cabinet. Said she stole two diamonds that were hidden in the bottom of a shoe closet. It was one thing after another; her lawyer even had her taking monthly urine tests so they could refute the drug allegations in court. She often feared someone was spying on her, and that she'd been followed.

In March 1986, Lita's longtime friend and former Spelman classmate Poppy Marable discovered that her husband, Marvin Marable, had wiretapped Poppy's phone, listening in on her conversations, many of which were with Lita. Poppy filed for divorce from her husband, who was later indicted on invasion of privacy charges. According to the FBI, Sullivan, a friend of Marvin Marable's, later admitted that he'd received copies of the tapes, sent to him in a big box to his Palm Beach home.

On January 16, 1987, a judge was going to address a pretrial motion on division of property and determine the validity of the Sullivans' postnuptial agreement. Judged in her favor, Lita stood to get half of Sullivan's assets.

SLATON DRIVE, BUCKHEAD

On January 15, 1987, Lita's mother and sister Valencia were visiting Lita and discussing the upcoming trial. Sullivan had scheduled to have someone take a video inventory of everything in the Atlanta home that day, but Lita got a call canceling the appointment.

That night, Lita grabbed a bite to eat with a friend at R. Thomas' Deluxe Grill. Later, Poppy and her young daughter came over to spend the night, to be with Lita before the trial. Though the women planned to stay up chatting, they fell asleep late while watching TV.

January 16, 1987, began as an unspectacular day, one of those postholiday days when the chilly wet air and steady drizzle keep one in bed a little longer than usual.

That morning, a Friday, two men drove up to the Botany Bay flower shop, then located on Peachtree at Pharr Road, about half a mile from Lita's house. They drove a white Toyota. One guy came in and said he wanted a dozen roses; he didn't care what color. The clerk, Randall Benson, felt anxious and hurried; he worried that he was going to get robbed, and so only wired five of the twelve roses. The customer told Benson to leave the shop's sticker off the box, so the clerk tied it with a pink ribbon. He let out a sigh of relief when the men left. It was just after 8:00 a.m.

Armed with the white, long flower box, a tall, white, balding man wearing a green work jacket and gray pants stood on Lita's stoop, looked around, and rang the doorbell at 3085 Slaton Drive.

Lita woke up that day in her Buckhead townhouse likely nervous about the coming afternoon. She was due in Superior Court at 2:00 p.m. to hear the important pretrial ruling. The trial was due to start in just ten days.

Maybe Lita didn't have time to think about anything that day, except perhaps that it was odd that the doorbell was ringing so early in the morning. She put on her housecoat, went downstairs, and answered the door. It was 8:20 a.m.

Lita must have seen the flower box because she opened the door wide, unsuspecting of anything more than an early-morning delivery. She took the box. She must have immediately noticed the man held a gun because she instinctively lifted the box to her face. Did she have time to think? Did she have time to taste fear?

Neighbors heard two shots. One bullet veered wildly into the family room, the other hit Lita's temple, on the right side of her head. The man fled on foot, "like a bat out of hell," said a neighbor who almost hit him with her car.

"I walked up and the door was ajar; it was probably opened six to eight inches, and I really didn't want to go in there but I knew I had to," Lita's neighbor Bob Christenson later told police. "I opened it up and Lita was lying in the foyer . . . I immediately went in and into the kitchen, which was just a few feet away, and called nine-one-one and then came back to see if I could—if I could make her more comfortable. But it was obvious to me that she was in pretty bad shape."

Poppy and her daughter were still upstairs when the shooting occurred. Hysterical, Poppy called Lita's parents.

"Poppy called me and she was screaming and crying saying Lita's been shot," says Jo Ann McClinton. "I was getting dressed to go visit my mother in the hospital. I called Emory and he got there before I did." Jo Ann pauses as she recounts that day. "They were putting her in the ambulance when I drove up. Emory drove his car and I followed to Piedmont Hospital. We were there a short time when they pronounced her dead." Jo Ann's voice trails off and she says quietly, "And that's when Emory said, 'That son of a bitch did it.' We knew right away it had something to do with Jim."

Forty minutes after the shooting, at 9:00 a.m., Sullivan accepted a collect call at his Palm Beach home from a pay phone at the northbound rest stop on 1-85 in Suwanee, about thirty-four miles from Lita's house. The call lasted a minute.

On January 13, 1987, three days before the shooting, three men checked into the Howard Johnson Motor Lodge at Roswell Road and I-285, at 7:24 a.m. They registered under phony names, and were driving a white Toyota. Southern Bell phone records later revealed that a call was placed at 7:44 a.m. from room 518 to Sullivan's house in West Palm Beach. Sullivan called the room back at 10:33 a.m. Minutes later, he called Lita's neighbor, Bob Christenson, and asked, "What did you hear this morning? Did you hear any loud knocking?"

Police later figured that the murder was planned for that day, January 13, and that Lita must have not answered the door. The shooter needed a way to gain entry. In Sullivan's day planner, FBI Special Agent Todd Letcher, who described Sullivan as a meticulous note-taker, later found a notation on January 14. It said: "Get flowers."

In a phone call to a friend a few days after the murder, Sullivan described the gun that killed Lita—a 9mm semiautomatic pistol. But information about the gun was never publicly disclosed, intentionally withheld by Atlanta Police.

WEST PALM BEACH

On the morning of the shooting, Sullivan's lawyer called him to announce that Lita was dead. That day Sullivan lunched with a business associate. At about 8:00 p.m., he dined with his girlfriend, South Korean–born Hyo-Sook Choi "Suki" Rogers at Jo's, a posh French restaurant.

Later, according to prosecutor Brad Moores, authorities found a note in Sullivan's diary that said, "Suki and I celebrate with champagne and caviar at Jo's." Another note, scrawled on December 12, 1986 (a month before the shooting), simply said, "pistol."

Eight months after Lita's death, Sullivan married Suki Rogers, her fourth marriage, his third. A recent divorcée, sexy Suki was reportedly as ambitious as Sullivan, and together they made progress on the Palm Beach social circuit.

It didn't take long before the life he'd so carefully crafted started to crack. In March 1990, three years after Lita's death, Sullivan got into a three-car fender bender while driving his Rolls-Royce. His driver's license had been revoked in 1989 due to more than a dozen traffic violations. Rather than dealing with the fines, he took the matter to court and said Suki had been the one driving. The traffic cop told the court that Suki wasn't even in the car.

Sullivan was convicted of two counts of perjury and sentenced to house arrest for a year, confined to his home except for "tennis court therapy" prescribed by his doctor. During that year, still seeking clues into Lita's death, federal agents searched his house and found four guns, including a sawed-off shotgun. Convicted on felony charges for firearms possession, Sullivan was sentenced to spend the remaining nine and a half months of his house arrest in the Palm Beach County Jail.

By this point, Suki had filed for divorce. At her divorce trial, she testified that after they got arrested for perjury, Sullivan admitted his role in Lita's death. In choppy English, she explained: "He turned the TV high. He say anybody can listen to this conversation . . . so he tell me he hired person to kill Lita. . . . He said let's sell this house as soon as possible and he say, we go anywhere you want, anywhere in the world." She later told lawyers, "He mention in Georgia in countryside you can hire those people for nothing, you can do anything you want to have done."

While in jail, Sullivan got into a jailhouse scuffle with convicted robber Paul O'Brien, who broke Sullivan's nose.

FULTON COUNTY

In January 1992, federal agents indicted Sullivan on interstate murder-conspiracy charges in Atlanta. Sullivan spared no expense in hiring Ed Garland and Don Samuel—two of the top criminal defense lawyers in the country. The duo's long list of clients include Baltimore Ravens linebacker Ray Lewis, acquitted of involvement in a post-Super Bowl Buckhead bar brawl that left a man dead; Larry Gleit, CFO of the now-defunct Gold Club, who walked away with a misdemeanor charge in his federal racketeering case; and Jim Williams, protagonist in the nonfiction tale *Midnight in the Garden of Good and Evil*, acquitted of murder in his fourth trial.

The federal charge of interstate murder conspiracy, by using interstate commerce to commit murder, put the onus on the federal government to prove interstate nexus. Despite the circumstantial evidence—primarily the collect call Sullivan received the day of Lita's shooting—prosecution could never prove the content of the phone conversation. Judge Marvin Shoob dismissed the case for insufficient evidence on November 23, 1992.

WEST PALM BEACH

Though a free man back in Palm Beach, Sullivan was reduced to riding around town on his twelve-speed Peugeot bicycle. He became reclusive, now shunned by the Palm Beach social circuit. One neighbor said Sullivan had lost weight and looked visibly stressed, that his face was gaunt and he looked "almost like a ghost."

Sullivan sold the Palm Beach mansion for $3.2 million and moved to a more modest place in nearby Boynton Beach.

In 1994, the McClintons and their lawyer, Brad Moores, took Sullivan to West Palm Beach Civil Court in a "wrongful death" suit. In civil court, judgments are based on the weight of evidence, whereas in criminal court, a defendant has to be deemed guilty beyond a reasonable doubt.

A few days before that case went to trial, Sullivan fired his lawyers, opting to represent himself.

"I think it was a strategic decision," says Moores. Lawyerless, saying that he lacked the funds to get proper representation, Sullivan hoped the jury would sympathize with him.

In his opening address to the jury, Sullivan pouted and said ". . . something else that is terrible and that is to be wrongly accused of murder, to have to live through that and with that is another form of death, another form of murder of the spirit." He added, "To be a husband and to lose your wife violently is the worst thing that can happen to a husband."

Because Sullivan represented himself, he questioned Jo Ann and Emory on the witness stand. Emory McClinton said, "It was horrible being questioned by the killer of your daughter."

The jury heard testimony from Suki and Paul O'Brien, the convicted robber who had broken Sullivan's nose in jail. O'Brien told the court that Sullivan confessed to arranging Lita's murder, and that the only thing he couldn't account for was the collect call made from the interstate.

It didn't take long for the jury to reach its verdict. On February 25, 1994, Sullivan was found guilty and ordered to pay the McClintons $4 million in compensatory and punitive damages. The McClintons were elated. "For us, it was never about the money," says Jo Ann. "We wanted Jim to be held accountable for what he did to our daughter."

Sullivan, now quick to hire lawyers, appealed. Devastating to the McClintons, in 1995 the Florida Supreme Court overturned the 1994 verdict, ruling that the court case hadn't been filed soon enough. Unlike in criminal cases, where there is no statute of limitations on murder, civil court has a two-year statute for wrongful death, and those two years had long passed.

Moores counterappealed, arguing that the statue shouldn't apply when Sullivan concealed his involvement in the shooting. "You shouldn't be able to beat the system because you're clever and fraudulent," says Moores. "Finally, the Florida Supreme Court agreed with us." In 1997, the court reinstated the guilty verdict.

The decision prompted a wave of media attention. After a story about Sullivan appeared on TV's *Extra*, authorities got a break in early 1998. A woman in Texas, Belinda Trahan, called Atlanta police and told them she recognized Sullivan. Her ex-boyfriend, Phillip Anthony "Tony" Harwood, was the same truck driver Sullivan had met when he first moved to West Palm Beach. She told the GBI that Harwood had met Sullivan in a Florida diner, shortly after Lita's death. She saw Sullivan slip Harwood an envelope full of money. The final payment. It was a link authorities desperately needed.

FULTON COUNTY

In May 1998, Sullivan and Harwood were indicted by a Fulton County Grand Jury for the murder of Lita McClinton Sullivan. With Harwood in custody, authorities called Sullivan's lawyers to get him to surrender. But by then, Sullivan had disappeared.

In September 1998, the state issued its intent to seek the death penalty against Tony Harwood. In 2003, Harwood pleaded guilty to voluntary manslaughter with an agreement to testify against Sullivan when he eventually got to trial. In exchange, Harwood's sentence was reduced to twenty years. He sits in the Georgia State Prison in Reidsville.

THAILAND

For nearly eighteen years, Sullivan has been a prime suspect in Lita's murder. At the top of the FBI's most-wanted list for four years,

Sullivan led investigators on an international manhunt throughout Central America to, eventually, Thailand.

In 2002, *America's Most Wanted* ran a segment on Sullivan and, incredibly, someone in Thailand recognized him. He was living in Cha-am, a luxury condo community about 150 miles south of Bangkok. He lived with Chongwattana Reynolds, a Thai divorcée he had met in West Palm Beach.

More than fifteen years after Lita's shooting, Thai police arrested Sullivan and took him to Lard Yao Prison, on the outskirts of Bangkok. There his lawyers fought extradition, hoping to use international laws to avoid the death penalty.

Thai prisons are notoriously crowded places. Amnesty International says that more than fifty inmates are held in cells built for twenty, that the prisons are plagued by rats, disease, and rotting food, and that guard brutality is rampant.

On his two visits to see Sullivan in Thailand, Samuel says the situation was better than he'd feared. "I never had the sense that the conditions were so bad that it would shock the consciousness," says Samuel. "It appeared to be in all respects humane." Reynolds visited him often during his more than eighteen months of incarceration. On one such visit, Samuel said, the couple got married, making Reynolds, Sullivan's fourth wife.

By virtue of his parentage, Sullivan has dual citizenship in both the United States and Ireland. Like other Western European countries, Ireland opposes the death penalty and the extradition of Irish citizens to any country that enforces capital punishment. When the Thai courts denied the citizenship motion, Sullivan's lawyers appealed to the Thai Supreme Court, saying that prosecuting Sullivan for Lita's death was a case of double jeopardy—Georgia's constitution states that a person cannot be tried for the same crime twice. Samuel says that because Sullivan was already prosecuted unsuccessfully in the 1992 case, which was dismissed for insufficient evidence, he should not be tried again. Again, the Thai courts denied the appeal.

In March 2004, extradition was finally granted, and a disheveled sixty-two-year-old Sullivan limped off the plane at Hartsfield before being transported to the Fulton County Jail. Sullivan wore handcuffs and shackles, a facemask and a single shoe. "He was being difficult," reported U.S. Marshal Richard Mecum. "He obviously didn't want to come back." Scott Page, one of three U.S. marshals who traveled with Sullivan from Thailand, said the fugitive read *Newsweek* the whole way, while grumbling profanity at the notion of returning to Atlanta.

A few days after Sullivan's arrival, Fulton County District Attorney Paul Howard Jr. served Sullivan notice of the state's intent to seek the death penalty against him.

Sullivan's lawyer, Don Samuel, said Sullivan's foot had swollen on the flight over, that the facemask was just a precaution in light of SARS. He said that Sullivan has a serious dental problem, one that the lawyers are "struggling" to get Fulton County to address. While he was incarcerated in Thailand, Samuel admitted, Sullivan did get into a fight.

Samuel says Sullivan's defense is simple: "He didn't do it. He is not guilty." Samuel argues that Sullivan did not flee, that he just happened to move at the time of his indictment, that he had left the country long before there was a warrant for his arrest. Apparently, he was unaware that he was the target of an international manhunt.

Today Samuel contends that the state's case is no better than it was in 1992, when it was thrown out for insufficient evidence. His contention is that Sullivan will get off, that some day he'll walk out a free man.

That thought makes the McClintons' blood boil.

The McClintons' lawyer, Brad Moores, says that when Sullivan fled to Costa Rica in 1998, he hired a private banker in Palm Beach who worked with a Swiss bank to hide Sullivan's money in offshore accounts. Those monies were funneled through a corporate trust account established in the small country of Liechtenstein. All statements from the corporation, Nicola Resources, were sent to

Sullivan in Thailand. Moores says a lawyer in Liechtenstein managed the funds and sent Sullivan money whenever he needed it.

"He's still a pretty wealthy individual," says Moores. Neither the McClintons, nor their lawyers, have ever seen a dime from the $4 million judgment they won in 1994 (which is now calculated at $8.8 million due to accrued interest). Moores is on a hunt to find Sullivan's well-hidden money.

While the McClintons believe in Sullivan's constitutional right to a lawyer, they think he shouldn't be able to use the money from the Florida lawsuit to pay for his high-priced criminal lawyers. Jo Ann calls it "blood money," while Moores calls it a lawsuit, one that's pending against Samuel and Garland for accepting funds from Sullivan that they knew were subject to the judgment.

District Attorney Paul Howard Jr. believes Sullivan should be court-ordered to pay his civil court judgment. "It is really obscene that you could take somebody's life, profit from it and then use the proceeds from it to defend your life in a trial involving that same person," he said.

Howard looks forward to the trial, which could start in early 2005. "I've talked to a lot of people in our county," he says. "I was surprised when Sullivan was returned that so many people I've never met would just walk up to me and say, 'We want you to make sure he understands that you just can't get away with something like that in Fulton County.'" Howard says the fact that Sullivan was living in luxury, basically vacationing, offends a lot of people and that anyone familiar with the case over the past seventeen-plus years wants to see it resolved.

"I think we've waited long enough."

ATLANTA

In the living room of Emory and Jo Ann McClinton's stately home on East Lake Drive, where they have lived for nearly thirty years, photographs of Lita are as prevalent as photos of Valencia, Emory, Jr., and the McClintons' two grandchildren. Portraits of ancestors line the walls. The home is furnished with antiques and heavy, brocaded furniture. In a bowl, the generous buds of their giant magnolia sit submerged in water. Talk radio murmurs in the background.

After fifty-three years of marriage, they are the kind of couple who finishes each other's sentences. They have been best friends since they met in seventh grade at their parochial high school.

Though it's nearly eighteen years ago, they remember that January day when they lost their oldest daughter. They remember her funeral, held at H. M. Patterson and Son on Spring Street at Tenth. Sullivan didn't come, nor have they ever heard from him. Catherine, Sullivan's first wife, who died last year, sent her condolences. The McClintons have kept in touch with Sullivan's four children who, they say, gave up on their father a long time ago.

They lament how they were never able to go through Lita's things. Because Sullivan was considered next of kin, he was able to get a judge to enjoin anyone from entering the townhouse. Sullivan had the locks changed on her condo before they could search for clues, or take keepsakes their daughter would have wanted them to have. Sullivan never contacted them after Lita's death, but because he was still legally Lita's husband, they had to seek his permission to have her cremated.

Their devotion to their lost daughter and the need to bring her alleged killer to justice never wavers. Their tenacity and commitment have kept Sullivan in the media. "He should have known," says Emory, wearing shorts and a green T-shirt, with sneakers and white athletic socks pulled halfway up his calves. He's a tall man with a gentle but determined voice. "He should have known that we would not let him get away with this."

For the McClintons, January 16 will always be a gray, drizzly day. Determined to shake the hand of justice when it finally arrives, they know they will never feel vindication. There is no end; the memories and dreams are nothing compared to embracing your child.

"Closure does not have a meaning to me," says Jo Ann. "There's no such thing as closure because our daughter is dead and that can never be erased or changed. To lose a child, there is never closure, because in the scheme of things you never think your children will predecease you—that isn't in the computer at all. We might fill in the missing pieces, but we will never have closure."

FULTON COUNTY JAIL

He attained riches, mansions, and fancy cars. He had wives and mistresses, friends and social status. He had charm, and he had dreams. Now, Sullivan sits in a prison cell, his tousled hair a dull gray, his body bent and strained from the burden of age. He has a family he no longer knows, a fortune he cannot spend. His shadow on the prison walls is only the dimmest reminder of that determined boy who played stickball in the street.

DEBRA MILLER LANDAU *is an award-winning travel writer who's penned eight books for Lonely Planet Publications. Born in Canada, she started writing about crime when she researched the lives of Canada's most infamous serial killers. She is a contributing editor at* Atlanta *magazine.*

Coda

I get a strange sensation when I think that James Sullivan sits in a jail cell just a few miles from my house. Even with Atlanta traffic, I could get in my car and be there in ten minutes. I'd like to look in his eyes, to see if there's fire, to see if he's still running away from himself, that working-class kid he despised so much it made him lead a life stranger than fiction.

What it would be like to talk to him? Would he be a crushed, aging man? Would he still be charming? Would he feign dignity, and plead innocence? Does he sit alone in the jailhouse yard, or does he have pals, buddies with whom he commiserates?

For a man who fought his whole life for control, how does he stand it, waiting for his lawyers to pass motion after motion, exploring the tiny cracks in the law, those little openings that give him a window of hope?

As the months tick by, with legal acrobatics and new extensions delaying the trial, details of Sullivan's segmented life come slapping him in the face. Just a few months after this article appeared in *Atlanta* magazine, district attorneys in both Atlanta and Macon announced their intent to exhume the remains of Sullivan's uncle, Frank Bienert, whose death by "heart failure" left Sullivan the liquor distributorship that eventually made him a millionaire. Did Sullivan have a hand in his uncle's death? If so, was it the trigger—the justification for everything that followed?

While combing through old court archives in Florida, reading about Sullivan's life of riches, I wondered how a guy like this could allegedly hire a trucker to kill his wife. It's a desperate story, not about one man's fall from grace, but one man's desperate attempt to get there.

It's past lights-out at the Fulton County Jail as I sit at my desk writing this. In the prison darkness, does Sullivan think about those heady days in the liquor distributorship, does he long to be sipping martinis at the Palm Beach parties? Does he, almost twenty years after her death, remember Lita's face? I wonder, as his death penalty trial approaches, if he fears death, or if his tightly woven cloak of invincibility continues to help him sleep at night.

Neil Swidey

THE
SELF-DESTRUCTION
OF AN M.D.

FROM THE *Boston Globe Magazine*

THE KID WAS BORN into medicine. He was on track to becoming one of Boston's next great spine surgeons, taking his place alongside his father among the city's medical elite. But on this day in January, the forty-three-year-old sits on the dark bench in the dimly lit gallery of Middlesex Superior Court in Cambridge, watching the parade of career criminals take their familiar positions, wearing expressions of defiance or boredom. Look in *his* eyes, however, behind the boxy glasses, and you can see flashes of bewilderment. How did *I* get *here*? He watches as a paunchy guy charged with conspiring to kill a cop asks the court officer if he can give the large, weeping woman in the front row "a kiss and my lottery tickets" before being led away. And then the clerk calls out his number: "Case number thirty-eight—David Arndt."

As the prosecutor and the defense lawyer take their positions before the judge, Arndt advances to his designated spot in front of a tattered computer printout that reads DEFENDANT, stooping his six-foot-two frame a little so his right hand can reach the railing. He is wearing a brown pin-striped suit. A taupe trench coat hangs over his left arm.

His appearance has rebounded from the unshaven, sunken-eyed mess that was on display in his mug shot last summer, though his physique is still a ways from the chiseled, rippled showpiece it was before everything fell apart. The pretrial hearing is over in just a few minutes, and he pulls his trench coat close to his chest and exits the courtroom.

You follow him into the hallway and call to him, "Dr. Arndt."

The words stop him in his tracks. *Dr. Arndt.* For the better part of a decade, that wasn't just his name, it was his identity. The domineering surgeon cutting his path—loved by some, loathed by others. But *respected.* That identity has been confiscated along with everything else he valued so much—standing, status, power. Now he's just another David standing in a criminal courtroom wondering what his future holds. He turns to look when he hears the words. But he recognizes you, throws up his hands to block his ears, shakes his head, and walks away. You suspect he'll come back. When you'd met a week earlier, in another court, in another county, he'd walked away then as well, at his lawyer's instruction, only to return and demand that you hold off on writing about him. "To do otherwise," he told you in his sonorous voice, "would be to engage in Murdoch-style journalism." You found it surprising that this man, given what he so infamously did in his operating room, not to mention what he's accused of doing in the weeks and months that followed, would choose to deliver a lecture about professional standards.

On this day in Cambridge he returns again, and the lecture is more expansive and comes with a reading list. "Are you familiar with Janet Malcolm's piece in *The New Yorker* entitled 'The Journalist and the Murderer'?" he asks. "It was published in two parts. Do you know her work?"

You shake your head no.

"You *should*," he says.

You ask him how he came across the article.

"I *read*," he says, narrowing his eyes. "Didn't you take any journalism courses?"

That's when, for the first time, you begin to understand the experience many of his former colleagues have described to you. Now you're the lowly scrub nurse—or even the seasoned superior—whose competence is being so pointedly challenged by Dr. David Arndt. And, just as they have explained it, he does it in a way that suggests he has no choice but to do it, and that he is confident, in the end, you will appreciate being made aware of just how far you've fallen short of his expectations.

There's an intensity to David Arndt that never seems to slacken, a way in which he seems both hyper-aware of his very public collapse and oblivious to it. Overnight, the high-octane, Harvard-trained Arndt became *the doctor who left his patient on the operating table so he could go to the bank to cash a check*. In an instant, that summer of 2002, the news went national. But the profound professional embarrassment would turn out to be only the beginning. Within two months, Arndt would be charged with statutory child rape, indecent assault, and drug possession. He would file a "poverty motion," the surgeon in one of medicine's most lucrative specialties asking the court to pay his costs. And then, in a separate case nearly a year later, he would face one more charge, this one for possessing methamphetamine with intent to distribute.

"His downfall is almost operatic in its tragedy," says Grant Colfax, a Harvard-trained doctor who was once one of Arndt's closest friends. As Arndt prepares to stand two separate criminal trials, Colfax is like many of the people who knew him well and are now left scratching their heads. Their emotions oscillate between two poles: There's the lingering disbelief that such a brilliant and compassionate doctor—some say the most brilliant and most compassionate they had ever known—could seem to self-destruct in such a spectacularly public way. Then, perhaps more troubling, there's that voice inside them, which had been muffled deep for so long, the one that kept telling them it was only a matter of time before David Arndt's self-absorption and sense of invincibility finally got the best of him.

DAVID CARL ARNDT was born on October 10, 1960, in New Haven. Kenneth Arndt was attending Yale medical school and living in student housing with his wife, Anne. Many of the other med students weren't even married yet, never mind parents. The couple's baby became an immediate attraction for Ken's classmates. "From the time he was extremely small, David was a very bright guy," says Jack Barchas, one of Ken's good friends at Yale and now chairman of psychiatry at Weill Cornell Medical College in New York. "And he just radiated happiness. We'd go over there for brunch—lox and bagels—and here was this little kid, always interacting."

When David was almost two, the Arndts packed up for Boston, so Ken could do his residency in dermatology at Massachusetts General Hospital. They had another child, a daughter. Ken would begin climbing the ranks of Boston medicine, joining the faculty of Harvard Medical School and eventually becoming chief of dermatology at Beth Israel Hospital. Years later, Anne, a psychologist, would also join the Harvard Med faculty. Friends describe the couple as charming, warm, stylish, and smart.

Growing up in Newton, David stood out. Extremely bright, no doubt about that. Tall too. Kathy Sias was his neighbor and one of his best friends. She ate dinner with his family, accompanied them on ski trips to their place in New Hampshire. Longhaired David was intense and intellectual but fun to be around. What did they do together? "A lot of drugs," she says, chuckling. "Just about everybody in our clique did during those days."

She and other friends say David, who attended Weeks Junior High School in Newton and the private Cambridge School of Weston, was always pushing limits. (He kept a boa constrictor as a pet, says Sias.) They also say Anne and Ken seemed hipper and easier for teens to talk to than other parents in the neighborhood. But Sias says that as she spent more time with the family, she changed her mind. "They were as unclued-in to teenagers as most parents, but they thought they were more clued in," she says. "His father was remote. His mother thought she knew everything because she was a psychologist. 'Oh, it's just a phase,' she would say about anything going on with David."

(Through their attorney, Stephen R. Delinsky, Ken and Anne Arndt declined to comment for this story, and David declined to talk beyond his brief conversations outside of the courtroom. "Dr. Arndt's parents respect, love, and admire him very much and are deeply concerned that your proposed article about David will seriously compromise his ability to achieve justice," Delinsky wrote. The couple "are confident that when all the facts are presented in court, David will be found not guilty in both cases.")

Though David would eventually become comfortable in his homosexuality, it's not surprising that his teenage years were more difficult.

"Looking back, I think he was aware of it, but I don't think he wanted to be," Sias says. "If he had admitted that he was gay, he would have probably lost a big part of his circle of friends." He dated girls, including Sias. "For about a week and a half," she says. "We went back to being best friends."

After logging time at the University of Massachusetts at Amherst from 1978 to 1979, Arndt left the state for San Francisco. He immediately soaked up the ethos of the city—part tie-dyed Haight-Ashbury hippie, part *Tales of the City* free spirit. The son of Harvard faculty members enrolled in a "university without walls" college called Antioch West. The downtown school awarded students course credit for their life experience. It no longer exists. He quickly earned a bachelor's degree and became a mental health counselor, working with the homeless who, in the parlance of San Francisco, were housed in "homeless hotels." Arndt's living quarters weren't much better.

On April 7, 1982, Arndt married a woman from India named Shobha Hundraj Nagrani. They would file for divorce four years later, and it became official in December 1987. Many of his friends say they knew little about the circumstances surrounding the marriage. What they did know about Arndt during this period was that he was into writing, literature, the arts scene. He was passionate, smart, insightful, *alive*.

And arrogant.

"One of a kind," says Harvey Peskin, who was a professor in San Francisco State University's clinical psychology graduate program when Arndt enrolled in 1983. What set him apart was the way he put everyone around him, especially the professor, on notice. "Professors tend to believe that students have to work to earn their respect," Peskin says. "David felt that the professor was the one who had to earn the right to have his respect."

As the yearlong class wore on, Peskin, who had initially been irritated by Arndt's chutzpah, found himself wanting to pass his brilliant student's test. David Arndt has that effect on people. "I don't think his behavior changed much," Peskin says, "but I think I changed."

But Arndt would begin changing in other ways. One day in 1983, he walked into a San Francisco clinic where Stephen M. Goldfinger, a psychiatrist who oversaw mental health services for the homeless, was presiding over a case conference. Afterward, they talked, and soon they were dating and then living together. Goldfinger was thirty-two, Arndt twenty-three.

Arndt earned his master's degree and turned in his tie-dye for extensive travel throughout Asia, gourmet cooking, and an intensified focus on his career. He began contemplating medical school and took some supplemental pre-med classes.

It was around this time that Jack Barchas got a call from Ken Arndt. Barchas was then the director of a prestigious research laboratory at Stanford. His old Yale med school pal told him that David was living in California and for the first time was thinking about pursuing medicine. "Ken, it's probably easier for me to talk to him about it than you," Barchas said. "Have him come see me."

As it turned out, Barchas's lab had just been given a very early and crude MRI machine, which the researchers were about to experiment with using rats. Arndt volunteered to help. In no time, he had all but taken over the project. "He was like a navy SEAL," Barchas recalls. "Just willing to do it and not waiting to be told." Arndt suggested to Barchas that they write an academic paper about their findings. When it was published, the name of David Arndt was listed first, followed by a bunch of respected researchers with actual titles after their names.

Years later, when Barchas was serving with Ken Arndt on the editorial board of the *Journal of the American Medical Association*, and he would ask about David, Ken would say, "It's all coming together for him."

IN 1988, DAVID ARNDT came home. He made his way to the hallowed ground of Harvard Medical School, where his father, one of the nation's top dermatologists, was a heavyweight. If relations between him and his parents had been strained during some of his time in San Francisco, they appeared to be back on track. But David didn't advertise his connections. Occasionally, a classmate would notice the author's name on their dermatology textbook. "Kenneth A. Arndt—any relation to you?"

"Yeah, that's my father," David would reply casually.

And no one who saw David in class—with his burning intelligence and remarkable self-possession—would question whether he had the goods to get into Harvard on his own. Soon after Arndt joined the medical school's class of 1992, Steve Goldfinger joined the Harvard faculty. They shared a gracious Victorian in Jamaica Plain that was well appointed with the artwork they had collected together on their travels—Balinese puppets, Burmese wall hangings, Borneo masks. They frequently had Arndt's med school friends over for dinner or cocktail parties. What those friends saw was a couple that seemed to enjoy life and each other's company. They had a couple of dogs and a garden that Goldfinger faithfully tended to.

This is not the average med student experience. "Most of us came as unformed characters, having spent all of our time studying to get to Harvard," says Timothy Ferris, a classmate of Arndt's who is now a primary care doctor at Massachusetts General Hospital. "We came as receptors of knowledge, not producers. David immediately stood out as someone who appeared to have a fully formed character. He could do the work. He was confident. Most medical students were still so afraid that they spent all their time studying. David was organizing parties. He had a life. He had a car. He had a nice house. While the rest of us were putting our personal lives on hold for four to eight years, David had balance. He was where we all hoped to be. The fact that he was gay only added to that. The most mysterious part of us— our sexuality—and here is a guy who has it all figured out."

Not that there weren't moments that gave his friends pause.

Grant Colfax appreciated Arndt's tremendous warmth and easy ability to talk intelligently about literature, politics, life. Like most of Arndt's friends, he found something magnetic about him. "But he had some clear character flaws," Colfax says. "To my dearest friend, he was outwardly rude and uninterested. He couldn't even exude the bare social graces. She asked me, 'How can you be friends with such a jerk?' I saw what she was saying, but he had always been really kind to me and fun to be around."

A few years into med school, Arndt accompanied Colfax to a gym near campus. "David was totally dismissive of the whole thing," Colfax recalls. "Then, overnight, he had to be the best." And so David Arndt, who up until this point had stood out only by what he said, also began to stand out by how he looked.

His nondescript physique was soon gone. He became even more

toned as his weight training intensified during his general surgery internship at Beth Israel Hospital. On a warm spring day in 1993, Alexandra Page, a med school friend and fellow intern, had brunch with Arndt and Goldfinger. Afterward, Arndt showed her the new gym he had just switched to. "We went inside," she remembers, "and it was just flush with attractive young men."

It's only looking back now that Page can recognize that visit as a sign of trouble ahead. Goldfinger, she says, "was a wonderful guy, incredibly bright and interesting, but he wasn't an Adonis."

The relationship with Goldfinger would last through Arndt's first year of residency. But friends detected a change in Arndt's priorities, starting with his surprising choice of residency. He had always talked about neurosurgery. But when he didn't get into the Harvard neurosurgery residency program, he decided against pursuing the field elsewhere and switched gears. He secured a spot in orthopedic surgery at Harvard. In medical circles, neurosurgery has the reputation—fair or not—of attracting the intellectuals and orthopedics, the jocks. Arndt's interest in fixing other people's bones and muscles dovetailed with his growing concern with developing his own.

The breakup with Goldfinger came in the summer of 1994. They had been together for almost eleven years. Their lives were interwoven. Arndt had found someone new and wanted out. He moved into an apartment in the South End. Goldfinger had an exhaustively detailed legal agreement drawn up providing for the division of their art collection, arrangements for the care of their dogs, and a financial settlement. For more than a decade, Goldfinger would argue, he had paid for nearly all of Arndt's living, travel, and entertainment expenses (but not his tuition). The expectation had been that Arndt would absorb more of their shared costs after he entered private practice. So the most controversial provision in the agreement was this: Beginning in 1998, Arndt would be required to pay Goldfinger 9 percent of his income over the next fifteen years, not to exceed $500,000. Arndt signed the agreement.

Given the punishing schedules that doctors in training are forced to endure, it's not uncommon for personal relationships to become casualties. But what Arndt's friends did find curious—alarming even—was the way he handled the breakup.

"Here David is, a very good friend of mine. I was not as close to Steve. But clearly David was the one responsible for the breakup. And David had absolutely no insight into it," says Grant Colfax. "It was all about his problems. It was shocking to me." He and other friends began to pull back from their relationship with Arndt.

Then there was the whiplash of seeing the guys Arndt dated right after Goldfinger. "He ran around with all these Barbie doll boys," says Colfax, who is also gay and is now the director of HIV prevention studies with the San Francisco Department of Public Health. "Is that any different from a straight man who gets divorced in middle age and runs around with trophy wives? No, but it was something that was disturbing to me."

It was as though his friends were seeing a David Arndt, version 2.0—a better-looking package but one that lacked the charm of the original release. "He once told me, 'I'm like Dorian Gray. I just get better looking as I get older,'" Colfax recalls. "It takes a certain personality to just state that. And I thought it was an interesting literary reference, considering what the novel was about."

The central character in Oscar Wilde's *The Picture of Dorian Gray* manages to defy age and remain youthfully handsome. But he loses his inner compass. In the end, Dorian Gray pays dearly for his vanity.

IF DAVID ARNDT sounds a little too intense, a little too arrogant, ask yourself this: Aren't those exactly the qualities you want in a surgeon? Because this is what his arrogance looked like for most of his time in the operating room: An intolerance for error. An eagerness to take on the toughest cases. A fearlessness about confronting anyone—be it an orderly or a chief of surgery—who he thought was underperforming. Even as an intern, he would routinely challenge the attending physicians. "Interns are supposed to always back down, but not David," recalls Alexandra Page. "The rest of us were like, 'You go, man!'"

As an orthopedic surgical resident, Arndt would finish a grueling shift at Massachusetts General Hospital and then, instead of going out for a beer with his coworkers, would head back to Brigham and Women's to check on a patient he had treated during his last rotation.

Sigurd Berven, one of Arndt's fellow residents, recalls a memorable case: A teenager was rushed to the emergency room with multiple fractures to his spine and pelvis. He had jumped from the roof of a tall building. Arndt operated on him, but that was only the beginning of his care. "David was the only person who figured out why he jumped," says Berven, now a faculty member and spine surgeon at the University of California, San Francisco. Turns out the boy had just been outed at school.

This, says Berven, was typical Arndt care, no matter who the patient was. Sure, he complained a lot. "But the physicians who get angry, who are difficult to get along with, are almost invariably the physicians who really care," Berven says. He compares Arndt to Eriq La Salle's Dr. Benton character on *ER* and wonders if his friend's intense compassion ultimately became an unmanageable source of stress. In the face of all the defects and demands of medicine, "there's no precedent for somebody surviving in the field who cared as much as David cared."

But here's another way to view Arndt's commitment, his determination to stay involved in patients' care even after they had ceased to be his patients. "He didn't necessarily know where to draw the line," says Stephen Lipson, who was chief of orthopedics at Beth Israel during Arndt's residency. Maybe that surplus of compassion and of self-centeredness came from the same place. "He wanted to be in charge," Lipson says.

Lipson had known Ken Arndt since their residency days at Massachusetts General Hospital, and thought the world of him. Now, here they were, both chiefs at Beth Israel, both watching their own sons follow in their footsteps. (Lipson's son was several years behind David at Harvard Medical School.) "Ken and I had a real kinship," he says.

Lipson found David to be a superior surgeon in the OR and intellectually stimulating outside of it. So he took him under his wing. While David would soar to great heights, it would be prove to be a bumpy flight.

"David wanted nothing but exceptional results," says Lipson, a soft-spoken fifty-seven-year-old who now works at Harvard Vanguard Medical Associates. But he says Arndt's interpersonal skills didn't always measure up, whether he was twisting around language to confuse people or tearing into them. "If a nurse was doing something and he didn't like the way it was being done—a dressing change, medications, or whatever—he might bark at them: "No, you shouldn't do this! It's wrong! Do it this way! He wanted to run the show. Some nurses would go away crying." Lipson would take him aside, tell him to cool it. "But he would just commit the same flaw another time," Lipson says. "He could not turn himself off from being himself."

Lipson was particularly troubled by one area of Arndt's behavior that arose as his residency progressed. Some male orderlies and nurses were complaining that Arndt had made what they felt were inappropriate comments to them, he says. "I had to warn him not to pursue sexual interactions with other male staff," Lipson recalls. "Otherwise it was going to be a problem, and he could be chastised and reported to the administration."

But still, but still: David Arndt was an extremely gifted surgeon. Lipson found him fun to teach—he would do research on his own, push relentlessly for higher performance from everyone, especially himself. Although some of his patients were put off by his manner, most loved him—they could tell he genuinely cared about what happened to them.

And around this time, friends say, Arndt began talking about needing to get his personal life back in order so he could be a good role model—for his son. Arndt told friends that the boy had been born during his early days in San Francisco, but that it was only after the boy was in his teens and wrote to Arndt that the connection was revived. Arndt kept a picture of him, proudly updated his friends on the teen's achievements in school. One time when Arndt was visiting California, Grant Colfax got a chance to meet the boy and his two female parents.

Things were coming together at work as well. As the capstone to Arndt's residency, Lipson advocated for him to be named chief resident at Beth Israel in 1997. Given his father's longstanding connections there, "it felt like home for David."

Lipson still envisioned Arndt becoming one of Boston's next top spine surgeons, if he could just keep himself in check. He helped arrange for Arndt to do his fellowship in spine surgery (the branch of orthopedics that is closest to neurosurgery) at Tulane University School of Medicine in New Orleans. When Arndt returned to Boston and began working at Harvard Vanguard and at a private group practice, Lipson sent him a steady supply of referrals—a crucial lifeline for a young doctor starting out in an over-doctored place like Boston.

Lipson and his wife, Jenifer, had always enjoyed socializing with Ken and Anne Arndt at hospital functions. "They're a nice Jewish couple," Lipson says, "and so are we." Still, his wife sensed trouble in his continued advocacy for David and cautioned him to keep his distance. Lipson would hear none of it. "I wanted to have to do with him," he says. "But my wife said, 'He's out of control.' Which, in the end, I think was true."

YOU WANT WARNING SIGNS? They were there. In fact, the year 1998 was packed with them, though many of the people who worked with David Arndt wouldn't find out about them until much later.

When Arndt returned from New Orleans, Stephen Lipson asked his protégé about his experience. Arndt told him it went great, neglecting to mention the federal law he had broken while he was there. On May 29, Alfredo Fuentes submitted a passport application under a false name, and Arndt filed a supporting affidavit. Fuentes had been Arndt's domestic partner for several years, and he had moved with Arndt from Massachusetts to New Orleans. But Fuentes was a Venezuelan who was in the States illegally. The fraudulent passport application, Arndt would say later, was their attempt to head off deportation.

Three months later, in the early morning hours, Fuentes was sitting on a bedroom couch talking to a man named Roger Volzer in Volzer's Provincetown home on Cape Cod. After Volzer got up to blow out some candles, Arndt, who had been staring at the men through a window, used his surgeon's hands to rip out a screen and climb into the house, according to the Provincetown police report. Volzer would tell police that Arndt punched him in the head, pushed him out of the bedroom, and then threw a chair at him. Arndt was charged with assault and battery, burglary, and malicious destruction of property.

Volzer eventually decided not to press charges in exchange for Arndt's agreeing to pay him $30,000 and to attend weekly anger-management counseling. Christopher Snow, Volzer's attorney, says Arndt's supporters lobbied his client, telling him a conviction could derail a promising medical career.

But if Arndt dodged a bullet, he hardly acted grateful during their meetings, says Snow. "In the 'if looks could kill' category, he was a murderer. He acted if the proceedings were an *incredible* invasion on his otherwise important life. He had absolute contempt for the fact that someone might have the audacity to hold him accountable for his bizarre and destructive behavior."

In the end, Snow has said, Arndt paid only $18,700 and failed to follow through on counseling.

In the fall of 1998, Arndt pleaded guilty to the misdemeanor passport violation in federal court in Louisiana. He was sentenced to three years' probation and fined $3,000. But because he had renewed his medical license a few months earlier, he would not have to report that conviction to Massachusetts authorities until his next renewal period two years later.

The fines and legal fees, meanwhile, were adding up. His breakup agreement with Goldfinger, the one that required Arndt to pay 9 percent of his income to his former partner, was slated to go into effect in 1998. So just when Arndt had finished up his lengthy medical training and was about to start making some real money—the 2002 median salary for spine surgeons was more than $545,000, according to the Medical Group Management Association—the financial vise was beginning to tighten.

Arndt argued in court filings that the Goldfinger agreement should be invalidated because he had signed it under duress. The case slogged through the courts and arbitration until a Superior Court judge upheld it in 2000. Goldfinger would never collect a dime.

Even with so many distractions, Arndt seemed able to wall off his personal problems from his professional work.

James A. Karlson, chief of orthopedics at Mount Auburn Hospital, had known Arndt since residency and practiced with him both at Harvard Vanguard and in their four-surgeon group practice. Arndt had privileges at most of Boston's top hospitals but began focusing his attention on Mount Auburn when the veteran spine surgeon there started to cut back. Karlson says there were a few low-level concerns about Arndt, such as tardiness, but no indication of his mounting personal problems. "He had certain problems that we didn't pick up on," Karlson says. "Should we have? 'Could we have?' is a better question."

The care of Raymond LaVallee-Davidson offered a few clues. In the summer of 2001, Arndt operated on his back at New England Baptist Hospital. LaVallee-Davidson says Arndt told him the surgery would take about eight hours. It took eighteen, and even after that, Arndt told him he had been unable to finish the job. Because

LaVallee-Davidson suffered serious complications, it wasn't until December that follow-up surgery was scheduled at Mount Auburn. Just after six o'clock on the morning of surgery, he was being prepped by hospital staff and about to be anesthetized. "I had asked them to hold off, because I had a few questions I wanted to ask Dr. Arndt before I went under," the forty-four-year-old recalls. Four and a half hours later, hospital staff told him they had been unable to locate Arndt, and so LaVallee-Davidson got dressed and made the four-hour drive back to his home in Skowhegan, Maine. Four days later, he says, he got a call from Arndt saying he had overslept. LaVallee-Davidson, who says that initially he found Arndt to be "probably one of the most compassionate people I have ever met," is now among Arndt's former patients suing him for malpractice.

EARLY ON THE MORNING of July 10, 2002, Charles Algeri, a former Waltham cabdriver with a history of back problems, arrived at Mount Auburn Hospital and was prepped for fusion surgery on his lumbar spine. Algeri says Arndt arrived late and unshaven, with dark circles under his eyes. "He said his car had been towed because he had parked in a bus stop," Algeri says.

Like most of the cases Arndt took on, the surgery for Algeri would be a complex, all-day affair. According to state investigative reports and interviews with some of the people involved, this is what happened: The first incision was made around 11:00 a.m. In the OR during the afternoon, Arndt twice asked the circulating nurse to call his office and ask if "Bob" had arrived. By the second call, the receptionist informed the nurse that "Bob" was Arndt's code name for his paycheck and told her to tell Arndt the check would be delivered to him there.

Just before 6:00 p.m., Leo Troy, one of Arndt's fellow orthopedic surgeons from their private practice, was passing by the front desk near the operating room when a secretary asked him if he could take the check to Arndt in the OR. Troy had a few minutes before he was scheduled to operate on another patient, so he had planned to look in on Arndt anyway. He went into the OR, handed Arndt the check, and then observed the surgery for a couple of minutes. Then, Arndt asked him if he would watch his patient for "about five minutes." At the time, Arndt was about seven hours into the surgery. Algeri was under anesthesia and had an open incision in his back. It's not unusual for surgeons doing long procedures like this one to step out to use the bathroom. Although he is not a spine surgeon, Troy says he had assisted Arndt before and was "qualified to close up the patient in an emergency." Arndt then turned to a salesman from a medical device supplier—sales reps often sit in on complex surgeries in case there are questions about the equipment—and said, "Let's go."

A few minutes later, a nurse walked into the OR and asked where Arndt was. Told he had stepped out for a few minutes, she said, "I bet he went to the bank." She had apparently overheard Arndt talking about it earlier. Troy and the rest of the OR staff were incredulous. They tried paging Arndt. Hospital administrators were notified. The decision was made to wait for Arndt to return and, if he didn't come in a timely manner, to try to find a spine surgeon from another hospital. Troy, who calls Arndt an excellent surgeon, says he never had any doubt that he would return.

And he did. Thirty-five minutes later. He admitted he had gone to the bank, and the OR staff said he seemed surprised that they would be upset with him. He finished the surgery about two hours later. Mount Auburn suspended Arndt's privileges the next day, and after an internal review process, the suspension was reported to the state medical licensing board.

"This has got to be a joke," Nancy Achin Audesse said after the report hit her desk.

It was July 25, 2002. Audesse is the executive director of the Massachusetts Board of Registration in Medicine. By the summer of 2002, she was more than familiar with the name David Arndt. The board's year-plus investigation into Arndt's conviction on the

passport violation was wrapping up. (He would get a formal repri-
mand.) He told the board he had no choice but to lie—if he didn't,
he said, his partner would have been deported to Venezuela, where
he said wealthy homosexuals are persecuted and killed. "He was always presenting himself as the victim," Audesse says.

Still, the reason for his suspension from Mount Auburn was so
outlandish that she was convinced someone was putting her on. *He
left his patient in the middle of surgery to go cash a check at the bank?*

After doing a round of interviews—Arndt told an investigator
he had some "overdue bills" and needed to get to the bank before
it closed at 7:00 p.m.—the medical board voted on August 7 to sus-
pend his license. Audesse issued a press release.

At 7:00 a.m. the following day, she was sitting in her dentist's
chair, getting extensive work done. At 9:00 a.m., she called her assistant, who was panicked. "You have to get in here now," she told
Audesse. "This place is crawling with TV news crews!"

"This story went national so fast," Audesse recalls. "I did sixteen
straight interviews, numb and drooling."

In the public, the jokes spread—*A Harvard doctor, and he never
heard of direct deposit?* And then the conjecture—*Overdue bills? Who
insists on cash these days besides drug dealers and bookies?*

As for Arndt's patient, Algeri had no idea what had happened
until he got a call from Mount Auburn officials the day before the
news was going to break. Told that Arndt had left him during surgery to go to Harvard Square, Algeri, a six-foot-five, 315-pound
guy who sports a Boston Bruins baseball cap, a goatee, and a ready
laugh, replied, "What, for a cappuccino?" He watched the media
circle around Arndt for a week before coming forward with his
lawyer, Marc Breakstone, who later filed a malpractice suit.

For a doctor who had always craved attention, David Arndt suddenly had more than even he had ever wanted. The news, when it
found its way to his med school friends scattered across the country,
took the wind right out of them. They had a feeling Arndt would

cause a stir wherever he went, maybe put his career in jeopardy by telling off a hospital chief. But *this?*

Nearly two years later, Alexandra Page still keeps a newspaper clipping about the interrupted surgery on the desk in her office outside San Diego. It's yellowed now, but when she refers to it during an interview, it produces fresh tears. "We all make mistakes," she says, "but this was so heinous, so volitional. I'm just aching for him, for whatever must have happened in his life that caused him to do this."

During his interview, Sigurd Berven breaks down at the same point. Same with another friend of Arndt's from med school, Saiya Remmler, who is now a psychiatrist in Lexington. "What could be more important? You know, the guy's on the table," Remmler says. "To this day, I don't know how anyone could do that, let alone one of my classmates."

But then how to explain Remmler's reaction when she first read about the incident, how she put down the newspaper, turned to her husband, and said, "It doesn't surprise me." Remmler says that Arndt was funny, charming, and really smart. "I felt lucky to have him as a classmate." But, she adds, "he was also really narcissistic, and I guess I knew there was this compulsive streak about him— addictive almost. And so deciding his needs are more important than his patient's life—that sounds narcissistic to me."

About a month after news about the check-cashing broke came another bombshell. Arndt would be charged with four counts of statutory child rape and one count each of indecent assault and battery, drugging a person for sexual intercourse, contributing to the delinquency of a child, and possession of the drugs ketamine hydrochloride ("Special K") and methamphetamine. Middlesex County prosecutors allege that on September 5, Arndt was driving through Central Square in Cambridge and stopped to invite two boys, ages fifteen and fourteen, into his car to get high. Then, they allege, after dropping off the fourteen-year-old, he had sex in his car with the fifteen-year-old. The boys waited four days before contacting police. They said that Arndt had given them his cell phone number and told them his name was David. According to court records, when police dialed the number, Arndt answered, and he later admitted to having the boys in his car but said he had no physical contact aside from brushing one of the boys on the shoulder.

Soon after came Arndt's "poverty motion," asking the court to pay his costs because, according to his lawyer, he was indigent and his parents needed to save for their retirement. (His parents disputed the lawyer's account; he is now gone, and their lawyer, Stephen Delinsky of Eckert Seamans, is representing their son.)

Then, in August 2003, almost a year to the day after he first made headlines, Arndt made a splash again. He was arrested on August 8 and charged with possession of methamphetamine with intent to distribute. According to the postal inspector's report and other court records, on the morning of August 7, Arndt reserved a room at the Chandler Inn in Boston's South End for that night and asked that a party by the name of Frank Castro be added to his reservation. He also asked if any packages for him or his guest had arrived. Around 8:30 p.m., Arndt checked in to Room 501 but apparently didn't stay there that night. Around 1:30 p.m. the next day, Arndt appeared at the front desk. Told that a package had arrived for Room 501 but that it was not in his name, Arndt signed for it and took possession of it. What he didn't know was that, the day before, postal inspectors in Los Angeles had found the six-pound Express Mail package addressed to Frank Castro in care of the Chandler Inn suspicious enough to get a federal warrant. Inside the box, they found a large, pink penis-shaped piñata. Inside the piñata, they found about two pounds of a white crystalline substance that tested positive for methamphetamine. That discovery led to a sting operation at the Chandler Inn, which in turn led to Arndt standing in Room 501, sweating profusely, trying to explain himself to a postal inspector.

The postal inspector reported that Arndt told him he had met Frank Castro online a few months earlier. When authorities went to Arndt's apartment in the South End, a man identifying himself as Alfredo Fuentes told them he and Arndt used to be partners but were now just roommates. He said Arndt knew a Frank Castro from med school.

In fact, authorities were able to track down Frank Castro, an orthopedic surgeon. Castro and his office manager explained that he had been in surgery in Tennessee for the entire time of the incident. Informed of the parcel containing narcotics that had been addressed to him, Castro told the inspector that of the few people he knew in Boston, "only one could be desperate enough to do something like that." David Arndt. He said he and Arndt had been friends since they were lab partners during their premed days in San Francisco but had not been in touch in some time.

David Procopio, spokesman for the Suffolk County district attorney's office, says that while the investigation is ongoing, Castro has been cooperative and "the only person against whom charges are warranted, according to the evidence now in our possession, is David Arndt."

Because of the new charges, Arndt was found to have violated his bail on the Cambridge case and it was revoked. (Earlier in the summer, Arndt had been found at Logan Airport carrying at least $12,000 in cash and his passport. The passport was revoked, but he was allowed to travel in the United States.) He would eventually be released, after posting $50,000 cash bail. But for two months, home for the surgeon and son of privilege was a cell in the Nashua Street Jail.

ONE WEEKEND after the blizzard of headlines, Stephen and Jenifer Lipson went out to brunch and bumped into Ken and Anne Arndt. (Ken, by this time, had left his post at Beth Israel Hospital for a private practice in Chestnut Hill.) "We sat at our separate table, formally said hello to one another," Lipson recalls. "But clearly nobody wanted to talk about David. It was too sensitive."

What does Lipson think happened to his protégé? "I think somehow he got involved in drugs and it ate him alive and he went over the edge," he says. "Beyond that I don't have an answer. And it's a shame."

If, as friends say, David Arndt has always viewed himself as the star of his own drama, what, in the end, drives the story line?

Is his a story of downfall by drugs?

It should be noted that neither of Arndt's criminal cases has yet gone to trial, and he has pleaded not guilty to all charges. But if the allegations turn out to be true, he would hardly be the first hard-driving doctor to get wildly off track because of a substance-abuse problem. John Fromson is a Harvard psychiatrist and president of Physician Health Services, the Massachusetts Medical Society off-shoot that provides support and monitoring services for doctors battling substance abuse and mental health difficulties. Confidentiality rules prevent him from discussing any one case, or even confirming a particular doctor's involvement with the program. But he has gained considerable insight from overseeing a program that has worked with about two thousand Massachusetts doctors over the last ten years.

This is not a great time to be a doctor. More than 40 percent of physicians surveyed in 2001 said they wouldn't go into medicine if they had to do it over again. With increased productivity demands and a tightening financial squeeze, doctors are under tremendous stress, and more of them are turning to drugs and alcohol for relief. An estimated 8 to 14 percent of physicians have a substance-abuse problem. In Massachusetts, surgeons are among the most affected.

Fromson ticks off the warning signs: verbally abusive behavior, tardiness, unexcused absences, inappropriate sexual behavior. The signs of strain tend to come first in a doctor's personal life. "When things happen at the workplace," he says, "usually they have been going on for a long time." Even then, he says, the problem may not be confronted, because most doctors are self-employed and only loosely supervised, and hospital management is often hesitant to call doctors on questionable behavior for fear that they will take their patient base to a hospital across town.

All of this means a doctor's substance-abuse problem can go unchecked and then trigger a downward spiral.

And if the drug of choice is crystal meth, or speed as it's also known, the narcotic at the center of Arndt's charges, the spiral can move at dizzying speeds. In his job with the San Francisco Department of Public Health, Grant Colfax has done some pioneering research documenting the prevalence of speed in the gay community. "For many gay men, crystal meth has just completely destroyed them," he says. "People bottom out. It's a question of how far down you've fallen, and if you can get back up."

"If you look at David's personality, speed is the dream drug," Colfax says. "It makes you feel invulnerable."

At some point in conversations about him, just about all of Arndt's friends and colleagues use that word or others like it to describe him and his self-image. *Bulletproof. Subject to his own rules. Unbreakable.*

Ultimately, that's what makes the drugs explanation, on its own, unsatisfying. After all, the same description fit him even during the long periods in his life when he was clearly not using drugs. Friends were often driven to distraction by Arndt's sense of invulnerability and need for control. But they also saw how those traits could be attractive, especially for patients in need—spurring him to take on the most challenging cases, to fight the toughest battles on their behalf.

But what happens if that need to be in control becomes more important than anything else? "David wanted people to pay attention to him and notice him," says Saiya Remmler, the psychiatrist and former med school friend. "To me, it sounds like a gradual, maybe even lifelong, struggle between greatness and tragic flaws." And what might be at the center of this Greek tragedy? She and other physicians who knew Arndt but haven't seen him in years suggest narcissistic personality disorder, where an exaggerated sense of self-importance masks a chronic emptiness. Then again, only the star of this drama knows the full story.

YOU DO as he tells you. And he is right. *The Journalist and the Murderer* is a gripping piece of nonfiction. (The original *New Yorker* piece was published in book form in 1990.) It examines the dance between a controversial figure and a journalist trying to persuade him to share his story—one that is always something of a tango through a minefield. The relationship at the center of Janet Malcolm's book is the one between *Fatal Vision* author Joe McGinniss and convicted murderer Jeffrey MacDonald. The first sentence of the book is a pretty clear preview of the analysis Malcolm will render: "Every journalist who is not too stupid or too full of himself to notice what is going on knows that what he does is morally indefensible." To be sure, the field of journalism is ill served by the selection of McGinniss as its emissary. This, after all, is a writer who, according to Malcolm, entered into a revenue-sharing arrangement with his subject and then peppered him for years with flattering, deceptive letters before crucifying him in the pages of his book.

The Journalist and the Murderer, David Arndt tells you, provides insight into his decision not to speak to you at length. It's hard to miss the casting choice he is suggesting for you in the role of this ethically challenged journalist. But his literary reference cuts both ways. After all, the other part to be cast is that of MacDonald, the physician convicted of murdering his wife, two daughters, and unborn son and implausibly blaming the carnage on a band of marauding drugged-out hippies.

In a way, the most thought-provoking portions of Malcolm's book do not involve her indictment of McGinniss but rather her own admissions. She concedes that it was easier to come down hard on McGinniss after he shut off communication with her early on.

Your own mind returns to the conversations you had with Arndt before he, too, stopped talking. "You have no idea what my life is like now," he says in the hall of the Cambridge court. "If you talk to anyone who knew me after residency, you know I am an excellent surgeon. I can no longer do what I do best, through a series of circumstances, some of them perhaps my own doing."

And then, as if on cue, his call for compassion is dislodged by a reassertion of control. "You must not do this story," he says. When you remind him that he can't control whether the story is written, but only how complete it is, he shakes his head. "You can control anything you want," he says.

How?

"Don't turn it in."

NEIL SWIDEY *is a staff writer for the* Boston Globe Magazine. *His assignments have included reporting on the Arab world during the run-up to the Iraq war. His previous profile subjects have ranged from former Red Sox shortstop Nomar Garciaparra to the general manager who traded him, from the brother of Osama bin Laden to the one American charged with putting a price tag on each of the lives lost on September 11.*

Coda

Spend enough time with David Arndt's story, and you feel as if nothing could surprise you.

His downfall has a cinematic quality to it. After being away from his story for awhile, I was curious to see how it had continued to unfold. The dramatic turns just kept coming.

Arrogant, compassionate, and reckless, David Arndt seems incapable of living his life in anything but capital letters.

Not long after this piece was published, federal prosecutors swooped in and took over the county drug case against him. They alleged Arndt was a serious drug dealer, part of a wider ring, and that the undercover sting at the Chandler Inn exposed just a glimpse of his illegal activity.

To support their case, they produced testimony in court papers from several unnamed witnesses. The most sensational allegation: that Arndt was supplementing his income by practicing "back-alley medicine." This image of Arndt, the once-rising star in the dazzling constellation of Boston medicine, furtively sewing up bullet holes in drug-trade players unwilling to go to the hospital might be dismissed as too implausible by even immoderate screenwriters. But for people who lived through Arndt's real-life fall, nothing could be considered too over the top. Even the language attributed to Arndt fits the part. One witness said the former surgeon had boasted he would have no problem "disemboweling," with just a "quick swipe of the scalpel," anyone who "ratted" on him about his drug deals.

With the new federal charges, Arndt was ordered held without bail. In the Middlesex County case involving charges of statutory child rape, a trial date was set for the fall of 2005.

Meanwhile, Arndt's malpractice insurer agreed to pay $1.25 million to Charles Algeri, the former cab driver Arndt left anesthetized on the operating table while he ran out to the bank. Algeri says Arndt botched his surgery so badly that he was left with excruciating pain and had to undergo two additional operations to try to correct the damage.

Having battled his own drug addiction years ago, Algeri says he often finds himself replaying in his mind the fateful morning when he went under the knife with Arndt. "The day he showed up, I should have known better. I said to myself, 'There's something wrong with this guy.' Dark circles under his eyes, unshaven—he was a mess. But what am I supposed to do? Ask him to pee in a cup? Piss off the guy who's about to cut me open?"

On June 29, 2005, after spending nearly a year in jail, Arndt walked into a courtroom and pleaded guilty to a host of federal drug charges, including conspiracy to distribute methamphetamine.

He did so knowing that sentencing guidelines will require him to spend a minimum of ten years in prison. The prosecutor said she will recommend a sentence of fifteen to nineteen years.

In court, Arndt was unusually contrite, telling the judge he had been addicted to drugs. "I was out of my mind," Arndt said, "and being incarcerated probably saved my life."

James Ellroy
_____

CHOIRBOYS

Writers' debts accrue over time. You determine the origins of your craft. You look back. You chart books read, style and theme assimilated, the big hurts that made you vow payback on paper. Crime writers get wistful over gas-chamber ghouls and sex psychopaths. Middle-age makes you mark moments. You rematriculate your criminal education.

Mine was more street than most and puerile in the long run. It was snafu as lifestyle. It was idiot kicks. It was books read, books read, books read.

The books were strictly crime books. They transmogrified my childhood grief. They supplied narrative transfusion. They gave me my world heightened and eroticized. Writers came and went. A few turned escapism into near-formal study. One man served as moral rebuke and all-time teacher. This is for him.

IT WAS FALL '73. I was twenty-five. I ran circumspectly wild in L.A. I vibed grotesque. I ran six-three and one-forty. My upper body weight was all pustule. My diet was shoplifted luncheon meat, dine-and-dash restaurant food, Thunderbird wine, and dope. I slept in a Goodwill box behind a Mayfair Market. The fit was tight. Discarded clothes provided warmth and minor comfort. I stayed west of skid row and mass street bum encampments. I carried a razor and shaved with dry soap in gas-station men's rooms. I took garden-hose spritzes and minimized visible dirt and stink. I sold my blood plasma for five scoots a go. I roamed L.A. I did sporadic pops of county-jail time. I swiped skin mags and jacked off by flashlight in my Goodwill-box condo.

I was on a minor misanthrope on a mission. My mission was READ. I read in public libraries and my box. I read crime books exclusively. My crime-study mandate was fifteen years tenured. My mother was murdered in June '58. It remained an unsolved sex-snuff. I was ten years old then. My mother's death did not inflict standard childhood trauma. I hated and lusted for the woman. The killing instilled my mental curriculum and beckoned me to full-time obsession. My field of study was CRIME.

Fall '73. Warm days undercut by smog. Cramped nights as a Goodwill-box dweller.

Joseph Wambaugh had a new book out. The title was *The Onion Field.* It was Wambaugh's first shot at nonfiction. Two punks kidnap two LAPD men. It goes way bad from there. I'd read a prepub magazine excerpt. I was half-bombed at the Hollywood library. The excerpt was brief. It slammed me and made me want more. Pub date approached. Two blood-bank jolts would glom me the cover price, with booze cash to spare. I sold my plasma. I got the coin. I blew said coin on T-bird, cigarettes, and kraut dogs. I raged to read that book. Inimical and more pressing urges interdicted it. Frustration reigned. Ambivalence grabbed me. My chemical/survival compulsions warred with my higher calling of reading. I got hammered and hitched up to Hollywood. I hit the Pickwick Bookstore. I wore my shirttail out and utilized my skinny physiogamy. I jammed a copy of *The Onion Field* down my pants and beat feet.

Fate interceded—in the form of LAPD.

I got eighty-odd pages in. Park bench reads by daylight, box reads by night. I met the two shanghaied cops and liked them. Ian Campbell—doomed to die young. A Scots-American bagpiper. Brainy, a bit mournful. Dislocated in '58 L.A. Become a policeman?—sure. Stand tall, touch the wild side, and rake in five yards a month. Karl Hettinger—Campbell's partner. A dry wit, surface cynicism, stretched nerves underneath. Gregory Powell and Jimmy Smith—a salt-and-pepper team. They're parolees. White man Powell's the alpha dog. He's a skinny-ass, long-necked stone pervert. Black man Smith's a hype. He's playing lapdog and porking Powell's bitch on the side. They're out heisting liquor stores. Campbell and Hettinger are working felony-car nights. The four-man collision occurs. Character is fate. It goes shit-your-pants, all-the-way bad.

Knock, knock—nightstick raps on my Goodwill-box door.

It's Officer Dukeshearer and Officer McCabe—Wilshire Division, LAPD. They've popped me before. It's a plain-drunk roust this time. Someone saw me hop in my box and buzzed the fuzz. Dukeshearer and McCabe treat me with the expansive courtesy that cops reserve for the pathetic. They note my copy of *The Onion Field* and praise my reading taste. I go to Wilshire Station. Copy Number One of *The Onion Field* disappears.

I got arraigned the next morning. I pled guilty. The judge gave me time served. This did not mean instant courtroom kick-out. It meant county-jail intake and release from there.

The intake took sixteen hours. Cavity searches, chest X-rays, blood tests, delousing. Intensive exposure to various strains of indigenous L.A. lowlife—all possessed of greater machismo and street panache than me. A Mexican drag queen named "Peaches" squeezed my knee. I popped the fucking *puto* in the chops. Peaches went down, got up and kicked my ass. Two deputies quelled the fracas. It amused them. Some inmates applauded Peaches. A few hooted at me.

I wanted to be back to my box. I wanted to be back on Crime Time. I wanted to get down with Ian and Karl and the killers.

I processed in and out of jail within twenty hours. Crime Time became Wambaugh Time. I stole a pint of vodka, got bombed and walked to Hollywood. I hit the Pickwick Bookstore and stole Copy Number Two of *The Onion Field*. I read some park-bench pages and hit my box at twilight. I was now 150-odd pages in.

Knock, knock—nightstick raps on my Goodwill-box door.

It's Officer Dukeshearer and Officer McCabe—Wilshire Division, LAPD. Kid, you hopped in that box. Someone saw you. Jesus, you're reading that Wambaugh book again.

It's the same process. The same plain-drunk roust. The same judge. The same time served. The same intake and outtake, twenty-plus hours strong.

Vexing. Exhausting. Wholly fucked-up. Lunacy defined: doing the same stupid shit over and over, but expecting different results.

I wanted to get back to that book. I was strung out on Wambaugh Time and juiced with Wambaugh-inflicted remorse.

You're a Scot like Ian Campbell. *But:* you can't play the bagpipes, because that takes discipline and practice. *And:* you're knock-kneed and bony-legged, and would look ridiculous in your ancestral kilt.

Yeah, but you're not scum like Powell and Smith. No, but you steal to survive. Yeah, but you're not vicious. No, but you lack the plain guts to rob liquor stores. A bantamweight faggot kicked your ass.

Wambaugh Time. Wambaugh-inflicted remorse. Learn from it? Change your life?—no, not just yet.

I got out of jail. I stole a pint of vodka, got bombed and walked to Hollywood. I hit the Pickwick Bookstore and stole Copy Number Three of *The Onion Field*. I read some park-bench pages and curled up behind a bush near my box. I was now 250-odd pages in.

Poke, poke—nightstick jabs on my legs.

It's two new cops—Wilshire Division, LAPD. It's the near-same process again.

I lose Copy Number Three. I go to Wilshire Station. I go to court and see the same judge. He's tired of my theatrics. My raggedy ass offends him. He offers me a choice: six months in county jail or three months at the Salvation Army "Harbor Light" Mission. I vibe the options. I opt for hymns on skid row.

The program was simple and rigidly enforced. Take the drug Antabuse. It allegedly deters the consumption of alcohol. You get righteously ill if you imbibe. Share a room with another drunk. Attend church services, feed bums, and pass out Jesus tracts all over skid row.

I did it. I took Antabuse, fought booze-deprivation shakes and stayed dry. My sleep went sideways. I kept brain-screening conclusions to *The Onion Field* text. I shared a room with a rummy ex-priest. He'd quit the church to roam, drink, and chase poontang. He was a big reader. He disdained my crime-books-only curriculum. He didn't know Joseph Wambaugh from Jesus or Rin-Tin-Tin. I tried to tell him what Wambaugh meant. My thoughts spilled out, inchoate. I didn't really know myself.

My blood bank was three blocks from the mission. Two plasma sales earned me book money. I walked to a downtown bookstore. I bought Copy Number Four of *The Onion Field* and read it through.

Ian dies. Karl survives, shattered. Jimmy and Greg exploit the legal system conwise and escape their just fate of death. Wambaugh's outrage. Wambaugh's terrible compassion. Wambaugh's clearly defined and softly muted message of hope at the end.

The book moved me and scared me and rebuked me for the heedlessness of my life. The book took me tenuously out of myself and made me view people at a hush.

I split the mission early. I wanted to roam, read, and booze. I went off Antabuse and retoxified my system. I fell in with an old buddy from high school. He had a right-on, can't-miss, criminal plan.

He had a pad south of Melrose. The Nickodell Restaurant was just across the street. The bar was rife with affluent juicers. I would waylay and sap drunks in the parking lot. I would run across Melrose and be at the pad in sixteen seconds flat.

I refused to do it. You do not wantonly raise your hand to another human being. My childhood in the Lutheran Church did not teach me that. Joseph Wambaugh did.

BOOKS AND I WENT BACK. My old man taught me to read at age three-and-a-half. I bloomed into a classic only child/child-of-divorce autodidact.

My first love was animal stories. This reading arc tapped out quick. My love for animals was wrenchingly tender and near-obsessive. Animals suffered cruelty and died in animal books. I couldn't take it. I moved on to sea stories. I dug the vastness of the sea and the specialized nomenclature of ships. I overdid this reading arc and got mired down in the unabridged *Moby Dick*.

Words and phrases baffled me. The narrative was hard to grasp. I grokked a fair portion of the text and rooted for Moby. Fuck Captain Ahab. He was this pegged-leg psycho cocksucker. He was fucking with Moby and trying to stick harpoons in his ass. The story got tedious. My old man finished the book for me. He said the ending got schizzy. Moby rammed the boat and only one guy lived. Moby caught some harpoons and skedaddled.

Sea stories, *adieu*. On to kid westerns. Cattle drives, gunfights, redskin ambushes. This reading arc ran concurrent with a bumper crop of western TV shows. *Gunsmoke*, *The Restless Gun*, *Wagon Train*. Frontier justice and dance-hall girls flashing cleavage. My book fixation up to the drum roll of fate on June 22, 1958.

Now she's dead. She's Geneva Hilliker Ellroy, age forty-three, farm girl from rural Wisconsin. She's my mother. She's a drunk. She's a registered nurse—*the* sexy archetype female profession. She's a gooood/looking redhead/she's got film-*noir* qualities/she's my kid-sex stand-in for all women.

She betrothed me to CRIME. My reading focus zoomed there instantly. I moved in with my old man. He catered to my newly wrought reading arc and bought me two kids' crime books a week.

I gobbled them, started shoplifting books to fill reading gaps and exhausted the kid-crime-book canon quicksville. I graduated to Mickey Spillane and cold-war psychoses. Crime was sex, sex was crime, fictional crime and sex was a sublimated dialogue on my hated and lusted-for mother. My old man got me Jack Webb's book *The Badge.* It lauded the LAPD and detailed their most notorious cases. Joe Wambaugh joined LAPD the next year. He was a kid-cop with an English degree. He stood a decade short of his writer apotheosis.

Crime. The redhead and me. My Wambaugh rendezvous years hence.

My mother's death corrupted my imagination. I saw crime everywhere. Crime was not isolated incidents destined for ultimate solution and adjudication. Crime was *the* continual circumstance. It was all day, every day. The ramifications extended to the 12th of Never. This is a policeman's view of crime. I did not know it then.

My *métier* was kiddie-*noir.* It's summer '59. Dr. Bernard Finch and Carole Tregoff whack Bernie's wife for her *gelt.* Bernie's 40-plus. Carole's 19, stacked, and leggy. She's a redhead. Redheads and murder?—I'm there. It's May, '60. Caryl Chessman eats gas at Big Q. It's a Little Lindbergh bounce—kidnap with sex assault. Limo Liberals lay out lachrymose—big boo-hoo-hoo. Joe Wambaugh joins LAPD the same day.

Kiddie-*noir* was couched in a dual-world constellation. The outside world was the alleged real world. This meant home life and my enforced school curriculum. The inside world was CRIME. This meant crime books, crime flicks, crime TV shows. Every encapsulated drama offers a tidy solution. I know this is bullshit. The glut of book crime and filmic crime means no surcease from crime ever. Joe Wambaugh's a rookie cop now. He knows this more than me.

It's April, '61. Country fiddler Spade Cooley's deep in the shit. He's jacked up on bennies. His wife wants to join a free-love cult. Spade beats her to death. Ella Mae Cooley vibed slow-burning fame. She had that "Oh, Baby" look my mom got with three highballs. Joe Wambaugh's twenty-four now. He's working University Division. It's all Negro and all trouble. The natives are *always* restless. Parking-lot dice games. Hair-process joints. Sonny Liston-manqués sporting porkpies. Nightwatch bops to a tom-tom beat.

The inside world was a fiend habituation. Racetrack touts, brain-damaged pugs, ice-cream vendors with kiddie-raper rackets. It's Winter '62. My old man takes me by the Algiers Hotel-Apartments. He says it's a "Fuck Pad." Whores work the rooms. It's a "Hot-Sheet Flop." Married guys bring their secretaries for nooners. I ditch school and surveill the Algiers. Every woman who enters is a siren, a temptress, a film-*noir* succubus. It's Summer '62. It's buy-school-clothes time. The old man takes me to the Wilshire May Company. Nature calls. I bop to a men's room stall to unload. There's a big hole in one wall. I wonder why. I find out toot-fucking-sweet.

A fruit sticks his dick through the hole and waggles it my way. I shriek, grab my pants, and lay tracks. My old man is equal parts aghast and amused. Joe Wambaugh works Wilshire Vice a year later. The May Company "Glory Hole" is a Fruit Mainstay, a Fruit Landmark, a Fruit Cup Supreme. He entraps fruits there. He writes a fruit-entrapment scene in *The Choirboys* years later.

It's March, '63. The Onion Field snuff occurs. It slipped through my radar then. Joe Wambaugh's working Wilshire. He gets obsessed.

Crime carried me through a failing school career and my old man's failing health. I read crime books, watched crime flicks, brain-screened crime fantasies. I neglected my schoolwork. I bicycle-stalked girls around my neighborhood. I peeped nighttime windows and grooved on stray women. I roamed L.A. I shoplifted books. I snuck into theaters to watch crime films. I grew into a big, geeky, acne-addled, morally-mangled teenage thief/scrounger. I craved mental thrills and sex stimulation. I boosted skin mags. I lurked. I leched. I ditched school. I called in bomb threats to other schools. I burglarized empty pop-bottle sheds behind local markets. I got kicked out of high school. I joined the army. The old man died. I

faked a nervous breakdown and got discharged. I came back to
L.A. It was Summer '65. I found a pad in the old neighborhood and
a handball-passing gig. I was free, white, and seventeen. I figured I'd
become a great writer soon. Logic demands that you write some
great books first. This fact eluded me.

I started drinking, smoking weed, and eating amphetamines.
My stimulation index exploded exponentially. I roamed L.A. I
shoplifted. I got popped at a market and carted to Georgia Street
Juvenile. It was July, '65. Joe Wambaugh worked there then. I might
have glimpsed my all-time teacher.

A friend's dad bailed me out. I got a lecture and summary probation. My day in jail scared me and taught me just this: Steal more
cautiously now.

I did. It worked. I shoplifted food, booze, and books and rocked
on, impervious. It's now August, '65. The Watts Riot goes down.
Moral exemplar Ellroy is appalled, enraged, aghast, and racially
threatened.

It's *baaaad* juju in Jungle Junction. I sense Commie influence. I
get giddy and righteously riled. This beats crime books, crime
flicks, crime TV shows. Nasty Negro Armageddon. The savage sack
of *my* city. The Watts Riot—what a fucking blast!!!!

I huddled with some pals. We armed ourselves with BB guns.
We were Mickey Spillane fans and rigorously anti-Red. What
would Mike Hammer do? *He'd fucking act.*

We got bombed on weed and T-bird. We drove south at dusk.
L.A. cringed under curfew. We violated it. We had meager fire-
power, but stern hearts. Smoke hazed up the southside. We hit
trouble at Venice and Western.

Two white cops pulled us over. They checked out our arsenal
and howled. They told us to go home and watch the show on TV.
Hit the road—or we'll call your parents.

We obeyed. We got more bombed and watched news reports.
Joe Wambaugh caught the show live.

He reported to 77th Street Station. He worked a four-man patrol car. They had sidearms and one shotgun. He went out into it. He caught the first shots fired.

Vermont and Manchester. Store windows shattered, alarms ringing, seven hundred to eight hundred fools in the street. A gun pops. Then another. Shots overlap in one long roar—*and it never stops.*

The cops barged through stores. They hurdled broken window glass and subdued rioter-thieves. Shots popped out of nowhere. Richochets ringed. They hauled suspects out of buildings and pulled them off the streets. Gunfire poured down. They couldn't make its origins. They couldn't dodge it for shit. They took their suspects to booking stations and Central Receiving. They got out of it. They went back into it. Wambaugh got scared, unscared, scared, unscared, scared. His adrenaline went haywire. The heat and flames and heavy riot gear leeched pounds off of him.

He held the moments close. He compiled notes later. He deployed them in his first novel.

The New Centurions tracks three cops for five years. The narrative covers 1960 to the riot. Policework vignettes force the action. It is crime as continuing circumstance and crime as defining circumstance writ intimately and large. The cops differ in temperament. Their worldviews converge along authoritarian lines and diverge in their need to touch darkness and disorder. The three posses near-disordered inner lives. They meet, subvert, interdict, and seek to contain crime every working day. The process serves to still their fears on an ad hoc basis and grants them a sometimes stable, sometimes troubled equilibrium. The novel concludes shortly after the Watts Riot. The riot has provided them with the context they have unconsciously sought since their first days as cops. They have aligned the opposing sides of their natures through enforced chaos. They have achieved momentary peace. That peace will die almost immediately. A non sequitur event, prosaic and deadly, will define them all in the end.

Crime as continuing and defining circumstance: '60 to '65. My own idiot crime life: '65 to '70.

I read crime books. I scoured Cain, Hammett, Chandler, Ross Macdonald. I nurtured a fatuous sense of my own future literary greatness. I viewed crime flicks and crime TV shows. I enacted crime in my own inimitable and Mickey Mouse manner.

Bottle-bin raids. Bookstore grabs. Stolen booze sold to high school kids at drastic markup. T.J. runs to score *pharmacia* dope and catch the mule act.

Pad prowls—*craaaazy,* Daddy-o!

It's '66 to '69. I'm a girl-crazed, fuck-struck, quasi-young adult virgin. I subsist in cheap cribs near swank Hancock Park. I grew up craving the girls there. I stalked them and knew where they lived. They were poised young women now. They attended USC and UCLA. They wore high-line preppy threads. They were bound for careers of marginal note and marriage to rich stiffs. I craved them. I was unkempt, unlovable, unloved. I possessed no knowledge of the simple civil contract. I lacked the social skills and plain courage to approach them for real. I broke into their houses instead.

It was easy. This was the prephone machine/alarm system/home invasion era. I called the pads. I got dial tones. That meant no one's home. I bopped over and checked access routes. Open windows, loose window screens, pet doors with grab space up to inside latches. Entryways to affluence and SEX.

I pad-prowled roughly twenty times total. Kathy's pad, Missy's pad, Julie's pad. Heidi's pad, Kay's pad, Joanne's pad twice. I raided medicine chests and popped pills. I hit liquor cabinets and poured cocktails. I snagged five and ten-spots from purses and wallets. I hit my love-objects' bedrooms and snatched underwear.

I never got caught. I always covered my tracks. My thefts were modest and always geared toward sustaining egress. I was a soul-fucked youth reared behind poverty and death. I wanted to see where real families lived. I wanted to touch fabric that touched lovely girls' bodies. I did not hail from an aggrieved perspective. I knew the world did not owe me shit. I was too mentally jazzed and sex-tweaked to indulge self-pity. I knew that crime was a continuing

circumstance. The redhead taught me that. I was pervertedly tracing her lead. I went at this pursuit sans remorse or compunction. I
was young and implacable in my fervor. I hadn't absorbed enough
deadening shit. I hadn't read Joseph Wambaugh yet.

I kept boozing and snarfing dope. I blew my rent roll and lost
my pad. I moved into public parks and slept under blankets. Cold
weather drove me indoors. I found a vacant house and crashed
there. Bam—it's November, '68. The LAPD comes in the door
with shotguns. It's overkill with a civil edge—the cops size me up
as a passive putz with poor hygiene. They treat me brusquely, de-
cently, dismissively. Say what? I thought the LAPD was a storm-
trooper legion. The press roasts them for strongarm tactics. They're
some Klan Klavern/ Bund hate hybrid. My shit detector clicks in.
My street and stationhouse instinct: it just ain't so.

I do three weeks at the Hall of Justice Jail. It's a potent crime
primer. I'm the geek that all the pro thugs disdain. I observe them
up close. It's the '60s. It's social-grievance-as justification-for-bad-
actions time. My cellmates have sadness raps down. I gain a notch
on my crime-as-continuing-circumstance notion. Crime is large-
scale individual moral default.

That means you, motherfucker.

Now you know it. Change your life behind the concept? No,
not yet.

I exited jail right before Christmas. I went back to books, booze
and dope. I pad-prowled. I stole underwear. I pursued the Panty-
Sniffer Pantheon.

I roamed L.A. by night. I got repeatedly rousted by LAPD. I
sensed that a cop–street fool compact existed. I behaved accord-
ingly. I denied all criminal intent. I acted respectfully. My height-
to-weight ratio and unhygenic appearance caused some cops to
taunt me. I sparred back. Street schtick often ensued. I mimicked
jailhouse jigs like some WASP Richard Pryor. Rousts turned
into streetside yuckfests. They played like Jack Webb unhinged.
I started to *dig* the LAPD. I started to grok cop humor. I

couldn't quite peg it as performance art. I hadn't read Joseph Wambaugh yet.

It's August, '69. The Tate/LaBianca snuffs occur. L.A. goes freaky-deaky. I note private patrol signs on Hancock Park lawns. I weigh the odds. They hit against the Pantyphile Panther. Don't do it again. You *will* get caught. County jail is no sweat. Don't risk the penitentiary.

I stopped it. I never B&E'd again. I trucked through to '71. I read crime books. I guzzled booze and snarfed dope. I did an honor-farm petty theft jolt. I heard about this cop. He wrote this novel. It's the inside shit on LAPD.

I left Wayside Honor Rancho. I prowled public libraries. I found *The New Centurions* and read it in one gulp. It confirmed and trashed and realigned all my criminal conceptions. It fully rewired me.

It was the moral and psychic cost of crime on an unprecedented scale. It was a anecdotal social history of '60s L.A. It was a merciless treatise on the lives of *men*. It was bottomless dark humor. It was a sternly worded defense of the need for social order and a rebuttal to the prevelant anticop ethos of the day. It was my crime-as-continuing-circumstance configuration expanded and made humanly whole.

It burned my mental world down. It took me back to my mother's death and all stops in between.

I reread the book. I took in Wambaugh's knowledge. It dovetailed with my knowledge and gave me a view of the flipside of the moon. I couldn't quite dodge its moral power. I routinely violated the rule of social order that Wambaugh eloquently expressed. Joseph Wambaugh would dismiss me on moral grounds, and rightfully so.

I reread that book. I did not alter my lifestyle one iota. Wambaugh's second novel came out. *The Blue Knight* was a first-person narrative. Bumper Morgan is a street cop set to retire. He's reluctant to go. He's fiftyish. He's engaged to a splendid woman. The prospect of one-on-one lasting love flummoxes him. He's hooked on the mundane and occasionally thrilling pleasures of policework. He's fearful at the core of his heart. The job allows him to live at a distanced and circumscribed level on his downtown foot beat. He rules a small kingdom benevolently. He gives and takes affection in a compartmentalized fashion that never tests his vulnerability. He's afraid to love flat-out for-real. His last cop days tick by. His reluctance to walk away increases. Violent events intercede. They serve to save him and damn him and give him his only logical fate.

Joseph Wambaugh, sophomore novelist, age thirty-five. A great tragic novel of the cop's life, his second crack out of the gate.

I read *The New Centurions*. I read *The Blue Knight*. I read *The Onion Field* in idiotically staggered intervals. I took them as great criminal and literary teachings, and moral indictments of *me*.

I was twenty-five. I ran on bad chemicals and bad, crazy blood. Don't change your life yet. It may hurt too much. Don't rip out your own ruthless and impotent heart.

HE WAS AN ONLY CHILD and a cop's kid. His people were Irish. His father worked factory jobs and joined the East Pittsburgh PD. It was the Depression. Jobs were short, crime was up. His father rose fast and bottomed out quick. He made Chief. He got mired up in local politics. Political shit taxed him and forced him out. He quit the PD in '43. He returned to factory work.

Joe was six then. Joe loved to read. Joe loved animal stories and kids' adventure books. His snout was always tucked in some book. He never read crime books. They just didn't jazz him.

His mother had five brothers out in the war. Uncle Pat Malloy's case was outré. He fought in World War I. He went from doughboy to town drunk. Uncle Pat never worked. Uncle Pat scrounged booze money. Uncle Pat got drafted in the Big War. He went from East Pittsburgh souse to army training officer. He met a rich woman and married her. They moved to California. They bought a chicken farm outside L.A. They boozed the postwar years away.

Uncle Pat always drove drunk. Career drunk driving lays tits-up odds against you. The odds crunched Uncle Pat in '51. He plowed an orange truck. He died. His wife died. Joe and his folks came out for the wake. They liked California. They stayed.

They settled east of the San Gabriel Valley. Ontario, Fontana—L.A. satellites with grape vineyards and orange groves. Joe's dad got factory work. Joe dug on the California weather, the California beauty, the California absence of grime. He attended Chaffey High. He graduated in '54. He did three years in the Marine Corps. He came home and found work. Kaiser Steel in Fontana—private-duty fireman.

Factory work, mill work, grub work—strictly the shits. He wanted to work with his mind. He wanted to take his love of books and extrapolate. He enrolled at Chaffey J.C. and L.A. State. He married his girlfriend. He got an English degree. He wanted to become an English teacher. Fate keestered him.

A simple ad. A page portion in the *L.A. Herald*. Police Officers wanted/$489 a month.

Adventure. Romance. Five yards monthly. It's like his favorite kids' book: *The Call of the Wild*.

Okay, you'll do twenty years. You'll retire. You'll become an English teacher *then*. You'll be forty-three. You'll be a two-career man.

No. Fate is more quixotic and complex than that. You'll witness crazy shit. You'll fight in a riot. You'll battle butch fags in moviehouse men's rooms. You'll get shot at. You'll kick ass. You'll get your ass kicked. You'll dig on more race schtick than 86,000 Redd Foxx albums. You'll nosh pickled pigs feet in Watts at two-fucking-a.m. You'll slop scorching chili verde on your bluesuit. You'll meet baby fuckers, dog fuckers, cat fuckers, penguin fuckers, wombat fuckers, turkey fuckers, syphilitic drag queens, sink shitters, public masturbators, tubercular pimps with six months to live, and geeks who shell-fuck three-hundred-year-old turtles. You will witness human bravery and honor in quick-march proximity to depravity and blasphemy of unimaginable measure. You will distill and contain your knowledge. You will give the world horrifying and hilarious books that only a cop could have written—books of deep and true human measure.

Officer/Sergeant Joseph A. Wambaugh. LAPD: '60 to '74.

He stayed fourteen years. He wanted to stay twenty. His celebrity sandbagged him. His author life fucked up his cop life. Suspects recognized him and begged autographs. Agent calls and producer calls swamped the Hollenbeck squadroom. He had to go then—but, oh Jesus—*the ride.*

It was a fully contained and wholly uncontainable funhouse tour, replete with shape-distorting funhouse mirrors. The distortions were human behavior rendered grotesque. A couple fights over custody of a child. Both grab the child and pull his limbs in opposite directions. The child almost disarticulates and snaps in two.

The severed-penis boy. The double amputee wino bragging that his dick hits the ground. Officer Charlie Bogardus, dying of cancer, short of twenty years on the job. His family needs his pension. He needs to die on duty. He blind-charges a burglary suspect and takes two in the pump.

Ian and Karl. The Onion Field. The funeral and bagpipe wail.

The transy whore on Chenshaw. His first Vice bust. He-she pinches his thighs beyond black and blue. Pain off the charts—let's kill him—no, let's don't.

The pool-hall caper. The cat with the shotgun. The orange flame and pellets over his head. Fred Early's his partner. Fred traps the cat and nails him between the horns. The cat's dead. Fred's shot and killed ten years later. It's still unsolved.

Jesus, the ride. The homos, the hookers, the hugger-muggers, the heist men. The wineheads, the wienie waggers, the pill poppers, the pachucos, the Jailbait Jills and the jittery junkies. The lazy daywatch tours, the late-nite losers, the lessons.

He brought fear to the job. It was the informed fear of the intelligent and imaginative. He surmounted his fear in repeated context. He learned that you never quash your fear for good. Cop work is always the next context.

He learned that boredom incites rage that leads to chaos and horror.

He learned that the strongest human urge is the simple urge to survive. He learned that this urge mutates. He learned that it induces pity in good people. He learned that it inspires brutal willfulness in the bad.

He learned that crime is a continuing circumstance. He learned that a cop's split-second choices poised him a heartbeat close to laurels and dishonor.

Joe Wambaugh. LAPD: '60 to '74.

He should have stayed longer. He couldn't. He had to write. He had to transpose his lessons. He had to share the ride in all its power.

He turned informal on-the-job notes into sketches and short stories. He submitted them to magazines. An editor at the *Atlantic Monthly* advised him to shape them into a novel. He wrote *The New Centurions* and sold it for a modest advance. The book was a critical sensation and a big best seller. He got packaged and somewhat pigeonholed as this anomalous cop-writer. The book portrayed policework as a troubling and morally ambiguous journey. Some cops hated the message. Most respected the inherent truth. The LAPD high command disapproved. That was a fucking heartbreaker.

The Blue Knight, The Onion Field. Big bestsellers, big bucks rolling in, big-time acclaim. Big movie sales, big hoo-haw, the disjuncture that big recognition always brings.

He wrote *The Choirboys.* It was scheduled for mid-75 publication. The job pulled him one way. The craft pulled him in reverse. The craft was the job. That consoled him somewhat. He shut down the ride.

———

MY RIDE WANED. Outdoor living and booze and dope sent my health south. Jails, hospitals, rehabs. The nadir of early '74 to mid-'75.

I read *The Choirboys* late that summer. I stole the book from a Hollywood bookstore. It was Wambaugh's finest work. The locale was Wilshire Division. A group of nightwatch cops unwind in Westlake Park. They call their soirees "Choir Practice." It's kicks and chicks for a while. An undercurrent sets in. They're too stimulated and tweaked by the job. The job sates their curiosities. They're public servants *and* voyeurs. The job gives them a steel-buffed identity. They're macho-maimed and frail underneath. They brought a surfeit of fear and hurt to the job. They're overamped and stressed and more than a little crazy. They're in over their heads. Crime as continuing circumstance claims them. Their collective fate is madness.

The book tore me up and oddly consoled me. It reindicted my moral default. It diminuitized my street-fool status. It put me at one with some guys as high up on a ledge as I was.

It forced me into a corner. It jabbed my imagination and made me cough up portents of a story. It was a potential novel. I knew I had to write it. I knew I had to change my life first.

I did it. I'll credit God with the overall save. I'll cite Joe Wambaugh and Sex as secondary forces.

I knew a couple named Sol and Joan. Sol sold weed, played the sitar, and pontificated. He was a gasbag hippie patriarch. Joan loved him heedlessly. I was in love with her. She haunted my head. I placed her in fantasy contexts with the cops from *The Choirboys*. She leaped from Wambaugh's pages to my prospective pages. She haunted my first novel four year later.

I was at their pad. Joan sat to my left. She wore jeans and a man's white dress shirt. She reached for a cigarette. Her shirt gapped. I saw her right breast in pure profile.

Oh, shit—you must change your life. No shit, you did.

That was almost thirty years ago. Joe Wambaugh's sixty-eight. I'm fifty-seven. I'm at that elegiac, debt-acknowledgment moment. My debt to Joe stands out brightly.

Joe and I are friends. We're cordial, but not close. He's a tough nut to crack. We share the same film agent.

He's thirty-one years gone from the LAPD. His book career sits at age thirty-five. He has produced a legendary body of fiction and nonfiction. His most recent novels portray exile. Aging ex-cops roam affluent settings. They fall prey to odd temptations and reach for the fortitude that fueled their cop days. Joe left the job early. He's always looking back. It isn't regret. It isn't nostalgia. It's something sweeter and deeper.

It's hushed visitation. It's the faint heartbeats of our lost ones. It's a feminine stirring in our male-crazed world. It's a woman's breath in ellipsis. Joan. The white-shirt moment. Another Joan nearing forty, dark hair streaked with gray. Joan.

I might visit Joe next month. I might cohost his screenwriting class at University of California, San Diego. We might sit around and talk, arriviste to arriviste. I can see it. I can hear it more. We're two word guys from Jump Street.

Joe's Catholic. I'm Protestant. I'll confess to him anyway. I'll urge him to forego exile and return to *Then*. I'll tell him my head is still full of fucked-up and magnificent shit. I'll describe the breadth of his gift. You granted me vision. You unlocked the love and dutiful rage in my heart.

Permissions and Acknowledgments